T0105490

GAIL SINCLAIR

No Safe Bet

iUniverse, Inc.
Bloomington

iUniverse books may be ordered through booksellers or by contacting:

iUniverse
1663 Liberty Drive
Bloomington, IN 47403
www.iuniverse.com
1-800-Authors (1-800-288-4677)

ISBN: 978-1-4502-7009-0 (sc)
ISBN: 978-1-4502-7011-3 (hc)
ISBN: 978-1-4502-7010-6 (ebook)

Printed in the United States of America

iUniverse rev. date: 11/30/2010

In memory of Stand Off

March 28, 1986 – December 25, 2008

Acknowledgements

There are many people that gave advice and support in this endeavour. My good friend, Dianne Fahselt, and my mother, Nettie Sinclair, offered sound guidance throughout my struggle to transform life on the backstretch into an interesting story. In addition, Sam Young helped to guide me with his fluent knowledge of the grammar and flow of language.

The editorial staff at iUniverse was very accommodating. Their initial editorial review process led to changes that enhanced the characters and content of the story. The staff was also very helpful with formatting.

I would like to thank my editor, Sharon Crawford, for her wonderful advice and recommendations. She gave valuable suggestions that allowed the flow, point of view, and many other aspects of the writing process to become clearer. She was always willing to answer my questions, counselling me in the correct methods.

The wonderful photos are care of Adam Grant and Grant Galleries. His ideas and proposals helped to enhance both the picture of me and the cover design.

Finally, I'd like to thank my family: Ron, Andy, and Michelle for their patience and support. Supper was often late because I was spending so many hours editing. I am grateful for their understanding and willingness to let me see this project to its end.

PART I

Woodbine Racetrack, August 1984

Chapter One

The air was vibrant with tension. Julia adjusted the tight seatbelt, shifted restlessly in her seat, and glanced apprehensively at her boyfriend Ken. He had made it clear that he wasn't impressed with the early hour. Yet he had insisted that she needed a job. Julia had also wanted a job, but had been procrastinating for weeks. The ultimatum had landed in her lap last night. Financially, Ken was unable to support them both. Get a job or get out. Julia peeked out the window and watched the dark buildings and streets glide by as Ken drove silently. Their recent argument was still ripe in her mind. Ken hardly ever shouted, but he had come close. Julia really did want to get out, to leave him, and perhaps she had given him some indication of this fact. Ultimately, she knew that he would be furious with her plans.

"Horses!" Ken had fumed. "Why can't you get a real job, like the pizza joint on the corner? Why does it have to start in the middle of the night?"

Reluctantly, he had agreed to rise at the ungodly hour.

It really was a glorious morning. The sky was clear with a hint of blue, as the glow of the sun lay just below the horizon. The grass cast long shadows in the still early morning light. Five in the morning was the coolest time of day, and the heat of a typical Toronto August afternoon had not yet warmed the grass, trees, and paved surfaces. The outside air was dry and crackled in anticipation of the rays of scorching sunshine.

Eager to be free of the tension in the vehicle, Julia jumped from the Jeep Cherokee as it rolled to a stop just inside the backstretch gate of Woodbine Racetrack. She glanced at the ominous bulk of the grandstand in the distance, nearly a quarter of a mile away. The slight early morning breeze caressed her brown hair as she pushed a few strands back from her face. Her lips parted in expectant excitement as she glanced at Ken. He nodded at her.

"Shall I leave you here, hon?" he asked carefully.

His words were clipped, anger and disappointment hidden under the endearment. She knew that this change in her life would seriously compromise their life together. This was a good thing.

"I'll be fine." The off-hand reply escaped her as she surveyed the backstretch in the gathering light. "I'll call if I need you." Hoping to relieve some of the stress of their drive, Julia smiled at him with a warm glow in her soft brown eyes. "Thanks for the ride."

The man reluctantly put the Jeep in reverse and waved. The dust gathered as he turned and left.

Friends at the stable where Julia rode had warned her about what to expect; yet she still felt eagerness and some trepidation about a morning of new experiences. Her friends had also given her a rundown of a typical early morning at the racetrack.

Work in most barns on the backstretch started at 6 a.m. and 5.30 a.m. in some of the bigger establishments. A steady flow of vehicles arrived and moved through the gate toward the barns 300 yards down the road. The security guard in the booth simply waved most trucks and cars through the gate. The workers called their morning greetings over steaming cups of Tim Horton's coffee.

Julia stared at the stream of workers heading towards the barns for morning training. They added to the aura of a country atmosphere in the midst of a metropolitan city that bustled and buzzed with vigour around them. The tall and lean ones were the grooms and hot-walkers, her friends had said, and the short and compact ones were the exercise riders. All appeared muscled and incredibly fit to work with the high-energy racehorses. Julia was in awe.

"Something you want, Miss?" a voice asked gruffly behind her.

She wheeled around towards the man in the security uniform. He had just come out of the security trailer, a mobile home permanently set by the roadway leading toward the gate.

"I'm here to meet with Roger Dongals, the personnel manager." The guard nodded to a trailer at the far end of the parking area beside the gate. It appeared closed, locked, and deserted. "That there is Dongals' trailer. Should be here 'bout five minutes from now."

Julia nodded her thanks and wandered slowly toward the trailer. Much smaller than the security trailer, this off-white trailer was only about 15 feet long. The entrance door was padlocked and set in the centre of the trailer in the long shadows cast by the rising sun. Unlike the busy gate only a few feet away, this quiet corner of the parking lot was devoid of people and activity. Julia sat on the concrete slab that fashioned a step to enter the trailer. She gazed longingly toward the barns, which were just beginning to bustle with activity.

Julia let her mind wander back to the last couple of weeks. Finished with Grade 13, Julia had been unable to decide exactly where her life was heading. Ken had been pushing her to find employment to help pay the bills, but Julia desperately wanted a job to make enough money to enter university, and escape Toronto and the suffocating relationship with her boyfriend. They had been together for nearly four years, and, at the age of 19, Julia felt that it had been a lifetime. Ken had been kind to her and she had been eager to move in with him last year, but she now wanted to experience life beyond the four walls of their tiny Etobicoke apartment.

During the last few weeks Julia had learned to ride a horse at a local stable. Enthralled with the country atmosphere surrounding the stable, Julia had begged them for employment that was different from the usual teenage summer jobs. Financially unable to grant her wish, the owners had suggested that she talk to Roger Dongals at the racetrack if she was that keen to work with horses.

So here she was, leaning back against the cold metal of the trailer, gazing out over the early morning grass. Although she didn't have a clear idea of her future or her long-term goals, Julia knew that she craved excitement and the unknown. Her dark brown eyes gazed toward the sun creeping over the horizon. Sometimes she felt old beyond her years; the long-term relationship with Ken had protected her from the harsh realities of life. Things had been comfortable. Her parents had moved north last year, and Julia had moved in with Ken. Disappointment had ultimately surfaced, as the mundane day-to-day reality of life had forced Julia to think seriously about her decision. Similar to other teens fresh from high school, she was naive in her romantic outlook on life. What had happened to the spark, the fire, the always wanting to be together?

A small brown Mazda drove into the parking lot and stopped beside the trailer. Coffee in hand, a plump man in his 60s opened the car door and stepped out. Slamming the door, he reached in through the open window to retrieve a dog-eared leather folder. With keys dangling below the folder, the man strode over to the trailer, nodded to Julia, and unlocked the padlock on the trailer door.

"Good morning," he said, smiling.

Julia moved off the cement step to allow Dongals to pass into the trailer. He dropped his folder onto a small metal desk across from the door, and coffee still in hand, turned to face Julia.

"May I come in... sir?" Julia asked, forcing a smile.

"Of course, my dear. Don't be shy." Dongals leaned back against his desk. "Your name?"

"Julia Reinhardt."

She stepped into the trailer and gazed around. Dark and dusty, the tiny trailer held just a small metal desk cluttered with papers and a couple of folding chairs. The only light was cast through the open door and a single small window in the opposite wall. Roger Dongals wore a plaid blue shirt pulled out over an old pair of jeans. His gruff appearance belied his personality. Beneath his thinning hairline, his blue eyes twinkled. Julia's taut nerves began to unknot. He held out a hand.

"Roger Dongals," he said as she shook his hand. "We're waiting for another girl who's also looking for work. It may be a couple of minutes before I take you back to the barns. Have a seat. I need to get my cart." He stepped out of the trailer and disappeared.

Julia felt very awkward. She sat on a metal chair and gazed around her at the rough surroundings. The racetrack was very different from what she had expected. Her limited impressions were based solely on Hollywood's version of the track, the occasional glimpses of a glorious Kentucky Derby run in May, and the few comments from her friends at the riding stable. The clutter and darkness of the personnel manager's trailer gave a hint of the unknown waters into which she was about to plunge. Although normally a determined, headstrong teenager, right now Julia felt nervous about the unknown. In fact, until just recently, she had nursed a healthy fear of horses—not the best fright to have in this particular line of work!

Julia shook her head to clear it of the negative thoughts. She wanted a job and she wanted out of the relationship with Ken. She had to focus on those things to be a success.

Hearing Dongals outside talking to someone, Julia moved to the door of the trailer. Roger was talking to another girl not much older than herself.

"Julia, climb aboard my cart." He gestured toward the other girl. "This is Kim, who is also looking for work."

Roger Dongals climbed into the driver's seat of the electric golf cart and, with Julia and Kim on board, set out for the security gate. He handed each of the girls a security visitor's pass to wear on their shirts, and the guard at the gate waved them through.

Their route took them down a gravel road flanked by fields towards the white barns in the distance. These barns were essentially shedrows, her friends had told her, stalls set back-to-back in long rows of whitewashed cement block foundations. The wooden roofs peaked in the centre of the shed and stretched down across an aisle in front of the stalls. Most of the sheds were enclosed with a three-foot wall surrounding the entire barn. The barns themselves were built in an "H" shape, with two shedrows of about a hundred stalls all together connected by an intervening section of building which had several doors set into the cement wall. Each barn was numbered at the end in large black paint easily visible against the whitewash. Dongals drove by the first few barns, waving and shouting morning greetings to many of the workers and trainers who were busily scrubbing buckets, sorting bridles, and feeding horses.

"We'll try you with Henderson, Julia," he called over his shoulder. "He's been looking for a new hot-walker, and his assistant trainer Lorraine is used to green help. They are a small stable, and you may find it easy to fit in with them."

Julia nodded quietly. She was completely in awe of her surroundings. She could not believe how huge the backstretch was. She began to realize just how many people were employed to care for the thousands of horses stabled here. Because she knew so little about racing and horses in general, many questions crowded her mind. She wasn't even sure what Dongals meant by the term "hot-walker," and assumed that "green help" referred to inexperienced workers.

"Kim, you've got a little more experience. I think we'll try you with Carlson. They're looking for a groom."

After passing several barns, Roger Dongals pulled up to a centre section of Barn 8 and gestured for Julia to exit. He wandered over to a blonde girl leaning against the entrance. Julia stood beside the cart and strained to see into the dark stalls. Many of the horses were munching their early morning meal, but an occasional animal gazed across the bottom door of its stall at the early morning excitement of the racetrack. Ears were pricked forward as if anticipating when they would be allowed to escape their confines to train, bathe, and feel the morning sunshine on their backs. And what lovely specimens of horseflesh these racehorses were! Julia had been riding a thoroughbred horse at her riding school recently, but the riding school horses were not these shiny, sleek creatures! Just the thought of these lively fresh young horses began to bring back the healthy fear that she had thought she had buried.

Roger Dongals was signalling for her to move towards them. He introduced her to Lorraine, who simply glanced at her clothing and footwear and nodded.

"Good luck to you, Julia. I'll be seeing you around." Dongals gave a parting wave and mounted his cart to take Kim to another barn.

Julia felt a moment of insecurity and loneliness as the only two people she even knew slightly were driving away. Yet the moment passed quickly as Lorraine started giving orders.

"Jim isn't here yet, but you'll meet him when he gets here around six. Any experience with horses?" she asked.

"Not much," Julia replied truthfully. "I ride at a local stable."

"You'll learn quick enough at the track." Lorraine nodded toward buckets sitting in the cement ditch in front of the barn. "You can start by scrubbing those water buckets. I'll get you to walk a cold one in a moment." With scarcely another glance at Julia, she walked into the shed.

Julia picked up the scrub brush and glanced around at the barns. It seemed relatively quiet in this area, yet she could hear sounds of activity. The morning was still and calm with the sun quickly warming the quiet air. Chattering birds flew through the shed. A horse and rider came down the road between the barns, the rider holding the horse closely on the bit as it pranced along the road. Used to riding-school horses, Julia noticed that this particular mount was moving down the road sideways more than straight ahead. She wondered how it was possible to control such high-spirited horses. Yet the rider did not seem to be bothered by the antics going on beneath him. He raised his whip in greeting to Julia as he spotted her closely watching him.

"Julia."

Startled, Julia jumped up at the sound of Lorraine's voice behind her. Lorraine stood in the shed beside a tall grey horse. She handed the end of the lead shank to Julia.

"You can walk this horse," she said.

Julia moved forward to take the lead from Lorraine. The lead was soft leather with a chain portion wrapped around the horse's nose. Her mind barely registered Lorraine's instructions as she stared at the young grey filly. Lorraine stooped to undo the bandages wrapped around the filly's front legs.

"You can walk the full length of the shed or if you are needed when a hot one comes in, take a half turn. Make sure you stop if you hear the words, "Hold up; coming through." Call that out when you take a half turn. Watch the horses down the shed. They have some biters and will nail you when you're not looking. What's the matter?" Lorraine sounded irritated as she glanced at Julia.

"I...uh..." Julia wasn't exactly sure what was the matter, except that everything was happening very fast and she wasn't sure if she'd made the right decision. However, she was here and it was employment, so... "Nothing."

"Walk her for 40 minutes unless a hot one comes in. I'll be busy tacking. The water bucket is across from the stall—number 37."

Lorraine pointed to a bucket hanging against the shed. She turned and shouted a greeting to another woman walking down the road toward the shed.

Julia felt dismissed. Glancing once more at the horse standing beside her, she dropped back to the left side of the animal and started forward.

Julia was not walking the horse. The horse was walking her! It didn't take her or the animal very long to figure that out. The young filly, eager to be out of the confines of her stall prison, was stepping right out. The lead shank tightened in Julia's hand, dragging her along so that she practically had to run to keep up. She scarcely had time to think about calling out any intention as the filly took a quick turn to the left and plunged through the middle of the shed. While the horse pulled Julia down the other side of the shedrow, she could hear the chuckles emanating from other grooms and hot-walkers.

"Henderson's got himself a new girl. Wonder how this one will do?"

"Make sure you call when you go through the centre, missy."

"You could slow that filly down, you know. She's been laid up a while."

Embarrassed that she had no control over the horse and no response to their comments, Julia quietly struggled to keep up with the grey horse. But that appeared to be the least of her concerns. Apparently word had travelled fast in the horse world that she was "green" and didn't really know what she was doing. Horses within the stalls lunged out at the filly as they passed closely, nipping her on her flank. The filly, in her defiance, would kick out at the guilty parties. Julia found herself ducking teeth and attempting to avoid the cow-kicking filly. By the time she was back in front of the home stalls, where Lorraine was chatting to a couple of other workers, she knew that she was going to need some instruction if she was to have any control over these high-spirited horses. The filly, knowing exactly her own water bucket, dragged Julia to the other side of the shed for a long drink.

"Mind she doesn't drink too much at one time," the girl next to Lorraine called out. "Watch her throat as she swallows and only allow seven to eight gulps every second full turn."

The filly dragged Julia towards the familiar voices.

"Hold up." Lorraine moved in front of the filly that came to an immediate quiet halt.

"Take her long turns, Julia. Short turns are too hard on her legs. Only walk her 20 minutes as I have a tracker that just went out."

Lorraine reached out to run a practiced hand down the horse's front legs. She signalled for Julia to continue.

"We got time for a smoke, Carla."

Twenty minutes seemed like an eternity to Julia after the first half turn. She and the filly left at a double march along the shed. She had a bad feeling that it was going to be a long day.

Chapter Two

Antonio Descartes had pretty much spent his entire life on the racetrack. His old man was a jockey at Waterford Park in West Virginia and hadn't wanted much to do with Antonio other than to brag to his buddies in the jock's room about how he'd scored with a prominent owner's daughter. Raised around the racetrack backstretch, Tony had walked hots, rubbed horses, and eventually helped to break youngsters at the local farms. He moved permanently to the track when he turned 14, having had no use for school in as many years. His father hooked Tony up exercising mounts with a trainer who rode him in afternoon races. This allowed his old man to have time to attend to other business. Tony didn't mind. It was an "in," and he didn't plan on spending a lot of time at a second-rate bullring like Waterford Park, anyway. Bullring racetracks were less than a mile long with tight turns. Generally, there were cheaper horses at those tracks and lower pay for exercise riders like Tony.

Tony worked the circuits for the next 10 years: winters in Ocala and summers on any number of tracks in North America. His favourite spot was Woodbine. Here the money was good, and he didn't have to compete with the crazy Jamaicans who would get on any horse with hair. Deciding to move permanently to Toronto, he'd found a trainer who treated him well and paid him enough to afford a place off track.

And the girls were good. And easy. Tony admitted that was a weak spot for him. The Toronto girls were willing and he prided himself on his prowess with the ladies. He thought with fondness of his conquests over the last few years. It was a better game than the money he poured through the windows, betting on the horses he'd breezed. Breezing a horse was a morning workout closer to the speed of the race. After that type of workout, Tony would know if he should bet the horse in its next race.

"Got your first mount, Tony."

Descartes fastened his helmet, picked up his whip, and got a leg up onto the two-year-old colt prancing in the shed. He crossed the reins in front of him and nodded to the groom.

"Take me out to the end of the shed. This colt is feeling his oats this morning."

"No problem, Tony. Boss says to just take him once round nice and easy today. He's got a race next week and he wants to work him tomorrow."

Antonio listened as he adjusted the irons. He had nerves of steel when it came to exercising thoroughbreds, and an inborn sense of what to do when the unexpected happened. Oh, he'd had his share of injuries. The worst occurred six years ago when a young horse flipped in the gate on him during morning training. The two-year-olds were particularly prone to rear, lose their balance, and fall onto the unfortunate exercise person. He'd broken some ribs and punctured his spleen. But that was racing. He was hooked and scarcely let the injuries heal before backing the next mount.

Out the end of the shed he hooked up with another rider headed toward the training track.

"Mornin', Tony."

"On the big mount, Thomas? Runner-up for the Plate and the Prince of Wales. I thought Matheson was going to lay her up for the rest of the year?"

The other rider grinned. "Still some big money for three-year-olds this year. You know Matheson won't miss a trick."

Tony laughed. It was a glorious morning to be doing what you loved. At 32 years of age he still enjoyed the early mornings and frisky mounts. Well, maybe not all the mornings. November mornings with workouts in whiteout conditions weren't much fun.

"Henderson's got some new blood. Cute little brunette. You should check her out, Tony."

Tony's mount bucked. Tony responded by bringing the reins down along the neck and sitting deep into the training saddle. The training track was busy already and the young horse was excited.

"Easy boy, just about there."

Nodding farewell to Thomas, Tony picked up a rising trot with the colt as he backed up—trotted him clockwise—to the three-eighths pole. The rhythm of his body kept time with the young colt beneath him. The sun, not yet warm, oozed across the track, casting long shadows from furlong poles and the rail. Other exercise riders saluted him as they breezed by in the opposite direction. Tony was an old-timer and very well-respected. He knew how to handle a difficult mount. The green and white pole came into his vision as he stood in the stirrups.

Slowing the youngster, he turned at a walk and then let the colt begin an unhurried, easy canter in the counter-clockwise direction around the training track. He let the horse take a hold of the bit and stood in the irons, body bracing against the colt's brute strength. God, it was good to be alive! The feeling of euphoria was better than any fix he'd tried. He had to admit that the muscular strength of the colt straining underneath him was almost better than any sex with the countless girls he'd experienced.

Tony pulled up the colt after a mile gallop. The colt reluctantly slowed, nostrils flaring. They turned and headed back to the barn as Thomas pulled up alongside him on the filly whose flanks were now heaving.

"Breezed three-eighths in a slow 44," Tom bragged. Tony cast him a dark look. Forty-four seconds was a fast time for three-eighths of a mile in a morning workout. His friend was always puffing up his own prowess. He smiled.

"Guess we better go to the windows, Thomas."

Thomas saluted him as he came alongside the barn. Tony turned in at the end of the shed, the warmth of the colt tight against his thighs. He could see the groom anxiously waiting at the other end of the barn. His mind wandered to the new girl in Henderson's barn. Maybe at break he'd check her out. It couldn't hurt to have a new piece of ass.

It had turned out to be a really bad first morning. Julia felt she had fortified her fear of horses rather than finally conquering the feelings of insecurity.

The first horse had reared, and the second horse had stomped on her foot and leaned into the toe so that her big toe had swollen to double its size. Lorraine had told her to keep her shoe on and keep walking so that it wouldn't swell. She never got much of a break. It seemed as soon as she was done walking one horse, there was another hot one in to be bathed. Her breaks consisted of running to get hot bath water or gathering hay and straw bales from the end of the barn. The unevenness of the shedrow was hard on her feet. The dirt floor was scuffed from horses and people walking, and a groove had begun to develop in the middle of the shed. She wished that she had worn running shoes instead of heavy boots. She thought that a blister was beginning to develop on her good foot.

Very few people had spoken to Julia. She knew that she was an outsider and felt excluded from conversations, either intentionally or simply because they knew she didn't know anything about racing or the racetrack way of life. Also, it seemed like many of the people who worked for Henderson were smokers. Julia didn't smoke, nor did she want to, which only made her feel even more of an outsider.

Jim Henderson had arrived at 6 a.m., as Lorraine had implied. He hardly said anything to Julia for the first hour, and then had done nothing but shout at her after that initial silence. At one point, when Lorraine was bathing a horse that had just returned from training, the horse kept pushing forward against Julia. When she had stepped back to avoid being bitten, Jim had sworn at her to keep the horse still so that it could be bathed properly. Julia had tried desperately to hold the colt in one spot but it pranced sideways as Lorraine moved the sponge toward the colt's flank, and Jim, scrutinizing her, starting yelling again.

"What the hell is wrong with you, girl?" He pulled the lead shank from her grasp. "If that horse kicks me, I'll have your head, you idiot!" The horse stepped back from Jim's voice, obviously aware that a different person now held him. Jim, already annoyed, shanked the horse several times, relaxing on the lead wrapped around the horse's sensitive nose and then suddenly jerking the shank tight. Both the noise of the chain tightening and the sharp pain of the brass hitting the colt's nose caused the animal to glance apprehensively at its handler. Julia was appalled at the violence in the manoeuvre, and watched as the colt trembled in anticipation of more punishment.

Jim yelled to Lorraine to hurry up and finish the job. Julia was given back the horse to walk through the break. Break time was when the training track closed for harrowing, and most of the workers from the barns headed to the kitchen for coffee or a snack.

Jim stood outside the shedrow having a smoke with Lorraine.

"I'm not convinced she's going to work out," he said. He took a long drag and watched Julia as she passed in front of them along the shed.

"Roger brought her around early this morning and said that she'd had some experience."

Lorraine's blonde hair shone in the sunshine. She had tied the hair back into a ponytail so that it couldn't fall in her eyes while she was grooming horses. Her breasts were practically spilling out of the tight halter top that she wore. She had cut-off shorts that rode well up the tops of her thighs. Jim gazed at her appreciatively. Lorraine was a great worker and gave him a little extra on the side. He'd made her assistant trainer but gave her no real power. He hired only women because he honestly believed they handled the horses better than most men. Except Julia. She seemed terrified.

"Not bloody much experience, I'd say. I thought she was going to cry when that horse stepped on her foot. And she walks them too fast. I don't need them having another workout after training."

"She's not likely to come back tomorrow morning, Jimmy."

"I sure hope not. I'll probably have to let her go." Jim threw the butt of his cigarette into the drain and wandered down the road in the direction of the racing office.

Julia walked five horses the first morning. When she was finished at around 11 o'clock, Lorraine showed her how to rake the shed. It had to be raked three times: the first by moving the dirt into the centre where a groove had been worn, the second angling into the centre, and finally down the centre to make a level dirt layer. To Julia it seemed as though they were extremely picky about even the raking of dirt. She was exhausted. It had been an early 4:30 start to the morning when Ken had brought her here, and she had felt constantly wary of the horses that she had handled. But, miserable as she was, she desperately wanted to keep her job and was determined to have Ken drop her off the next morning. She had heard that there was a dormitory for women up by the gate that was reasonably inexpensive.

Lorraine came out of one of the stalls. She approached the bale where Julia was sitting.

"I'll take you over to the racing office and have you fingerprinted and licensed. Jim pays his walkers $115 a week. He likes all his help back for afternoon feed at 3 p.m. You may not be ready for coming back today. Where do you live?" Lorraine asked.

"I live in Etobicoke. I was planning on taking the bus home," Julia answered. She stood and followed Lorraine to the end of the barn. "I'll plan on staying 'til feed time tomorrow. I was wondering who I talk to about a room in the dorm."

Lorraine looked surprised. "If you're planning on staying, you're going to have to get a lot tougher, girl. The racetrack chews up people like you and spits them out. I doubt you'll even hack it a week!"

Lorraine turned on her heel and headed towards the racing office. Julia, fighting a mounting discouragement, followed behind. She knew that she had to do this. Anything was better than a continued life with Ken.

Chapter Three

Julia had been walking hot horses for four days. The weather at least remained wonderful. August in Toronto was often hot and humid, with very few rainy days. She still felt like an outsider on the backstretch and had yet to make any friends. Each day had brought its share of traumatic events. Her toe that had been stepped on by the horse on the first day had been repeatedly assaulted on the second, third, and fourth days. The toenail on her big toe was turning black. It was very painful to walk on the uneven dirt of the shedrow. Horses lunged from the back of their stalls to try to bite her because grooms neglected to close them behind the screens. Someone had called to her on the third morning, temporarily distracting her so that one of the horses managed to bite her on the shoulder, leaving a tender bruise.

Each night, exhausted, she had returned home to Ken, telling him imaginary stories of the fun and excitement behind working on the backstretch. Happy for her and the prospect of a paycheque, he would rise early the next morning to take her to work before heading out to his own job. Last night she had finally told him of her desire to move into the women's dorm at the track.

"Just trying to make things easier for you," Julia explained.

Ken acted shocked, and then scowled.

"I don't mind taking you in," he said. "I wanted you to get a job, not move out."

"But you've complained every morning about 4 a.m."

"I'm getting used to it," he said, his voice louder than before. "By the time I drop you off, it's pretty much time for me to go to work anyway."

"You complain every night as well." Julia could see that Ken was barely containing his anger.

"Sounds like you want to leave. We haven't even been living together a year and you want to move out. Is this permanent?" Ken, usually so placid, was actually shouting.

Julia had remained quiet after that. It had been a rough night, with Ken sleeping on the couch. She just had to get through the next couple of days. Then she would finally be free.

There would be racing today, and Jim Henderson had a horse entered. Julia had never seen a live horse race, and the excitement of walking a horse that had actually run a race was mounting in her throughout the morning. She had the last walker of the morning, what was considered a "cold one," a horse not sent out under saddle that particular morning for training. Instead, she had to walk the horse for 40 minutes, longer than normal. This young colt was turning into a problem. The first round in the shed had resulted in a bucking incident where the walker behind had nearly been kicked. Terribly apologetic for her lack of control, Julia had walked a little faster, knowing full well that if Jimmy spotted her, she would be reprimanded.

Having walked the colt for 26 minutes, Julia finally believed that maybe he was settling down, but as she turned out of the centre of the barn, taking the forbidden half turn, the horse spotted something fluttering in the breeze outside the shed. Spooked, it reared up and shot straight backwards, the lead shank tightening in her hands. Appalled, Julia hung on to the horse as it dragged her backwards down the shed. She was so certain that she wouldn't be able to stop the horse from backing completely outside and breaking away from her grasp.

"Release!" a voice behind shouted. "Give the horse some lead and he'll stop pulling back from you."

The voice was beside her now as she struggled to hold the horse. A dark-haired man dressed in a red plaid work shirt reached out and placed his hand on top of hers.

"Follow my hand movement," he said quietly as if talking to the spooked horse. "You have to give them their head and they will come back to you. Like this....

"Easy, boy…easy."

The stranger's voice was soft and soothing as he loosened up on the shank. The horse, ears pricked forward as he listened to the new command, immediately stopped backing. The stance, though tense, showed that the man had the colt's complete attention and obedience. The man turned finally and smiled at Julia.

"I'm Antonio," he said. "You're new here?"

Julia, shocked that someone was actually treating her civilly, was overcome with shyness. The stranger appeared to be in his 30s and had the rugged good looks of a person used to living outdoors. His shaven face had the beginning of stubble and his hazel eyes gazed at her kindly. Similar to many racetrack employees, this man was not particularly tall, only around five foot seven. His helmet with red silk cover told her that he was probably a morning exercise person. He had a muscular build, but too stocky to be a jockey like those she had seen in the last couple of days.

"Julia…," she stammered an introduction. "I just started here four days ago."

Antonio let go of the lead shank, and Julia moved beside the colt to resume walking along the shedrow. Antonio fell in beside her.

"Don't worry; you'll catch on," he said; then he cut through the middle when they approached the centre of the barn, and headed off.

Julia was sorry to see him go and became once more acutely aware of being alone. The colt seemed to realize that the man was gone and began to act unruly again but at least not lunging backwards. Julia rounded the shed at the end where hay and straw were stored. She could see Lorraine and Jim chatting together in front of the stalls. Antonio was there as well, listening to the conversation and nodding his approval every now and again.

"Put that horse away," Jim commanded as Julia approached.

Julia knew that she had not walked the horse long enough and was afraid that Antonio may have mentioned the episode on the other side of the shed. Jim, however, did not allude to any incident.

"Rake the shed," Jim said.

Julia picked up the rake, acutely aware that Antonio had his eyes on her. Still feeling tied to Ken, she wasn't sure how she felt about his scrutiny. She moved away from the group as she began raking the loose dirt into the central groove. She had no trouble hearing the others' conversation.

"Chances today, Jimmy?" Antonio was asking.

"The filly's in over her head, Tony, but she needed a race. It's been nearly three weeks since her last start."

"Doesn't sound like she's worth a bet."

"I wouldn't count on her being there. Never know in a horse race. I have to go to the draw. I entered one for Friday. See you around, Tony."

Jim headed down the shed. Julia gave a sigh of relief to see him go. It seemed she couldn't please him, no matter how hard she tried. She tensed up every time Jim walked into the shed and only relaxed when he left. The only thought that kept her going was that Friday was two days away, and she would finally get paid.

Antonio and Lorraine started talking in lower tones. Julia glanced at them and strained to pick up what they were saying.

"How's the new girl working out?" Tony asked.

Lorraine shook her head as she looked towards Julia.

"Not great. In fact, I'm surprised she's still here. She's definitely green, and she lacks good horse judgment. But I gotta hand it to her—she's a hard worker. She gets here on time every morning and stays as long as Jimmy wants."

"Cute little thing, isn't she?" commented Tony, staring at Julia's breasts. "Not too confident around the horses, though, I've noticed."

"No kidding. She's definitely scared of horses, although she tries to hide it. I don't get why she wants to work here, anyway. She's way too soft, Tony. I think Jimmy's going to let her go."

Tony took his eyes off Julia and glanced at Lorraine. "That's too bad," he said. "I was hoping she'd be around for awhile." He looked back at Julia and smiled appreciatively.

"Gotta go. See you around." Tony smacked Lorraine on the butt as he left.

Chapter Four

Friday finally arrived. Lorraine told Julia that Jim Henderson usually gave out the paycheques after the morning break. Meanwhile, Julia was walking the same colt she'd been with when she met Antonio. The colt was not acting any better. The horses seemed to sense that she really didn't know what she was doing.

The colt alternately lunged forward or dragged her backwards. Each turn heightened her fear of what the horse would do next. Stopping to allow a horse out of a stall, Julia felt the colt lean against her. Pushing her against the stalls, the horse squealed and bucked, pinning Julia helplessly against the barn.

This was Julia's limit. The pain and humiliation peaked as Jimmy Henderson happened to walk in the end of the shed at that moment.

"What the hell is going on?" he yelled at her.

She couldn't help herself. Tears were streaming down her face.

"I can't walk him, Jim. He's hurting me." She began to sob.

"You useless bitch!" Jim strode up to Julia and snatching the shank from her hand, he savagely kicked the horse in the stomach as he screamed at her. "You're not cut out for this. I want your licence back, and I don't want to see you again. Get the hell out of my barn!"

Shanking and yelling at the horse, he led it back to its stall. The grooms in the area had slipped out of sight.

The shed was unusually silent except for Julia's quiet crying. Now what would she do? What a miserable boss! He was really unfair! She was all set to move into the dormitory tomorrow and had said her good-byes to Ken. What was she going to do now, with no job and no licence to work on the backstretch?

Lorraine appeared beside her and silently handed Julia her paycheque. With nothing else to do or say, Julia gave her the backstretch licence and walked into the August sunshine. She began a slow fatigued meander back to the main gate.

As Julia approached the last set of barns, she spotted Roger Dongals' cart. What the hell, she thought; it was worth a try.

Roger was busy talking to a trainer, so Julia stood just apart from them to wait until he was finished. Smiling at her, he finished his conversation.

"How are things going at Henderson's barn?" Dongals asked pleasantly.

"Not so great," Julia admitted. "He let me go. I was having problems handling the horses."

Dongals nodded thoughtfully. "Some people aren't really made for this type of work," he began sympathetically. "It's dangerous and some people here think more of the horses than those around them."

"Please, I know that I can do this," Julia began in despair. "I'm supposed to be moving into the dorm tomorrow and I know that if I have a chance with another trainer, I can learn how to handle the horses. I just need to be told what to do." Her brown eyes, so recently in tears, were pleading with him.

Dongals got into his cart.

"All right. I'll see what I can do, but no promises. Not many outfits want women, and they certainly don't like beginners."

To Julia it seemed as if the situation might be hopeless again.

"I have an idea though. Come to the gate at six tomorrow morning if you really are serious."

Dongals drove away.

The next morning, Roger Dongals took Julia to one of the last barns on the racetrack, Barn 12. There he introduced her to the assistant trainer of Wilf Cunningham—better known as Wilf the Weasel. The assistant trainer scarcely looked at her. He simply grunted and told Dongals they would give her a try.

Cunningham's outfit was much larger than that of Jimmy Henderson. Wilf trained 32 horses and took up a large part of one end of the barn. He hired six grooms and had another hot-walker, but none of the help were female. Unlike Henderson, he seemed to prefer male grooms and hot-walkers.

His assistant trainer, Rob, hardly spoke to anyone and certainly didn't give orders the way Lorraine had to Julia. Most of the help were older men in their 50s who had worked their whole life on the backstretch. That first day, Julia asked them many questions, and she was glad that they enjoyed showing off their expertise to a willing learner.

The other hot-walker, George, was a retired jockey in his 60s who immediately took Julia under his wing. He put her on the end of the shank to a quiet filly and walked around with her for the first 10 minutes.

"You're going about this the wrong way," he said as he watched her walking the horse. "Always have your right elbow against the shoulder so that the horse knows you are there. If they happen to step sideways, they won't get your toe. Keep the horse's neck turned. They don't have as much strength with the neck twisted. Once they straighten their neck, they can get their head down to buck. Also, your voice is the most important thing in controlling a horse. Keep your voice quiet but strong. The horse will always listen. The voice can accomplish more than beating on them."

As the day wore on, if a horse that was a little spunky came in after the morning workout, George made sure that he was the available hot-walker. Cold horses that were laid up or feeling frisky were walked by either George or one of the grooms. Julia found that she was most often on the shank with quiet horses or tired ones. The grooms in this barn were good about closing their screens so that the horses in the stalls would not bite her or the horse that she was walking.

"It's one of the racetrack rules," a groom said to her. "We could be fined if security or the stallman came down the shed. Trainers don't want to annoy the stallman. The stallman could permit, move, or take away stalls from trainers. Having stalls on the backstretch is critical to survival in the racing business."

The best part of working for Wilf Cunningham was at the end of training hours when Old Donald, the ancient horseman who lived in a tack room by the outfit, would throw a bridle and blanket on the pony. The pony was a retired horse no longer used to trot beside the thoroughbreds as they warmed up immediately prior to races. Old Donald said that Julia could ride under the trees in a picturesque area behind the barns. The old horse was nearly as ancient as Old Donald and walked placidly, allowing Julia to smile and relax, enjoying the beauty of the backstretch for the first time.

It was three days before Julia got a chance to meet "the Weasel." An ex-jockey, the trainer drove a leased Mercedes. He wore a three-piece suit and oiled his greying hair back on his head.

Cunningham strode over to meet his new employee, a sly smile on this face.

"You're a nice looking girl. The boys must like having you around. How about a roll in the hay some time?"

Julia was appalled by this explicit openness. She wasn't quite sure what to say.

George, on the other hand, laughed brusquely.

"Wilf, leave the kid alone. She doesn't need that kind of crap when she's just starting. Besides, you've already got a wife."

Cunningham gave a sly chuckle.

"I see you're fitting in quite well with the boys," he said.

Cunningham didn't seem to care how she handled the horses and what her experience was. She found out later that he kept a closer eye on his help than it first appeared. She had obviously passed inspection. Getting a little more used to the backstretch attitude and not quite as naive, Julia realized that sex appeal might have helped Wilf Cunningham in his judgment of her expertise.

Julia's favourite groom was Carl, who rubbed horses for Wilf on the backside of the barn. She spent much of her time after morning training hours listening to his stories and admiring the horses he groomed. She had a particular fondness for a horse that Carl had nick-named "Mama Goat." The filly was extremely nervous and lived with a goat in her stall to keep her calm. Carl explained that when they ran the horse, the goat travelled along beside the horse to the paddock where she was saddled for the race. The racing name of the filly was Northern Snowdrop, which Julia thought was a beautiful name. Carl suggested that the next time the horse started, maybe Wilf would let her "run" the filly—walk it over to the paddock. Carl would be beside her to prevent any problems.

Julia couldn't believe how kind the men who worked for the Weasel were. Their treatment of her, each other, and the animals they cared for was completely different from the degrading beatings that she had experienced at Jim Henderson's stable. Although still nervous of the high-strung thoroughbreds, Julia found that she was learning effective ways to handle the horses, and her fears were beginning to dissipate.

After working for the Weasel for five days, she was raking the shed in front of Carl's stalls to help him out, when Antonio happened to walk into the barn. Julia smiled to herself and continued to rake the shed as she ignored the man walking down the shed, helmet in hand.

"Hey, Julia," he said. "How's it going? I hear you're fitting right in here with the Weasel."

Carl laughed. "Tony, you scoundrel," he called. "I haven't seen you in a donkey's age. How about coming back to mount some horses in your old outfit?"

Astonished by the conversation, Julia looked up at both Carl and Antonio. So Tony had worked for the Weasel in the past.

Tony winked at Carl. "Maybe the occasional filly," he suggested, as if Julia was not there.

"Have you warned her about the Weasel?" he asked Carl.

Julia stopped raking the shed and glanced inquisitively at Carl. He shrugged.

"You know the Weasel is the same as most of the scoundrels on this racetrack. Just wants you on your backside. You should know that after working for Henderson and his gang of whores."

Julia was appalled at Carl's candid speech, the first that she had heard in this barn. She had no idea that others on the racetrack had that opinion of the Henderson barn. Still rather naive, she was shocked at some of the language and suggestions.

Antonio smiled at her, his warm hazel eyes capturing her attention as they had only a short week ago. His T-shirt showed the muscles in his chest and arms, taut from years of riding racehorses. Aware of a sudden attraction to this man, Julia quickly subdued the desire. She felt totally unprepared for any relationship right now— specially with someone like him. He was too old for her anyway. But he did have a certain rough appeal….

Carl was still rambling on about Henderson. "Everyone knows that Lorraine is screwing Henderson so she can run his barn."

Julia looked at Carl with complete surprise.

He chuckled. "Shouldn't be news to you—you worked around them both."

Antonio picked a piece of hay from a nearby bale and stuck it in his mouth. His teeth worked the strand as he watched Julia carefully.

"You'll like working for the Weasel. He's got a good crew. Just take care to be first to the bank with your paycheque. After the first two, the rest of 'em bounce," he said; then turned to Carl. "Has she met Old Donald?"

"First day," Carl replied. "He saddled up the old pony, and she's been riding bareback every day after training hours in the ring. I think the old geezer has got a soft spot for the girl."

"There's a new racing movie out called *Phar Lap*." Antonio was talking to Julia again. She steeled herself for his invitation. "Wondered if you wanted to check it out on Friday? Provided Cunningham hasn't got any horses running."

"Sounds like fun," Julia heard herself saying. What an idiot! Didn't she know that this was a date? What did she think she was doing, going out with another man after just getting rid of the previous one? She saw Tony smiling at her and turned quickly away, like she didn't even want to acknowledge that she'd accepted.

"I'll pick you up at the gate at six," Tony said. "See you then."

Carl whistled and went back to currying Northern Snowdrop.

Chapter Five

Woodbine Racetrack was located in adjacent industrial and commercial sections of Metropolitan Toronto. It was obvious to Julia each morning that the track was hidden in the shadow of the large airport. Yet she was thankful that the horses became immune to the loud engines of jets and the drifting dark shapes of planes as they flew overhead. The 600-acre parcel of land encompassed the massive grandstand, a mile-long dirt track, a regular turf course and a mile-and-a-half Marshall turf course reserved for specialty stakes races. Racing was held at Woodbine at 4 p.m. every Wednesday and 1:30 p.m. Thursday through Sunday. There was no live racing on Mondays or Tuesdays, traditionally called "dark days" by the Ontario Jockey Club.

Julia had yet to wander through all the 24 main barns in the backstretch, which housed over 1500 horses. Each morning she walked past the mile-long training track with its starting gate and a smaller oval dirt ring. This allowed for morning training without disrupting the layers of the main track needed for the afternoon racing card. There were also several smaller sales barns and a sales arena where multi-million dollar colts and fillies were sold every September.

She'd learned that more than 1000 workers made their living on the Woodbine backstretch. About half of those workers lived on the backstretch, primarily in the tack rooms adjacent to the main barns. Some of the older horsemen saw little of the outside world. They kept their meagre possessions in their rooms, venturing out only to eat in the kitchen. The Horsemen's Benevolent and Protective Association

(HBPA) helped to pay for a minister, doctor, dentist, and any other amenities to make the backstretch workers' lives easier.

In Wilf Cunningham's outfit, Julia found that George, her fellow hot-walker, had a surplus of information when it came to other barns, their workers, and where to get what you needed on the backstretch. George seemed particularly cozy with Roger Dongals, who stopped by the barn regularly to chat. Roger was the representative for the horsemen, appointed by the HBPA. Julia assumed correctly that Roger was the source of much of George's endless supply of information.

One morning, waiting for the first hot horse to come back to the barn following the morning training break, George sauntered over to where Julia sat on a bale of straw opposite the empty stall.

"You know Marissa who works for the outfit at the other end of our barn?" George asked.

"Of course," Julia replied.

Marissa was the hot-walker for the noisy outfit in their barn. The trainer generally hired migrant workers from the Caribbean, in direct contrast to most of the Woodbine outfits. Marissa was the exception to this rule. She was an older woman who kept to herself but had gone out of her way to befriend Julia. She wore her thick red hair in a long braid down her back. She would bring Julia a coffee when the canteen truck arrived during break and drop hints on handling the horses as they passed each other walking through the centre of the barn. Julia didn't know a lot about Marissa other than that she lived with her cats off the racetrack.

"She's been working for that trainer for a number of years. Rumour has it she's leaving."

His voice was lowered conspiratorially to her and he rolled his eyes to the far end of the shed. Everything was always a big dark secret with George. But he always managed to pique Julia's curiosity.

"Why?"

George slunk up to her and leaned in towards Julia as if he had the most interesting information in the world.

"She's got a kid, you know. Rumour has it she screwed the trainer years ago."

Julia was beginning to become accustomed to George's rambling but his crudeness still took her by surprise.

"Her trainer?"

"Cunningham."

Oh, great. Just the information she needed wandering inside of her head the next time her boss walked down the shedrow. She shook her head and glanced sceptically at the squat, chubby man.

"So what?" she asked, in typical racetrack fashion.

George straightened up with authority. "So...apparently the kid is sick. Really sick. Must be six or seven years old by now. Marissa doesn't have much money, so she's putting the screws to Cunningham to support her while she supports her boy. You get it?"

"Hot horse in," someone called.

George picked up his shank and moved into the corner of the empty stall as a horse came in from training.

Julia was thinking things about Cunningham that she didn't want to consider. After all, he was married to a wonderful woman whom she'd met more than once in the last week.

George led the horse out of the barn for Rob to bathe. Julia tagged along, confused. George was once again leaving her with more questions.

"Why would Marissa...?" she began, but George cut her off, knowing full well that Rob was all ears.

"Let me tell you something about racetrackers and the backstretch, honey. It ain't all glory, fancy owners, and winning races. There's a dark side to the racetrack. Extortion, fraud, rape, murder—you name it. You stay here long enough, you'll see it all. And I'm talking only a couple of years."

"No place for a woman," Rob added. "Should've never let women on the backstretch."

George's words rang home ominously for Julia. Extortion, fraud, rape, murder...? Was he just stringing her along?

Unfortunately, Julia would find out firsthand that his words were only too true. And sooner than she thought.

Chapter Six

Julia had not been out on a date in at least five years. She had been with Ken since she was 14 years old and had essentially been shielded from the dating game of other teenagers. Now she stood contemplating her limited wardrobe in the tiny dorm room. In the end, she chose jeans and a blouse. The jeans were worn and cheap and the blouse evoked repulsive fashion trends from five years previously—pillow-like sleeves and a V-neck. Julia stood in the bathroom and brushed her shoulder-length hair until it shone. She paused reflectively to gaze at her complexion in the mirror. The deep brown eyes shone back to her in a nervous sense of anticipation. She had never seen the need for makeup, and Ken had never asked her to enhance her natural olive skin. Julia held her breath and watched the lines around her mouth crease in the need for release. She was the two-year-old filly held in check in the starting gate, listening for the sound of the bell to ring into her sensitive twitching ears. She let the air out in a sudden expulsion. It was time to go.

Julia gathered her keys and, pushing a few dollars into her tight jeans' pocket, left her room in the dorm to meet Tony at the security gate. Arriving at the foot of the outdoor stairwell, she walked gingerly across the gravel past Dongals' locked trailer, not wanting to stir the dust from the gravel onto her clean clothes.

Antonio drove an old white Chevy. He pulled into the dorm parking lot as Julia stopped, poised against the backdrop of the white trailer. He was very cordial, and got out to help her into the car on the passenger side. She quietly stood back, not sure what to say to a man from the racetrack who was treating her respectfully.

He held the door, and Julia felt an unexpected urge to flee before it was too late.

As he drove, Tony talked about the outfit where he worked, the horses he galloped and the bets that he had made, particularly the good ones. With a growing interest in racehorses and racing, Julia quietly absorbed the information. She was overcome with an unusual silence. Normally, she would be asking many questions about the horses, the people, and the racetrack. Tony talked fondly about a recent stakes winner that he helped condition. Julia was in awe of his prowess. Her nerves were as taut as Northern Snowdrop's nerves when away from the goat.

The theatre was only a short drive from the racetrack and they arrived early for the show. Tony suggested they adjourn to the restaurant next door for a drink. Julia was trying to relax and she knew that alcohol might be the remedy to calm her. She was also deeply interested in the tales that Tony's ego was weaving into her imagination. She wanted to hear more about life on the backstretch.

Tony appeared to be totally relaxed and at ease with Julia. His wavy brown hair fell into his eyes periodically, but he would brush the strands back with a finger as he smiled at the young woman across the table. Her nervous reactions seemed to boost his confidence. He unfolded his tales of the track slowly which served to further enhance Julia's admiration of an admittedly hard existence.

The movie *Phar Lap* was a horse-lover's dream, and both Julia and Antonio sat quietly enraptured as the story of the Australian rags-to-riches racehorse unfolded. The movie was over early—a necessity for backstretch workers, and Julia followed Tony slowly back to his car, regretting that the pleasant evening was over. Tony was just as cordial, helping her into the car, although his hand rested on her arm a little longer than necessary.

Tony drove towards the racetrack. Julia was not sure what to expect when he left her at the backstretch gate, and her heart thumped in anticipation. Passing the entrance to the backstretch, Tony continued along Rexdale Boulevard.

Julia was a little disturbed at this turn of events.

"Where are we going?" she asked timidly as she looked out into the deserted streets of the industrial neighbourhood.

"Thought that you might want a coffee after the show," Tony suggested casually. Julia relaxed significantly. Coffee at the local Tim Horton's did sound like a rather pleasant ending to the evening.

Tony, however, had different ideas. Driving farther from the track, he finally turned into an apartment complex not far from where Julia and Ken had lived in Etobicoke. She began to get very anxious.

"Where are we? What are you doing?"

"I thought you might want to meet my roommates," Tony said. "They used to work with racehorses—Standardbreds rather than Thoroughbreds." He gave her his warm friendly smile.

She was not completely convinced that his intentions were in her best interest. Yet if he had roommates, then it must be reasonably safe. Right?

Julia allowed Tony to lead her up the stairs to the dimly lit corridor outside the apartment. Tony opened the door to a hockey game playing on the TV set in the centre of the room. A couple lounged in front of the TV, drinking coffee and cheering on the Maple Leafs.

Introductions made, Tony suggested that Julia give him a hand in the kitchen to make the coffee. Julia's heart was pounding. She had a pretty good idea of where this evening was going, but she wasn't sure how to stop the progression. Julia paused at the entrance to the kitchen. It seemed safe enough, but she was far from feeling safe at this point.

Antonio turned and smiled at her, beckoning her to join him as he filled the coffee maker with fresh water. Julia took an unsteady step towards the vibrant man.

Turning out the overhead light, Antonio pushed her against the wall and roughly kissed her.

Julia pushed back. "I'm not ready. This is way too soon." She was shocked and disappointed in this man she had naively thought only wanted to help her and treat her kindly.

Antonio ignored her. His hand shot up under her blouse and grasped her breast, kneading the nipple in an expert grip. Julia gasped in shock as he kissed her again.

"You are ready, honey. That's why women go out with Antonio Descartes."

Julia was not used to this type of forwardness. She pushed at him but felt her unwilling body starting to respond to the attention. She couldn't understand what was happening. This man was forcing her into an uncompromising dilemma, and a part of her was responding to this unwelcome situation. It didn't make sense.

"Please don't," she said again. "I need to go home."

Her thoughts turned to Ken and the safeness of that relationship. No fear of the unknown or a man who would not take no for an answer. Tony's roughness and determination made Julia wonder if it was only old-fashioned sex that was being demanded. Again, Antonio was ignoring her protests. It didn't seem to matter to him what she said or how she pushed on his solid biceps.

Tony had her wrist and was guiding her down the hallway. His roommates scarcely gave them a glance as they watched the hockey power play in dogged anticipation of a goal. Julia found herself in his bedroom. Tony was very strong, the years of galloping horses having developed his muscles beyond that of the average man. He pushed her onto the bed and in a swift move was on top of her. She felt helpless in the onslaught, and for the first time that evening was truly afraid.

Tony stopped briefly and sat up to look at her.

"Don't be afraid, Julia. I just want you so bad I can't help myself." His eyes were devouring her body, undressing her first before his hands began the task.

Julia knew she was in over her head but figured that it was far too late to say no again. She decided that it was better to lie still and let the inevitable happen. She berated herself for being stupid enough to allow this situation to get this far.

While she hesitated, Tony took the initiative.

Chapter Seven

It was raining. The backstretch was dark and gloomy, which matched Julia's mood as she walked through the barns to work. Horses whinnied to her for food as she passed close to the shedrows. She meandered past the red brick of the kitchen, the odour of grease from early morning bacon and home fries drifting out. The rain was not heavy but rather a light continuous drizzle that, nevertheless, got her quite wet by the time she reached Barn 12. Carl was already at work organizing bales of straw and hay outside his four stalls. George had yet to make an appearance.

"Mornin'," Carl called a greeting. "Wilf put the filly in for the Sunday race. Want to take her for a stroll?"

"Sure," Julia replied and went into the tack room to retrieve a lead shank.

Looping the chain of a shank around the filly's nose, Julia talked quietly to this special horse. Thin because of nervous walking around the stall despite the presence of the goat, Northern Snowdrop anxiously pushed her nose towards Julia. Maybe it was the fact that this horse was nervous too that drew Julia to it. She took the filly out into the shed and walked past Carl as he adjusted the radio to a favourite morning program.

Julia was beginning to find walking the first couple of horses in the morning relaxing. There was little activity in the barn as the riders had yet to make an appearance. She could reflect on her few experiences at the track and closely watch the work of grooms and trainers. Afraid that she would begin to cry, she pushed the previous night's experience with Tony furthest from her mind. She had left him sound asleep shortly after midnight and walked back to the racetrack. Tony had not said a word as he used her, and didn't seem to care how she felt as she lay there rigidly waiting for him to finish. She had just wanted to leave, and get as far away from the man as possible. The walk had taken her three hours, and she was running on adrenalin this morning after a fitful two hours of sleep.

Snowdrop pranced along beside Julia, looking carefully for any excuse to spook. Julia talked to the filly like an old hand. Carl smiled as she passed him.

"Do you want to run the horse on Sunday?" he asked. Julia paused walking the filly and gazed at Carl, realizing the implication of his suggestion. He was asking if she wanted to take the horse over the paddock for the race.

"Do you think I could handle her?"

"Sure." Carl smiled again. "I'll be there to help if you need me."

Snowdrop stomped her foot in the soft dirt and Julia began to feel marginally better. The rain softly drummed on the metal roof of the shed. Yesterday she had seen a horse gelded and the groom had insisted on throwing the testes onto the roof—for good luck, he claimed. She couldn't help but think of that now as she listened to the rain.

The Saturday morning continued quietly, as most horses in the barn did not go to the track to train. George failed to make an appearance. Carl figured that he was hung over. In typical racetrack fashion, he hadn't even called to say he wouldn't be in to work.

As she approached the centre of the shed, Julia glanced at the tack rooms. These rooms were small, only 8 by 12 feet, and usually had metal bunk beds at one end. At Woodbine, only the men were supposed to live in the tack rooms, as the women had the option of living in the dorm. Tack rooms were allotted to the trainers based on the number of horses stabled at the track. Like most racetrackers, George had not started the season working for the Weasel, and so stayed in another barn. Carl suggested that maybe this was planned so that the grooms couldn't wake him up after a night of over-indulgence.

Wilf came into the barn at the end of training, around 11 o'clock. Directly behind him strode Antonio. Spotting him, Julia moved to the other side of the barn where Carl's stalls were located. However, she made her move too late, as Tony followed her closely. Carl was nowhere in sight.

"I was worried about what happened to you last night."

Julia stared at him. Didn't he realize that she had not wanted to go as far as he had pushed?

"I walked back to the track," she said quietly.

"I would have driven you," he said.

Julia did not answer him but sat down on a bale of straw. She was beginning to feel weary from the long night and early morning. Tony drew a hand under her chin. The gesture was far too intimate for her, and Julia jerked her head away.

"What's the matter?" he asked.

"How could you ask that? You pushed me into doing something that I didn't want. I feel used." Angry but afraid she would cry, Julia looked away.

"If you didn't want to sleep with me, why did you come home with me?"

Julia was furious. "I didn't have much choice."

Carl appeared from around the corner with the lunchtime feed in hand. Julia immediately stopped talking. She did not want the men in the outfit to know what had happened. She knew from experience that the walls of the shed had ears, though. Carl had probably heard enough to be able to figure out the rest of the story. Julia stepped back, away from both of the men. She felt barely accepted on the backstretch, particularly after her experience at Henderson's barn, and she suspected that Carl, George, and the other members of Cunningham's outfit would respect her even less after hearing about her night with Antonio.

"Tony, my man," she heard Carl greet Antonio. "How's that outfit treating you? You seem to be spending some time around here lately. Thinking about coming home?"

Tony laughed and smiled towards Julia. She turned her back to him. It seemed to her that he was indifferent about anything that had happened between them the previous evening. He was back to his old charming self, appearing kind-hearted and unthreatening.

"I like your Julia here. She went out with me last night, and I just came to see if she still likes me today."

"Knowing you, the answer is probably no." Carl chuckled drily.

Julia could hear footsteps and when she took a quick peek, Carl had moved up closer to Tony.

"I have a pretty good idea what your game is, Tony, and I don't particularly like it," Carl said in a lower voice. "Don't let me find out that you've hurt her."

Antonio saluted him in a mocking gesture, and turned toward Julia, who quickly put her back to him.

"I want to see you again, Julia," Antonio said. "Come by the shed and visit me sometime."

Julia didn't answer. She completely ignored him as he moved past her down the shed.

When he was gone, Carl asked. "Did he hurt you?" Julia heard the concern in his voice.

Did he hurt her? No, not really, although he was kind of rough. But he forced her to do something she didn't want to do. Was that rape? It wasn't violent. She hadn't fought him. She just felt abused, disrespected, violated.

"No," she answered. She wanted to change the subject. Carl knew far more about her personal life than was necessary. "Can you show me how to groom?"

Carl smiled at her and picked up his grooming kit.

"Go into Mama Goat's stall, and I'll tell you what to do."

Julia bent under the webbing and talking quietly to the horse, tied her to the chain at the back of the stall. The dark bay filly stood quietly waiting to be brushed.

Carl handed Julia the curry comb.

"Circular motions. Just curry where the saddle has left a mark. Then use the hard and soft brushes alternately on the whole body. That stimulates the skin and massages the muscles."

Julia responded by currying the girth mark still slightly visible from yesterday's training. Carl leaned on the webbing.

"I should've warned you about Antonio. His reputation precedes him. He's been with a lot of women in the years that I've known him, and he's half in love with most of them. But it's not real love, Julia. He's not a stayer. I think he'll treat you okay, but it's short term. Please remember that."

Looking up from what she was doing, Julia glared at him suspiciously.

"Why are you being nice to me? Do you want to sleep with me as well?"

Carl laughed.

"I'd love to, honey, but I know that's not an invitation. I have enough skeletons in my closet. I don't need a woman. I'm a reformed alcoholic. Belong to A.A." Carl pulled a tiny black book from his back pocket.

"This is a tough racket, Julia. You're going to have to develop some thick skin if you want to survive here. I think you have a knack with the horses. You have a quiet voice and a kind touch. That's probably partly what attracted Tony."

Chapter Eight

Sunday came very quickly for Julia. She had never been over to the grandstand yet to see a live race. However, she had spent some time in the backstretch kitchen watching the races simulcast on television. Avid bettors watched anxiously and ran for the betting windows set up next to the kitchen one minute to post. Julia couldn't really understand the shouting and excitement that occurred as the horses turned into the stretch and headed for the wire. She didn't see the point of yelling at a television monitor when the horses were running live down the backstretch only a short distance away.

The morning work finished early and Julia headed back to the dorm to clean up for the special afternoon ahead. She shared a room with another girl whom she hardly knew. Much to Julia's surprise, she had only seen her twice in three weeks. Apparently her roommate spent most evenings elsewhere. The room was quite large and had a separate bathroom. The women were allowed to have a refrigerator and a toaster oven in their rooms to make meals, unlike at the barns, where all cooking equipment was strictly forbidden because of the fire hazard.

George was good about including all the barn help in the weekly race to the bank to cash their paycheques. As a group, they usually went for brunch at the local pancake house and then grocery shopping. Julia had the opportunity to pick up a few meals for the coming week.

Similar to the barns on the backstretch, the women were not allowed to have a phone in their room. The Ontario Jockey Club had created this rule to discourage outside betting. Considered an inconvenience by most, Julia enjoyed the complete separation from Ken, but had made a point of phoning him every few days. She was loath to completely cut off a man who had been with her for a number of years. They had even met briefly for dinner a week ago. Unfortunately, it had been a bad decision. Ken had begged her to return home, and then responded angrily when she had refused.

Julia made herself a sandwich and changed into a blouse and clean jeans for her first experience at taking a horse to the paddock. She was to take the skittish Northern Snowdrop. Carl told her not to worry about handling the horse as he would be there to help if she had any trouble. George was scheduled to walk the horse following the race. Julia had wanted to walk the horse then as well, but Carl claimed that the walk to the paddock was tiring enough without a horse and could be gruelling with a difficult horse.

Northern Snowdrop was to start in the fourth race. Post time for the first race was 1:30 p.m., and they had to take the horse over during the third race. That meant that the filly had to be at the tunnel by 2:10. The tunnel was the route that took the horses below the Marshall Turf course to the main dirt track. Instead of going for lunch, Carl was staying behind at the barn to prepare the horse for the race and keep her calm. Julia was anxious to get back there as soon as possible.

Julia wasn't sure how she would be handling the horse. Snowdrop had been a little jumpy just that morning. Carl said that the horses were treated differently prior to a race, and they were excited by the changes. Julia herself was somewhat tense in anticipation of the event. She was beginning to feel more confident about handling horses, but this experience was bound to have its surprises.

Arriving back at the barn, listening for the PA speakers to call the horses for the first race, Julia found Carl outside Snowdrop's stall icing her ankles. The filly's front ankles and legs were wrapped in red cloth bandages dripping wet with icy water.

"She won't have anything to do with the ice tub," said Carl. "She's always jumping out so I just use cold water bandages." He sporadically splashed another cup of ice water from the bucket beside him onto the bandages.

"Why do you ice her?"

"Wilf likes icing them all prior to the race. He hopes that icing them might take any heat from unseen injuries out of their legs."

Julia nodded. She wondered when the Weasel would make an appearance prior to the race. He usually wandered in at the last moment before the horse went to the paddock. Unlike Henderson, who was always watching every move that Lorraine made and giving constant orders just before a race, the Weasel seemed to trust his crew to do the right thing for the horses. They were experienced horsemen and had been doing this type of job all their lives. George had disagreed with Julia's deduction.

"Don't be silly. He's just taking every opportunity possible to rub shoulders with the owners. Doesn't matter that much whether they win or lose just so long as they are paying that 30-dollars-a-day stall rate."

"Doesn't the trainer get 10 percent of the winnings?" Julia had asked.

"When he thinks the horse has a shot, he'll be hanging out at the barn—you wait and see. He'll be anxious to see just how much to bet on the horse."

Julia sat down on a bale opposite the filly's stall. The horse watched Julia carefully, giving her sleek dark bay head a toss every now and again. The filly had no white on her head at all but did have an extra unusual whirl in her hair in the centre of her forehead. A chain attached her to the wall at the front of the stall so that she wouldn't try to eat any straw bedding just prior to the race. Her nostrils flared with the Vicks that Carl had rubbed into them and she was trying her best to blow out the irritating substance. Carl explained that some trainers believed that the Vicks would help to keep the nasal passages clear for the race.

Both the horse and Julia could hear the crowd gathering in the grandstand a quarter of a mile away. Post time was nearing for the afternoon racing card, and the horse twitched in anticipation. Carl pulled his rub rag from his back pocket and stroked the filly carefully above her eyes.

"She knows what's going to happen." He tickled her under her muzzle. "I don't think a horse ever forgets racing even if it lives beyond 30 years."

Carl sat beside Julia and pulled a piece of straw from the bale to chew while he watched the filly. He had taken the goat from the stall and tied her outside the shed to graze.

For the first time in nearly three weeks, Julia felt at ease with the racetrack world, but her body tensed in anticipation of the race. Mama Goat looked at her with her soft brown eyes and Julia yearned to reach out and stroke her velvety neck as they waited for the call to post. Muscles rippled beneath the filly's chest and little quivers of longing for freedom made her shiver.

"Easy, girl," Carl said soothingly.

He was a tall man for the track, over six feet, and he stretched his long legs across the bale of straw. His short, well-groomed hair was greying, but he brushed a couple of strands that had shifted out of place. Many grooms dressed in their racetrack best to paddock horses that had a chance at winning, but Carl tended to wear clean jeans and a clean shirt as often as possible, even for the morning training hours. He hardly ever sported the manure-encrusted boots or torn pants that seemed commonplace on the backstretch.

Julia watched Carl close his eyes and doze. There was still some time to post, and a relaxed groom helped to relax the horse. Horses seemed to be good at picking up on their handler's emotions, as Julia knew too well—whether it was relaxed, happy, or nervous.

"Attention, horsemen! Bring your horses over for the first race. Bring over the horses for the first race. Twenty minutes to post," the loudspeakers announced.

Snowdrop's ears twitched and she turned her head towards the speakers.

Carl rose and stretched. "Not much time for a nap around here, is there?" he asked the horse affectionately. He glanced at Julia. "I'm going to get her bridle ready. Keep an eye on her for me, okay? You can put some cold water on her bandages every 15 minutes or so." Not waiting for an answer, he headed down the shedrow to Wilf's main tack room where the racing bridles were kept.

The filly watched Julia closely. Julia's heart was pounding in anticipation. She didn't move, and attempted to look relaxed, hoping that Mama Goat wouldn't pick up on her nervousness and would be easy to walk over to the paddock. She had seen some of the horses at the tunnel on previous race days, rearing, bucking, and dragging their handlers back and forth. She was glad that Carl was going to be close to help her if there was a problem.

The loudspeakers continued to announce the races, either calling the horsemen over to the paddock or giving results and naming the horses that were to proceed to the test barn. The winner and another horse from each race were always called to the test barn where they cooled out, and then urine was collected from the animal so that a laboratory test could be performed. Many of the drugs that trainers employed to get the animals to perform at their peak were illegal for use in the actual race. If a horse tested positive for a drug, the owner forfeited the winnings, and the trainer lost his licence for at least a month.

In her limited experience, Julia had yet to hear of this happening. Most test results were "negative," a sign that most trainers knew the limits of drug use. Several veterinarians worked on the backstretch, and it was a daily occurrence for a vet to come into the shed to administer some sort of medication.

Carl returned with a clean racing bridle. As the speakers announced that horsemen should prepare their horses for the fourth race, Carl rinsed out the filly's mouth with water and slipped the bit behind her teeth. He pulled the bridle up over Snowdrop's ears as he talked quietly to the horse. The filly was prancing and pacing, the excitement beginning to make her muscles twitch.

Julia watched the filly with wide eyes.

"Take the cold water bandages off her legs, please." Carl motioned to the bandages. "It's easier with two of us. I'll keep a hold of her for you."

Julia moved under the lone crossbar in front of the filly's stall and removed the wet bandages.

"Can you hold her?" Carl asked quietly. He had run the lead shank through the D-bit. "I have to get the goat." Julia nodded and took hold of the leather lead.

The strength of the horse vibrated into her hands. She could easily feel the tense anticipation. Carl appeared at the end of the shed with the goat on its tether.

"Bring her down the shed," he said.

Julia unlatched the crossbar and Snowdrop bounded out of the stall into the shedrow. Julia pressed her elbow into the filly's shoulder and loosely held the shank, so the bit wouldn't pull at her mouth. The two of them made their way towards Carl, who was nodding approvingly.

"You're beginning to look like a natural in handling these animals. It won't be long till you'll be one of the best hot-walkers on the backstretch." His quiet praise meant a lot to Julia, and she was glad she hadn't given up when Henderson had fired her. Carl kept pace beside her as they headed down the road towards the tunnel.

Walking Northern Snowdrop outside the shedrow was a whole new experience. There were a multitude of new sights and sounds that made the filly twist her ears and prance beside Julia.

As they approached the tunnel, the third race could be heard running on the other side. Mama Goat stopped and stood very still, ears pointed directly at the sounds of thundering hooves and the roaring crowd.

"Talk to her, Julia," Carl said. "Try to get her attention away from the race and get her focused back on you."

"Easy, girl. Easy." Julia stroked the horse and tried to reassure her as they continued ahead.

Carl took the number clip from the official at the gap to the tunnel and, stroking the filly's neck, reached up and clipped the black tag on the right-hand side of the bridle.

"The third race is over. Time to get a move on. Are you going to be okay with her?"

Julia nodded. She wasn't really all right but she wasn't about to admit that to Carl. She was very nervous that something might go wrong, and she would startle the horse and not handle her correctly. Her worst fear was losing her grip on the shank. Her hands were sweating in the warm late-August sunshine, more from nerves than from the heat of the day. Yet Snowdrop pranced beside her without making a wrong motion. The filly was more experienced at the game of racing than Julia, and knew exactly where she was going and what was going to happen once they reached the paddock. They moved through the tunnel with the other horses and emerged onto the main dirt track.

It was more difficult to manoeuvre in the soft track dirt. They kept to the outside white rail that encircled the track and began the half-mile walk to the crowded grandstand. The horses were beginning to buck and prance with greater intensity. Carl was careful to keep the goat within Snowdrop's line of sight. The filly danced around Julia until they were facing the wrong way.

"Take her in a little circle when she does that," Carl said. Julia circled the filly around and continued walking towards the grandstand.

As they approached the end of the grandstand, Julia became aware of individual patrons leaning over the fence.

"You got a winner there, sweetie?"

"What post is that horse?"

"Any chance with that one today?"

Julia felt bombarded with questions and shouts from the crowd. She nearly missed Carl's next set of instructions.

"I'll take her when we get into the paddock. The goat will have to stay there, and Snowdrop is a bit hard to handle when she's being saddled. You watch closely so you'll know what to do next time."

Julia followed the other horses through the dirt track that led between the clubhouse and the main grandstand. The horses trotted alongside their handlers as the crowd pressed in from both sides. There were many new sights and sounds surrounding Julia, but her attention was completely absorbed by the filly. Carl had moved ahead to tie the goat to one end of the paddock area. He returned and took the shank from Julia, who finally breathed a sigh of relief.

Carl winked at her. "You did a great job. Even Wilf noticed."

Sure enough, Wilf Cunningham was standing in the paddock outside one of the saddling stalls. Beside him stood an older gentlemen dressed elegantly in a pin-striped suit. Julia assumed that this was Snowdrop's owner.

Carl stood in front of the filly and talked quietly to her as the jockey's valet and Cunningham saddled the horse. He pulled on the bit to get the filly's attention as the elastic overgirth was tightened.

"Riders up!" came the call.

Wilf gave a leg up to the small, light jockey and threw him onto Snowdrop's back, and they headed toward where Julia stood. Carl smiled at her. He handed her the rein. He had thrown the lead shank over his shoulder.

"You take her to the track. You deserve the glory since you brought her over."

Tentatively, Julia took the rein and fell in beside the filly as they walked towards the track. The trumpeter sounded the familiar voluntary as they passed through the grandstand.

The jockey was busy adjusting his irons. "She's feeling pretty good today, isn't she?" he asked Julia.

Julia was amazed that he was talking to her. After all, she was just a hot-walker, the least important worker on the backstretch. She smiled up at the little man perched on Snowdrop's back. He stood in the irons to test the height and then tied the loose ends of the reins into a knot. He smiled back at Julia and winked.

"Turn her loose, honey," he said, before she had a chance to answer his first question. "The pony will pick me up on the track for post parade. I'll see you when I pull up."

Julia let go of the rein and backed against the wall of the grandstand as the other horses in the post were released by the grooms to the waiting pony riders. Carl moved beside her and pointed towards the track.

"There's a place by the rail where grooms and hot-walkers can watch the race," he said as the track announcer began to call out the horses and riders for the post parade.

Julia felt on top of the world. The crowd behind her buzzed with excitement and the horses broke out of their formation to begin warming up for the race. She leaned against the rail and watched "Mama Goat" trotting beside the pony rider. The pony girl had looped a leather strap through the chin strap of the bridle so that she had a hold of the horse without interfering with the jockey's reins.

The horses moved to the backside of the track towards the three-quarters pole. The race was a short six-and-a-half furlongs, and the starting gate had been moved close to the pole.

"Three minutes to post," the announcer called so that last-minute bettors could make the windows.

The horses gathered behind the gate, where the gate crew took them one at a time from the pony people to load into the starting gate. Carl had been chatting to another groom and turned his attention back to the race as the horses were being loaded into the gate.

"That's one of the most dangerous jobs on the track," he told Julia. "Some of those horses are so wound up that they just go nuts when they get loaded into the gate. The gate crew guys are crowded in between the loading stalls, perched up on the bars trying to hold the horses still. They could be trampled or flipped on by a bad gate horse."

"They're at the post," came the announcement, "and…they're off!" A bell rang and the starting gates swung open, releasing the confined horses and jockeys. Excitement exploded in the grandstand, and the announcer gave the positions of the horses.

"She's in seventh place," Carl yelled over the crowd. "Wilf told the jock not to move her until the top of the stretch. She might place with any luck."

The horses rounded the far turn, with the leading front-runner well ahead of the rest of the pack. As they came into the stretch, Julia could see her filly towards the back but on the outside, trying gallantly to make a move.

As they approached the wire, the sounds of the jockeys' whips hitting the horses' flanks and the shouting as they urged the fillies forward assaulted Julia's ears. The crowd went wild. Behind her, people were yelling at the riders or calling out the number of the horse they had bet for that race.

Nostrils flaring, the fillies shot across the wire, the riders immediately standing in the stirrups to pull them up as the outrider cantered forward to pick up the winner.

"Sixth." Carl moved under the rail to wait to pick up Snowdrop. "She just missed the money. I'll take her back, Julia. Can you go and get the goat from the paddock? I'll meet you back at the barn."

Carl didn't wait for an answer as the jockey pulled up in front of him. He ran the lead shank through the bridle and the rider jumped off and loosened the girths. Julia was disappointed that the filly had not won. It would have been nice to see a winner in the first horse that she took to the paddock. She quietly turned back towards the paddock to retrieve the goat.

Chapter Nine

It had been two weeks since Northern Snowdrop's race, and Julia was beginning to get accustomed to the morning routine in the sheds. When a horse was particularly lively to walk, George showed her how to run the chain of the lead shank through the animal's mouth. He claimed that made it easier to walk them without the hot-walker getting hurt. Julia noticed that horses from other outfits in the shed were often walked that way to keep them quieter.

Wilf Cunningham was getting three new horses in from the farm, and had asked Julia if she wanted to try grooming the following week. She had eagerly accepted, knowing that it would double her pay and allow her to get close to some of the animals she had grown to love.

Julia had spent the afternoons of the "dark days" sleeping in her dormitory room, and on race days she began to stay in the backstretch kitchen watching the post parade and racing on the monitors. When Cunningham had a horse running, she offered to walk the horse after the race. Wilf would sometimes bring the owner back to the barn and brag about how good his workers were in caring for the horses.

It didn't take Julia long to realize that Wilf would say anything to make a buck. Carl chuckled when she voiced this opinion.

"That's why he's known on the backstretch as the Weasel. He came by the name honestly."

It was annoying to Julia that many of the backstretch workers were always explicitly asking her to go out with them. Many of the men in adjacent outfits would be discussing their sexual exploits rather boisterously, with little regard for the women who worked in the barn. The older men in Cunningham's outfit seemed a little different. Most of them quietly did their own work and went their separate ways at the end of the day.

As Julia had done since the first day in Barn 12, she finished her morning by riding the old outrider pony. Old Donald, the ancient horseman in Wilf's outfit, whose only jobs were to feed in the early morning, water off at night, and look after the pony, would seek out Julia at the end of training hours, bringing her the pony to ride under the trees just behind the barn.

Julia enjoyed the old horse, and the ring was a lovely setting with trees and grass surrounding the dirt track. It was still a good way for her to forget about the barns and morning commotion in a relaxing walk through the trees. By the time she returned to the barn, the horses were quietly eating their lunch, and most of the grooms had departed.

Julia might watch Carl groom for a while, but she often went to the track kitchen for lunch. She made it a point to avoid the barn where Antonio worked.

The track kitchen was a bustle of noise and commotion, even at the quietest times. The Greeks who ran the business were constantly hollering at each other or the horsemen to come and pick up their orders. Run as a cafeteria line, the food was a typical-greasy spoon restaurant: home fries, bacon and eggs for breakfast, and hamburgers with French fries and gravy for supper. The food didn't really appeal that much to Julia, but from Woodbine it was a long walk to the nearest restaurant. Wilf's outfit did a weekly trek down Rexdale Boulevard to the bank and the pancake house every Friday following morning training, but it was a long wait between Fridays for a hot meal. Like most of the backstretch workers, Julia soon learned to appreciate the kitchen.

George, the other hot-walker from the barn, would often join Julia as she ate her lunch following morning training. He seemed to savour the greasy food. He would sit across from her, greedily dipping his toast into his eggs.

"How you enjoying working for the Weasel?" he asked Julia.

"It's better than Henderson's barn."

George wasn't really listening. He grasped a piece of bacon and pushed it into his mouth after the toast.

"Got any ketchup?"

Julia grimaced and pushed the bottle across the table. He poured the ketchup onto his plate, flooding the home fries in red.

"You been out with Antonio?"

Startled, Julia glanced at George more closely. "Yes," she answered tentatively, not sure where the conversation was going. George was not paying any more attention to her than he had when he'd asked for the ketchup.

"Not a bad guy," he began. "Some women don't think much of him though. Especially his wife."

Julia carefully put her fork down beside her plate. Her face was drained of colour.

"What did you say?" she stammered as she stared at the man.

George glanced briefly at her and then went back to his home fries.

"His wife don't think much of him. That's why she divorced him. Ask her yourself." He pointed with his egg-encrusted knife. "That's her over there."

Still shocked by George's revelations, Julia had walked quickly back to the dorm. She knew that she would have to leave the track. Sitting on the narrow bed in her dorm room, she counted carefully on her fingers. She was past the date. Past due. Her period had been due nearly a week ago and she was never, never late. Her skin felt awash with a cold sweat, contemplating the consequences. Tony. A wife. An ex-wife, it was true. Yet still, a wife. Why had she ever gone out with him? She had been so naive.

Before Antonio, her only boyfriend had been Ken. Ken had never pushed her. They had dated for nearly two years before becoming lovers. Then it had just been a natural extension of their friendship. Ken had taken care not to get her pregnant, after her brief battle with birth control pills. They had made her violently ill, with agonizing pains in her legs. Ken had been kind, safe, and comfortable. There had not been the passion, the craving that Julia had sensed in Tony. There had not been the undercurrent of excitement that she had sensed in herself, despite the fact that Tony had pushed her too far.

Where to go? Her parents had moved nearly a hundred miles north, so they were not an option. Besides, Julia couldn't be sure how they would react to this type of news. They had been raised in a different age, when women were virgins until their marriage beds. Her father had been angry enough when Julia had moved in with Ken a year ago.

What to do? She couldn't have a baby. She wasn't ready. Julia felt too young, too unprepared. Wasn't marriage supposed to happen first? Or love? Should she tell Tony? No. That was out of the question. Whatever happened, she would not breathe a word to that man. She needed to make her decision without him being aware. He hadn't cared when he'd pushed her that night, so why would he care now?

Julia lay back on the bed and gazed sorrowfully around the room. Why had everything gone so wrong when she had struggled so hard to make it right? She finally felt that she was being accepted on the backstretch. She finally felt that she could handle the horses. Now she had to go away. There was no choice really. Despite her resolve, Julia felt a tear escape her eye.

She would find somewhere to have an abortion. Alone.

PART II

Greenwood Racetrack, April 1985

Chapter Ten

Antonio sat in the kitchen of Greenwood Racetrack in east Toronto and enjoyed the camaraderie of the other horsemen at this first meet of spring. This kitchen was warmer and more pleasant than the one at Woodbine. Tony had given up his apartment last fall, and as usual, had spent the winter galloping horses in Ocala. That was a much better option than breaking yearlings at Woodbine in February. There had been the usual assortment of girls in Florida, but none had possessed that warm, newcomer's charm he had experienced in Julia last summer. Her reaction to him following their evening out continued to confuse him. Tony took a long swallow of his coffee. Women! You could never predict what they really wanted.

Another horseman sat down with a coffee opposite Tony. Tony smiled.

"Eric, it's been a while," he said.

Eric was a short man in his mid-30s. He wore the helmet of an exercise rider and a padded green vest against the early spring morning chill.

"Where's your helmet, Tony?" Eric asked. "Don't tell me that you've given up backing the fillies."

Tony chuckled. After all, he did have a reputation to keep. "I'm trying my hand at training. Found a man with a lot of extra cash who's willing to take a chance on a greenhorn like me," he said to his friend. "I got tired of backing morning mounts. Those horses are too damn unpredictable, especially the young ones. I've seen too many riders get badly hurt on them. It was time for a change."

"How many are you training?" Eric asked.

"Four. The owner's looking at claiming. Maybe at the meet in the Fort." Tony referred to Fort Erie, the "B-meet" of Ontario for broken-down horses or horses unwilling to pull their weight at Woodbine.

Tony thought about what he was considering. A move to Fort Erie was not such a bad thing depending on what a man's ambition was in the racing industry. Fort Erie was a laid-back track, featuring a mile-long oval as opposed to the traditional bull-ring tracks (½ to ¾ mile) found in the States. The track was respectable to a point, but had a reputation for sex, sun and fun for racetrackers in the summer. It was a good place for beginner riders and trainers to start their careers without losing a great deal of money.

Eric took a sip of coffee. "What's your old stable going to do without you, Tony?"

"You know, when it comes to horses, nothing's a sure win, Eric. My trainer understood that I had to take my chances to make something more of my career, instead of busting my bones on some crazy two-year-old's back." He grinned. "They've turned the lights off and the sun's rising."

Sure enough, the large bright lights surrounding the familiar dirt track at Greenwood had been dimmed.

"Is that a hint? What are friends for except to remind me that it's time to get to work?" Eric laughed.

The morning was dawning clear and crystal clean. Tony knew the exhilaration of galloping horses as the sun rose over the morning frost.

Eric nodded to Tony affectionately and rose to leave the backstretch kitchen. The odour of fresh bacon lingered in the air, and he could hear Eric's stomach rumble in anticipation. Tony smiled.

"You've got two hours of galloping before breakfast."

It was nice to know that he didn't have to rush away into the cold dawn, mounting as many horses as he could to try to make a living.

Eric grimaced.

"I'll be back at break if you're around," he replied.

As Eric left, Tony took another sip of his coffee and surveyed the odd assortment of people in the backstretch kitchen. The short spring meet here preceded the meets at both Woodbine and Fort Erie, so workers from both Toronto and the Fort were mingling. However, as transfer vans transported horses each race day from Woodbine, many Woodbine trainers chose to remain at the main track and simply ship the runners to Greenwood on race days, so there were more racetrack people from Fort Erie than Woodbine living on the backstretch at Greenwood. That suited Tony just fine, as he enjoyed the laid-back approach of the small-town horsemen. It would be nice to get away from the rat race at Woodbine this year to a calmer atmosphere in the border town. Maybe his Waterford roots were deeper than he'd first thought.

Antonio stood and stretched. He still felt a little odd not wearing an exercise helmet, but his horseman's cap was a good substitute. It was time to go have a look at his newly acquired horses.

At Woodbine, Wilf Cunningham had divided his outfit for the Greenwood meet. He sent Carl to manage the 12 horses at Greenwood and left the remainder of his stable with his assistant trainer at Woodbine. Carl had made a deal with Wilf over the winter, having acquired a couple of his own horses. He had stalls in Fort Erie and planned to leave Wilf's outfit to go back to training for himself. He let Wilf know that any horse he wanted run at the B-meet he'd look after provided that Cunningham let him have a couple of stalls at the Greenwood meet. Stalls were hard to come by in the reduced barn space at the Greenwood meet, and the stallman had brushed Carl aside for the more prominent owners and trainers. There were only 12 available barns because the standardbreds that normally used this racetrack predominantly shipped their horses in from the farms for racing. The "cold-blooded" standardbreds did not need the exciting atmosphere to prepare for races in the same way as their "hot-blooded" thoroughbred counterparts.

Julia knew that Wilf was surprised when she suddenly reappeared last week at Woodbine asking if she could walk hots for him again. She felt that she was a good worker, and Wilf didn't hesitate to hire her back and send her to Greenwood to work under Carl's direction.

Working at Greenwood was a whole new experience for Julia. This track was much nicer than Woodbine. The atmosphere of the track and the attitude of the horsemen seemed less stressful. The barns were completely enclosed and the tack rooms were heated. The food at the kitchen was wonderful, and horsemen could simply walk across Queen Street to eat in one of the many restaurants or bars in the area.

Julia loved Greenwood. She stayed in the tack room with the saddles and bridles, but she didn't mind. Wilf was hardly ever in the barn, and Carl was an easy-going boss. During the brief five-week meet, she'd risen early enough in the morning to head to the kitchen for a coffee before training hours. Carl would feed the horses their early morning grain, and meet up with her and the other two grooms who worked for the outfit. Wilf had not sent his exercise people down from Woodbine, as most of the horses would be racing or breezed by the jockeys who wandered the barns.

Some of the horses that Julia had worked with the previous fall were still in the outfit, but there were also quite a few newcomers. Northern Snowdrop had been claimed in November, Carl had explained, and the new owners had come later to the barn to buy the goat. Despite new horses, Julia found that she was getting better every day at handling even the craziest youngsters.

Julia felt better about the track and backstretch workers. She was glad that she was a long way from Woodbine and the possibility of running into Tony. At least that was what she thought until he walked into her barn one cold, bright Friday morning.

Julia had just put a horse back into its stall and was waiting for a hot one to come in from the track when she saw him come into the barn. *What is he doing here*, she thought with despair. She turned her back, hoping that he hadn't seen her, but it was too late. She could sense that he stood directly behind her.

"Hello, Julia."

Julia turned around to face Tony. She couldn't think what to say to him.

"I was sorry to see you leave Woodbine last year. I didn't even get the chance to say good-bye," Tony was saying.

"I didn't think you cared that much," Julia replied bitterly.

Tony responded by looking hurt.

"How was your winter?" Tony asked.

"I went away to see some friends in the States. I took a couple of courses while I was there."

"Courses?" Tony asked. "Sounds like a waste of time. Who needs courses? Let real life teach you all you need to know."

Julia didn't say anything. She knew the attitude of most horsemen towards schooling. She had better reasons for leaving the racetrack so quickly the previous year, but wasn't sure if she should tell him why. What the hell, she thought.

"I was pregnant, Tony."

He gazed in shock at Julia.

"Was it mine?" he asked.

Julia saw red. She couldn't believe his response. So typical of him and his over-inflated ego!

"You bastard!" she yelled. Heads turned in their direction from other horsemen working in the shed. "How could you possibly ask me something like that?"

Carl appeared beside Julia. He hadn't heard the whole conversation, but had heard enough to know the general context.

"There's a hot horse coming in."

The rider could be seen coming down the shed, and Julia handed Carl the lead shank. Tony moved to the other side of the stall door as the rider took the horse into the stall. Julia glared at him and ducked into the stall behind Carl. Carl pulled the bridle off the horse and threw the halter and shank quickly onto the animal. The rider removed the saddle and, nodding at Carl, beat a hasty retreat from the tension in the stall. Carl handed Julia the end of the shank and rubbed some straw on the gelding's heaving flanks.

"Get him walking, Julia," he said. "I'll sponge him in a couple of turns."

Julia was ready to cry, but something in her had hardened in the last six months. She was no longer the naive baby who had first entered the Woodbine backstretch last August. She could see Tony waiting outside the stall.

"Julia, we need to talk about this," he began as she brought the horse out of the stall.

"I have nothing to say to you," she said.

Julia stopped by the water bucket to let the gelding drink, carefully counting the gulps as the horse swallowed thirstily.

Tony tried again. "I need to know what happened. What did you do?"

Julia glanced at him. For the first time in their brief relationship, she knew that she had the upper hand.

"You didn't care about what happened to me that night you took me out." Her voice was barely above a whisper. "Stop pretending you care now. I did what I had to do. It wasn't your problem."

Julia pulled the gelding's head from the water pail and turning her back to Antonio, strode down the shedrow.

Tony was left with mixed feelings. What the hell was wrong with him, letting some chick get under his skin? The problem was, he had really liked her. She was cute. She seemed to honestly like the racetrack and the horses. She didn't have the bitterness of some of the women born and raised around the track.

He had to admit that Julia was not the only woman who could make him feel this way. He was used to one-night stands, and rarely did he go out of his way to ask the same woman out more than once. It wasn't that he didn't care. He tried to be polite and cordial to all the women, whether or not he spent time with them in the future. It made him feel that he wasn't just taking them out to use their bodies.

The fact that Julia had avoided him following their night rendezvous had bruised his ego. But only a little. He had a pretty healthy ego and felt that he could have her back if the chase was worth the effort. Tony shook his head to rid it of these depressing thoughts. He was beginning to think that Julia might be worth the effort. Silly man! He must be getting soft in his old age!

It was a full two days before Julia had the misfortune of running into Tony again. The grooms from the barn had asked her if she wanted to join them for lunch at a favourite sports bar on Queen Street. She had gladly accepted. It was a chance to get off the backstretch and into the real world. The group enjoyed lunch and were walking back across the track parking lot when Tony approached them, hands stuck nonchalantly in his jean pockets.

"I need to talk to you, Julia," he said to her even before she had a chance to avoid the confrontation.

The men with her nodded to Tony in greeting but watched Julia warily. The racetrack was ripe with rumours, and the Antonio/Julia story was gathering momentum each day. They knew only too well how she felt about the man.

Julia sighed and stopped walking. She was going to have to face this creep sooner or later. Maybe it was best to get it over with now in the middle of the deserted parking lot rather than on the backstretch with listening walls.

"Go ahead, guys," she said. "I'll catch you back at the barn."

The grooms waved farewell and left Julia alone with Antonio for the first time since he had been with her last August. Julia walked away from him towards the high steel fence surrounding the dirt track.

"I would have married you, you know," Tony called after her.

Julia stopped and turned to face him.

"I didn't want a shot-gun wedding. I didn't love you. There was a good chance that you would've ruined my life more than you already have."

"You can't mean that." Tony sounded exasperated. "I cared about you. I still do."

Julia laughed.

"You're not serious," she said. "Quit bullshitting me. It worked once. It's not going to happen again." Julia leaned against the metal fence. It was much easier to face this man in the daylight and the open.

"I assumed that you were on the pill. I thought most girls protected themselves."

"You assumed wrong. You didn't even bother asking."

Tony moved closer to Julia. "What did you do?"

"I had an abortion. There was really no choice. But having an abortion does something to a woman, you know; it leaves her scarred. I wonder if I can ever have a child again. I wonder if I'm a murderer, like the pro-life people tell me I am. I lie awake some nights wondering if I made the wrong decision. But I really had no choice."

Julia stopped. Why was she explaining herself to this man? He had used her and deserted her. Digging at the wound inside herself wasn't going to help her deal with Tony now.

"You should have told me, Julia. I would have helped. I am not quite the bastard that you think I am."

Julia made the mistake of looking Tony right in the eyes. They were soft and pleading. Either he was a hell of a good actor, or he was being sincere. She had to admit that he had never tried to pretend to her about his intentions or feelings. Even on that fateful August night, he had told her exactly the way he felt.

"Oh shit," she muttered.

Tony took a chance. He moved towards her and put his arms around her.

Julia couldn't respond. It was as if this man had regained control of her body. She let him hold her as she fought anger and frustration. Why was this happening? Why couldn't she have just left him and all that pain behind? Why was she letting him do this to her now? She was terrified that he might rope her back into his snare.

"Let me buy you a coffee," Tony was saying. "I'm not used to women as innocent as you. Maybe I should have moved a little slower last summer. I'm a different person now. I don't gallop anymore. I'm going to get my trainer's licence and try to be respectable."

Taking Julia's hand, Tony guided her towards the backstretch gate. As they approached the guard, Julia pulled away from him and flashed her licence in the direction of the security man. She needed some time to sort out the confusing feelings running through her body. She hadn't anticipated that she would respond to Tony in this way. It would have been so much easier to steer clear of the man.

For the first time in Julia's life, she was free of a relationship, and she was enjoying this new-found freedom. Now Tony had walked back into her life and demanded an explanation for decisions she had made last fall. Did he deserve to know what she had done? Maybe she should have hidden the full truth from him. He really wasn't such a bad guy, despite pushing her into a corner. She still wondered if she'd inadvertently given him the wrong idea. Maybe it had subconsciously been a reaction to her fallout with Ken.

Yes, now Tony was back. He seemed just as tough, forceful, and egocentric as he had first appeared to her last summer. Yet he still had that energy and enigma that had attracted her to him originally.

As they reached the backstretch kitchen, Tony led her to a table and then went to get the coffee. Julia glanced around the room. There were only a couple of other men in the corner. At 1 o'clock in the afternoon, most horsemen were catching a couple of hours' sleep in anticipation of the evening racing card.

Tony sat down opposite Julia and handed her the mug of coffee.

"Do you hate me?" he asked.

"No."

Tony was staring at her intently, and she refused to meet his gaze.

"Are you going back to Wilf's outfit at Woodbine after the Greenwood meet?"

"That's right. Wilf is going to let me groom again."

"Are you seeing anyone?" Tony asked casually.

Julia finally looked right at him.

"Were you married?" she queried in return, already knowing the answer.

Tony sighed, leaned back, and took a sip of his coffee. "How come it always comes down to this?" he mumbled. "I don't understand women." He shook his head and looked out the windows towards the grandstand.

"It was nearly six years ago. It wasn't right. She and I both figured that out."

Julia pushed the cup of coffee toward him and stood up.

"I need to sleep. We have a horse running tonight in a late race."

Tony glanced at her and reached as though tempted to grab her hand, but Julia backed away from his advance. Tony stopped.

"Am I going to see you again?" he asked.

"I don't know. I need to come to terms with what you did to me," she answered. "At this point, I don't think I want a relationship with any man."

Julia turned and walked away. For the first time, she felt in control of the situation. It left her with the option of the next move. What she didn't realize was what that move might be, and how soon she would make it.

Chapter Eleven

Julia loved living on the backstretch at Greenwood. There was optimism in the spring that exuded through the horsemen. The horses breathed excitement. The backstretch hummed with activity as training hours filled the main track with the chestnut and bay colts, geldings and fillies. Julia could wander out of her barn to lean against the fence and watch the horses galloping around the dirt track. The early spring morning light would filter through the dew as the breath of hot horses poured through their nostrils. It felt so good to be alive, to watch the power and energy, knowing that she was working with multi-million-dollar animals that were bought and sold on the whim of the owner. The money and the power appealed to her young 20 years. Oh, to be able to control your own destiny!

The Greenwood meet was cold and wet at the best of times. Nestled on a narrow strip of land between Queen Street and Lake Ontario, it was in the area of east Toronto known as "The Beaches." Stiff breezes from the lake blew in rain, sleet and snow. The land was often inundated with water, to the point where staff in the backstretch kitchen served morning breakfast from their perches on pallets.

Formerly called Old Woodbine, the racetrack had once seen the running of more than 70 Queen's Plate Stakes. This was the birthplace of thoroughbred racing in Ontario, where the Ontario Jockey Club originally made its home. The racetrack itself was unique; stretching only five-and-a-half furlongs. It was well known in North America for the tight turns and long backstretch and stretch runs.

World-famous horses such as Northern Dancer once graced the old shedrows. However, when the new Woodbine racetrack was built in Rexdale (partly funded by E.P. Taylor's Windfield Farms), Greenwood became predominantly inhabited by standardbred horsemen who built a stone chip track to accommodate the buggies. The deep mud of a dirt track did not suit the standardbred sulkies.

The thoroughbreds still raced at Old Woodbine, but only for a few weeks in April and December, at the beginning and the end of the thoroughbred racing season. Many horses were not yet fit enough to run the short four-and-one-half furlong spring races, and many trainers used the track as a training ground. Late December races saw cold, ice, and blizzard conditions. There were nights when Conner Tate couldn't call an entire race because of reduced visibility. December racing was a brutal existence for the horsemen, and only the die-hards saw the last night of the season. But spring was different, Julia thought. Spring brought hope.

Julia saw the big trainers, Cavanaugh and Turner Farms, as they took charge of the owners, jockeys, and the low-life of the backstretch. She knew that she was one of the low-life: hot-walkers, grooms, and exercise people. There was part of her that wanted to rise above her status, become a trainer or owner. But she knew better. She was still the naive newcomer that scarcely knew the head of the horse from the tail. Wilf made sure that she was aware of this fact.

Races were generally at night during the Greenwood meet, with the exception of Saturday and Sunday. Julia would open the door of her tack room and watch the races from her cot. The powerful lights encircling the track would illuminate the horses as they strove for position along the backstretch. Often, the starting gate would be set up close to the barn, and she could hear the oaths of the gate crew as they loaded the high-strung animals. Carl had shown her the gate was actually a few metres behind the pole that indicated the length of the race. This was because thoroughbreds would be allowed a running start to the race, a fact few betting patrons realized. Carl also told her that the starting gate was wired so that the power was on to hold the gates closed, and when the starter pressed the button, the power was shut off allowing the gates to open and the horses to be set free from their confines. This was a safety precaution in case there was ever a massive power outage at the track and the horses were in the starting gate.

Julia was watching the gate being loaded two days after her encounter with Tony, when Tony himself appeared at her open door. He tapped politely on the wooden door.

"Watching the races?" he asked, although this was obviously what she was doing.

Julia simply nodded.

Conner Tate began to call the race as the gates opened. Although muffled, they could easily hear the names of the horses. The sounds of jockeys' whips and shouts filtered back to their ears. As the race ended with a roar from the crowd in the grandstand, Julia's attention refocused on Tony.

"What do you want?"

Tony leaned against the door frame.

"I was wondering if you were interested in seeing the horses that I'm training."

Always eager to see racehorses, Julia grabbed her coat and moved to the door. That was the primary reason she worked on the backstretch.

"Sure," she said as she put the padlock on her door.

Tony led her along the backstretch to Barn 10, the second last barn. His four horses were stabled in the central section of the barn. Antonio moved easily into each individual animal's stall and introduced them to Julia. Julia rubbed their noses and talked softly to the horses that were relaxed despite the sounds of the races filtering into the barn.

"You've come a long way since last August," Tony said. "You seem to have the touch."

Julia knew that her fear last summer was mostly due to a lack of knowledge. She didn't say anything to Tony, but quietly tickled one of the fillies behind her ears. The filly leaned her head towards Julia, and her soft muzzle quivered.

"I'd like another chance, Julia. I guess that I moved too fast last summer. I didn't mean to spook you and I sure didn't mean to get you pregnant. Maybe we could just talk somewhere. Start over."

"I'm not sure that I can trust you, Tony."

"I won't try to touch you," Tony said. "God knows that I want to, but I'll be good. I can keep myself in check."

Julia wasn't convinced.

"Unless you want me to, of course." He smiled.

There he was using that charm to try to get her into bed. Julia glared at him.

"I don't want you to touch me. I'm not entirely sure that I want to go out with you again. You hurt me."

"Why don't we go over to the grandstand then? Have you been to the races yet?"

Tony seemed to always know the right thing to say, Julia thought in frustration. No, she hadn't made it over to the grandstand yet, and she really wanted to check out that aspect of racing. It would be rather fun having someone experienced and knowledgeable at her side.

"All right," she said.

Tony pulled a racing program from his back pocket and handed it to Julia. He had picked it up at the racing office that morning.

"They just called them over for the sixth race," he said. If we hurry, we can cut along the track rather than walking through the parking lot."

The grandstand proved to be a lot of fun. Julia mingled amongst the betters who quickly became aware that they worked on the backstretch. Tony had chuckled at her surprise.

"We have a certain look," he said. "I guess you are officially a 'racetracker' now. Congratulations, I think."

Tony bought her a cheeseburger, and then began to explain how to read the program and the basics of making a bet. He explained that the odds on the board and TV monitors were based on a one dollar bet, but you couldn't bet less than two dollars. That meant if the odds were two to one, you got 10 dollars back if you bet five dollars to win on that horse.

It was fun to hang out with Tony on an otherwise lonely night. Julia loved to watch the horses and was developing an interest in racing. Her head was soon filled with exactors, triactors, and daily doubles. Tony pointed to the third horse in the eighth race.

"I used to gallop that colt. He's a long shot, but has already started this year. Maybe we should put some money on him."

Julia shook her head.

"You go ahead. I don't bet."

"Make you a deal," Tony said. "I'll put two dollars across the board on the horse and if he's there, I'll give you half the winnings. Your job is to bring me luck."

Before Julia had a chance to reply, Antonio had moved to the betting windows and pulled six dollars from his wallet.

Because she now had something at stake in the eighth race, Julia renewed her interest in the horses as they walked into the paddock. She gazed with seriousness at the number three horse as the trainer tightened the girth. Her heart jumped in anticipation as the horses were loaded into the starting gate. Antonio stood beside her and placed a hand on her shoulder as he pointed to their horse in the gate along the backstretch.

Julia was acutely aware of Antonio's touch, but didn't pull away. Her attention was focused on the race. He was being kind to her, but part of her still didn't trust his actions or movements. However, she felt more capable of stopping this man now in the cool spring evening than she had that hot August night.

"They're at the post," came the call. "And...they're off!" Tony's hand tightened on her shoulder as they leaned forward to see the horses racing down the backstretch. Tony pointed to the television monitor above their heads.

"He broke good and is fifth right now. May have a shot."

Julia clapped her hands together as the horses turned into the stretch.

"Oh, Tony, he's moving up!" she said.

Sure enough, the jockey had taken the colt to the outside and the horse lengthened its stride racing past the other horses along the rail. The crowd was yelling in disbelief as the number three horse easily passed the favourite. Tony and Julia shouted along in the din, cheering the horse and rider to the wire. As the horses thundered across the finish line, it was hard to tell whether their pick or if the number two horse had won the race.

"It'll be a photo. I think that we may have got beat at the wire, but we'll make some money just the same." Tony pulled Julia to him and kissed her.

Julia at first went rigid. She was not really that shocked at his approach, but rather at the public format. She could feel his hard muscled body around her as he ran his hands through her hair and down her back. She felt her body responding to him despite her mind telling her that she was being a fool. For a brief moment she kissed him back and then pushed him away.

"Thanks," said Tony quietly. "You are driving me crazy, you know." He backed away and smiled at Julia. He handed her the ticket. "You cash it. The racing stewards will make their decision in a moment."

Julia took the strip of paper and looked away from Tony. She was confused about how she felt towards this man. She had thought that she hated him, but he was being so kind to her, like the day when she had first met him in Henderson's shed. Maybe Tony wasn't such a bad guy. Maybe he just had a hard time controlling his desires.

The horse finished second. The payout was over thirteen dollars for the place and show portions of the ticket. Julia brought the money back to where Antonio was standing. She held out the cash and he shook his head.

"You were kind enough to kiss me," Tony said. "The money is the least I could do."

"I can't be bought." Julia said.

"I'm not trying to buy you. Why don't you put the money back through the windows? We'll pick a triactor box."

Somewhat satisfied, Julia looked at the racing program as Tony pointed out the horses most likely to be close in the final race. He told her what to say and sent her to the windows to make the bet. In the end, a long shot came from behind to win the 10th race. Tony crumpled the ticket and tossed it over his shoulder.

"Time to go home."

They walked back along the track with the horses that had run in the final race.

"I hate working the last race," Tony said. "The horses aren't cooled out 'til nearly one in the morning."

He stopped outside her tack room and Julia unlocked the door.

"Do you have a bolt on the inside of your door?" Tony asked.

Julia looked a little startled. Why would he want to know?

"Yes," she answered. "I keep it locked."

"Good. There are some bad people on this track. I don't want to see you hurt."

Julia wanted to point out to him that he had been the one to hurt her in the past, but Tony pulled her into his arms again. He held her briefly and then released his strong grip.

"It was a great night, Julia. Thanks."

Antonio turned to go and Julia grasped his wrist. She drew him into the door frame and wrapped her arms around him. She was terrified that he might take advantage of her forwardness but reached up and kissed him. He responded forcefully and passionately. Tony did have the ability to touch her and set her on fire, but she was determined not to let him go too far. This time when she pushed him away, it took nearly all her strength before he got the message.

"Not tonight." Julia was firm although her voice quivered.

"You sure know how to hurt a guy." Tony reached for her again.

Julia stepped back.

"Stop, Antonio. You're scaring me." She had raised her voice to emphasize her words.

"Sorry. I really don't want to hurt you. I did have a good evening." Tony turned and walked down the slight incline from the barn. He smiled back at her and waved. "Lock your door. I'll bring you a coffee at 5:30 tomorrow morning."

"Goodnight," Julia replied with relief.

She quickly closed her door and slammed the bolt home.

Chapter Twelve

Other than coffee on her doorstep each morning, Julia saw little of Antonio Descartes over the next few days. Wilf Cunningham had begun to enter more horses into the races, and Julia found that she was very busy many evenings cooling out hot horses.

By now it was mid-April and Julia knew she would soon be returning to Woodbine for the main racing season. She felt a little sad that Carl would be going on to Fort Erie. She knew that George, Donald, and Rob would be at the barn with the Weasel, but it just wouldn't be the same without Carl. He had always been helpful and kind to her. He didn't pass judgment, although she was sure that he knew about her relationship with Antonio. She could see that Carl was getting impatient to be away from the outfit and on his own. He spent his afternoons grooming his own horses and talking with other trainers that were moving to Fort Erie. He had already arranged transport and obtained stalls in one of the barns at that racetrack.

Curious about the older, large barns beyond the kitchen, Julia wandered down the backstretch to Tony's barn at the end of training hours one morning. As she entered the barn, she noticed that the atmosphere was very different from Wilf's shedrow. Despite the late hour, many of the horses were still out in the shed, some of them under tack. She stood at the end of the barn and watched the bustle of morning work in front of her. Music from radios hanging beside the stalls added to the commotion in the barn.

Antonio came around the end of the barn with one of his horses under tack.

"Hold up." He stopped the filly and smiled to Julia. "Hi there. How about a leg up?"

Julia felt a little shy in the strange barn but moved around the prancing filly to take hold of the rein. Tony latched his helmet and bent his knee so that she could take hold to throw him onto the horse.

Just as she leaned to grasp his ankle, the horse shied to the right. Startled, Julia let go of Tony to try to hold the horse still. She became aware that Tony was laughing.

"You've never done this before, have you?" he asked, not unkindly. Guiltily she shook her head. "Let's keep the filly walking. I have lots of spring. When I bend for the jump, I just need you to guide me into the saddle."

Julia walked the horse forward and did as Tony had directed. She scarcely knew that she had lifted him as he sprang into the saddle. He was all business as the filly paced beneath him. Julia realized that she had never seen this man on a horse, in spite of his previous position as an exercise person.

"Take me a turn, please," Tony said as he moved his left leg forward to tighten the girth.

This was also something new for Julia, but she wasn't about to admit that to Tony. She continued to walk the filly forward down the shed watching what Tony was doing as he adjusted the irons. His hands were gentle and loose as he held the rubber of the crossed reins. The horse seemed to be enjoying herself as she bounced along beneath him.

Julia felt the filly tense as Tony stood in the irons and took hold of the bit.

"Turn me loose."

Julia let go of the rein and backed against the stalls. Tony smiled to her again as he held the prancing horse lightly.

"Wait for me. I'm only shedding this filly. I'll be done in 20 minutes."

Tony released the horse so that it trotted down the shed. He straightened his legs and leaned over the filly. Julia had seen lots of exercise people as they galloped the young horses each morning, but it was different watching Antonio. She watched as his powerful muscles came into play holding the horse in check. She couldn't help thinking about those same arms around her just recently. In an odd way, she was a little jealous of the filly. However, she also felt sorry for the horse, knowing what it was like to be in Tony's grasp.

Julia walked towards Tony's stalls. She was aware that some of the other workers in the barn were watching her closely. She found a bale of hay outside his feed room and sat down to wait for him to finish. Every couple of minutes, Antonio would either trot or walk past her on the filly. He would smile and nod in her direction.

An older horseman wearing an exercise helmet walked over to where she was sitting.

"Hey there," was the stranger's greeting. "You Tony's new girl?"

Julia was a little embarrassed.

"Not really," she answered.

The man dropped down beside Julia and pulled a piece of hay out of the bale to stick in his teeth.

"Name's Bill. They call me Crazy Bill." The man introduced himself to Julia.

"I'm Julia Reinhardt."

"You moving down to the Fort at the end of the meet?" asked Bill.

"I'm going to Woodbine. I work for Cunningham."

"Going with the big leagues? It's more fun at the Fort. Relaxed. Lots of dark days. The beach. You should try it out. You could hang around with my crazy girlfriend and me if Tony doesn't work out."

Bill hadn't seemed to acknowledge that she didn't see herself as "Tony's girl." Julia didn't bother trying to explain again. She knew what racetrackers were like once they had an opinion. Tony came down the shed and turned into the filly's stall.

"Give me a hand here, Julia," he said as he jumped off the horse.

She walked into the stall as he pulled the saddle from the filly's back.

"Pull the bridle," he said. "Make sure that she drops the bit before you take it right off."

Tony threw the saddle over the bottom door of the stall and picked up the halter and shank. Julia noticed that he had already cleaned the stall, and the horse stood on clean fresh straw banked professionally around the sides. She worked at loosening the throat latch and nose band. Tony was back at her side watching her approvingly. She became acutely aware of the musky smell of leather and horse dander.

"Place your left hand on her nose and pull the bridle with the right hand. Don't forget about the bit."

Sure enough, the filly tried to toss up her head as she felt the bridle slide off her ears. Julia had a firm grip on her nose and held her there until the bit fell out of her mouth. Tony had moved right against her as he hooked the halter around her neck. In this way the horse was never completely free to break away and out of the stall. He slid the halter onto the filly's nose and fastened the lead shank. He brought an arm around Julia and held her as loosely as he had the filly by their side. His breath tickled her ear.

"Thanks. I think you're great."

Antonio released Julia and tied the filly to a chain at the back of the stall.

Julia jumped as a voice boomed in her ear.

"You are so full of shit, Antonio."

Crazy Bill leaned against the stall door. He still had the piece of hay between his teeth. He grinned at Julia. She turned to dunk the bit in the water pail. This was done to briefly clean the bit so that it could be used on the next animal waiting for the tack.

"I'd be willing to bet that he tells all his girlfriends they're great."

"How many girlfriends does he have?" asked Julia.

"Who invited you in here?" asked Tony.

Bill ignored him.

"There appears to be only you right now, but he's had lots in the past."

"Get lost, asshole."

Tony rubbed the filly down with straw. He didn't appear particularly angry. Crazy Bill made no move to leave.

Not sure how serious the argument was between these men, Julia stood uncertainly holding the bridle. Crazy Bill took the bridle from her and threw it across the saddle.

"I must admit that you're a little cuter than most of them. I don't understand why Tony's letting you go back to Woodbine. I would have thought that he'd want you at the Fort where he can keep an eye on you." Bill chuckled in a good-natured way, his clear blue eyes twinkling. "Or at least keep his hand on you." Bill laughed at his own joke.

Tony glared at Bill, but Julia could see that he was laughing. She hoped that the laughter was not at her expense.

"Isn't it time you had your morning beer?" Tony tried to get rid of Bill again.

"That was a couple of hours ago before I got on Nickel's crazy colt." Bill shrugged.

Julia looked a little shocked. She knew that many of the backstretch workers were drinkers or had been alcoholics, such as Carl had once admitted to her. She was shocked that the men would drink so early in the morning when they knew that they were going to work around the high-strung horses.

Tony released the filly from the chain and turned the animal towards her hay in the front corner of the stall. He shooed Bill out of the stall and hooked up the webbing and cross-bar. Picking up the saddle and bridle in one hand, he grabbed Julia's hand and led her towards his feed room.

"If you don't mind Bill, I'm going to buy my helper some lunch. Greenwood's finest for the lady."

Julia was starting to enjoy the banter between the men. If this was the mood at the Fort Erie racetrack, maybe it would be a nice place to work. She shook her head to rid it of those crazy thoughts. She had a job with Wilf Cunningham, not a Fort Erie outfit. She'd be going back to Woodbine in less than two weeks.

Antonio closed up his feed room.

"Maybe I'll tag along," Bill said. It only took a moment to get a reaction out of Tony.

"Beat it," was the reply.

Bill chuckled again and wandered down the shedrow whistling to himself.

Tony still had the saddle and bridle over his arm.

"I'll clean these later. I meant what I said about lunch. It's the least I could do to say thanks."

"I didn't do much…," Julia began but Tony was already walking away from her.

"I have to lock these up in my tack room. It's at the front end of the barn."

Curious, Julia followed him to the front of the barn and watched as he unlocked one of the central tack rooms. She looked in at his cot and belongings spread rather haphazardly around the room amidst the saddles, bridles, shanks, and other horse equipment. Perhaps a little messier, but similar to the room she occupied in her own barn.

"Come in," Tony said. "The heater is on and I'm trying to keep the cold damp of the barn out there."

Julia was not sure if this was a good idea but had been feeling better and better about their relationship over the past few days. She walked into the room and Tony closed the door. He hung up the bridle and threw the saddle onto its saddle horn.

Antonio held a hand out to the room in a mocking gesture.

"Welcome to my domain. All I have in the world is in this room."

He took a step towards Julia and encircled his arms around her. He gently pulled her to him and held her more tenderly than he had on past occasions. She could feel his heart beating against her ribs and breasts. Julia knew that her own heart was racing. Partly from fear, and surprisingly, partly from excitement. Antonio was no comfortable Ken. He was unpredictable, demanding, and focused. His energy appealed to her. His strength appealed to her. His way of life appealed to her. But Julia was terrified of what he might do and the power that he obviously knew how to wield. He could take control and push her into a corner before she had a chance to escape. Julia had watched him with the filly. She knew that he had the same control when dealing with the horses.

Julia could sense how much Antonio ached for her, but at least he was exercising great control, allowing her to make the first move. He brushed his lips chastely across Julia's forehead, and she felt him reluctantly release his hold. Tony opened the door.

"Let's go for lunch."

Chapter Thirteen

Julia was in the test barn on the last Sunday of racing cooling out the winner. Wilf had told her that there were only three more possible races for the horses stabled at Greenwood, so the outfit would move back to Woodbine no later than Friday. He'd arranged for a girl's dormitory room for her at the backstretch gate. She would help to pack equipment on Friday and he'd send Rob, the assistant trainer, to get her early Saturday morning.

Julia had mixed feelings about moving back to Woodbine. It would be nice to be settled and back into the routine at the track. She was also looking forward to being a groom again. Her one misgiving was that she was beginning to fall for Antonio. Although it was obvious that he wanted her, he had been the perfect gentleman at the Greenwood meet. He had brought her coffee every morning and often stopped by to chat with her following training hours. He was around enough that Carl was definitely taking notice.

"Be careful of that man, Julia," Carl said one morning as she put the shank on a hot horse. "He may seem fun and full of charm, but there's a part of Descartes I know you won't like. You're a good, honest hard-worker and a decent person. It's too soon for the racetrack to chew you up and spit you out. You should probably steer clear of Antonio."

Julia was a little annoyed that Carl was interfering with her personal life. She already knew the bad side of Tony and was beginning to believe that she could handle that part of the man. She had a pretty good feeling that she was going to let Tony take the next step in their renewed relationship. This time she would be very, very careful.

Tony was happy to see Julia walk into the backstretch kitchen that evening after the last racehorse was safely back in the barns. She no longer shied away from him but approached his table.

"I need to talk to you, Tony. Preferably alone."

Tony pushed his plate back and stood up.

"Your place or mine?"

"I'd rather go to your room, if you don't mind."

"No problem."

Julia walked beside Tony as they moved in the darkness towards Barn 10. He opened his tack room and she moved inside. As he reached to turn on the light, she caught his wrist.

"Leave it off, please."

Taking a deep breath, Tony closed the door and leaned against the wood. He was having a hard time thinking with a clear head. There could be no mistakes. That much he knew for certain.

"You know, Julia. Once I start, I find it very difficult to stop." His voice was scarcely a whisper.

Tony moved towards her in the darkness. He could see the fear in her eyes. For him, this reaction was new. He was used to having to dominate women, but most of the girls he had known were rock hard both mentally and emotionally. Too many years on the racetrack. Maybe that was why Julia turned him on.

"Don't be afraid, Julia. I'm not going to hurt you. You won't get pregnant. I'll make sure of that." His words were tender. "I care, Julia. More than you think."

Tony took her hand and led her to the cot. His breathing had increased. He exercised more control than he had thought possible. His words were sincere. He did care. Julia was under his skin and he desperately wanted her to be a part of his life. He couldn't understand what it was about Julia that nearly drove him mad. Maybe it had been her ardent opposition to his advances, or perhaps just her fierce independence. He was becoming tired of the lonely one-night stands.

Antonio pulled Julia down onto his cot. He drew his strong arms around her body. He was simply holding her, allowing her to make the first move. Julia moved on top of him and kissed him. Tony's grip tightened around her and he kissed her back, his passion draining him to his core.

Tony pulled away and looked directly at Julia. He could see that she was fighting tears, her eyes reflecting mixed emotions.

"Take off your clothes, Julia. I'm going to make love to you." Tony wiped her eyes and whispered in her ear. "Please don't run away from me tonight. I only have five short days left. I want to hold you every chance I get."

The heat from her body finally got to Tony. He lost his control and pulled her to him. There was no turning back. But this time, Antonio made sure that it was much better.

Chapter Fourteen

Friday came far too quickly. Julia had spent every spare second in Antonio's arms. He was still rough and demanding, but he was consistent. She at least knew what to expect. He had spent the last few days trying to convince her to come to Fort Erie. That was too big a plunge for her. She didn't want to take that kind of chance. To leave her job and everyone that she worked with and go to a strange racetrack in a strange town a hundred miles away was a big step. She still didn't trust Tony that much.

Carl was busy sorting equipment and getting the horses ready for transport. Julia wasn't sure if Carl was aware of how seriously involved she was with Antonio. She already knew how he felt about Tony and was glad that he was too busy to interfere. Carl was a good man and she would be sorry to see him leave.

Friday dawned clear and warm—a hint of what the summer would bring. Carl sent the trackers out before the break so they would be cooled and bandaged when the transport van arrived at 11. Julia wanted to hurry away to Barn 10 but knew that her own outfit needed her there to help load horses.

When the time came, Carl and the grooms loaded the 12 remaining horses into the transport truck while Julia scrubbed and loaded water and feed pails. The grooms waved good-bye and climbed into the trailer with the horses. Julia was to be picked up by Rob the next day.

The barn seemed so empty with the horses gone. Only Carl's two geldings remained in the end stalls. He walked down to feed them their lunch.

"I'm leaving at seven this evening, Julia. I'll help you finish packing Wilf's equipment so that you can take the evening off."

Julia followed Carl down the shed to get to work.

Julia watched Carl load his horses at the loading dock at 7 o'clock. They quickly returned to the barn where his car was piled with equipment and his own personal belongings.

"I have to beat the transport to Fort Erie to unload the colts," he said. "It's going to be a long night by the time I have them bedded down and happy at the new track." He moved down the shed to collect his crossbars and webbings from the stalls.

Julia was sitting in her tack room with the door open so that she could see him return. The racetrack just wouldn't be the same without Carl. She stood up as she saw him approach. She knew that he would be in a hurry to leave.

Carl walked to her door.

"Give an old man a hug, girl," he said as he held her for a brief moment. Julia smiled. She knew that he wasn't really that old, barely more than 40, but years of hard drinking had taken their toll on Carl.

"If you're ever in the Fort...maybe for the Prince of Wales if that Weasel has any decent horse flesh this year...you look me up. I'd love to buy you a coffee."

Julia nodded. She didn't know what to say.

"I'm going to miss you, girl. Old George is a gossip but will look after you at the outfit. If you want a change of scenery, come to Fort Erie. I can hook you up with a decent trainer."

Carl gave her another hug and then started for his car. Julia was acutely aware that she still hadn't said a word. She ran after his tall lanky back.

"Carl," she said. "Thanks for everything."

"No problem, sweetie. I guess this is good-bye." He climbed into his car, started the engine and rolled down his window. "Take care of yourself. And...." He put the car into gear. "Don't let Tony fuck with your mind."

Carl drove away.

The backstretch was more than half empty as Julia wandered through the barns to see Antonio for one last night. Tony had begun to pack his own gear even though he wasn't leaving until Sunday morning. That was the soonest that he could arrange transport to Fort Erie. Julia found him in his tack room sorting bridles.

His face lit up and he crushed her to his body.

"I've missed you. I haven't seen you all day."

Julia pulled away from him and sat down on an overturned bucket.

"I'm feeling kind of sad, Tony. The outfit's gone. Carl's gone. The racetrack is clearing out."

"I'm not gone, Julia. Think of this as a beginning rather than an end." Tony sat down on his cot. "We need to talk."

"I'm not going to Fort Erie, Tony. We've already discussed this. I wouldn't know anyone there. It would be worse than living at Woodbine without you."

"I want you to come. You'll know me. I can look after you. I think I'm in love with you."

"Jesus, Tony, don't make it worse!" Julia said. She ran a hand through her hair in despair.

Tony caught her hand and pulled her to him. He kissed her tenderly.

"I think I'm in love with you," he said again.

Julia kissed him back.

"Then make love to me and forget about this conversation."

Tony pushed her roughly onto his cot as he pulled her shirt off over her head. Julia was a little worried. He had been pretty good to her all week, but his attitude tonight was different. He took her breast in his mouth, teasing it tenderly. She relaxed. Maybe she was just imagining things. She closed her eyes and let the sensations he was so good at creating move through her body.

The pain hit her like a brick. Tony had bit down hard on her nipple.

"What are you doing?" she cried as tears came to her eyes.

She remembered him promising that he would never hurt her again. She tried to pull away but Tony was strong. He pinned her arms down. He was angry and frustrated.

"You're not going anywhere, Julia. I hurt you because you hurt me. I declare that I love you, and you essentially slap me in the face. After I'm finished with you tonight, you'll never forget me. No man will ever be the same."

"Please, Tony, I don't like what you're saying. I never meant to hurt your feelings."

Julia was terrified. She had an idea of how far this man would go with her, and she suddenly felt very vulnerable. She was more afraid than she had been last August.

Antonio let go of her suddenly and got to his feet. He stood facing away from her but still effectively blocking any escape route through the tack room door.

Julia pressed her shirt into her aching breast. She could see his shoulders shaking but didn't know if it was from anger or sadness. She was beginning to understand what Carl had been trying so hard to get through to her infatuated mind. There was another side to Tony. If she could survive tonight, she'd be at Woodbine tomorrow and safely away from this man.

When Tony turned to face Julia again, there was clear sadness in his eyes. He looked at her for a long moment before saying anything.

"I'm sorry. I shouldn't have done that. I guess that I've ruined everything now. I can see the fear in your eyes. Please stay with me. I'll just hold you and I won't force myself on you. I was just so frustrated. I want you to come with me, but I guess the chances of that happening are pretty slim." He stopped.

Julia drew a deep breath. She was shaking, but not from any cold.

"I thought that you said you loved me."

"I do." Antonio took a step towards her. Julia shrank away from him.

"Then why did you hurt me?" she asked quietly.

Tony sat down next to her and slowly moved his hand onto her fingers which still clutched her shirt. He used his strength to pull her fingers away. Knowing it was useless to resist, Julia let him take her hand. He kissed each of her fingers and then drew her into his arms.

Always the charming romantic, Julia thought with regret. She couldn't understand why she wasn't making a dash for the door. Why was she still beside this man who had just intentionally caused her pain? She remembered the last few nights with Tony. He had been kind to her but not gentle. This man was like a Jekyll and Hyde. She wondered if he knew what he truly wanted out of their relationship.

Perhaps what scared Julia the most were Antonio's words. She may have understood the pain in her nipple as a fit of passion, but the poison he had spoken to her following that pain left no doubt in her mind that Tony was someone she could not completely trust.

Antonio pulled away from Julia.

"You can stay here and have the cot," Tony said. "I'll sleep on the top bunk. Just don't leave me yet. Give me just one more chance... please."

"I'll stay," Julia said. After all, she had been with him for the past four nights. "You don't need to move to the top bunk. You can be beside me. I'll stay with you tonight, Tony."

Julia knew why she was making her decision. The racetrack was a lonely place, especially with most of the outfits gone. Her own barn had none of the familiar sounds of horses moving or men snoring. Perhaps it was better to stay here with Tony. She sensed that he was more in control of himself, more like the man he had been just last night.

Tony rose and turned out the light. He pulled his ragged familiar comforter around her shoulders and lay down beside Julia. He didn't know what was happening to his emotions. He had always used women and then walked away. Julia had for some reason changed his strategy. Maybe it was that the transient life of exercise person was behind him. He felt deeply depressed. He knew without a doubt that tomorrow evening would see this woman he loved at Woodbine. And he would still be here.

PART III

Fort Erie Racetrack, May, 1985

Chapter Fifteen

Woodbine felt like a homecoming to Julia as Rob drove her in through the west gate towards Cunningham's barn. They had stopped briefly at the dorm so that she could drop her bag of meagre possessions in her new room. Training hours were over and the trainers had rushed to the racing office for the first draw of the Woodbine season. Rob pulled into the parking lot outside Barn 12.

Julia opened her door to the quietness of the barn.

"I'll show you the four horses you'll be grooming. They've been fed their lunch but I expect you back for 4 o'clock feeding."

Rob was gruff with her. Julia didn't mind. He had treated her exactly the same the previous year. He was pretty easy to work with because he basically ignored you if you did your job.

Rob pointed out three fillies and a colt in stalls 61 through 64. Julia memorized the stall numbers and tried to remember the names of the horses. Rob mentioned that the president of a major bank owned the horses, but the owner rarely showed around the barn.

Julia gave Rob a hand unloading the equipment from Greenwood. He helped her find a set of brushes and grooming equipment. Julia pulled the feed tubs from the stalls and washed them. Then she lay down on the bales across from her horses and observed their behaviour so that she could learn something about their personalities.

Julia tried not to think about Greenwood, but the memories were vivid. Antonio had made love to her one last time in the early hours this morning before the track opened for training. He had taken her to the kitchen for breakfast and said his good-byes. Julia closed her eyes briefly and remembered this man who had confused her so much over the past few weeks. He was gone now and she probably wouldn't see him again. Part of her still lived in fear of Antonio, but part of her had been deeply attracted to his harsh reality. He was a good man with horses, and had showed her kindness on more than one occasion.

In the end, she had begun to wonder if she might have fallen in love with Antonio Descartes. The colt she had been watching tossed its head in her direction. He turned his head sideways and tried to reach the clean halter hanging on the top open door of the stall.

"No you don't, you little scoundrel," Julia said to the colt.

He looked at her with big innocent brown eyes. Julia climbed off the hay bales and began the 20-minute trek back to the women's dorm. She had a couple of hours until feed time and wanted to see if she could sleep away the loneliness and sorrow that she was beginning to feel. Besides, she had spent nearly all night awake with Tony and needed the rest.

Julia was in the barn the next morning by 5:30 even though Wilf's outfit didn't officially begin work until 6 a.m. She tied up each of her four horses and removed their bandages. She pulled the feed tubs and water pails and scrubbed them with a stiff brush. By the time she was re-rolling the bandages, George had wandered down the shedrow. He had already taken a lead shank from the tack room and was busy making a knot in the leather end of the shank.

"Aren't you a sight for sore eyes," he greeted her. "How was Greenwood?"

Julia smiled, genuinely glad to see her fellow hot-walker. He obviously hadn't changed at all since last fall.

"We only won one race," she said.

George snorted.

"Wilf only entered about 10 horses. The OJC isn't going to be too happy with the Weasel after they gave him 15 stalls. Need to fill the racing card."

George looked into the stalls of her horses.

"How about we get a cold one out before the riders get here?" he asked.

Julia nodded, grateful that her horses would be taken care of by George. It was nice to get them out early so that she would have less to do in the afternoon.

"I think the colt's down to walk this morning," she said.

George nodded and walked towards the stall. He tied back the webbing on the screen and ducked under the crossbar. Julia watched as George slid the chain of the shank through the colt's mouth and doubled it back on the right side of the halter.

"You got to watch this colt," George said. "He's a biter."

Julia dropped the crossbar for him. Whistling, George moved out of the stall and into the shed.

Julia adjusted her trouble light so that she could see into the stall. She picked up her pitchfork and began to muck out the soiled straw. After a few minutes, she became aware of Rob watching her from the doorway.

"Mornin'," he said gruffly. "Cunningham likes the stalls disinfected every day. I left the solution in your bandage box." He pointed at the walls of the stall. "Make sure you bank them. That colt has a tendency to get cast."

He walked away to begin his own horses. Julia had no idea what he meant by "cast," but wasn't about to confide that to Rob, knowing how he felt about women on the backstretch. However, she did know how to bank a stall, she thought, as she tossed the straw up against the walls.

Half an hour later, George put the colt back into the fresh stall.

"Have you heard the latest?" he asked Julia.

"Of course not, George; I've been at Greenwood," she replied, knowing full well that he would fill her in on any juicy details.

"Marissa left Sig's outfit down the shed last fall, you know," George began in his conspiratorial whisper.

"Get on with it, George. You told me that was going to happen last summer. Remember, she was after Wilf to help care for her son?"

"Yeah, yeah, but she didn't leave as soon as I'd thought. She was still at Greenwood in December."

"Really?"

"And, you know that nut-bar that Sig hired from the islands?"

Sometimes Julia had a hard time seeing the gist of George's story through all the gossipy details. Which nut-bar was he referring to? As far as she was concerned, all of Sig's workers were from the islands, with the exception of Marissa, of course. And they were all nuts.

"Who?"

George was talking so quietly that Julia had to lean forward to hear what he was saying.

"The tall nut."

"Oh."

That explanation didn't really help her distinguish one of the workers from another in that barn.

"Is this going anywhere, George?"

George looked hurt.

"Of course. Well, Marissa was one of the last ones at the track. I think it was around the eighth of December. Some wicked blizzards off the lake."

Julia knew that she would have to be patient for George to get to the end of his story. She closed the screen on her colt. She tuned George out and began filling her water pails. George followed her still chatting away.

"...brutally raped."

Julia froze and looked at the man.

"What did you say?"

"Yeah, apparently he forced his way into her tack room and began hitting her over the head with a brick. Left her for dead when he was finished with her."

Julia turned the water tap off. The water had been pouring over the edge of the bucket.

"Barn 10 I think it was, one of the last barns there and a long way from the kitchen and help. Hey, I got to go. Rob's got one in."

George had walked away. Julia's face was completely drained of colour. She grabbed the rail of the shed as George's words began to bring pictures into her already tortured mind. So recently she had been in that very shed, those very tack rooms! She couldn't understand why she hadn't heard anything about this until now. After all, she had been at Greenwood the very next season.

George brought Rob's horse past where Julia was standing and moved him out into the warm sunshine for a bath. Rob motioned him onto the cement where buckets of warm water and shampoo were standing. George beckoned to Julia as Rob began soaping down the hot horse.

"I never finished my story."

Julia moved towards the pair of men. She wasn't sure that she wanted to hear any more of this particular story.

"Well," George began again in a matter-of-fact voice. "After the guys found her, they say she was in pretty bad shape. As a matter of fact, I think one of the men that found her was Antonio Descartes. Remember him from last summer?"

Julia took a step back. She definitely didn't want to hear another word. She thought she was going to cry. She just couldn't believe what George was saying.

"Jesus, George," Rob reprimanded the old man. "Leave the poor girl alone. Can't you see that you're scaring the shit out of her? Julia, go put the tack on the Ruckus filly. I'll send her out next."

Julia stumbled back and moved into the dim shed, a new feeling about Tony beginning to form in her mind. Why hadn't he told her? Why had he hidden something so important to her own safety?

Julia numbly went to collect the saddle and bridle from in front of Rob's stalls. She wished that Carl was there to listen to her fears. Yet, why hadn't even Carl mentioned Marissa to her? He must have known. Julia felt betrayed, especially by Tony who had claimed that he was falling in love.

Hanging the saddle on the stall door, Julia took the bridle into the Ruckus filly's stall. The horse seemed to sense that there was something the matter and shied away from Julia's hand. Not thinking about what she was doing, Julia grabbed for the filly's halter again. The horse responded by rearing. Julia was cornered in the back of the stall. She ducked below the horse's slashing front feet.

"Whoa there, easy girl," a voice from outside the stall said soothingly.

The filly came down with a snort and the stranger took hold of the halter. He smiled at Julia.

"You okay, miss?" he asked.

From the helmet and chaps, Julia knew this was one of the new exercise riders. She took the horse from him.

"Yeah, I'm fine. I just moved too fast." She didn't want to mention how absent-minded she had been just a moment ago.

She hooked the reins over the filly's neck, dropped the halter on its chain, and began to work the bit into the horse's mouth. The rider placed the saddle cloth and pads on the filly's back while Julia adjusted the throat latch and clipped the bib to the racing martingale.

"What's your name?" the rider asked pleasantly as he gently put the saddle on the filly's back.

Julia moved to the other side of the horse to buckle the girth. She passed the loose end below the horse to the rider.

"Julia," she replied. Her answers were short and clipped. She really didn't feel like talking. Her mind was still fuzzy from lack of sleep and George's revealing gossip.

"I'm Thomas. I started with Wilf Cunningham this spring. Used to gallop for Matheson. The big stakes winner from last year. The Dancer filly, Northern Reflection." Thomas tightened the girth.

"Take her a turn for me, hon, in case she's cinchy?" he asked.

He glanced into the shedrow.

"Head's up, George, we're coming out."

George stopped the horse he was walking so that Julia could lead her filly out of the stall.

"Never finished my story," George complained as he walked along behind Julia. "It's the best part," he went on, appearing oblivious to her discomfort. "Marissa will be back next week. She's coming back to work for Sig again in this very barn. Isn't that just too much?" He turned into one of Rob's stalls with his horse.

Julia stopped the Ruckus filly and gave Thomas a leg up. She got back to work quickly. She was looking forward to escaping back to the dorm.

Chapter Sixteen

Woodbine was proving to be a lonely place. Julia's roommate at the dorm was hardly ever in the room, and Julia spent most of the dark day afternoons and all of her evenings alone in the room. The track was so huge and far away from the rest of the city, that without a vehicle, the backstretch workers lived in isolation. Even the city buses didn't bother to drive within three kilometres of the racetrack. Barn workers tended to stick together, but it was generally a man's world. Without Marissa, Julia was the only woman working in Barn 12.

As training hours finished around 11 a.m. each day, Julia would walk down to the kitchen for lunch, and then head back to the barn to groom her horses and sometimes graze them during the afternoon. George would disappear, and Rob was often around but not terribly friendly.

Thomas was the exercise person assigned to gallop both the Ruckus filly and the colt that Julia groomed. He was friendly, and unlike many of the other riders, he helped her to tack up the horses. She had learned that exercise people on the backstretch often considered themselves the prima donnas of the racetrack, second only to jockeys. Most exercise people expected the grooms to be at their beck and call, having the horses ready as they walked into the barn. When something went wrong, and a rider got dropped, inevitably it was the groom's fault.

The Ruckus filly that Julia groomed was proving to be a handful. Like the first morning, she was showing a tendency to rear at the slightest provocation. Thomas asked Julia to walk the filly out the end of the barn after the first morning because of her previous silliness as he tied the reins and tightened the girth. Rob was good about sending her out before break so that she was less of a handful for both rider and groom.

Julia was putting the saddle on the filly as Thomas ducked under the crossbar into the stall. He stuck his whip in his belt behind his back and began to put the bridle on the filly.

"You hardly smile or laugh you know," he said.

Julia didn't say anything. She wondered why he would say something like that when he hardly knew her. She moved to hold the horse's head still while Thomas checked the saddle and girth. She had been told by George that good riders always checked their equipment.

Julia led the filly out of the stall and took her a turn. She threw Thomas onto the horse and keeping hold of the rein, took the filly through the centre and down the backside of the barn. Thomas tightened the girth.

"I used to gallop with Descartes, you know," he told her.

She glanced up to notice him watching her as he tied his reins in a knot.

"He thought a lot of you. He told me that you were one of the best women he'd ever met on the backstretch. You didn't know much but he had a feeling that you would go a long way. I think he was right."

Julia didn't get a chance to answer. They had just walked out of the end of the barn into the morning sunshine when they heard a commotion down the road.

"Loose horse!" came the shouts along the shedrows.

Sure enough, a riderless horse was barrelling along the road towards Thomas and Julia. The Ruckus filly went crazy. She lunged backwards and reared. Thomas's feet came out of the irons and he desperately tried to shift his weight onto her neck to bring her back down to the ground. The filly's neck was twisted and it looked as though she was going to flip onto her back.

Julia reacted instinctively. She could see Thomas sliding to one side and pulled in the opposite direction as hard as she could on the rein she still held. This placed her directly beneath the filly's slashing front hooves. She could see the toe grabs for added traction on the racing shoes as the filly panicked above her head. Julia didn't back down but kept pulling, the newly developing muscles in her biceps straining against the filly's overwhelming strength.

The horse came down with a crash, sending Julia flying backwards into the ditch, finally losing her hold on the rein. Thomas had somehow managed to regain his stirrups and brought the horse's head down onto the bit. She pranced in the one spot but was finally under control.

"Are you okay?" Thomas asked Julia as she picked herself up and shook the loose grass and dirt from her arms and legs.

"I think so."

"You saved my hide, girl. If that horse had flipped on me, I would have been out of commission for at least a month. I better get her to the training track." Thomas walked the prancing filly onto the road. "Tony was right. You've got more balls than half the men on this backstretch. I owe you one."

As Julia walked back down the shedrow, Rob stormed up to her.

"What the hell did you think you were doing? "he asked. "Next time there's a loose horse, you get your ass out of there. You could have been killed under that filly!"

"What about Thomas?" she yelled back, surprised at herself. "Don't you care that he may have been hurt?"

"Thomas is paid to handle those horses. He's paid well to take his chances. Your job is in the barn. God, Cunningham's gonna have my head if he finds out about this." He glanced at George walking a cold one up the shed.

Julia didn't understand why these men cared so much about her welfare. She wandered back to her stalls and picked up the buckets to fill with water for the filly's bath when she returned. She was confused about how she was treated by the men at the racetrack. They wanted her to be strong and able to handle the horses, but when a problem arose, they didn't want to see the woman in the dangerous spot.

Filling the bath buckets half full of hot water, Julia lugged the buckets to the cold taps. She poured cold water into the buckets as George came out of the shed with his lead shank over his shoulder.

"I'll do that for you if you want to start the stall."

"Thanks," Julia replied, leaving the tap running.

She lugged a bale of straw back to the stall. Thomas was due to come back with the filly in only 10 minutes. That didn't leave her much time to completely clean the stall.

Julia heard Rob's voice long before she was aware that the filly and Thomas had returned to the shed. Thomas turned into the filly's stall, calling to Julia and George. As Julia walked past the colt that she groomed, she noticed that he was lying down. Unusual for this particular time of morning, she paused to take another look. The colt was tight against the side wall with his legs curled up against his body. She wondered if he was able to get up while cramped against the wall of the stall in this manner.

"Rob, I think there's something wrong with the colt," Julia called down to the assistant trainer.

Rob came down the shed mumbling under his breath. He took one look at the colt and ducked under the webbing.

"Thomas, give me a hand here," he yelled at the next stall. "We've got a cast horse."

Thomas appeared at the door and handed Julia his whip.

"What do you want me to do?" Julia asked.

"Stay the hell out of the way," Rob said. "I don't need some woman getting hurt."

"Get on the tail," he said to Thomas. "I'll take the head."

The colt didn't even try to move as the two men took up their respective positions. Thomas had a firm grasp on the horse's tail with both hands, bending the tail tautly backwards over the colt's back. Rob had a hold of the halter and forced the head away from the wall.

"On the count of three," Rob said.

"One, two..."

Julia watched as the two men braced themselves against the horse's weight.

"Three."

Thomas pulled the hind quarters away from the back wall as Rob tried to move the head forward as far as possible.

"Careful, he looks like he's going to come up kicking," Thomas said.

The colt began to struggle, lashing back and forth with all four limbs. With a final tug, the two men fell backwards as they dived for the door. Julia moved back just as they came under the webbing. The colt had scrambled to his feet and was bucking and striking at the stall kick-boards in a mad frenzy. He lunged at the audience in front of his stall with bared teeth.

Rob was furious.

"I thought I told you to bank the stall," he shouted at Julia. "You'd better hope that colt doesn't have a scratch on its legs. Aside from trying to get us killed!"

Julia didn't want to admit it but she had forgotten to bank the stall. She was only human after all. She did make mistakes.

Rob moved towards her and spoke slowly directly into her face. He had lost some of his natural colour.

"I don't know what sort of game you're playing here. Maybe you think you're some kind of superwoman but I remember a girl not so long ago in this barn afraid of horses. Stop trying to be a hero, and just do your job for a change!"

Rob stormed away. Julia was embarrassed. She didn't even want to look at Thomas after Rob had berated her in front of the man. She shifted her gaze down the shed towards George who was taking the filly a turn.

Thomas reached forward and took his whip out of her hand. She hadn't even realized that she was still clutching the whip tightly.

"Don't let him worry you too much there," he said quietly. "Some of the racetrackers around here are old school. Don't like women around the sheds."

Julia just nodded in agreement, scarcely hearing his words.

"I still think you're pretty special. You're Tony's girl and you saved my hide."

Julia stared at him.

"What makes you think I'm Tony's girl?" she asked, glaring at him.

"Why he genuinely cared about you. Didn't you two connect at Greenwood?"

Julia looked away from Thomas again.

"I have to bathe my horse," she said.

Chapter Seventeen

Julia socialized less and less as the days at Woodbine dragged by in the clear May sunshine. Even George commented on her gloomy attitude when he couldn't get her to laugh at his crazier gossip stories. Rob scarcely said a word, speaking only when giving Julia direct orders. Thomas continued to try to get her to open up to his conversation, but she continued to withdraw into herself.

Julia reflected on her experiences at Greenwood with Carl and Tony, and life at Woodbine just didn't seem to come close. Carl had been straightforward and honest, expecting little but an honest day's work. He had been a friend as well as a boss.

And Tony had loved her.

Julia was grateful that Wilf Cunningham had made very few appearances at the barn since her return to Woodbine. She knew that he had suspected her relationship with Antonio on his few brief visits to Greenwood to saddle horses. However, her relief ended with his appearance one fateful day after she had been at Woodbine for nearly one week.

Wilf had chatted with Rob for nearly an hour before moving down the shed to the stalls where Julia worked. He made his cursory pass at her and then apologized.

"Antonio might not be too happy with me." He laughed.

Julia didn't say a word but her silence appeared to verify his remark.

"Absence makes the heart grow fonder. Do you miss a man in bed at night? Will I make do?" Wilf chuckled to himself again.

Julia was furious. She was having a hard time containing her anger. How dare he think that she was mourning after Antonio? How dare he think that she would even consider sleeping with the likes of him? How dare he think that she should stand there and take this kind of trash? She didn't care if he was her boss. She wasn't going to let this man walk on her.

"I'm going to Fort Erie," she said to Wilf.

What was she saying? Was she completely crazy? She hadn't even considered this as an option. Yet here she was, essentially telling her boss that she intended to quit her job.

Wilf looked at her curiously. He didn't appear that upset.

"When?" he asked.

"Tomorrow," she said with more certainty than she felt.

Wilf seemed to contemplate briefly what she said.

"Must be love. Good luck to you."

Julia wasn't sure how exactly she was going to get to Fort Erie. George proved to be a wealth of information. He suggested that she go to the racing office and use their direct phone line to the track in Fort Erie to call Tony and let him know she was coming. He also informed her that on race days, a transfer van from Fort Erie came to Woodbine with horses to race in that card. The trick was to find out when the van was leaving, and simply hop on for the free ride to the Fort.

That night Julia packed her few belongings in her one small bag and went to see the manager of the dormitory. The woman who ran the dorm usually wanted two weeks' notice but realistically knew that the racetrack would never conform to normal rules. She let Julia know that she had broken the rules of notice but didn't seem to care beyond that rule. There were plenty of women who wanted Julia's room.

Arriving at work the next day, Julia was a little fearful that Cunningham would not pay her, since his reputation was to weasel out of financial commitments, and she had given him very little notice. However, Rob handed her a cheque as she finished her morning work.

"No guarantee that it won't bounce. Not many banks left that will cash the Weasel's cheques. I'll miss you around the shed."

Julia stared at the man. She assumed he must be lying after his degrading treatment in the last few days. Rob must have sensed how she was feeling.

"No, really. You are a good worker, on time, sober. They're few and far between on the backstretch."

George spent the morning humming excerpts from love songs. She would give him a whole new line of gossip; that much she knew. As her morning drew to a close, she said some bittersweet good-byes to her horses. As short a time as it had been, she had grown attached to the animals.

Afraid to miss the transfer van, Julia grabbed her bag from her dorm room and hurried back to the loading dock as the first race was being run. She sat in the sunshine by the door of the transport and waited for nearly five hours before cooled and bandaged horses arrived to be loaded.

Feeling that she was invading another person's space, Julia timidly asked the driver if it was okay to ride the van back to Fort Erie.

"I really don't care what you do, honey," had been his reply.

The two-hour trip seemed to take forever. She spent most of the time standing by the open door, gingerly avoiding the urine rolling along the floor from the tired horses. She knew that soon she would be back in Tony's arms. That's what kept her going. It was the hope that she clung to when she had given up the world that she knew, the job and people who had worked with her. Greenwood was indeed a million miles away.

The transfer van unloaded quickly at the Fort Erie loading dock. Julia stood on the dock and watched as the horses disappeared and the driver swept out the trailer and pulled the transport away and out the gate. She was still standing on the dock 10 minutes later, observing an essentially deserted racetrack. There was no one there to meet her. In fact, there was no one in sight at all. She felt so alone, so deserted. Julia picked up her bag and walked towards the first barn in hopes of seeing a human face. She wasn't sure about where to go or what she would do when she got there.

The barns at Fort Erie had a more open concept than those at Woodbine. The shedrows were simply closed in with a single rail. Horses whinnied to Julia as she walked through the sheds, oblivious of the direction that she was taking. As she walked through a completely deserted first barn, she crossed a roadway to an adjacent barn, finally hearing voices.

"You no good piece of shit. Just come here and say that!" The woman's voice was yelling angrily.

"You get your black ass over here!" yelled back a man's voice.

"When I get a hold of you, you're going to beg me to let go!" The woman yelled again.

Julia had stopped in the roadway, unsure whether to proceed into the next shed. Through the centre of the barn ran a white man, thin, tall, and older followed by a short, plump, black woman. The tall man, catching sight of Julia, stopped so suddenly that the black woman nearly crashed into him. The woman had huge thick arms and she immediately grasped the man's wrist and twisted it painfully.

"Jesus, Vern, wait a sec," the man said. "This here is...oh, you're Descartes' girl from Greenwood aren't you? Julia, I think it was?"

Standing in front of Julia was Crazy Bill.

Julia had been hoping that Antonio would be waiting to greet her, but she knew that Crazy Bill was perhaps the next best thing. He was from Fort Erie and knew that she had been seeing Tony at Greenwood. Bill wrestled his arm free of the black woman's grasp.

"Julia, this here is Veronica, Vern, the black trash. . . Ow!"

Veronica had punched him hard in the arm.

"I mean the love of my life," Bill said. "Ow!"

Another punch landed in the same spot.

"Stop saying shit!" Vern hollered at Bill. "You know you don't mean any of it."

She chuckled, a deep throaty laugh. She was obviously having fun at Bill's expense. What was interesting was that Bill appeared to be enjoying the rebuttal.

Julia was immediately attracted to Veronica. This woman wasn't going to take any backlash from a man. She let him know with her voice and her fists. Yet Vern had a natural humour and good-nature about her. She seemed not to be bothered by the insults and laughed just as heartily at Bill's as well as her own expense.

"He says stuff just to get me going," Vern said to Julia.

"Antonio expecting you?" asked Bill.

Julia put her bag down.

"I called from Woodbine and left a message but he doesn't appear to be here." She felt a little upset and deserted.

"Maybe he didn't get the message," Bill said.

"Not bloody likely," Vern said.

Julia looked distressed.

"Shut up, will you!" Bill glared at Veronica.

"Any idea where his tack room is?" asked Julia. She was beginning to feel really weary.

"Yeah; it's right in this barn."

Bill headed back through the middle to the tack rooms on the back side. Julia picked up her bag and quickly followed.

"I think it's just past the can," said Bill.

Reaching the appropriate tack room, he pushed on an unlocked door and it opened to reveal what appeared to Julia to be Antonio's equipment. The bed was neatly made and the assortment of bridles and saddles lined the walls. The tack room was empty and dark. Bill flicked the light switch and discovered that no light came from the overhead bulb.

"He should talk to the stallman about that and get it fixed," Bill mumbled.

"Don't look like the man's at home," said Vern as she walked up behind Bill and Julia.

"Maybe I'll just wait here for him."

Julia moved into the tack room and sat on the bunk. Bill looked at her sceptically.

"Why don't you come out with us? We're going to the local watering hole, the Pit Stop, for some dinner and a couple of beers."

Julia pulled her sneakers off. She was bone tired—emotionally and physically.

"Thanks, but I'd rather just wait for Tony."

"Suit yourself," Vern said. "Let's get outta here." She motioned to Bill.

The two of them left and Julia could hear them begin to bicker again before they were out of the shed. She glanced around at the tiny room. Tony appeared to keep his equipment a little more neatly than he had at Greenwood. Julia realized that she knew very little about this man who somehow had attracted her. She knew that he had been around horses and racing for most of his life. He appeared to be naturally adept at handling even the highest strung thoroughbreds. He must have been a loyal and responsible worker because of the outfit he worked for at Woodbine. She knew some trainers would hire only the best.

Yet there were so many unknowns in her relationship with Tony. He claimed that he loved her but often forgot that she was a part of their physical relationship. He could be kind and charming, but also very selfish. He seemed used to being in charge, and although he often acted as if she had a choice, she knew there would be no opportunity for her to argue with his ideas.

This was perhaps the most important day of her life, the day when she quit her job and everything she'd known to move to a strange track and strange town. She had no idea what she would do or where she would work. She was going to rely totally on Tony to give her a place to stay, food to eat, and a direction for her life. Maybe that's what he had wanted. But she didn't know if she had made the best decision. It had been a long time since she had totally depended on another person.

Darkness had fallen. Julia glanced at the digital alarm clock. The red numbers indicated that it was nearly 10 o'clock. The barns seemed ghostly quiet. Occasionally, she could hear a horse moving in its stall. This track was so different from Greenwood or Woodbine, where there was always some sort of bustle. However, she had never been on the backstretch at Woodbine so late in the evening and maybe things quieted down there as well.

Thinking briefly about Greenwood, Julia wondered about her safety on this backstretch. Tony didn't appear to have any types of locks on either the outside or the inside of his door. She could hear someone coming and glanced nervously but expectantly at the door. The sounds of footsteps approaching the door made her sit up a little straighter, her heart beginning to beat faster. Sure enough, the door swung open and Antonio stood there, his strong muscular body framed in the dim shedrow light.

Julia breathed a sigh of relief. She was having a hard time fighting back the tears of joy that wanted to fall. At last things would be okay. She was with someone who loved her and would look after her needs. They could work together and build a great life on this backstretch or anywhere else they chose. She felt Antonio's eyes graze over her and at last he spoke.

"What are you doing here?"

Chapter Eighteen

Antonio rose early. Even for the racetrack, Julia realized as he pushed her out of bed at 4 o'clock.

"Time for coffee," he said in a brusque voice.

He seemed unconcerned about the lack of emotion he displayed despite their intimacy the previous night. He pulled jeans on over his underwear, his back to Julia. She quickly donned her T-shirt from the previous evening in an effort to hide her naked breasts.

Tony moved swiftly in the dark of the tack room. Julia struggled to make out the scattered items to avoid stumbling over boxes or clothes. Tony opened the door. Dim light from the shedrow filtered into the room.

Julia found her comb and quickly pulled it through her tangled hair. Tony was already outside, impatiently waiting for her to finish.

"We'll stop by the barn to give morning feed before we go to the kitchen."

Julia had still not said a word to this man who seemed to have such control over her feelings and actions. She was confused. Antonio had claimed that he had loved her while they were together at Greenwood. He had practically begged her to come to Fort Erie with him, and had appeared heart-broken when she insisted on returning to Woodbine with the Weasel's outfit. Yet Tony was treating her indifferently now that she was finally with him on a more permanent footing. She was beginning to wonder if she hadn't acted too foolishly.

Julia watched from the shed as Tony opened his feed room and made up the morning feed to the chorus of nickering horses.

"Tony," she said, casting her eyes towards the hungry horses.

Tony glanced up.

"What's the matter?"

Julia swallowed her nervousness. It was now or never. She began quietly, moving into the dim feed room and gaining confidence as she talked to the man.

"You act like you don't care about me anymore. Other than necessary things, you've scarcely talked to me since I've gotten here. I don't understand why your feelings have changed so much in just one week. Did I make a mistake in coming to Fort Erie?"

Julia knew that she had to ask this question. She also knew that she was desperately afraid of the answer. Tony watched her carefully for a moment before he moved towards her in the dark feed room. Julia tensed, not sure what to expect from this man.

Descartes took Julia in his arms. As Tony held her, Julia's tension began to dissolve.

"There is no mistake, Julia. I still love you. It's just that you surprised me. You were so certain that you were going to stay at Woodbine that I had given up hope. Then, suddenly, you're here, and I'm not sure how to get used to that idea. I'm sorry if I'm confusing you, but I do want you to be a part of my life and work here at Fort Erie, a part of my fresh start."

Julia felt bad. Obviously she had misjudged this man. She looked into his eyes. This time, Tony didn't avoid her gaze.

"Can I help you feed?" she asked.

Tony nodded and pulled away from her. He handed her one of the feed buckets.

The backstretch kitchen at Fort Erie was not as pleasant as the kitchen at Greenwood but was certainly not as crazy as the kitchen at Woodbine. Tony liked to spend nearly an hour sitting in the kitchen in the early morning, from when it opened at 5 a.m. to just prior to the track opening for training an hour later. Many of the backstretch workers greeted Julia and Tony as they sat sipping their coffee.

Charming and pleasant again, Tony introduced Julia to the new faces she had not met at Greenwood. He chatted to her about how the horses that he was training were coming along in their various levels of fitness. Although feeling a little estranged in her surroundings, Julia was beginning to realize that the rhythm of the racetrack was pulsing in Fort Erie just as evidently as it did on any other backstretch in the world. This gave her a sense of well-being and belonging despite the new images and names.

Morning training was pleasant and relaxed. Julia at first credited this feeling to the fact that there was far less work to do with only four horses and two people to handle the daily tasks. However, she soon realized that the atmosphere was commonplace in the quiet town of Fort Erie. Fellow backstretch workers took the time to stop and chat, and invitations abounded for dark day afternoons. Woodbine and Greenwood had been all business, with big races and million-dollar horses. Fort Erie was home to the cheaper mounts, broken-down geldings and fillies, and its own brand of "homebreds." A homebred was a racehorse that was bred and raised by one individual rather than a large racing stable or company. These horses tended to be spoiled and difficult to handle once they reached the track.

Julia enjoyed walking Tony's horses around the open shed with the sunshine streaming in under the rail. The male exercise riders whistled from their mounts, and the grooms talked politely, making her feel at ease and welcome. As training hours drew to a close, Julia began to realize that she had made the right decision when she had left Woodbine.

Tony took her back to the kitchen for lunch at 11. Julia had a toasted Western sandwich, what was to become a favourite of hers in that backstretch kitchen. An older man came to their table and sat across from Tony, discussing various aspects of training. Tony fired off questions to the man and Julia listened carefully, absorbing the obviously knowledgeable conversation.

Finally, the older man smiled at Julia.

"I'm Ernie. I understand that you are Tony's new girl from Greenwood."

Julia nodded at the man.

"He used to groom Seattle Slew. You know, the Triple Crown winner," Tony said.

Julia glanced at him. She might be naive but she wasn't stupid, she thought irritably. Of course she'd heard of Seattle Slew. Ernie was laughing.

"Actually, I rubbed him after he won his big races, just prior to his retirement to stud," he said.

Julia didn't say anything. She was still impressed. The men turned back to their discussion about illegal medications.

"What about Lasix?" asked Tony.

"These are just about the only tracks left in North America that don't allow that one. Twenty-four hours. Get a good vet. The timing is critical. You can't give them any water once they've had the shot."

Tony pulled a tiny book from his pocket. Julia could see the emblem of the Ontario Racing Commission on the front cover. He leaned back in his chair and opened the book, searching for a particular page. Stopping, he glanced up at Julia.

"Why don't you go back to the barn? I'm going to be here a while, and I'm sure that you don't want to hang around listening to old horsemen talk. I have to study for my trainer's test."

Julia felt dismissed. She had really wanted to stay. At last, Tony had seemed to be treating her as an equal in a conversation. Maybe he was feeling a little pressured with her presence. She knew how much it meant to him to get the trainer's licence. She pushed her chair back and, mumbling good-bye to Ernie, headed out of the kitchen.

Julia didn't know what she would do back at the barn. She felt very much alone and friendless at this track. It seemed that her sole link was Tony, and he confused her with his reactions. He appeared to want her around, yet he often chased her away from his conversations and activities. Approaching Tony's stalls, she noticed that Veronica was across the road in the opposite shed.

"Hey, Julia," Vern said.

Julia walked across the road to where the woman stood rolling bandages.

"You wouldn't know how to pull a mane by any chance?" Vern asked. "My boss wants me to pull the mane on my colt and I know that I'll screw it up."

Julia had come to the track with limited horse knowledge but that was the one thing that the hunter/jumper people had taken the time to teach her. When a mane is cut with scissors, the hair will stand straight up on end. To keep a mane flat, even, and neat, horseman wrap the hair around a small metal comb and pull it out by the roots rather than cutting the hair. Julia didn't mind helping out Vern. It would give her something to do while she waited for Tony to return to the barn.

"I think I can help you."

"Great," Vern said. "Let me grab a shank. You saved my ass."

Julia laughed as the black woman moved down the shed in search of a lead shank.

Vern returned with the shank and handed Julia a pulling comb. She unfastened the webbing on the stall where they stood and ducked under the crossbar to put the shank on the horse in that stall.

"I'll hold this son of a bitch. He likes to bite," Vern said.

Julia was beginning to wonder if this woman could say a single sentence without swearing. She never appeared angry. She just used the words as part of her normal vocabulary.

Vern had pulled the horse toward the entrance to the stall.

"Ready when you are," she said.

Julia moved into the stall and standing on the right-hand side of the horse, reached up to grasp the beginning of the mane behind the bridle path. The colt's eyes rolled towards her and he tried to pull his head away, but Vern had an iron grip on him.

"Let him pull the other way a little," Julia said. "It helps me so that I don't have to pull so hard."

She wrapped another section of hair around the comb and moved quickly back to avoid the colt's stomping foot. He was aiming for her toes. Vern shanked the horse.

"You no-good bastard." She growled at him. "You'd be worth it if you could win a race." She laughed in a good-natured way.

Julia began to realize that Vern was quite fond of the colt. Much of her aggression and swearing was simply for show.

It only took her about 10 minutes to pull the mane. She took pride in keeping the line of hair straight and thin. Vern was impressed.

"Hey, Charlie," she yelled down the shed at a neighbouring horseman. "Look at the great job that Julia did on my colt's mane."

Another groom walked down the shed to view Julia's handiwork.

"You're good," he said. "How much do you charge? I've got a couple that need doing."

"A sawbuck for each mane," Vern said before Julia had a chance to answer.

Julia had no intention of charging Vern anything for the basic 10-minute job. It was simply a way to pass time until Tony returned to the barn.

"You got time now?" Charlie asked.

Julia glanced over at Tony's horses. Vern noticed and gave her a knowing look.

"That man won't be back for at least two hours. You've got lots of time. Charlie, it's money up front. Don't be cheap."

"And who are you?" Charlie chided back to Vern.

"Her agent, asshole. Give her the 20."

Charlie laughed, dug into his pocket and handed Julia a 20.

Julia was surprised but took the money and followed Charlie down the shed to his stalls.

"I'll grab you a beer," Vern called after her.

Julia turned briefly.

"I don't drink beer," she replied.

"This is Fort Erie. It's a good time to start. I think the bootlegger's got some coolers; I'll get you one of those instead."

Before Julia had a chance to answer, Vern had disappeared around the corner. It wasn't even noon yet, a little early to start drinking. However, it was turning out to be a warm day, and she had been up since 4 a.m. Maybe a cooler would taste good after she pulled the manes.

Antonio arrived back at the barn an hour later to discover Julia laughing and chatting with Vern, Charlie, and Crazy Bill in the shed across from his stalls.

"Your old man's back." Vern nodded to Tony as he walked towards the group.

Julia stopped talking and turned to face Tony as he approached.

"You been up at the kitchen shooting your mouth off while Julia here has been making money."

Vern's grammar was deteriorating with each beer that she consumed. Tony looked at the empty beer bottles and the cooler in Julia's hand.

"Looks like you've found some friends," he said with a smirk.

Julia felt chastised. She put her bottle down and glanced towards Vern.

"I asked her to pull a mane," Vern said. "And she did such an excellent job that Charlie here hired her to pull two more."

Tony smiled. "Really?" he asked Julia.

She nodded, not sure how he felt about her working when she was supposed to be helping him, but hoping that he would be pleased.

"Freelancing already?" Tony asked.

"Good money in it, Tony," said Charlie. "The girl's a real horsewoman. Managed to get me for a 20."

Crazy Bill pushed Vern playfully on the arm.

"I wish I had a girl that went out to do extra work for me."

Vern lashed back at her lover, her powerful thick arms backing the punch with some intensity.

"You get plenty out of me, asshole. You should be paying me for all I do for your ugly hide."

Both Charlie and Crazy Bill laughed.

Julia was still not sure what Tony felt about her new-found friends. He didn't seem that impressed with the situation. He watched her closely.

"Twenty dollars. That should help to pay for a few things."

Julia took the hint and reached into her pocket to hand him the money. Vern caught her wrist before she had a chance.

"Now just hold on a moment there, honey. This man is getting plenty of work out of you, and that isn't even going into what happens behind that tack room door. You keep your money. Don't be handing it over to some man just 'cause he thinks he owns you."

Antonio stomped away from the group towards his own horses. Julia was feeling bad. After all, Tony was looking after her. She quickly said good-bye to the group and followed Tony across the road.

Julia stood outside the stall where Tony was setting out the bandages by the front legs of a horse. He didn't look at her as she waited.

"You don't need to work, you know."

"They asked me and offered to pay me. I thought that it might help us. We are a team, aren't we?"

Tony rubbed alcohol into his hands and began to massage the filly's legs. For a moment he didn't answer her.

"Doesn't feel like much of a team when I'm working to study for a trainer's test so that we can have a better life and you're at some barn drinking with the likes of Crazy Bill and his black American girl."

The malevolency of his remark shocked Julia. She hadn't realized that he might be prejudiced. Tony stopped and glowered at Julia. When he spoke it was so quietly that she had to strain to her him.

"Let's get one thing straight, girl. As far as the racing stewards are concerned, you are here with me, working for me. You live in my tack room and I pay for your meals. If you want to remain on this racetrack, you need to remember that. I didn't ask you to come here. But now that you're here, you need to understand where you belong. You can freelance if you want, but make sure that if I need you, you are free to help me."

Julia gasped. She couldn't believe what she was hearing from this man who had claimed just that morning that he still loved her and wanted her to share his life. What he was saying now didn't sound like much of a partnership. She remembered her earlier thoughts of Tony as a Jekyll and Hyde personality. It was becoming clearer to her each day that she didn't know this man as well as she had imagined on those lonely nights in her dorm room at Woodbine. She felt tears sting her eyes as she turned away from Tony and walked blindly down the shed. She had to think. She needed time to sort through her feelings. She couldn't understand why Antonio Descartes had such a hold on her life. Why was she letting him do this to her? Why couldn't she just walk away from him?

"Julia!"

Her name was being called and she rubbed her eyes viciously before looking around to realize she was in an unknown barn.

"Julia!" the voice called again. "Over here…"

Julia glanced in the direction of the summons. Leaning against the shed rail, holding a horse for a blacksmith, was Carl. He beckoned to her to come closer. She felt embarrassed by her tears and rubbed her face again, hoping that Carl wouldn't notice as she approached.

"Aren't you a sight for sore eyes," Carl said. "I saw Crazy Bill this morning and he said that you were around."

Julia nodded. She looked at the horse that Carl was holding, remembering the gelding from Greenwood. The blacksmith let go of the foot he held between his knees and grinned up at Julia as he stretched his back.

"Who's the nice young lady that comes over to talk to an old geezer like you, Carl?" the stranger asked.

"Forgive me, Julia." Carl laughed. "This is Gus, one of the best blacksmiths on the backstretch. Gus, meet Julia. She worked for the Weasel with me at Greenwood this spring and Woodbine last year."

"Who are you working for?" Carl asked Julia.

"I'm just helping out Tony. We are looking after his horses together." She didn't go into any more details. The look that Carl gave her was enough.

"Taylor Anderson on the backside of this barn is looking for someone to walk some hots before break each morning," Carl said. "He pays by the head, strictly freelance. I'll put in a good word for you if you're interested. You'll still have time for Tony after break."

Julia looked away from Carl's intense gaze. She was having a hard time pretending that nothing was the matter.

"I don't know, Carl," she replied. "That's kind of you. I'll have to ask Tony what he thinks."

Carl was silent again. Julia could have cut the air with a knife, his disapproval was so vibrant.

"How's that man treating you?" Carl asked quietly.

"Everything's fine," Julia said. "I should get back to the barn. Nice seeing you, Carl."

"Just remember what I said. Anderson's is a mom-and-pop operation. Nice wife. Quiet horses. You'd like it there. Don't forget to come by and visit sometime. Now you know where I am." Carl turned his attention back to Gus and his gelding.

Chapter Nineteen

Tony took Julia to Grace's for supper. Grace's was a rambling old house converted to a hotel and bar. Located just beyond the Niagara Boulevard that ran along the waterfront on the quiet back streets of Fort Erie, Grace's was a quieter retreat away from the bustle of the Prince Hotel on the main drag. It got its name from some of the backstretch workers and was one of the many Chinese restaurants in Fort Erie. These restaurants, especially the cheaper establishments down by the Peace River, catered to the Americans who streamed across the border to pour their money in through the betting windows, and retired broke after a hard day.

Grace's, however, catered to the racetrack workers and was a favourite haunt for Antonio Descartes. He would take a taxi to the hotel every night following afternoon feed and listen to the tales of the group of horsemen who drank their beer and ate their evening meal. True to Fort Erie style, the cook was Chinese, but served up a different special every night. The kitchen was too small to accommodate a regular menu, but the fare was popular with the locals.

The woman who drove the cab was friendly with Tony and talked to him about his horses as they drove along the back roads down to the hotel. Julia couldn't help feeling a stab of jealousy at their apparent familiarity.

"It's a small town," Tony said when he sensed Julia's reaction to the taxi ride.

Grace's was quiet but seemed to be a men's club. There wasn't another woman in the establishment. The men seated around the one main table turned to look at her curiously as she followed Tony into the restaurant. Ernie, the trainer whom Tony had introduced her to just that morning, sat at one end of the table, his eyes already glazed over from the effects of alcohol.

Tony sat down in the chair next to Ernie and ordered himself a beer.

"Do you want a drink?" he asked Julia as she positioned herself across from the men.

"No thanks." Julia still felt that Tony was annoyed about her drinking with Vern and Crazy Bill earlier.

"Liver and onions is on the menu this evening," Ernie said. "If you don't like that, I think the alternative is Salisbury steak."

Ernie and Tony lapsed into a heated conversation about the various bones in a horse's legs. Both men completely ignored Julia. She watched the limited activity around her and found that the television channel had been switched to *Wheel of Fortune* so let her attention get directed to the game show playing out above the bar.

Julia found the evening long and dull and the cab ride home left her feeling like a third party outside Tony's life. She offered to pay for the cab with the money she had earned that day but Tony promptly refused, suggesting that she find a better way to repay him for his cordial performance. Julia already knew what this comment meant. She would submit fully to Tony's passion that night in return for his supposed kindness. His passion, despite its borderline cruelty, never failed to arouse something in her that Ken had never found. She wondered briefly if that was what held her so tightly to this strange man.

The next few days of life at Fort Erie were similar to Julia's initial experience. She rose early in the morning to sit in the kitchen with Tony's friends as he prepared himself for the trainer's test. She would clean the horse's stalls, brush and tack them, and cool them out following training hours. She had yet to ask Tony about the possibility of employment for herself and made it a point to avoid Carl's barn. His disapproval of her relationship gave her feelings of remorse.

The evenings were spent at Grace's as Tony discussed horses and racing with Ernie, who slowly drank himself to sleep each night. Julia had yet to see another woman at the hotel. Each night, after the four-dollar cab ride home, Tony would close the tack room door and become a different person to Julia. When he wanted her, his attention was focused and demanding. Sometimes Julia wondered if he thought about her at all as they lay together. Yet she was grateful for the small things, knowing that Tony took care not to get her pregnant again.

One night, as she lay with her back pressed against the cement block wall, she finally had the courage to ask Tony about Marissa. She still wondered why he had not told her about finding Marissa when they were together at Greenwood.

"She was a friend. She worked in the same barn at Woodbine."

Julia felt that she had to explain why she wanted to know. However, Tony often left her feeling intimidated, and maybe it was better not to talk about her fears.

Tony lay quietly on his back in the narrow bunk for a moment without answering. Then, slowly, he turned toward Julia and pulled her into his arms. She was so close to him that she could feel the steady beating of his heart. She began to realize that he held her not to still her misgivings, but rather, to bring the comfort that he needed from her at this moment.

"When you spend enough years on the backstretch, you eventually see the horses and people that you love either get hurt or killed. It's just part of the game that everyone accepts. They say that time heals the wounds and dims the memories. That isn't always true. What I discovered last fall will stay with me for the rest of my life."

Antonio stopped talking for a moment and pulled away from Julia so that he could watch her face. His voice was so quiet that it was barely above a whisper.

"What happened to that girl was horrible. I hope that black bastard rots in hell." Tony's voice had become almost malicious. He stopped once more to regain control of his emotions.

"I didn't want to frighten you while we were at Greenwood. I knew that while you were with me, you'd be safe. Don't you remember me asking if you had a lock on your door? I cared about you even then."

Julia didn't know what to say. When Tony was kind to her, she wanted to believe that they would be together always. Yet there were days when he treated her so differently, almost with an underlying cruelty. He had claimed that while she was with him, she would be safe. Yet who would protect her from him?

His personality was so complex, so confusing. Did he really love her? Did he even know what love was supposed to be? For that matter, did she?

Saturday afternoon, as the races were called over, Julia stepped out of a stall to find Carl standing there. She looked down the shed nervously, knowing that Tony would disapprove of this man in his shedrow. However, Tony was nowhere in sight. Carl seemed to notice her discomfort.

"I stopped by because I have a horse in tomorrow. I need someone to run the horse and wondered if you were interested. I'll pay you twenty dollars, the going rate."

Julia wasn't sure what to say. She felt that she should ask Tony if he minded, but the man didn't seem to pay much attention to her desires these days because he was so caught up in studying. She knew that normally they spent their afternoons sleeping or talking to other horsemen. She didn't see what harm it would do working for Carl for a couple of hours.

"I'd love to run your horse," she answered.

"Good," Carl said. "I'm in the fourth race. Come by the barn when they call them over for the third. I like to walk over with the horse so I'll be beside you if you have any problems."

Carl left and Julia walked through the barn to see if Tony had retreated to the tack room. Standing outside the tack room, Tony was in a heated conversation with one of the jockeys who came to get on their horses each morning. As Julia approached she noticed that the two men were smoking. Startled, Julia paused briefly but approached as the men stopped talking to look in her direction.

"I was looking for you, Tony; didn't know where you were...," she began, not wanting to look either man directly in the eye. It quickly became obvious that they were smoking pot.

"I'm smoking a joint." Tony was gruff with Julia.

The other man held out his hand. "Do you want a drag?"

"I don't do that," Julia stammered, embarrassed. Before she knew what was happening, Tony was within inches of her face, his hand gripping her arm painfully.

"If you breathe a word of this to anyone, I'll fuckin' kill you. Do you understand?" he said.

The pain in her arm brought tears to Julia's eyes.

"I wouldn't tell anyone, Tony," she replied quietly. "You know that." Maybe this wasn't such a good time to let him know about Carl's employment opportunity.

Tony released her and turned his back, taking a long drag on the joint.

"She's getting too goddamn defiant," he mumbled to the rider in explanation. "Didn't really want her to catch me having a toke."

He finished his smoke and said farewell to his friend. Julia followed meekly behind.

Tony liked to walk to the track to watch the horses train each morning. Julia would remain at the barn to clean the stall and prepare bath water. In a barn so close to the track, there was always lots of excitement to watch as horses and riders passed by on the central road. Julia could easily see the gap where horses entered and exited the track. The woman who served as outrider would be perched atop her pony watching for loose horses in the early morning sunshine. Unlike Woodbine with its training track, Fort Erie horses must train on the main track. This aspect of Fort Erie reminded Julia of Greenwood, where you could watch horses in their morning training as you sipped your coffee.

One morning, Tony had thrown a rider onto the skittish filly for training. Having walked the previous day, the filly was especially rangy under saddle as Julia took her for a turn around the shed. Tony threw the rider up and followed the horse out the end of the shed. A moment later, Julia heard a commotion on the main road at the end of the barn.

Glancing up, she could see the filly twisting away from Tony's grasp on the rein as the rider attempted to tighten the girth. A noise from the opposite barn unnerved the filly and she reared, taking the rider by surprise. He shifted in the saddle, grabbling to stay on the horse's back. Tony was beside the filly, trying to regain a hold of the rein. Other horses and riders were avoiding the commotion in the centre of the road.

Julia watched, shocked, as the filly lost her balance and flipped over backwards. The rider lost his hold and crashed to the ground with the horse on top of him. Even from the distance, Julia could hear the distinctive crack as bone broke. There was shouting from nearby sheds as some people rushed to help the injured man while others attempted to catch the loose horse. Julia could see Vern appear in the barn across from her to observe the saga before them.

Julia saw Tony in the swirling dust on the road, a firm grip now on the filly who danced in circles around him. People still shouted as the ambulance pulled alongside the injured man. He had still not risen from his prone position on the road. Julia knew this was a bad sign. She regretted that one of their horses had hurt this rider.

Tony walked along the road between the barns towards Julia, the filly rearing and lunging in his iron clasp.

"Julia," he called. Julia put down the pitchfork.

"Take this damn horse," he said. "I'm going to get my helmet."

Scarcely looking at her, Tony handed the rein to Julia. Worried, she took hold of the filly, knowing that she could lose her grip on the horse easily without a shank. Her nervousness at handling these high-strung horses still returned on occasion, and she could feel her heart racing.

Julia led the filly into the shedrow and retrieved a lead shank from the rail. By this time Tony had reappeared with his helmet and whip. As she pulled up beside him, he stooped to feel the filly's front legs for any scratches.

"I'll get on her in five minutes. The ambulance won't be back from the hospital yet, and the track will be closed. Take her a few turns to try to calm her down." Tony began to walk away.

Julia didn't respond immediately.

"Tony, please," she said. "That rider got hurt on this horse. Next time it could be you. You don't need to get on her."

Tony spun around to face Julia.

"Don't be telling me what I can and cannot do. I've backed horses that no rider has dared to go near. I am in charge here. You need to remember that."

Julia was astonished. He was truly angry, yet her concern for his safety had been real. If something happened to Tony, she didn't know how she would survive on this strange backstretch. Not having any other choice, she moved away with the filly dancing beside her.

Five minutes later, Tony beckoned to her to exit the shed to the roadway between the barns. The filly had settled a little in her stroll around the shed. As Julia approached, Tony pulled her to him with one arm and held her for a brief moment. He seemed calmer and more in control of the situation.

"You need to trust me. I know what I'm doing."

Julia felt a little relief at his words, but she still anxiously worried about the potential for a mishap.

Tony put the whip behind his back in his belt.

"The track will be open," he said. "Give me a leg up."

Julia held the rein securely and reached down to throw him onto the filly.

Tony had his whip out, and with his legs tightly encircling the horse's belly, he raised his hand high above the filly. The air sizzled as he brought the whip down across the filly's flanks. Julia managed to get out of the way just in time as the filly reared and lunged forward.

"For Christ's sake, Descartes, take that damn horse to the track if you're going to do that," Vern yelled from her shedrow. "You're spooking my horses."

Tony glared at her as the horse lunged and pitched beneath him. Feet still not in the irons, he hit the horse again, harder this time. Julia could see welts appearing on the flanks.

"Back away," Tony said. "This filly needs to be taught a lesson, and I intend to do just that."

He rushed the horse to the main road, and Julia could hear the hiss of the whip as he drove her to the track. Julia was upset by Tony's treatment of the horse. The violence disturbed her. It was a part of this man she had never seen before. Vern appeared beside her as she prepared the bath water.

"That man is amazing on a horse, but I don't agree with the beating. I hope he doesn't treat you that way."

Julia couldn't look at her friend. She felt that Vern could see right through the thin fabric of her relationship with Tony. Something about his behaviour today warned her that maybe she needed to truly fear this man.

Carl was glad to see Julia when she came down the shed in clean jeans and a blouse for running the horse. He was all business, attempting to keep the gelding calm as each race was called. Julia sat on an over-turned bucket as she watched the final preparations for the race. Carl did little to upset the horse, foregoing the Vicks' and cold-water treatments that the Weasel had favoured. He waited until they called them over for the fourth race before he pushed the bit into the horse's mouth. He handed the newly-oiled shank to Julia. The chain was doubled back in the D-bit.

"All yours. You've got enough to worry about with the horse. I'll look after the halter."

Carl glanced at Julia. "Are you nervous?"

Julia shook her head, watching the gelding. The horse must have picked up the excitement, and his muscles quivered in anticipation of the race. Carl looked at her critically, wondering briefly if she could handle the gelding.

Julia moved in close to the gelding, talking in a low voice to the horse. Carl could see that she had completely lost the fear she once held for racehorses, and treated them with an esteem that was seldom seen in the backstretch workers. Her love of the animals oozed from her pores, heightening his sense of respect for this caring woman.

Carl was unnerved. This warm-hearted girl that he admired was awakening a response in him that he hadn't felt for years. He grappled desperately at the present, and the gelding that he had to saddle.

As if sensing his thoughts, Julia hugged him suddenly. Carl couldn't resist the feel of this woman so close to him. His lips brushed against her forehead chastely but that was the last thing that he was feeling.

"Oh Julia, please. You don't know what you're doing to me." Carl knew that she belonged to Tony. "They called us over five minutes ago, Julia. We're in Barn 8. We have to make the gap." Carl's words seemed strangled, foreign, as he struggled to gain control. He couldn't believe how badly he wanted this woman. It was enough to drive him back to the bottle.

Julia appeared at ease for the first time since she had arrived on this backstretch the week before. She headed over to the paddock, the gelding prancing alongside. Carl walked a few steps away from the pair, at last focusing his mind on the race.

The gelding was an experienced racehorse. He stood like a gentleman as Carl tightened the over-girth. The horse appeared to understand that he had to save his energy for the race. He didn't act up and cause Julia to look bad in front of Carl. Carl noticed Julia's glances in his direction. She seemed to want so badly to impress him with her ability to run a horse. As she walked around the paddock, waiting for the "riders up" call, Carl was watching her handling of his gelding. He was noticing. In more ways than one.

Carl was not the type of trainer to wander into the clubhouse with owners, ignoring the workers of the track. He took Julia with him to the owners' box (the owners being absent), and together they watched the race and cheered on the gelding as he crossed the finish line in fourth place.

The gelding dragged Julia home. They were asked to report to the test barn, and Carl belatedly requested that she walk the horse if her schedule permitted. He needed to get back to his barn for afternoon feed and the gelding's stall.

He left Julia walking the gelding in the tight circles of the test barn, letting him sip from the green bucket every four turns. Julia finally returned to Carl's barn with the cooled horse nearly an hour later.

Carl handed her the promised twenty dollars and an extra ten.

"It's like he never ran a race," he said as the horse bucked in the shed. "Maybe he needs distance."

Julia glanced apprehensively at her watch.

"I need to get back to Tony. It's nearly 5:30."

Carl reached out to Julia and pushed a strand of hair away from her cheek.

"Take care of yourself," was all he said.

Antonio had been furious. He had awakened from his afternoon nap to discover that Julia had slipped from their bed. With a few inquiries, he had discovered that Julia had run a horse for none other than Carl, he had thought with a stab of jealousy, and had the insolence to not show up for afternoon feed.

"Don't you know where you belong?" he had shouted at her.

Then he had ignored her. This was almost worse than his anger. He had walked off the backstretch to his nightly rendezvous without suggesting that she come for supper. Crazy Bill had discovered her crying in the feed room as he walked through the barn to pick up Vern.

"That no good piece of shit," Bill said. He moved to pull the reluctant Julia off a hay bale. "Come with Vern and me to the Pit Stop. You can have a beer and supper, and we'll make sure that you make it back here before that bastard man of yours is home."

Julia shook her head. She didn't feel like celebrating. She felt like she had betrayed Tony. She deserved the way that she was now feeling. She drew her knees into her chin and gazed sadly at Crazy Bill. Vern appeared in the dwindling light of the shed.

"Can we at least bring you back a sandwich?" she asked.

Julia shook her head. It was better if she didn't eat.

"You don't need to stay with that man. He doesn't respect you. You've got friends here. You can find a job. The creep is using you and you're letting him. Have some backbone, girl. Walk away from him."

Julia didn't answer Vern. The couple left, squabbling between themselves.

Veronica was upset. She'd seen a lot of bad things happen in her years on the backstretch, but she didn't like what was happening to the woman that she now considered a friend. Crazy Bill was shifty and unreliable, but he treated her decently. Most nights he held her tenderly, a surprisingly sane man.

Vern liked to dine at the Pit Stop. They served up a wonderful helping of spaghetti and meatballs with sausage, a portion that her ample appetite could appreciate. The bar was a hole-in -the-wall, she had to admit, but it was packed with racetrackers and in spite of her dark skin, she felt welcome.

Sitting with her back against the wall, Vern let Crazy Bill know what she thought of Antonio Descartes.

"You gotta do something," she said. "He's goin' to chew her up and spit her out. He's a loser, and he's goin' to take her down. She's too good a person for that to happen. We should have made her come here. It's better than that feed room. That jerk probably wouldn't even let her back into his tack room. Christ, Bill, ain't you listenin'?"

Crazy Bill had his eyes closed.

"God, Vern," he mumbled. "Let me alone to drink in peace. Do you have to carry on like this? Yeah, you're right. Tony is an asshole, no doubt there. I just don't know how to get that crazy broad away from him; she was so taken with his charm."

Crazy Bill took another gulp of his beer. Vern could see the alcoholic state of peaceful equilibrium appear in his eyes, she thought with frustration. Bill smiled at her and continued.

"You know, she didn't take any crap from him at Greenwood. I don't understand why she's like this now. Too bad she wouldn't come here tonight. We could have shown her the other people on this backstretch are pretty decent."

Vern landed a punch on his arm.

"No they aren't, you stupid asshole. That's not gonna cure her."

Bill pulled back from the aggressive black woman.

"God, Vern, could you go a little easier? You're hard on a man, you know."

Vern waved at the man behind the bar.

"Get me an Alabama Slammer."

"Jeez, Vern, don't start drinkin' those," Bill said. "You know you always get a little crazy after the shooters."

Vern laughed.

"Just one, and then I'm heading back. I want to see if Julia's still in the feed room. You coming with me or hanging here?"

"I'll come," Bill said. "I've got another tack room. There's a mattress on the bunk, and she can stay there if she needs a spot."

"What? You got another room, and you didn't tell me? Where?"

Now Bill was laughing.

"Drink that Slammer and let's blow this joint."

Antonio Descartes didn't return until 11:30 at night to the tack room, dark save for a scantily clad compliant Julia. The beer on his breath fuelled her submission. She felt the walls tremor as Tony slammed the door.

Tony did not waste time but grasped her thin shirt and tore it from her body. Julia shivered in trepidation. She was beginning to know this man and his dark moods. She lay on the cot, using the sole blanket to cover her nakedness and closed her eyes, indifferent to the feelings that she knew Tony would force on her. Tonight, however, there was something unusual. Tony had stopped and was sitting beside the bed.

"I want something more from you," he stated as he looked above Julia's face to the whitewashed wall.

Julia didn't understand. What more could she give? What more could he demand?

Roughly, he pushed her away from him and pulling the cover from her body, moved behind her. Julia felt a new horror. Was this to be her punishment?

Julia was turned, with Tony's desire hard against her buttocks. Fear coursed through her veins. She felt more a virgin than she had been that first time with Ken at the tender age of 15. Maybe it wouldn't be as bad as she imagined. Searing pain ripped through her body, forcing a scream from her lungs as Tony clamped a hand over her mouth.

"Bear it," he whispered angrily in her ear. "I'll be done with you in a moment, and the pain will subside."

Chapter Twenty

Maurice La Chance was not from Fort Erie. Originally, he was born and raised in Montreal, close to where the Blue Bonnets Racetrack had once stood in its infamous career. Maurice had been a young pleasant Frenchman when the racetrack closed. No one had suspected this jovial, good-looking man was a key player in the drama that unfolded in the last few weeks before the crowd rebelled against the momentous conspiracy.

Blue Bonnets was 10 years ago. Maurice had discovered the easier road to making money. He had fallen into a crowd that taught him the finer points of lifting money from those who hoarded the commodity. He envisioned himself as a modern day Robin Hood. The obliging girls loved a man who had the money to give them whatever they wanted. Six years in a federal penitentiary had hardened his view of the world, but he was still taken with the women. The old adage wasn't true. Money could buy you anything—if you had enough.

Maurice had a great respect for the dollar. He spent many hours wondering how best to obtain the maximum yield for a minimum amount of work. Life had been too easy back in the days of Blue Bonnets. The races were easy to fix. No one was the wiser as they raked in the dough, until some crazy do-gooder blew the whistle and the top dogs took the fall.

Maurice could remember that fateful day when the racetrack crowd went berserk. The patrons pulled benches from the grandstand out onto the finish line. Horses running in the race didn't have a hope of stopping. Then in a horrifying climax, the grandstand itself was set ablaze. A dramatic gesture that angered him, but he knew that he had to leave the city or be a scapegoat to the blood-thirsty audience.

Crazy Frenchmen, Maurice thought as he reminisced.

He had not frequented a track for years, knowing that distance would help to alienate him from possible connections with the Blue Bonnets' disaster. Yet he had maintained a trainer's licence, sought after each year by his wife. His wife would do anything for him. She never questioned his judgment. She was the daughter of a judge in a small town, and Maurice knew things that would shame and dishonour the local family. His wife recognized that her disobedience would result in political suicide. Maurice appeared a civil, well-respected man, but never failed to allow those close to him to realize the consequences of staggering away from his expectations. He could maim or kill. He had done so in the past.

Maurice picked Fort Erie for several reasons. First of all, it was a small town, and easily moved by his personality. Then there were the easy women. Maurice didn't care what his wife thought. He fully intended to exert his masculinity on any willing participant. If his wife dared to comment on his actions, she would pay dearly for her advocacy. Finally, the atmosphere at Fort Erie reminded Maurice of Blue Bonnets, and the camaraderie of his fellow conspirators.

Maurice arrived at Fort Erie in the spring of 1985, working inconspicuously for a no-name trainer, walking hots, cleaning tack, and grooming his own homebred colt. Maurice demanded nothing from the man he helped save a stall and tack room. Ever watchful, Maurice knew that the rhythm of the backstretch would be his ticket to exploitation. He wanted vulnerable young men and women who would succumb to his French accent and language, and the lure of making a dollar.

Compared to prison, life on the racetrack backstretch was a simple game. There was just enough evil to make it interesting. During morning training hours, Maurice would watch his trainer as the man struggled to ensnare young boys in sexual escapades for the promise of riding the winner. A sorry promise for a trainer, who won maybe two races each season. Maurice had experienced enough boys while behind bars, choosing to be the predator rather than the prey. For sexual favours, he granted smokes, alcohol, drugs, or protection. It was interesting to watch the feeble old man try to work his magic with the naive youth. It was no contest. The boys always bared their souls.

The devil's advocate, Maurice enjoyed taking the boys in hand and showing them the true meaning of defiance. He would engage them in gambling games each night, taking their paycheques before they had the chance to earn the money. The smoke-filled nightly rendezvous would meld the youths to him, allowing him to take whatever he wanted from them or the outfits they worked. His suggestion of a ring bit or an exercise saddle would bring that object within his reach from a grateful youth wanting to pay his gambling debt. Maurice encouraged the youth to fulfill their obligations with alternatives to legitimate work.

Maurice was a man of few words who always watched and waited. He had no problem with claiming a horse from his best friend, and then fixing a race to make a killing. He had no regard for the horseflesh. He didn't particularly care if his friends were angry or sad when he acquired their possessions. As far as Maurice was concerned, it was every man for himself. If they couldn't take the punishment, they needed to get out of the game.

The youth in his barn called him "sir." He encouraged this form of respect. Maurice had only been at the track for three weeks when one of the tiny boys greeted him in the shed, eyes focusing on the dirt beneath their feet.

"Sir, I need your help."

Maurice didn't say a word. It was better if he didn't let people know how he might respond.

The youth swallowed nervously.

"The boss says there's no money," the boy said. "I've done all that I can for him. He's offered me dinner and a … bed. While, I'm not sure as I want to accept that offer no more."

"Don't like being his boy?" Maurice was harsh but a straight-shooter. "I'll loan you a sawbuck son, but remember that you owe me. One of these days I'm gonna call."

Maurice handed the youth 10 dollars. Inside, he was glad that the lad was escaping the manipulative trainer. He really didn't like the man's treatment of the boys.

Maurice headed back to his tack room. He made it a point to avoid frequenting the kitchen, preferring to stay in the vicinity of the barn. If people wanted to see him, they generally came to find him. He kept an electric frying pan in his room. He would throw a nightly meal into the pan, knowing that the security people would turn a blind eye. He had paid them off the first week. Everyone liked him because he was quietly compromising and stuck to himself. He chuckled. If only the backstretch knew what a bastard he really was, they'd have never let him in the gate.

Maurice had lots of time to make his move. Meanwhile, he'd try to find the correct people to control and the right horses to claim. Fort Erie would be well aware that he was there when he chose to come out of his shell. Perhaps the biggest problem for others was that Maurice wasn't afraid of its consequences. He'd already seen the worst that life had to offer. And he rather enjoyed living the life of a villain.

Chapter Twenty-one

Julia stayed at the barn throughout morning training hours. She felt that the eyes of the backstretch were scalding her, knowing what Tony was doing when they weren't watching. Tony was kinder than usual, almost as pleasant as he had been at Greenwood or even Woodbine before they watched *Phar Lap*. He brought her favourite breakfast of a toasted Western back to the barn, and made sure she had a hot coffee as she cleaned stalls, using the trouble light.

Tony's kindness only served to confuse her more. As 11 o'clock approached, Tony pulled her into the feed room.

"You need to do something for us," he said. "Ernie is in Barn 1. You need to go and ask him for a sawbuck so we can eat tonight."

Julia was upset. She hated to ask other people for money. She felt like she was begging. She would have rather worked an extra hour.

"I made some money yesterday, enough to eat. Why don't we just use that?"

"I'm not eating on what you made from Carl. We can use that for cab fare if you want."

"Tony, why don't we just eat in the kitchen and save ourselves the cab fare? Or better still, go somewhere close like the Pit Stop where most other people seem to go. We could probably catch a ride with someone."

"I'm not going to that crappy place. I have to study for my trainer's. The date is next Thursday for the test. You need to ask Ernie for the money."

"But he's your friend, Tony...."

Tony looked annoyed.

"Here's the deal. I told Ernie you'd shed a horse for the next three days. When you're done, ask him for the money."

"Shed a horse?" Julia couldn't believe what she was hearing.

"Yes. You know how to ride, don't you?"

"Of course," she answered. "But that's not the point. I don't have a licence to gallop, and I've never been on a racehorse."

"Security won't nail you for the shed. A horse is a horse. If I didn't think you could handle it, I wouldn't have recommended you to him."

Tony turned and began to walk away from her as if the issue was finished. Julia couldn't believe that this man was treating her this way. She had trusted him so much at Greenwood. He had always been considerate of her feelings. What had happened to their relationship in the last two weeks? Why had his affection for her deteriorated so much?

"Tony." Julia called down the shed after the man.

He stopped and waited. Julia approached him, not sure what she really wanted to say, but knowing that she had to say something. He was still as intimidating as when she had first met him, perhaps even more so now that they were living together.

"Tony, I want to get a job and make my own money. I could work just until 8 o'clock, and then come down to help you. I need some freedom to make my own decisions. I think that being so close to you has made you resent me."

"That's not true," Tony said in a low voice.

Julia looked around to make sure that no one could hear them.

"I think you were angry with me last night. You hurt me. You made me afraid of you."

There. She had said what she really wanted to say. She swallowed and waited for this man's reaction. Tony stared at her, his eyes boring right through her brain and into her heart. The intensity of his look took her breath away. She wasn't sure what he was transmitting into her body, but hoped that she hadn't once more provoked his anger.

"I didn't mean to hurt you."

Bullshit, thought Julia. He had told her that he was going to hurt her. She didn't argue with him but let him continue.

"I thought that we were a team, working together, living together. You don't need to work. I told you that I would look after you. But if you really feel the need to get away and work, I won't stand in your way."

Julia felt the breath that she had been holding release as he granted her some freedom. Maybe he wasn't such a bad man.

"I didn't realize that you were still a virgin in that way last night. You should have told me." He seemed to be accusing her, but his voice remained quiet.

"You never gave me a chance…," Julia began. Hadn't they had this conversation just recently?

"You seem to have no problem speaking up right now. You don't appear particularly afraid of me."

Julia was angry. Sometimes it was so difficult to talk to Tony's egotistical arrogance. Tony appeared to soften a little. The hard penetrating glare left his eyes. He took a step toward Julia.

"I'm sorry I hurt you," he said. "If you don't like it, I won't touch you that way again."

Julia couldn't believe what she was hearing. Now it was her turn to stare. This seemed just too simple. This man who was aggressive with her in the dark hours of the night was being surprisingly compliant in the morning sunshine.

"Weren't you angry with me?" she asked.

"I was annoyed that you ran a horse without telling me. I expected you around at feed and didn't know what had happened to you when you didn't appear."

Again the answer was simple. And inconceivable. Julia knew in her heart that Tony was lying to her, but she wanted desperately to believe in him and his self-proclaimed love.

"Will you go get on that horse for us?"

"If you think that I can handle riding a racehorse, I'm willing to try," Julia responded.

Actually, she was thrilled. She had anxiously watched the exercise people since the day she had first arrived on the backstretch, hoping someday that she would have the chance to experience riding the powerful animals.

Tony laughed at her. This time it sounded genuine. He reached forward to give her a hug.

"Old Donald said you were a natural on that pony at Woodbine. I wouldn't put you on anything that might hurt you. I really do care about you, Julia."

"I'll need a helmet," she said.

"You can borrow mine. Just make sure you ask for that sawbuck when you're done."

The reminder wasn't necessary. Once more, the reality of their true relationship reared its ugly head.

Ernie was glad to see Julia. He pulled an exercise saddle from the rail and ducked under the crossbar into a stall. Julia moved in to help him, but he waved her away.

"You're the rider. I'll tack him and take him a turn before I throw you on."

Julia felt a little embarrassed but stood by the rail waiting for Ernie to finish putting the saddle and bridle on the gelding. The horse stood calmly in the shed, and Julia timidly moved beside Ernie. She bent her leg allowing Ernie to grab her ankle, and then bent her other knee for the spring.

"Good God, woman, you've got no spring," Ernie said as he threw her onto the gelding's back.

Julia leaned on the withers so that she came down softly. At least she had learned something from watching the riders. The horse beneath her felt so different from the hunter ponies she had ridden briefly last summer. This gelding was pure muscle. She quickly put her feet in the irons and drove her heels down into a secure position. She tied a knot in the reins and nodded to Ernie who was still walking the horse.

"Tighten your girth before I turn you loose," he said.

Julia drew her left leg forward and reached down to tighten the straps. Sure enough, they moved up two more holes.

Ernie turned her loose.

"He's all yours. Half an hour should do it."

Julia took long turns, trying gravely to relax. As she rounded her third turn, she noticed Tony standing just outside the shed. He smiled and nodded. Julia was filled with pride. Maybe this was the type of respect that she craved from the man. By the next turn, he had moved into the shed.

"Old Donald was right. You are a natural."

Julia stopped the horse as she came alongside the man.

"Do you have any suggestions?" she asked shyly.

Tony took hold of the rein.

"Your knot in your reins is too far back. It looks like it has slid. Let me show you how to tie them properly." Grasping both reins, he quickly undid her knot and showed her the correct distance from the rubber to begin the knot, and how to loop the reins and draw the end through the loop.

"If the horse lunges suddenly, the shorter distance allows you to regain control much easier," Tony said. "A loop prevents the knot from slipping."

He leaned across the horse's withers and crossed the leather portion of the reins so that they were doubled. He showed her how to flip the reins over, allowing her thumbs to rest on top on either side of the withers.

"If the horse throws his head back or rears, the reins will catch against the neck. I've seen riders with a black eye or broken nose because they haven't been holding the reins properly. Also, this crossing allows for even tension on the bit with little effort. Make sure that your thumbs are facing forward. A fast move could break them if they're across the withers." He released his hold on the reins and stepped away from the gelding.

"Keep your heels deep to secure your seat. Your centre of gravity is just behind the withers. Use that for balance. Relax, Julia. You look so tense."

Tony paused as he gazed directly at Julia. She was trying to relax. For a brief moment, Julia thought he felt true remorse. The horse began to move underneath her.

"I love you. Be confident. You know a horse can sense fear."

When Julia rounded the shed the next turn, she felt much more secure and in control. Tony had disappeared.

Chapter Twenty-two

Maurice sat on a folding chair just outside the shedrow of Barn 9. Training hours were over and he had sent a boy to the kitchen to get him some lunch. He noticed a young girl shedding a horse in the next barn. He watched her intently, realizing that although green, she displayed a natural ability. Her long hair cascaded down her back beneath her helmet. He admired her body as she moved the horse down the shed. He knew the horse belonged to a drunk who the boys told him had once groomed Seattle Slew. He mused briefly about the usefulness of that knowledge, but quickly dismissed any ideas. He had learned years ago never to trust drunks or drug addicts. They would turn their mother in for a fix. He didn't need that type of problem.

He would stick to the young boys who were close to him each day. They were beginning to assume he would offer them protection from the man he was helping. Inwardly, Maurice was happy. He loved to disrupt this man's system of recruitment. He would watch as the trainer would bring a new young boy, barely 16, to the backstretch and promise the lad that he would let him ride a winning racehorse. Then the boy would work long hard hours for the man, walking hots, cleaning stalls, and grooming horses. Eventually, the man would throw the boy onto a homebred, and if the boy didn't get hurt, he would gallop all the horses in the outfit, about 12 in total.

That type of treatment didn't bother Maurice. He had used many people in the past in a similar manner—making them work long hours for nothing except protection, or possibly the fix that they needed. At the end of a long day, Maurice knew the boy would be taken to a local establishment for food. He would be promised the stars if that was what he desired. Then he would be taken back to the trainer's hotel for the night. None of the boys ever had much choice. The cost of food, lodging, and stardom was very high.

Maurice became the recruits' protection. He would offer to drive the lads out for supper, thus allowing them to return to the backstretch that night rather than the trainer's bed. He also made sure that these boys always had a little money of their own, usually by acquiring some item that he desired for his own horse. The boys would do favours for Maurice without a suggestion because they were so grateful to be free of the trainer. Eventually, many of them got jobs with other outfits, although few ever became jockeys. However, they never forgot about Maurice and remained indebted to him. The boys often returned to a game of poker that became a staple event in Maurice's tack room each night. In this way, Maurice ensured that their debt was never completely paid.

Maurice realized that most of the women who frequented the backstretch fell into two categories. They were loose—sexually promiscuous, or queer. He would occasionally engage a woman in conversation, his soft French accent lulling them into an invitation, but he had yet to find someone he truly desired. Maurice was a patient man and had no trouble biding his time until the right female crossed his path. He knew that, despite his age, he could have whomever he wanted. He had learned long ago that everyone had a price, monetary or otherwise.

As he watched Julia shedding the horse, Maurice began to think that hope might not be completely lost on this backstretch. Here was a girl worthy of pursuit. He decided that he would have to send his boys to find out more about this woman. If she proved to be a good game, he would set his desires on ensnaring her. If she already had a man, it would be even more fun. Maurice never let previous commitments stand in the way of something he wanted. He simply took what he wanted anyway, and laughed at the unfortunate person who had crossed his path.

Vern had been watching for Julia to return from Ernie's barn before she approached her friend that afternoon. She had an overnight in her hand. The overnight was a printout of the racing card in two days time, showing trainers the post position for the horses entered, as well as the list of also eligible horses. Also eligible horses were horses that had not made it into the race, mostly because the least recent runners had priority.

"My trainer put in two of my horses for Tuesday," she said. "They're back-to-back in the fourth and fifth of the card. I might need a hand if you're available. I'll make sure it's worth your while."

Vern knew that help in her barn was easy to come by, and they didn't really need Julia, but she wanted to do something for her friend. She felt that if Julia had her own life and her own money, she might feel better about leaving Tony. Vern knew that Tony was an unreliable shyster. She couldn't understand the power he seemed to hold over Julia.

"I can help you out, I'm sure," Julia answered pleasantly. "I'll make sure Tony knows where I am this time. I guess he was a little worried yesterday."

"Worried?" Vern's voice was incredulous. "Worried? This is Fort Erie for Christ's sake. It ain't no Hialeah."

"One of my friends was hurt on the backstretch at Greenwood last fall and…,"

"I know all about Marissa, my dear. That Jamaican put all of us coloured to shame. However, this is still Fort Erie. Probably the safest backstretch on the continent. Tony's no fool. He knows that."

Julia knew it wasn't worth trying to explain to Vern how she felt when her friend was in one of these moods. Nevertheless, she still wanted to help her out the next day.

"What time do you want me to come over?"

"When they call them over for the fourth, I guess. Listen, Julia, why don't you come with Bill and I tonight? Maybe you need a change of pace from the way Tony's been treating you lately."

Julia looked a little annoyed.

"Tony's been wonderful today. He brought me lunch. He was helping me as I got on my first horse. He was just having a bad day yesterday."

She was defending a man that last night she had considered leaving. But Tony had been so kind to her in the last few hours. She would get a job and some freedom, and things might return to the way they had been at Greenwood.

Crazy Bill turned into the shed with a couple of beers just as Julia finished her explanation to Vern.

"What's this I hear?" he asked as he approached the girls. "You on a thoroughbred? I guess they'll give a licence to anyone."

"I was trying to talk Julia into coming with us tonight," Vern said as Bill opened the bottles on a stall door latch. He offered one of the beers to Julia, but hung on to the other. Vern landed a punch on his shoulder.

"Ow!" Bill muttered. He handed over the second beer to his girlfriend.

"I usually don't drink beer but I kind of feel like one tonight," Julia said.

"It's okay," Bill replied. "I'll go back to the bootleggers. It's easier than a broken arm." He rubbed his shoulder vigorously where Vern had hit him.

Julia took a swig of the brown lager, letting the malt settle down the back of her throat. The day was looking brighter each moment. She was beginning to feel that she had friends on this backstretch, something that had never happened at Woodbine other than her association with Carl.

Vern sat on a bale of straw.

"How much are Tony's owners paying you for the work that you do?" Vern asked.

Julia was a little surprised at the question. She was simply helping Tony and let him deal with the owners. He had never really even talked to her about the man who owned the four horses that they were training.

"Nothing," she said. "I've never even met the owners."

Never met the owners?" Vern sounded like she couldn't believe what she was hearing. "You're kidding, I hope."

"I don't think they've been around too much. I'm sure Tony will introduce me the next time they're here." Julia took another drink, beginning to relax as the alcohol worked on her cells.

Vern put down her bottle and stared at Julia.

"That man is using you, girl. In more ways than one."

Not sure quite what Vern was talking about, Julia decided that it was time that her friend knew that Tony really cared.

"Tony loves me. He's always around to make sure that I don't get hurt. He makes sure I have enough to eat. That's more than most men on the backstretch."

"What about last night?" Vern asked.

Julia didn't say anything. She was trying to forget about what had happened to her last night. She was going to assume that it was the end of a rough couple of weeks for their relationship. Now things would get better. She'd get a job until break each day, and then they would meet up later in the morning to look after Tony's horses. Tony had already shown her today that he was willing to change.

"I'm going to tell you something about Descartes that you're probably not going to want to hear," Vern began. She was watching the shedrow carefully as if to make sure no one would be listening.

"His owners have been here a lot lately. They are essentially telling Tony what to do, how they want the horses trained. Tony won't have a problem getting his licence next week because the owners have made sure that he'll have an easy test. They don't pay Tony by the stall the way most trainers work. They are just giving him a paycheque, and last night when they were here, they gave him some money to pay you as well."

"He probably didn't have a chance to give me the money yet," Julia said.

She was beginning to get a little upset with the notion that Tony's owners had been in the barn and she'd yet to meet them. Even the Weasel had been good enough to introduce her to the rich individuals who owned the horses she had rubbed.

"Probably not before they took him to that fancy restaurant for supper. I seem to recall him leaving you in the feed room. I'm also not surprised that he didn't say anything to you later in the evening. I think that he fully intends to keep the money for himself while you continue to work for free."

The flavour of the beer had turned sour in Julia's mouth. She was staring at her friend, unable to comprehend what she was hearing.

"That man must be pretty good in bed for you to be putting up with all this," Vern commented jokingly.

"Sometimes..." Julia was talking from the back of a long tunnel, the alcohol burning in her stomach. "Sometimes he seems a little distant. Sometimes he hurts me."

"Oh shit, girl," Vern said. "No man has the right to hurt you. Especially when you work so hard for him. God, Julia, why are you still with him?"

"He loves me," Julia answered quietly.

"You got some fucked-up notion about love. He is using you. How can I get that through your head?"

From behind them they heard someone clear his throat. Both women swung around. Crazy Bill stood behind them.

"Your old man is coming, Julia. Vern, we should get a move on."

Julia looked up at Bill. She was beginning to want to go with the couple, but three was a crowd. She needed to talk to Tony. She needed to sort through what Vern had told her. She knew Tony wasn't perfect, but she found it hard to believe that he could be as deceitful as Vern was implying.

Tony approached as Vern and Bill ducked under the rail, talking quietly to each other for a change. They usually left bickering. The seriousness of her situation began to worry Julia. Every day she discovered how little she truly knew about the man she trusted. She realized that she needed to get a real job and stand on her own feet so that she could make some clear decisions about her relationship with Tony.

"What the hell were those two saying to you?" Tony asked. "You look as white as a ghost!"

He glanced at the beer bottle in Julia's hand and pulled a joint from his pocket. Julia didn't say a word to him. She disapproved strongly about his use of drugs. They'd had a heated argument about the subject, but he wasn't about to quit. He lit the joint and inhaled deeply.

"Can I try?" asked Julia. Tony looked shocked.

"You want a drag?" He raised his eyebrows.

"Yeah."

He handed the drug to her and she sucked on the rolled paper, holding the smoke in her mouth as she had seen Tony and some of the others doing. She handed the joint back to Tony and exhaled, coughing. The drug was working on her brain. A slow, easy feeling of relaxation moved across her limbs. She sat on the bale of straw that Vern had recently vacated.

Julia took another drag as Tony sat next to her. This time he bent to kiss her as she exhaled, taking the smoke into his mouth.

"Feel good?" he asked.

Julia nodded. It was a wonderful escape from the reality of her life. It seemed to be giving her an unusual burning desire for the man next to her. She was thinking of the good times that had been. She reached up to kiss him again as he exhaled.

Tony had his hand in her hair, drawing her closer towards his muscular body. Julia had become putty in his hands. She already knew he could do whatever he wanted. The logical side of her brain was fighting to reason with their relationship, but the alcohol and drug were relaxing her into a feeling of euphoria.

"Tony," Julia began. "Has the owner of these horses ever been around?"

Tony broke away from Julia.

"That's what those two no-goods were saying." Tony glared at her. "Yes, the owner was here just last night. I didn't get the chance to introduce you cause you were running that horse for Carl." He stood up and finished his smoke. "They made sure that I got paid. Maybe I'll take you someplace different tonight for dinner."

Julia was fighting reality. It was the first time she'd ever tried a drug, and she was feeling out of control with the strange, relaxing feelings.

Tony was looking at her strangely.

"You never smoked hash before?" he asked.

Julia shook her head. He still hadn't mentioned that some of the money had been given for her work.

"Don't fight it, Julia. Just relax. It's kind of like riding a racehorse. The first hit is always a little hard to get used to."

Tony had her by the hand and was leading her down the shed towards their tack room as Carl came around the corner. Tony put his arm around Julia protectively, and she smiled at the sight of Carl as he came to a halt in front of the couple. He stared at the beer bottle in Julia's hand and the look in her eyes. For a moment he didn't say anything, and then he moved closer to Tony.

"What the fuck have you done to her?" Carl asked.

"That's none of your business. She doesn't work for you anymore." Despite his bravado, Tony acted a little nervous.

"It is my business," Carl said. "I happen to care about her. I will not stand by and watch you get her hooked on some shit."

"What makes you think I'd do that?" Tony said. "She's her own person. She's old enough to make her own decisions."

Carl ran a hand through his hair. He looked as though he wanted to say something more, but stopped himself before continuing in a more even tone.

"I came by to ask her to run the gelding again. There's a race for him on Saturday, and if he gets in, I want to make sure she's available. She handled him beautifully yesterday, and the owners will be there next week."

"If we don't have a horse in, Julia might run your horse. Maybe you should have some kind of backup in case she's busy." Tony was answering for Julia before she had a chance. She placed her hand on his arm.

"I might have smoked some hash, Tony, but I think I can make a decision," she said in a clear voice.

She was beginning to realize that the drug had similar effects to alcohol. She hated that these two men were talking to each other as if she was somewhere else.

"Carl, I will gladly run the gelding again. I appreciate the offer. I don't think we'll have anything in. Tony has yet to work a horse. I'll let you know when the overnights come out."

She felt heat rising to her face as Carl studied her intently. He wasn't smiling in his usual way. Rather, he looked disappointed. She felt badly that Carl had seen her so obviously out of control. She knew that the beer bottle did not impress him. She pushed the brown bottle self-consciously behind her leg.

Carl nodded to her when he saw her reflex.

"You don't need to hide anything from me, Julia. I'm no saint and I'm not about to pretend that I ever was." Carl looked pointedly at Antonio. Tony refused to meet his look.

"I'd appreciate it," Tony began slowly, his voice ominous, "that you refrain from coming down this shed. My owners are a little concerned about someone claiming their horses."

It was a lie, but the warning was clear. Backstretch workers ignored the cardinal rule: you stayed out of other people's sheds. Rather, most horsemen thought it was an unwritten rule that you didn't claim any horses from friends or well-known acquaintances. Carl glared at Tony and turned to walk away. Julia was beginning to feel that she was making the wrong decisions as she let Tony lead her back to their room. What she didn't realize was that far worse was yet to come.

Chapter Twenty-three

Julia rose the next morning fully revived and ready for a new day of work. Tony smiled at her as she carefully plaited her hair into French braids, and then tied them up beneath her horseman's cap.

"No one is going to care what you look like. As long as you show up and you can handle the horses, you'll get a job."

Julia didn't answer. She had yet to tell Tony exactly where she was going to ask for a job, in Carl's barn. She knew he wouldn't be happy about that when he found out. Part of her acted defiantly, possibly because he was still hiding the details of the owner's visit from her.

Julia followed Tony to the kitchen for their early morning coffee, but kept a close eye on her watch so that she could arrive in Barn 8 well before 6 a.m. She hoped that Carl started as early as he had at Greenwood and Woodbine so he could introduce her to the couple he had mentioned previously.

As 5:30 approached, she excused herself from the table where Ernie and Tony were discussing the finer points of how to bandage a hock injury. Tony scarcely glanced at her.

"Don't forget that you need to shed Ernie's gelding at 11," he said as she left the kitchen.

Barn 8 at first appeared very quiet. As Julia entered the barn, she noticed Carl scrubbing feed buckets outside the shed. He looked up at her as she approached.

"Are you all right?" he asked, looking concerned.

"Actually, I'm looking for a job. I remembered your suggestion about the couple in your barn."

Carl smiled.

"They are early starters. Follow me, and I'll introduce you."

It took only two minutes for Taylor Anderson to hire Julia. Carl's recommendations carried a lot of weight on the backstretch. He was a well-respected horseman.

"I pay three dollars a head. I'll expect you here at 6 o'clock sharp each morning, and we'll be mostly out by break so you'll be finished by then. If we have horses in, you can earn an extra 10 dollars in the afternoon if they are back-to-back, or my wife is too busy to walk them. Does that suit you?"

"No problem. Who runs your horses?"

"I have a man come by to run the horses. Some of them are a little hard to handle. They require a nerve line or iron halter. If we are back-to-back, and the horses are easy to handle, I'll give you first call. Okay?"

Julia nodded. This was better than she had expected. Carl had disappeared to his side of the barn, but she knew that it was easy to hear through the walls of the shed.

"When can you start?" Taylor asked.

"I can start right now if you want," Julia replied.

Taylor handed her a shank.

"Third stall down from us. It's a filly who's been off a while. Put the chain through her mouth. If you handle her well, you're on."

Julia and the filly were the same personality. The filly bounced along beside her as she happily walked the horse for 20 minutes. After the first couple of turns, Taylor's wife, Miranda, introduced herself to Julia.

"I'm impressed with how quietly the filly is walking," she said.

Riders were arriving at the barn to gallop the horses as Julia put the filly back into a clean stall. She quickly went to get bath water in an effort to help the outfit.

"This one is a keeper," Julia heard Miranda comment to her husband. "She's willing to help out wherever necessary even if it's not part of her job."

The best part of working in Barn 8 was seeing Carl again on a regular basis. He didn't say much to Julia but always made sure to acknowledge her presence. A kind "good morning" or "How are you doing today?" went a long way to making her feel as if she belonged in the barn. He was a one-man operation, tacking horses, doing stalls, bathing, and walking the animals that he appeared to know and love. Carl would often graze his horses well beyond the training hours if only to give them a few more moments outside their stall prisons.

Taylor and Miranda provided a wonderful place to work. They genuinely cared about their help. Miranda would often slip up to the kitchen for a mid-morning coffee. They were quick to pay Julia for any additional duty that she performed. Julia never had to ask for her money. On Friday, Taylor would hand her a cheque for the number of horses that she had walked that particular week.

The outfit had pleasant horses, and Taylor didn't shy away from using the proper techniques to handle the difficult animals. Julia found that she was learning improved methods while working for the couple. Each day brought a new confidence in her ability to handle the high-strung thoroughbreds. The uneasiness she once felt for the animals scarcely a year ago seemed a thing of the distant past. Julia realized that the Anderson outfit was a place she would want to work for an extended period of time. In fact, she worked for the couple for nearly eight years.

John Lawson prided himself on his ability to find out information by simply observing and listening quietly. He figured that Maurice La Chance would soon consider him a partner in whatever enterprise they undertook. John was almost always the first to return to Maurice with the desired information.

As he entered Barn 9, John noticed that the tack room Maurice occupied was closed. Disappointed, he quickly scanned the shed. Sure enough, Maurice was standing beside his horse carefully grooming its mane. John moved to just outside the shed. He waited for Maurice to notice that he wanted to speak.

Maurice ignored the lad for a moment, and continued focusing on the knots in his colt's mane. Finally, he looked up and carefully slipped under the webbing.

"What do you want?" Maurice asked.

"You wanted some information about the girl shedding the horse for Slew." John referred to the nick-name the track had given to Ernie.

Maurice simply nodded. He was a man of few words.

"Her name is Julia Reinhardt. She's only been at Fort Erie for two weeks. Hangs with Antonio Descartes, Barn 4. I saw them smoking dope last night."

"She didn't strike me as the type to be hooked on drugs. Descartes her old man?"

John nodded. "Yeah. They share a tack room together. Same barn. No lock."

"Interesting. Good work, kid. I'll remember this. I want you to find out everything you can about Descartes."

John was a little disappointed. He didn't expect to be sent away on another mission. However, if the boss wanted it done, he'd make sure that he was the first. Maurice had lowered his voice so that John had to listen carefully to catch what he said.

"I want the dirt. Everything dirty about Descartes. Don't disappoint me, lad."

"I won't, boss."

"I'll let you on my colt when you come back with the information."

That final announcement made John happy. Maurice had promised that he would find John an agent and let him ride the colt. It sounded like he intended to keep that promise.

John left the shed a happy man. He would make sure to find out every secret that Antonio Descartes had ever kept. Anything for the boss.

Julia made her way over to Vern's barn just before the fourth race was called. For the first time, she felt like a new person on this backstretch. She felt respected and independent although she knew that the others would probably treat her no differently.

Vern had one of the horses standing in the ice tub.

"She was a bitch to get in," Vern said. "She needed a little extra persuasion, if you know what I mean."

Julia laughed at her friend. She noticed that one of the other grooms was helping with the gelding that was in the fifth race.

"If you could kinda help out getting bath water, running a halter to the test barn, you know…."

"A halter to the test barn?" Julia asked, raising her eyebrows.

"The filly will win."

"How the hell do you know that?"

Her friend glanced at Julia as if she were dense.

"My boss dropped her in for $2500. She just ran third for $4000 last week."

Julia knew that Vern referred to the claiming prices set for each race. The trainer had dropped the horse in for a lower claiming value which meant cheaper horses, and supposedly, an easier race. However, Julia was still sceptical. Vern laughed.

"The owner is generous," Vern said. "There'll probably be a hundred in it for me. I am definitely taking you out tonight." Vern moved towards a white bucket that was full of ice. "If you want a beer, there's lots in this bucket."

The PA system called them over for the fourth. Vern collected the bridle from the stall door. The soft leather had been treated and the ring bit shone. The other groom moved forward to help get the filly out of the ice tub. Julia reached into the stall and pulled the heavy tub into the shed.

The filly quivered with excitement; white foam oozed out of her mouth as Vern used a syringe to rinse around the horse's teeth. The filly's eyes darted back and forth amongst the small group of horsemen gathered in the shed; her ears twitched nervously. Vern put Vicks in the nostrils, a habit she had admitted to Julia that she despised but was instructed to perform. She rubbed Vasoline around the eyes, and then fastened the green racing blinkers into her belt loop.

Carefully unsnapping the webbing, Vern ducked under the crossbar into the filly's stall. Looping the reins over the neck, Vern carefully worked the ring bit into the horse's mouth and then secured the noseband and throat-latch. Julia handed her a freshly oiled lead shank. Vern doubled the shank back on the ring bit.

"Time to go." Vern gestured to Julia to step aside as she dropped the crossbar. "See you in the test barn."

Julia grinned at her friend. She herself had yet to run a winner. Tony still promised her that the first horse she ran for him would be a winner. A romantic notion, but Julia was beginning to realize that Tony sometimes spoke a different reality from the rest of the backstretch.

It was turning out to be a hot June day. Julia sat on an overturned bucket and glanced longingly at the trees casting shade along Thompson Road just the other side of the high fence surrounding the track. She recalled Crazy Bill teasing Vern, "They built the fence to keep us in, not the outside world out." She was beginning to think there was some truth in that statement.

It hadn't rained in over a week. The watering trucks had already passed along the main roads to the gap but had failed to water the side roads. Julia watched dust kick up in tiny swirls on the road in front, tornadoes of fury in an otherwise calm backstretch. The people and the horses of the racetrack were similar to the tiny swirls. Life on the backstretch was a truly relaxing atmosphere but a lifestyle that became upset with the high-stakes gamble of racing.

It all came down to the money, Julia thought. The money involved in racing—to be lost or won—was what turned a peaceful summer afternoon into a bloodthirsty fight. Owners and trainers would enter their stock, betting the odds of a good post position, the correct track conditions, and weather. Grooms and hot-walkers would pour their money in through the windows, hoping that the mounts they've cared for would be in the picture. The only real losers in this winning game were the horses. If they defied the odds and won the race, they were pushed up into races with larger purses and tougher competition. They were forced to run in all conditions with some pinhead rider perched above their back beating them. There was no mercy for sore muscles, bleeding lungs, or broken legs. If they made the mistake of losing too often, Gregory with his meat wagon would be waiting to take the horses to the glue factory. Win or lose, the horses always finished last.

Julia loved the doomed horses. She loved their spirit and their fight. She loved their strength and endurance. That's why she had stayed at the racetrack more than any other reason. It wasn't because of an escape from a cloying Ken or an attraction to a demanding Tony. It was simply for the love of horses and their plight. Julia could sympathize with being forced into doing something you didn't want to do. Like the animals in the stalls behind her, Julia knew that she had to win in this male-driven world or suffer the consequences of losing.

The loudspeakers came on overhead, effectively splitting her thoughts as results of the third race were given along with the call to get them ready for the fifth. Julia grasped the bucket she had been sitting on and went to the tap for hot water. She could see Tony and Ernie deep in a heated conversation at the end of the shed. She wiped the sweat from her own forehead. Vern's offered beer was beginning to have some appeal.

Tony moved along the shedrow toward Julia. He appeared to be in a better mood today. He had treated her with decent respect last night, and their separation for work this morning appeared to have had a positive effect on the man. Julia couldn't help but still be attracted to this dynamic individual. At times he appeared to love her deeply. He was possessive, caring, and passionate. He never shied away from giving her a hug or holding her hand. However, the other side to Antonio was just as vibrant. His possession of her could be cruel and demanding. He often acted as if he wanted absolute obedience from Julia, a concept that she internally rebelled against.

Tony smiled as he approached.

"Three days." He seemed jubilant.

Julia assumed correctly that he meant the time left until he took his trainer's test.

Surprisingly, Tony didn't demand anything from her but turned and walked across the road to his stalls. A few minutes later Julia listened to the results of the fourth race. She laughed as she picked up the halter. Vern's filly had won the race.

Chapter Twenty-four

Life on the backstretch was turning into a rhythm for Julia. Each day she carried her hot coffee into work at least 10 minutes early, ready to walk the first horse. She really enjoyed her job with Taylor and Miranda. They treated her decently and trusted her to use her own judgment in handling a horse. She grew fond of the horses and especially enjoyed the friskiness of the young ones in the brisk early June dawn. Julia found a special attraction to a particularly nervous filly that reminded her of Mama Goat.

Carl was watching Julia as her eyes lit up, the horse that she was walking dancing away when a saddle cloth fluttered in the breeze.

"Hey, the old Julia I knew at Greenwood is reappearing." Carl had said quietly as she passed. The haunted look was at last leaving Julia's eyes.

Thursday morning dawned with a steady drizzle. Julia left an anxious Tony pacing in front of his stalls. She wanted to help and comfort him as he prepared to go for his oral examination on general knowledge about the horse and racing. He spurned her help and asked her to stay away from the barn during his practical test. Julia was a little upset by this unusual treatment, but shrugged it off as a nervous response.

By the end of the day, Tony was holding Julia close to him as he reported the good news. He had passed the first two parts of the trainer's test. All that was left was the racing stewards and questions about the rules of racing. He already had a time booked for the next day to complete that portion of the test. Tony took Julia to the Grace Hotel to celebrate as he bragged with Ernie and the other men. To the other trainers, the third test was simply superfluous. To them, Antonio was already a trainer.

The third test went as predicted. By the end of Friday, Tony had his new trainer's licence in his hand and, grasping Julia around the waist, he told her that he was going to take her out for dinner to one of the classier places in town. Actually, it was out of town. Ernie picked up the couple at their barn at 6 o'clock, and the three went for supper at the Walton Hotel. This hotel was 10 minutes from the backstretch and situated by an old pier and the ruins of a former American amusement park that once graced the beaches of Fort Erie during the roaring '20s. Julia gazed longingly across the expansive beach and clear water, mesmerized by the waves lapping onto the cool evening sand. She wished that she had time to run in the sand and splash in Lake Erie. The freedom of the water beckoned to Julia as it ebbed and flowed in a dynamic undertow that was the start of the great Niagara River.

The Walton was a rambling old building that didn't appear to house anything special. Yet when Julia entered, she knew that finally Ernie and Tony had brought her somewhere that afforded some night life and fun. Inside was a vast bar and dance floor. A live band was setting up at the far end of the room. The men led Julia into the restaurant area where she dined on the house specialty of ribs and sauerkraut.

"Can we stay for just a little while to hear some music?" Julia was almost afraid to ask. She knew that 4 o'clock came early, and most racetrackers were in bed by 9 p.m. Ernie seemed to be enjoying the spot and answered before Tony had a chance to reply.

"I think we can stay a little while if you'd like. Right, Tony?"

Tony didn't really have a choice as Ernie had driven them out to the hotel and a cab would cost nearly 20 dollars to take them home.

The evening turned into the best experience with Tony since Greenwood. Julia listened to the band play a set, and both Ernie and Tony bought her a drink to celebrate. The ride home in Ernie's car was wonderful with Tony curled around her body in heated desire. Julia felt wanted, loved, and for the first time in a while, appreciated.

Veronica was upset with Crazy Bill. He had acquired his name on two different accounts: he went a little nuts when he was drinking, which was pretty much every night, and he would ride any horse, no matter how difficult or ornery. True to his name, Bill had attempted to gallop a horse known for a tendency to flip on riders. Bill had come off three times before the trainer had finally told him, "Forget it." The last time he landed hard on the main road. Vern applied salve to his bruised backside.

"Are you still drunk from last night?" she asked. "What the hell were you getting on that stupid colt for? You've got nothing to prove!"

"Aw, hon, just give me a damn beer for my pain," Bill said.

Vern handed him the beer.

"You need to lie down and get some rest instead of acting like some 20-year-old."

A tap sounded on their tack room door.

"Come on in," called Bill and Vern together.

Julia opened the door and peered in at the couple.

"I'm sorry. I thought you were alone, Vern."

"I am," Vern replied. "He's just leaving."

Bill got up from the bunk.

"Thanks a lot," he said. "Love me and leave me." He had a smile on his face.

"Go back to your own room," Vern said. "I'll see you after feed."

Reluctantly, Bill left.

"Have a seat." Vern tossed Julia a beer from her fridge.

Julia pried the lid loose on the metal edge of the bunk bed. Vern picked up a tub of hair gel and lathered the ointment into her already glistening black curls.

"How's your man treating you?" Vern asked.

"He's been pretty good lately. He's found a car and thinks that we should buy it."

"Wheels? That's cool. Do you drive?"

"No," Julia answered reluctantly. "I never had the money for driver's ed. He got a deal through Ernie. Only $400 and already certified."

Vern was impressed.

"Four hundred dollars is a pretty good sum for a racetracker to have available. Maybe your old man is better than I thought."

"Actually, I'm giving him the money. I still had a bit in my bank account, and with what I've been paid from Anderson these last couple of weeks, we'll have enough."

Vern stopped greasing her hair and stared at her friend.

"You're shitting me!"

Julia stared at her hands, her face flushed.

"You've got to be out of your mind, woman!" Vern said. "After the way that man's treated you, and you're going to buy him a car so he can leave? You're crazier than Bill!"

"He's not that bad. He's been good to me lately, and now that he's training horses, we'll start making lots of money."

"Not with those cheap owners," mumbled Vern.

"Besides, I have a good job…"

"That's your money. At least you don't have to beg his friends for a loan anymore while he returns the money like some big dealer. Makes you look like shit while he's getting the glory."

"Vern, we have a horse in on Sunday. Antonio thinks that it'll win. That's 10 per cent of the purse for us."

"That owner will never give him 10 per cent. Stop kidding yourself. I know of at least three trainers that have steered clear of that cheating bastard. How much does your old man owe the vet and the blacksmith?"

"Those bills are the owners. Tony doesn't have to worry about it."

"The backstretch doesn't think that way. The trainer hires the vet and blacksmith, and the trainer pays them. I'd not want Gus after me for money. That's one big strong guy. Tony won't be able to push him around the way he likes to push you around."

Vern's words were cutting.

"Why do you never have anything nice to say about Tony?" Julia sounded irritated.

Ignoring her, Vern didn't stop. "Old Doc Adams is a nice guy, but he won't hesitate to put a bill into the stewards and Tony will have to pay or lose his licence. Worst case, he'll be ruled off…."

"Jesus, Vern, will you stop! I love the man. I don't want to see him lose a licence that he worked so hard for, and I sure don't want to see him ruled off. Where would we go?"

Vern shook her head and twisted the lid back onto her gel.

"Ain't love grand," she mumbled, "and so blind. So fucking blind."

Vern stared in pity at her friend. She knew without a doubt that tragedy would ensnare her friend's world and turn it upside down.

Julia had given Antonio the money to buy the car. Tony said that he would look after the licence and insurance. Julia was beginning to feel more like they were a team. She worked for Taylor Anderson until break, and then helped with Tony's horses. The owner had entered one of their horses from Toronto, and Tony was to saddle his first horse in the seventh race on Saturday. In the four weeks since she'd arrived at Fort Erie, this was the moment that Julia had been waiting for—to run a horse that Tony was training and, hopefully, saddling a winner.

Tony had finally introduced Julia to his owner just after feed one evening. The man was very overweight and looked right through Julia as though she didn't exist. He spent most of the time telling Tony how he wanted the horses trained. Even Julia could tell that the man knew very little about training racehorses. She watched Tony smiling and nodding in agreement, knowing full well that he would do whatever he thought best when the morning came.

"What about the $600 you owe Doc Adams?" Tony asked. "He's not likely to pre-race the filly if you don't pay him."

The owner glowered at Tony.

"I don't think that filly needs anything. I've got the vet covered. You know there's more than one vet on this backstretch."

Tony didn't say anything. The vets talked to each other and respected their opponents' business. If Doc Adams wouldn't treat the horse, no vet would come near the outfit. Julia was beginning to realize that everything Vern said about this owner was true. She wondered why Tony was letting the man tell him how to do his job.

Saturday was a clear, sunny day with fast track conditions, horses running the quarter in 21 seconds and the half mile in 45 seconds. Antonio acted nervous. At last his big day had arrived, and Julia knew that he was concerned the filly might be in over her head. Julia arrived back at the barn in time to jog the filly for the commission vets. The commission vets were hired by the Ontario Racing Commission to examine each horse entered in the racing card for that day. Horses entered could not show any signs of lameness or sickness or they would be "scratched," cut from the racing card that day. Passing the vets was not a problem as the horse had never shown any unsoundness other than bucked shins as a two-year-old.

Julia went to get lunch as Tony refused to leave the barn. The filly had been fed early in anticipation of the race. Julia tied her at the front of the stall to prevent her from picking at the straw. The horse's ears twitched as she listened carefully to every sound, seeming as anxious as Tony for the race to move forward.

It was a long wait to the seventh race. Julia picked up an overnight from the box outside the racing office and noticed that Carl had entered his gelding in a race for the next day. The horse was in the 10th race and had drawn the fourth post position. Carl had told her that morning that he had dropped the gelding in for $2500 hoping it would finally win. He wanted Julia to run the horse, and she'd been glad to accept. Taylor had mentioned the possibility of running a horse on Monday as he was entering two in the same race as a combined entry. Julia felt that she was finally getting into the freelance work of running horses, a lucrative line of employment where she could make upwards of $80 in one racing afternoon.

Tony went to change into clean clothes as the call came over the speakers to get ready for the seventh. Julia was left at the barn to run a rub rag over the horse, clean out the nostrils and syringe the mouth. She picked up the bridle when they called them over, and was tightening the throat latch as Tony reappeared.

"I'm going to walk through the parking lot," he said as he watched her slip the shank through the bit.

"I'll take her a turn before I head over," Julia said. "I don't want to get caught on the road with this filly as the horses run by the gap."

Tony nodded his approval. "I guess I'll see you in the paddock."

"How about giving me a kiss, Tony?"

Startled, Tony gave her a sharp glance, and then leaned over to peck her on the cheek. Julia felt strangely unhappy as she dropped the crossbar and took the filly for a turn around the barn. She watched as Tony disappeared out the end of the shed.

The filly was proving to be a handful. As soon as Julia got out of the shedrow, the horse skidded sideways and reared. Julia didn't get upset but used her leverage on the shank to bring the filly back down to the ground. Julia's nerves were on edge. It had been a while since she had felt so alone dealing with a troublesome horse. The filly jogged sideways as the pair started down the main road towards the gap. Every few steps she would strike out with her left front leg, narrowly missing Julia's shin. Frustrated, Julia shanked the horse and swore under her breath. The filly's attention was brought back momentarily, but another horse walking to the gap began to buck, causing Julia's horse to rear again.

"Son of a bitch, you damn filly."

The filly had twisted her arm painfully. Julia used the other end of the shank to slap the filly across the neck. The filly responded by bolting backwards. The shank slipped through Julia's hand until the knot that she had carefully tied at the end caught in her palm. Julia leaned forward to release the tension on the spooking horse, and then snatched the shank as hard as she could. By now the pair was halfway down the main road. The horse had briefly paused. Taking advantage, Julia shanked the horse again.

"You get loose of me, I'll never hear the end of it, you no good piece of…," Julia could hear someone laughing from a nearby shed. She had managed to grasp the filly closer to the bridle, and turned to see who was watching.

Carl was just inside the shedrow closest to her, leaning on the rail talking with another trainer. He was laughing as he gave Julia a thumbs up.

"Watching you handle that horse, I'd hire you any day of the week," he said.

Julia didn't have a chance to answer. The filly reared again. It was going to be a long walk over to the paddock.

Julia was exhausted by the time she reached the paddock. Sweat was rolling down her back and the filly next to her was also glistening with perspiration in the heat. As she entered the paddock, Julia took the horse right to the stall where Tony and the owner stood.

"Heads up, I'm coming in guys," she said.

Tony looked slightly annoyed. He motioned for her to walk the horse around the paddock. Julia ignored him.

"Tony, I'm coming in," Julia entered the stall and turned the horse to face out. Tony stared at the horse, a nervous look in its eyes as Julia held it firmly by the reins.

"Did you have some trouble?" Tony asked Julia.

"Remember the stunt she pulled on the rider a couple of weeks ago?" Julia asked rhetorically. "Same crap, different person."

"I'm glad you didn't get hurt," Tony said.

Julia smiled for the first time that afternoon.

Not to be outdone, the filly reared and lunged forward. Julia couldn't stop the horse's forward momentum but managed to turn her back into the stall.

"Let's saddle her facing in," said Tony.

This proved to be good advice. The horse was much easier to hold as the jockey's valet appeared with the saddle and overgirth.

The filly ran seventh. Seventh in the seventh race, Julia couldn't help thinking. The owner wasn't impressed with the finish. He yelled at the rider, and then he yelled at Tony. It was everyone's fault that the horse hadn't finished in the money. You could feel the tension in the barn after the race, and Julia took the filly long turns to avoid the conversation. The horse was tired. She had obviously run the best that she could, although Julia wondered if the craziness on the way to the paddock might have taken away her edge.

After the horse was cool, Julia took her out on the grass to graze. The owner had finally left, and Tony finished the stall before he brought her a beer.

"Warm afternoon," he said.

Julia didn't answer. She held the shank loosely against the filly's neck as she took a long drink from her bottle.

"I'm thinking I'll stay in this evening. Grab something to eat from the kitchen and call it a night."

Julia was surprised. This was so uncharacteristic of the man standing at her side.

"You're kidding? I thought that you'd be wanting to celebrate the first horse you'd saddled."

Tony leaned against the rail.

"I'm tired, Julia. I'm surprised you have the energy to think about celebrating. Why don't you go out with Vern and Bill tonight. I'll see you back here later."

Julia looked at Tony suspiciously. He was confusing. She knew that he didn't particularly like Vern and Crazy Bill, and his suggestion that she leave him at home while she went for supper with those two was beginning to border on unbelievable.

"I don't need to go out, Tony. I don't mind staying with you for the evening. Is something the matter?"

Antonio wouldn't meet her eyes. He glanced towards Thompson Road as the results of the final race were announced.

"I was thinking that maybe we need a little break from each other," he said slowly.

"What?" Julia couldn't believe what she heard. Her ears hurt as she began to comprehend his words.

"We've been seeing quite a bit of each other, and I need some breathing room," said Tony as he turned to look at an astounded Julia. "It's not that I'm saying I don't want to see you anymore. I just need to be by myself for a while."

"What?" Unbidden, tears sprang to her eyes. Of all the things that Tony had done to her, this had to be the cruellest.

"You asshole." Julia's voice was subdued and quiet as she handed him the shank. Even in her misery, she wouldn't turn a horse loose and see it get hurt.

Tony quickly took the shank, and grasped Julia's arm with his other hand. Julia snatched her arm away, surprised at her own strength.

"I still love you, Julia. This is just temporary."

Julia put her hands in the air in frustration.

"Don't you talk to me about love," she said. Tears streamed down her face. "You don't have any idea what that means."

Julia turned and walked away from Antonio Descartes, sadness welling inside her heart as a numbness took over her body. She couldn't believe her own stupidity in trusting this man. Vern and Carl had both tried to warn her about Tony, but she hadn't taken heed. Part of her still wanted to believe that the last 20 minutes of her life was just a joke, and Tony would come running after her, laughing and holding her like the man she had once known.

Julia got only as far as their tack room. She sat on the step with the door at her back and sobbed. Why had she changed so much of her life to chase after a man who didn't really love her? Why had she been so blind to Tony's real personality? He had used her. He had hurt her. He had raped her as clearly as Marissa had been raped. He had raped her heart, her soul, her money. She felt empty. There was nothing left. Nowhere to live. No one to turn to.

Becoming aware of someone watching, Julia looked up to see Crazy Bill standing just outside the shed.

"What's going on, Julia?" he asked. "Why are you crying?"

Never had Julia seen Crazy Bill so serious. He was usually the joker, the clown of the party.

Trying to get a hold of her feelings, Julia stood up and weakly rubbed her eyes. Suddenly, she was very tired; bone weary.

"I...I don't know what I'm going to do, Bill. Ton...Tony just dropped me. I don't know where I'm going to live." Julia was beginning to feel a sense of panic as she realized her plight.

Bill looked really angry.

"Get your stuff out of that room and stay here," he said gruffly. "Don't leave. Okay?"

Dumbly, Julia nodded and pushed open the door to the room. Bill had left quickly, and she was alone as she faced the now familiar four walls. It didn't take long to gather her belongings and press them into the bag that she had brought into the room only four short weeks ago.

Julia quietly closed the door behind her and moved away from the room into the cooling June evening. She now had a man with a crazy name to look to for the help that she needed. Vern appeared first coming through the middle of the shed with Crazy Bill close behind.

"That no good piece of shit…" Vern began in her usual manner.

"Please, Vern, I know," Julia said. "You were right. I don't want to hear about it."

"Bill's got a room down in Barn 10. You can stay there for as long as you want."

Julia began to cry again as she looked at her friends.

"Thank you so much. You wouldn't know how grateful I am."

"I've got a pretty good idea," Vern replied drily. "I'm just grateful you're finally away from that creep. You were way too good a person for him."

Bill cleared his throat.

"Let's get a move on. There's a cold one waiting for us at the Pit. We'll drop your stuff off on the way out the east gate."

Maurice La Chance stood in the dim light of the shedrow. He smiled to himself as he watched the threesome depart down the road. John had proved as good as his word. Antonio Descartes had almost been too easy to manipulate, almost not worth the chase. However, now Julia Reinhardt was at last free for him to pursue.

Chapter Twenty-five

Julia picked up the lead shank and wrapped the chain around the gelding's nose. The jockey who had jumped off the horse's back pulled the saddle from the horse, and took the bridle that Julia held.

"Glad to see that you finally dropped Antonio. I heard that his owner fired him. Rumour has it that he may try riding. Never make the weight, if you ask me."

Julia didn't answer the man. She had heard the rumours. It had been nearly two weeks since she had walked away from Tony. She worked almost exclusively in Barn 8 now, first walking hots for Taylor Anderson, then doing stalls, walking, or any number of things for a trainer at the far end of the shed.

"Take him a turn and then bring him out for his bath," called a voice from outside the barn. The rider had stepped into the shed. "You're clear. I'll see you in the winner's circle tomorrow."

Julia moved into the shed, the large gelding bowing his neck and striding out despite the training. Cutting through the centre, she saw Carl sitting in his feed room nursing a cup of coffee as he read the conditions book.

"Got the big horse, Julia?" he asked.

She nodded. "Track favourite. Tom says he'll win again tomorrow. I get to run him."

Julia was happy to get the chance to run Rattrap. The horse had already won seven races this year. He was entered for five-and-a-half furlongs, the perfect distance for the speedster. They were forecasting clear weather and a fast track. Mud or slop, and Julia knew that Tom,

Rattrap's trainer, would scratch the horse. His ankles wouldn't hold up on an off-track.

She moved out of the barn into the morning sunshine. Tom stood by the buckets of steaming water, the sponge and scraper in his hand.

"How's the Rat feeling?" he asked Julia.

"Pretty cocky. Someone told him he was going to win again tomorrow."

Tom chuckled as he lathered the horse with shampoo.

"It's a tough race, but I don't think he'll have a problem. Every day I'm thankful that he's eligible for those starters. Otherwise someone would have claimed him by now. Hey, don't be turning him into a suck."

Julia laughed. She'd been stroking the big red horse on its velvety nose. The horse turned his lip in the air, showing her his identification tattoo.

"You won't have any trouble taking him over to the paddock. He obviously already likes you, and he walks over like a gentleman. He knows to save his energy for the race."

Julia wasn't worried. She knew that she could handle the gelding. Tom had told her that the crowd chants the horse's name whenever he comes over to the paddock.

"Make sure that you come around the barn after the races. The owner is always generous, and there'll be some extra money for you." Tom finished scraping the horse.

"I'll be here. I'm running a horse for Carl in the eighth," Julia answered as she took the wet gelding back into the shedrow. Tomorrow was going to be a great day.

Julia thought briefly about Tony. She'd seen him just two days ago driving the car that she had bought. Each morning there was a coffee on her tack room doorstep. Vern had called him a sick puppy when Julia showed her the cup with the words "I love you" scrawled across the side. Just yesterday, Tony had approached Julia and asked if he could borrow $20.

"You are unbelievable," she'd said before turning away. Afterward, as she had walked to the Pit Stop with Vern and Crazy Bill, Tony had driven by with one of the female grooms from Barn 5.

"That man doesn't appear to be missing you much," said Bill.

Rattrap spooked as Carl came out of a stall. The horse seemed to know that Julia wasn't paying much attention.

"Whoa there," said Carl. "That horse is sure acting like he wants to run again. Julia, can you do me a favour and hold a horse for Gus today? He's supposed to be here at three and I want to feed."

"No problem."

She knew that blacksmiths were notoriously late, and Carl probably wouldn't need her services but she was glad to help him whenever she could.

"There's five dollars in it for you."

Julia was beginning to realize how easy it was to make money on the racetrack. She walked horses, cleaned stalls, shed horses after hours, pulled manes, and held horses for the blacksmith on dark days. Race days always held lots of opportunities for running and walking horses for someone willing to work. She found that she could make nearly $600 a week by being available and willing to do just about anything. Easy money, easy game, Julia thought as she continued around the shed with the Rat. Correction: easy game if you were tough enough to survive.

Doc Adams came to find Julia after training hours. He told her that he'd put a complaint into the racing office about Tony's unpaid vet bills.

"I suggest you put in about that car you bought," he said.

"It's not worth it. I don't want to deal with that man anymore."

She just wanted to wash her hands of the whole situation.

Carl caught up with Julia just before she left the barn.

"I wanted to give you a shank because I may not be here right at three."

He walked over to his tack room with Julia close behind. She knew that he lived off the backstretch in an apartment by the lake. Julia stepped inside the room as Carl reached for a lead shank. Julia shut the door and reaching for Carl's hand, she gave him a kiss. Shocked, Carl froze for a moment, and then he gathered her in his arms and kissed her back gently.

"Why are you doing this?" he asked. "Why me?"

Julia didn't completely understand why she had turned to Carl. Perhaps it was because he had always been kind, the understanding person when no one else seemed to care. Perhaps it was simply to fill a lonely need with someone she trusted. She didn't understand her actions, but knew that Carl would treat her with dignity and respect.

"You're so good to me, Carl."

"You don't have to do this. You don't owe me anything, Julia."

She stopped him by kissing him again.

"Oh sweet Jesus, girl, you're killing me," Carl whispered in Julia's ear as he pulled her close. "I want you, but this isn't the place."

Julia began to cry.

"What's the matter?"

He pushed back her hair as he gazed into her eyes. Julia didn't answer him but reached for Carl again. He pulled away.

"No," he said. "Tell me what's the matter."

"I feel like I can trust you. You're being so gentle with me, so kind to me." Julia wasn't sure how to explain to Carl what she was feeling.

"Why shouldn't I be? That man must have really screwed with your head, Julia."

Carl opened the door, letting the late morning sunshine drift into the room. He handed her the shank.

"Why are you stopping me?" Julia was confused. She wasn't used to a man stopping and letting her leave.

Carl held her gently for a brief moment.

"I want you too much but you need time to heal. As I said before, this isn't the place."

Carl stepped out of the tack room. He couldn't believe how angry he felt. He needed a chance to calm down. He'd heard about how Tony treated women, particularly from his ex-wife. Despite her advances, Carl had sensed a fear and desperation in Julia's actions that were deeply saddening. She was too young to be feeling that way about men. He didn't know what cruelties Tony had inflicted on Julia, but he knew that he wanted that man far away so that he couldn't hurt her again.

Carl crossed to his car, partly angry with himself for stopping the woman. Before he quit drinking, the doctor had told him he would probably be impotent for life. Julia had awakened a desire that he hadn't felt in a long time. Instead, he had chosen to work and live alone. If he hadn't stopped her, Carl knew that he could have proved his doctor wrong. He hadn't lied to her—he had wanted her too much.

Carl hadn't touched alcohol for more than 10 years, and every day he thought about drinking, but today the craving was worse. He slammed his car door and started the engine, noticing that Julia still stood in the open tack room door that he'd neglected to lock. Swearing under his breath, Carl knew he had to go back to the room to put on the lock. Julia pulled the door shut and twisted the lock as she waved at him with the shank. She was such a good woman, Carl thought tenderly. He put the car in gear and drove out of the barn parking area.

Chapter Twenty-six

The next day Antonio Descartes left Fort Erie. Julia was glad when Crazy Bill told her that Tony's room was empty and the car was gone. At last there would be no more morning coffee on her doorstep. There was an extra spring in her step as Julia entered Barn 8. Today, she hoped, was the day that she would finally run a winner—Rattrap.

Carl hadn't returned to the barn yesterday, Julia thought. Late in the afternoon, she had held his filly for Gus to shoe. The horse had stood quietly while he pulled the shoes and hammered new racing plates onto the filly's feet. Julia didn't say much as Gus recited the latest of the never-ending list of blacksmith jokes. She assumed that Carl didn't return because she had embarrassed him earlier that day. She wasn't sure what he'd say to her this morning. She was supposed to run his horse in the eighth today.

Taylor and Miranda greeted Julia as she walked down the shed. She looped Carl's shank around her shoulders and took the horse that Taylor had just brought out of a stall. Miranda was busy unwrapping overnight bandages from the front legs. She glanced up at Julia.

"You running the Rat?" she asked.

"Yes, and a horse for Carl."

"Carl's gelding has a shot," Taylor said. "I think you'll be running two winners today."

When the bandages were off, Julia turned through the centre of the barn with the horse. On the other side, Carl scrubbed buckets in his usual morning routine.

"Where do you want your shank?" Julia asked.

Carl stopped and threw down the scrub brush. He crossed in front of Julia and put his hand over hers on the shank that held the horse she was walking.

"I wanted to say thank you to you," he said.

Julia felt confused and a little nervous. It was still early and no one else hung around in the shed.

"You made me feel like a man again yesterday. It's been a long time since I've felt any sort of passion. Thanks."

Carl let go of her hand and took his lead shank, stepping out of Julia's path. He leaned over, his voice tickling Julia's ear as he whispered.

"Next time I won't stop."

The horse beside Julia stomped impatiently. Her breath caught in her throat as she stared at Carl.

"Better get walking that horse." He chuckled. He pressed the five dollars that he owed Julia into her hand.

Suddenly everything was all right. Julia knew this man would make no demands on her. He would continue to treat her decently, regardless of what happened between them.

True to form, Rattrap leapt out of the starting gate first and ran wire-to-wire in the lead. The jockey had grinned at her when he pulled the horse up as if to say, "Told you so!" Julia led the gelding past the other horses as the rider released his grip on the reins. She stood proudly in the winner's circle, her hand on the rein of the great horse as Tom and the owner joined them for the picture. This was quickly becoming Julia's best day on the racetrack. She was being paid to do something she loved.

Julia finished walking the Rat at the test barn and got back to Barn 8 just as they called to get them ready for the eighth race. Tom took his horse and paid her $50 for running and walking the winner. He reminded her to stop back at the outfit after she was done with Carl's horse.

Running to the backside of the shed as they called them over, Julia saw that Carl had the bridle on the horse already and was hosing down the gelding with cold water.

"It's a warm day," he said as Julia took the horse from him. "This will keep him cool until he gets to the paddock. He'll be dry by then."

Julia noticed that Carl had changed into a clean shirt.

"Are you walking along the track or through the grandstand?" she asked.

"Along the track of course," he answered. "The owners can talk to me when we get to the paddock." He picked up the halter, and they started down the road to the gap.

Carl's horse won. Standing beside Julia in the grandstand, Carl turned and gave her a big hug.

"I had 10 to win on that horse. Not a bad payoff at six to one odds." He smiled and gave Julia another hug. "You okay to walk this horse?"

The security guard at the winner's circle picked up the phone that was a direct line to the racing stewards at the top of the grandstand.

"Test barn," he told Julia as she headed onto the track with the gelding.

"Of course," she replied to both Carl and the security guard.

She should be feeling tired but instead she felt on top of the world. Antonio was gone, and she had not just run one winner but two, and made nearly $200 for the afternoon of work.

Carl bathed the horse at the test barn and left with the bridle to clean the gelding's stall. It took Julia only a half-hour to get out of the test barn and head home with the gelding. It was getting late, nearly 6:30, but it was still very warm. Julia was finally tired as she entered the barn with the second winner.

She walked around to Carl's stalls and took the gelding out to graze. Carl was nowhere to be seen, but she noticed that the stall had been cleaned. It didn't take long for Carl to appear. He was carrying a beer. Julia looked at him in surprise.

"It's for you, silly," he laughed as he handed her the bottle. "Tom sent it over along with some more money." He handed her a roll of twenties. She counted the money and smiled. It was another hundred dollars. Carl reached into his pocket and handed her what he owed her for running and walking his own gelding.

"Let me put the water bucket into the stall, and then I'll take him from you."

The sun was behind the barn. The hot-walking machine beside Julia cast long shadows across the grass and parking area. Carl returned to take the horse.

"Anything I can do for you?" he asked as she stood sipping her beer.

"I want you to take me home with you, Carl," Julia whispered.

The man stopped stroking his horse and stared intently at Julia as if reading her mind.

"If that's what you really want."

Julia nodded. She was ready. She needed to forget completely about Tony.

"I want you to understand something, Julia," Carl said in a low voice as he scratched the gelding behind its ears. "You don't have to do anything that you don't feel comfortable about. If you want to stop and come back to the racetrack, all you need to do is ask."

Julia nodded again. There were tears in her eyes. Carl was such a good man. She was afraid to speak.

"Go let your hair down, my dear, and grab a jacket. I want to take you somewhere special before we go home. Be back here in half an hour. I'll be done with this gelding then."

Carl was true to his word. Julia trusted him completely. He was a perfect gentleman and took her across the Peace Bridge to the oyster bars along the Niagara River in Buffalo. They sat on the patio overlooking the river, talking quietly about Carl's horses and reminiscing about Cunningham's outfit.

Carl had taken Julia home, but not before making sure that was what she still desired. He made it clear that she didn't need to feel any obligation for the evening they'd spent together. Julia was surer than she had ever been. She was startled by her own desire for this quiet, older gentleman that she had known since her first week on the backstretch at Woodbine.

A steady rain brought the couple back to the racetrack before dawn. Carl stopped at a local coffee shop to get the morning coffee and dropped Julia at her own room before he drove up to Barn 8. Relaxed, Julia moved about her own room, braiding her hair and pinning it beneath her horsemen's cap. She was so happy. Even the thought of running horses in the rain today could not dampen her joy at being wanted and appreciated. Carl had been a man of few words that morning. He had reached across and kissed her gently when he dropped her off at her own room.

"You've made me a happy man," was all he had whispered.

In her heart, Julia knew there would never be a permanent relationship for the two of them. They were too different—he a reformed alcoholic with no family, and she who now wanted to live her life having fun with Vern and Crazy Bill. However, they had found something special that made each of them feel complete. In the end, that mattered more to her now than anything a relationship had to offer. She still felt bruised from Tony's abuse.

Julia had no idea of the high esteem that Carl held for her as a woman and a fellow backstretch worker, but would come to realize how deeply he cared. More than anyone else, Carl was the kindest, most undemanding person on the racetrack backstretch that Julia ever called a friend.

Fort Erie Racetrack

July 1986

Chapter Twenty-seven

Leaning against the solid cement block wall, Maurice carefully watched the men and boys gathered around the game. He lifted a bottle of beer to his lips and smiled as the cold liquid coated his throat. Maurice provided the cards, the room, the cigars, and the beer for a reasonable price. His tack room was an open invitation to anyone who wanted to chance their luck at the game.

The crowded room was hazy with smoke from cigarettes and cigars. A board lay atop an overturned bucket serving as a makeshift table. Spectators standing in the doorway of the tack room jostled for a better position to view the cards on the table. The tension in the room was obvious. The boys sitting on the bunk beside the table clutched their cards, sweat oozing from their palms. It was five-card draw with the jacks wild.

Maurice glanced at Crazy Bill framed against the door jam. It had taken the man a few weeks to make an appearance at the game, but the promise of beer helped to draw him to the room. Maurice knew that Bill liked to associate with some of the gamblers in the room when he wasn't hanging with black Vern and Julia. His thoughts briefly caressed Julia. Not a day went by when she didn't cross his mind, but Maurice was a patient man. He had waited nearly a year, and his plan was already beginning to fall into place. Maurice turned over his hidden card.

"Looks like I win again, boys."

Dark days were the best for Julia. She liked to meet Vern, Crazy Bill, and Sandra to head to the quarry. Armed with coolers and beer, the group waited for John and Kyle to arrive with Kristina, the life of the party. They would assemble on the flat grassy area opposite the main swimming zone because it stood away from the main beach and the watching eyes of the teenage lifeguard.

Julia spread a clean horse cooler on the rough ground and sprawled beside the radio, twisting the dial until she found a Buffalo station that suited her mood. She pulled a Wildberry cooler from the box and opened it using Bill's Swiss army knife. It was a hot July day, well over 30 degrees. Vern sauntered over to the blanket.

"Bill is putting his beer in the bucket of ice," Vern sat beside Julia. "Horses are going to be a bitch to run in this heat tomorrow."

Julia nodded. "Especially with all the rain we've had lately. That track is heavy mud. I think only two horses breezed this morning. Too hard on the legs. I've got three to run. It's gonna be a long day."

She took a long swig of her drink. It was better not to think about tomorrow. One of the horses that she had to paddock was especially difficult.

John and Kyle had arrived with the feed truck. Crazy Bill, beer in hand, helped the men back up until the five-ton truck was parked. Julia had placed her blanket where the rocks allowed swimmers to scramble back up the 40-foot cliff. This gave her an easy leap to dive into the clear, deep water. The first time that Sandra had invited Julia to the quarry, Julia had stood at the top of the cliff timidly, wondering if she dared to try the jump past the craggy rocks jutting from the bottom of the cliff. Crazy Bill had shoved her off the edge, not realizing that Julia had grabbed desperately onto his shirt. Vern had howled with laughter as the two of them plunged into the water.

Julia let the cool red liquid caress her throat as she baked in the hot sun. Her lean, muscled brown body was scantily clad in a bikini. Men on the backstretch teased her for never stepping out of her jeans, but those who frequented the quarry knew a different Julia. Her hair fell around her shoulders and she debated diving into the water as sweat beaded up on her forehead. She glanced at the white feed truck. She wasn't drunk enough to climb to the top yet. The truck added an additional 20 feet to the drop from the cliff—intimidating when you were sober.

Kristina threw down a horse blanket beside Julia. She tossed her substantial blonde tresses over her bronzed shoulders as she grinned at Julia and Vern.

"It's a roaster today. John said the sweat on the horses was brutal this morning."

"How many did he get on?" Julia asked. She knew that John had taken out his jockey's licence and was trying to get mounts. He still had the 10-pound allowance given to new riders.

"Only six today," answered Kristina. "I wish he'd get ridden. Only one possible race coming with his buddy Maurice."

Vern glanced at Kristina. Kristina was the type of girl that most men drooled over. She had an hour-glass figure with magnificent breasts that she pressed into the skimpiest tops and flaunted in front of every man and woman on the backstretch. Kristina talked continuously, but both Vern and Julia had yet to hear anything intelligent come out of her mouth. However, Julia and Vern didn't care. Kristina was always good fun, and amusing on most occasions.

In sharp contrast to her friends, Vern refused to part with her track clothes. She was willing to drink a few beers at the quarry, but her jeans and T-shirt remained a fixed part of her image.

"We should go to the beach sometime." Kristina was rambling. "They say the swimming is good off the old pier."

"Can't drink at the beach," Vern said.

Julia laughed. "Depends what time of day you go. If we go after dark, no one is going to give a shit what we do."

Vern looked sadly at her friend. Julia knew what she was thinking and could feel Vern's disappointment.

Yes, she had changed. She was no longer the sweet girl that Antonio Descartes had used so badly, but had become tough as nails. She stomped on anyone who stood in her way, and was vicious with her treatment of men. Julia carried a razor-sharp knife with her everywhere and made it known that unwelcome advances would be cleaved—quite literally. She smiled as she thought about the rumours circulating that she had recently cut a foolish individual in Barn 5. The rumour was true.

It wasn't that she stayed completely away from the opposite sex. No, now she used them. Men who wanted her paid a very high cost, and weren't always rewarded. Julia used both her mind and body to get the things that made life easier on the backstretch, the area she laughingly called the step beyond hell.

"You hear the latest on Conner Tate?" asked Vern.

"He's going down," replied Julia. "Touting. Knew which bloody horses to bet. I just wish I had a share of the $240,000 those boys won. Some things are worth the risk."

"He was just a race caller. What would he know about winning horses?" asked Kristina.

John was listening and wandered over to where the girls lounged. Vern stared at Kristina as if she couldn't believe her naive stupidity.

"You crazy, girl?" Vern asked. "We're talking Conner Tate. Thirty-one years calling races at Woodbine. He knew trainers. He knew owners. He knew jockeys. He just got caught. Crooked business this racing. They're fixing races every day, every card."

"No one would have blamed him if he hadn't been the race caller. Only reason he's going down is because he's Conner Tate," said John as he stood behind Kristina, massaging her shoulders.

"I'd risk it," said Julia as she rested on her elbow. "That's a lot of money. Sweep six or triactor—as long as you come out the winner."

"Yeah," said Vern. "Behind bars you'd be a good loser."

"Don't get caught," Julia replied.

"Tate isn't an idiot," John answered. "Bet he's been involved in this before. This time Simpson and Griffin turned him in."

"Don't trust anyone."

"Didn't you trust Tony?" asked Kristina.

The others were quiet and stared in shock at Kristina. Julia scowled at Kristina, throwing down her empty bottle. Rising, she sprinted for the cliff. Vern watched as Julia dived over the edge, her lithe body stretching over the water. Her arms broke the water cleanly, and she dived down into the depths. The water closed around her as the darkness increased. So cool, so cold, so brutal. Julia's lungs screamed. Instinct took over, and she felt her body change direction, the bikini bottoms tugging down as she strained for the surface and air.

Julia surfaced and thought briefly about swimming the width of the quarry, a good mile across. However, she decided she wasn't yet drunk enough. She struck out in a strong determined crawl toward the cliff. Assholes. Bringing up Descartes.

Vern met Julia at the top of the cliff with another cooler.

"Relax girl. Sometimes you take this hell-hole too serious."

"Tom offered to unload a horse on me yesterday, Vern." Julia had grabbed her towel and wrapped it around her shoulders despite the blistering heat. "It ain't no Rattrap, but may have a couple of wins. I need someone to put their name as trainer for me."

"What about Carl?" suggested Vern. "I think the man has a soft spot for you."

"He's not in the same barn this year. I hardly ever see him. I was thinking of a scoundrel. Someone like Ricky VanNes."

"Are you out of your mind, girl?"

Julia laughed. As a matter of fact, she was crazy. It felt good to have that reputation. She was trying to make the world forget that she was the woman who got bruised by Tony. Ricky VanNes was a ruthless horseman, caring little for the horses that he trained and even less for the people he hired. Julia knew he wouldn't care what she did to the horse as long as he didn't come up with a positive. It would allow her the freedom to train the horse the way she thought best.

Crazy Bill had approached the women at the end of their conversation.

"What are the horse's conditions?" he asked.

Julia glanced at him. "Non-winners of two this year."

"No lifetime conditions?"

"He's won four. A four-year-old gelding by the name of Cranky Dickson."

"I know the horse," said Vern. "Didn't come down from Woodbine. He's American bred from Finger Lakes. "

"Injuries?" asked Bill.

"He's bowed."

Vern turned away and flopped back onto the blanket. "Now I know you're crazy. What would you want with a bowed horse?"

"It's a high bow," said Julia. "It's more of a knot than a bow."

"Could bow out," Bill said.

"There's a chance, but he's racing fit. Just ran last weekend. All he'll need is light training. I was thinking of swimming the horse."

One advantage to using Ricky VanNes was that he controlled a pool across the road, easy walking distance with a horse from the backstretch. Julia knew that she could swim the horse fit with no risk of injury to the bowed tendon.

"I'll sign for you."

Vern threw her hands in the air. "I don't want to hear no more craziness. You haven't saddled a horse in years, Bill. The stewards might not let you back in the paddock; you were so drunk last time."

"Deal," said Julia. She had been hoping Bill would take the bait. She really didn't like VanNes's attitude but he had offered.

"Don't get me ruled off." Crazy Bill took another swig of his beer. "Let me know what you'll be pre-racing with."

"I'll steer clear of Bute," Julia said. "Probably Banamine 48 hours prior."

Bill frowned at Julia.

"I'll make sure you're looked after if the horse hits the board, Bill," said Julia as if reading his mind.

Bill grinned as he finished his beer.

"I'll talk to the stallman tomorrow morning," he said. "Are you ready to go off the top?" He pointed to the roof of the feed truck.

Julia threw down her towel and handed her drink to Vern. She was ready.

Chapter Twenty-eight

John Lawson reported back to Maurice after he dropped Kristina at her tack room. Maurice was sitting in the shed eating beans from his frying pan. He knew that it had been an additional advantage to introduce John to Kristina. Now the boy was completely loyal to him, especially with the promise of a mount.

"She's buying a horse." John was excited. It had been a while since he could provide interesting information about Julia.

Maurice made it a point to not let the boy see any response. This practice worked just as well outside the poker room. He was a little surprised that the girl would jump into horse ownership, but this fact opened up some new possibilities for his own ambitions.

"Who's training for her?"

"She was going to go with VanNes, but Crazy Bill offered and she accepted."

Maurice was quiet for a moment as he finished his beans. John waited impatiently. There were a number of ways that Maurice could approach Julia, and the time was coming when he would make his move.

"I want you to offer to gallop that horse, John."

John scowled.

"The bloody thing's bowed, boss. There's no guarantee that he'll run again, and I don't know if she'll ride me."

Interesting, thought Maurice. Why would she buy a bowed horse?

"She'll ride you," Maurice said.

He knew that he could apply some pressure to Crazy Bill. Alcoholics were easy prey. They'd sell their mother for a drink. However, he would have to use a method that sold Julia on the idea, a more difficult task. Maurice enjoyed the game. A challenge always made the racing business a little more interesting.

"There's a race for my own horse on Tuesday," Maurice said. "I've entered him with you as the rider."

John's face lit up. "Thanks, boss. This is great!"

Maurice scowled at the boy. "Just make sure that you make the weight."

Morning training hours were heavy with the humidity in the air. Julia worked until break for Taylor and Miranda, and then collected her horse from his stall to transfer down to Barn 4 where Bill had found a new home. The muscles in the gelding's neck rippled as Julia tickled him beneath his mane. She had a tenderness for the horse that she had not felt for anything in a long time. She deposited the horse in his new stall, and then walked to the racing office to meet Tom. They needed to transfer ownership, and she had to approach the racing stewards to get her owner's licence.

Thinking briefly about the afternoon racing card, Julia was almost wishing that she didn't have to run as many horses. She wanted to spend time with her new horse. However, it was easy money. The first and last horses were for Taylor Anderson, and she was running one for Tom in the fifth. Taylor's last horse required a nerve line and was often a handful to paddock. She knew that it would be especially tough because it was the last horse after a long day of paddocking in the mud. Miranda was the owner of the filly, and Julia now appreciated the special tie that she must feel with her own horse.

Julia transferred her new licence to her back pocket where she kept her hot-walking licence. Security never asked to see licences. They knew who belonged and those who were strangers. She stopped at the kitchen for a toasted Western sandwich. With a horse in the first, Julia knew that she didn't have much time to spend with her new horse.

Julia stopped at Gus's tack trailer in the central parking lot. There were two tack shops by the loading ramp. Gus always had the best deals. She had recently purchased her own lead shank from him. Most freelancers didn't have their own shanks, but it was nice to not have to rely on some trainer's dilapidated equipment when handling bad horses. Most of the outfits she worked for knew the necessity of keeping their gear in good repair, but there was the odd cheap trainer. She always asked for money up front from the scoundrels.

Gus was in his trailer gathering his gear for an afternoon of shoeing. He greeted her fondly. Julia had held several horses for him.

"I need a halter, Gus. I bought a horse and need to return Tom's."

"At the back, Julia," replied Gus. "So you're a horse owner now? What's the name of the horse?"

"Cranky Dickson," Julia said as she wandered down to the back of the trailer. "He was just shod, but I'll be calling on you in three weeks. Hope you'll give me a deal."

"For you, sweetie, always a deal."

Julia smiled. Gus was a good guy but liked taking too many chances through the windows. She picked up a new leather halter and brought it to the front of the trailer. Gus nodded approvingly.

"That's a good halter. Doubled up the leather."

"I pay cash, Gus. Give me your best price." Julia knew that the halter was listed for $60.

"Forty-five. You're going to be a good customer."

Julia pulled the money from her pocket and paid the man.

"You seen Carl around lately?" asked Gus as Julia turned to leave.

"I ran a horse for him two weeks ago. I haven't talked to him since."

She often saw Carl in the kitchen talking to other trainers or at his barn, but rarely approached the man. They had a quiet understanding about their relationship that they successfully kept hidden from the rest of the backstretch.

"He's in Barn 4A now," Gus said. "I guess you're not in that area much?"

"My new horse is in four. Vern's room is still in the area. I'm around. What do you need, Gus?"

"Nothing. Just wondering where you were. I'm shoeing a horse for him this afternoon. I might stop by to see your new acquisition."

"You're welcome. I'm not likely to be around. I have three horses to run."

Julia jumped down the steps of the trailer, letting the heat of the day envelop her body. It was so hot. Any movement caused her to sweat. She headed for Barn 4 where Cranky was awaiting his lunch. She had borrowed a feed and water pail from Taylor until she could get her own; flagged down the feed man for straw, hay, and oats to be delivered and had Bill watching the barn for her in case the feed man came early. However, he was usually on the same schedule as vets and blacksmiths—two hours later than expected.

Cranky was looking over the closed bottom door of his stall, waiting patiently for Julia to return. Bill had found a webbing and crossbar and was busy outside the stall attaching clips to the ends of the crossbar.

"Too hot to have that door shut," he said. "I scooped this from Vern's trainer. You can use it as long as you need it."

"Thanks, Bill," replied Julia as she dumped the oats that she'd borrowed from Taylor for the gelding's lunch.

Cranky pricked his ears forward and nickered at her. She laughed and attached the bucket to the horse's screen. Cranky didn't waste any time. His nose was lost in the oats that he savoured.

"He has a nice disposition," said Bill. "He doesn't spook easily and he's not cranky." Bill laughed at his own joke.

Julia already knew this about the horse. She had run him a couple of times for Tom. Seventy percent of the thoroughbreds at Fort Erie were crazy because they were so inbred or over-medicated. It was nice to have a minority.

Crazy Bill opened the bottom door and clipped the crossbar and webbing onto the welded hooks in the stall frame. Julia sat on the straw bedding just inside the stall underneath the webbing. The horse reached down, sniffing her and nuzzling as she tickled him behind his ears. She pulled her sandwich out and joined him for lunchtime.

It was a brutal day to be running horses. The sun penetrated every pore, sapping the strength from the most hardy individual. By 2 o'clock, after Julia got back to Barn 8 with Taylor's first horse, the temperature had risen to 34 degrees Celsius and the humidity made it feel like 45, the radio stations were broadcasting. Miranda took the horse to walk after Julia gave it a cool bath. Julia passed through the centre of the barn to meet up with Tom for running the horse in the fifth. The gelding was very quiet, and Julia, knowing the track conditions, was grateful. There had been considerable rain the day before. It was a hard slug over to the paddock in mud that clung to your hiking boots, pulling you down while the horse dragged you onwards. Tom had the bridle on, and Julia carefully tied a knot in the end of the shank in case the horse got away from her. This technique had saved her from losing a horse on more than one occasion.

Tom hosed the horse with cold water, a common practice on hot days to keep an excited horse cool before the race. Julia had often pulled horses from stalls even on dark days to hose off in an attempt to keep them cool. Tom's horse was good to paddock, but as Julia called to an inquiring friend, he ran "hot and dirty," not coming anywhere near the lead at any point in the race.

Julia moved back through the middle of Barn 8 to run the Anderson's horse in the ninth. It was the big race—an allowance for maiden three-year-olds. Miranda was on edge. It was only the second start for her filly that she had nick-named "Backwards" because of the horse's increasing tendency to run backwards instead of walking forwards in the shed.

Miranda was jumpy, pacing in front of the stall as Taylor adjusted the nerve line. Julia didn't like running horses with a nerve line. The thin, cutting wire was wrapped over the horse's poll, behind the ears, and then over the fleshy gum-line under the top lip. If the line came off, Julia knew that she didn't have a hope in hell of holding the horse.

Julia now stood just outside the shed. The late afternoon sun was unrelenting. She yawned and craved a cold beer but knew better than to drink and run horses. She quelled the craving and focused her attention on the wild-eyed filly. Miranda was not helping the filly's temperament. She snapped at Taylor more than once for mundane reasons.

Finally the call came, and taking the shank, Julia led the horse onto the road. The filly was focused as Miranda stepped into place behind the pair. Now Julia was on edge, knowing the horse could lunge backwards or forwards. It was so hot. The horse was pouring sweat by the time they made the gap. Julia shifted the uncomfortable halter over her left shoulder, looping her arm through the throat strap so that the halter was around her neck. She wanted two hands to handle this horse and didn't want to worry about carrying a halter.

The trip over to the paddock was remarkably uneventful. The filly respected the nerve line and walked carefully beside Julia and Miranda, who talked soothingly to the horse every few steps. Julia left the nerve line in place as the trio entered the paddock area. This filly did not go into the paddock stalls, but was saddled as she walked to distract her from the tightening girths. Taylor and the jockey's valet had to be quick. The filly's ears twitched as the over-girth was pulled tight, but Julia had increased pressure on the nerve line. Thankfully, Miranda had stepped back out of the way.

"Not much of a warm-up," Taylor said to the rider. "It's too damn hot out there."

Once the ambulance pulled onto the track, Julia settled in behind the rail to watch the race. Miranda had disappeared with her husband into the clubhouse. Julia had noticed Vern running a horse in the same race. Vern leaned on the rail beside her friend. Sweat was pouring out from under her black curls down her face and into her eyes.

"Isn't it a son of a bitch today?" Vern mumbled. "Lucky you gets some crazy with a nerve line."

"She walked over like a pussycat. The work is done. I'm looking forward to a beer."

"We got to get them back to the barn yet."

The race was a mile and a 16th. Julia glanced at the starting gate almost directly in front of them. Miranda's filly was to be loaded last. The pony rider had already removed the nerve line.

"And...they're off!" The voice of the race caller boomed from the grandstand loud-speakers.

The filly broke well and ran in fourth position as the horses entered the clubhouse turn. By the time they made the top of the stretch, Miranda's filly was two lengths in the lead.

"Would you look at this?" said Julia over the roar of the crowd. "This filly might have a shot!"

She moved so that she was directly by the wire. There was a horse coming from behind on the outside. She was rapidly overtaking the Anderson's filly. The racing fans were ecstatic: both horses were long shots. The riders hit the horses every stride in a desperate attempt to cross the wire first.

"Beat at the wire," said Vern as the horses flew past them with the jockeys standing in the irons to pull them up. "Too bad. Would have made the day worthwhile. My donkey ran dead last."

"Hot and dirty. Hope I don't have to go to the test barn. When you done, Vern?"

"Probably not 'til seven. I'll have to do the horse up in mud."

"I'll meet you at your barn then, and we'll head down to the Pit for dinner."

Julia slipped under the rail as Miranda and Taylor walked from the clubhouse to where the horses pulled up.

The filly had obviously run her race. Her eyes were wild as her flanks heaved trying to get a breath. Julia doubled the shank back through the bit as the rider undid the girths. The horse suddenly lunged backwards as the saddle came off her back. Thank goodness Julia had a good hold on the shank. Taylor looked concerned.

"What the hell? Are you going to be all right with her?"

Julia was angry. It was damn hot and the end of a long day. She didn't need a bad horse.

"I've got her," she said to the couple. "I just need to get her walking down the track."

"I'll go back to the barn with Taylor," said Miranda. "I want to get her bath water ready. We'll see you there."

Julia was already heading down the track with the filly. The dirt was finally beginning to dry out, and walking was a little easier.

She was only halfway to the gap when the filly lunged backwards again.

"I don't need this shit!" Julia yelled at the horse as she released the pressure on the shank. The horse stopped backing and just as suddenly ran forward, nearly running over Julia, who jumped out of the way at the last second.

The filly had a demented look in her eyes. She stumbled as she came alongside Julia. Julia's heart pounded. It suddenly occurred to her that they were in serious trouble, and she was still 50 feet from the gap.

"Oh, my God!" she screamed as the filly lunged backward again. "Heat! This horse is going down from heat! Someone get the horse ambulance! Fast! I need water!"

The filly reared and jumped high into the air. Julia didn't feel anything as a powerful hind leg connected with her skull. The shank slipped out of her hands as the world around her went black.

Chapter Twenty-nine

Julia's eyes opened slowly to shouting.

"Someone help. Julia got kicked." The voice sounded like Vern's but Julia felt far away and something pressed down on her nose. She opened her eyes and saw a horse's hoof resting on her nose. It took a moment for her dazed mind to realize that she was lying underneath the filly that she had been walking back from the paddock. The filly started to twitch and the foot in front of her began to move. Realizing she was in danger, Julia tried to roll out from underneath the horse's foot. In growing fear, she realized that she couldn't move. The filly's other hind leg was caught in the halter she had looped around her neck.

The horse was beginning to kick in earnest now, attempting to get her feet beneath her to stand. The halter tugged at Julia's throat. Fear motivated her and she slipped towards the horse to squirm out of the tightening halter. Feeling freedom from the leather, Julia rolled as fast as she could out from under the horse's legs. She got onto her knees, dizziness and pain finally hitting her body. The filly had risen only to collapse again onto the track. People were rushing towards Julia as she saw the horse ambulance pull alongside the animal. Horsemen jumped into the back of the truck and started the pump, water gushing from the hose onto the unresponsive horse. Julia could feel the spray from the powerful hose as strong arms lifted her onto her feet. She swayed and leaned on the people who helped her towards the gap.

Julia heard a French accent shout from behind. "She's up. Look out!" She tried to glance back to the horse but dizziness overcame the attempt.

"It's all right," said a voice in her ear. "Maurice got the horse up, and they're trying to get her to the gap. The vet was paged, and he's waiting there."

Julia looked ahead at the gap, now only 15 feet away. The gap attendant stood ready with a hose running, and she could see Doctor Nichols' truck parked by the opening. Julia watched as Taylor Anderson pulled into the parking lot of Barn 1, the closest barn to the gap. Taylor and Miranda jumped from their truck and ran towards the gap. Miranda's face was streaked with a look of panic. They didn't notice Julia as they ran towards their horse.

Julia reached the gap and grabbed the rail. She glanced at the two strangers who had helped her off the track. She could hear the filly directly behind. Still feeling woozy, Julia watched the drama unfold before her eyes. The horse began rearing again, front legs slashing at the older, tall horseman who loosely held the end of the shank. Julia assumed this man was Maurice. The horse ambulance was directly beside the filly, water still pouring onto her head.

"Look out, she's going over!" yelled the man driving the truck.

The filly lost her balance and flipped over backwards. In the scramble, she landed almost directly below the rail. The horse thrashed below the rail, twice hitting her head on the metal pipe that ran below the whitewashed wood.

Julia could see Miranda approach the horse, sobbing.

"My horse!" Miranda said. "Please, Taylor, do something. Get her out of there!" Taylor pushed Miranda out of the way.

"Grab the tail!" yelled Maurice as he took a hold of the bridle. "We're got to get her out from beneath the rail or she'll kill herself thrashing around like this."

Others ran forward to help as the men braced themselves against the dirt and pulled. Slowly, they managed to bring the filly back onto the track. Julia could see the sweat running from their skin as muscles tensed and flexed. The horse got her feet under her and was up and back in the air. With a huge jerk, Maurice pulled the horse down practically on top of where he was standing. The filly responded by lunging forward.

"Get behind her," said Maurice. "Keep her moving. We're just about there."

"They've delayed the tenth," said the driver. "At least until we're off the track."

Julia began to see a pattern in the filly's behaviour. She would freeze, rear and lunge. Sometimes she ran backwards and sometimes she flipped. The wild look never left the horse's eyes. The men managed to get the horse beyond where Julia stood and outside the fence that surrounded the gap.

A sickening ache was beginning at the back of Julia's head. She brushed some of the dirt from her arm as she reached back and probed her skull. A large bump was still rising where she'd been kicked. Using the rail for support, Julia headed towards the grassy ditch beside Barn 1.

Taylor had finally seen Julia and helped her over to the grass.

"Are you all right?" he asked.

"I'm sorry. I should have read the signs sooner."

Taylor shook his head. "It's not your fault. We all should have read the signs. She was showing them when she pulled up."

Doctor Nichols had a needle in his hand, but he couldn't get close to the flailing horse. Maurice still had the shank as the filly reared again and lost her balance. She went over backwards on the road, her head cracking sharply as it connected with the asphalt. Miranda screamed, and Taylor ran for the horse.

Julia sank into the grass and watched in dismay. Things appeared to be getting worse for the filly. Doc Nichols was shouting orders.

"She's unconscious. Quick, sit on her head and hold her legs. As many of you as it takes. Carol..." he called to his assistant. "Get me three saline jugs."

The vet reached down to the horse and injected her with the needle he carried in his hand. He motioned to the gap attendant still holding the hose.

"Keep the water on her forehead directly between the eyes. Her brain is swelling."

Julia knew the horse was in serious trouble. She looked down at her clothes, now filthy from the track mud. The heat of the day still beat down on the group, and she could feel the ground beneath her oozing warmth with reflected radiance. The air shimmered. The horsemen had jumped onto the filly and held her as still as possible as the first IV line was put into her neck.

Startled, Julia felt a hand on her arm.

"She's not going to make it," Carl whispered in her ear. "You need to come away from here." Gently, he guided her up so that she was standing beside him.

Julia didn't realize that she was crying.

"I should have known, Carl, but she's such an idiot that I thought it was normal."

"You did the best you could. Most horsemen would have let go." He drew his arm around her and began to lead her down the road.

"I can't leave, Carl," Julia said.

"It's over, Julia. The brain is swelling. Doc Nichols knows it's over. He's just waiting for Taylor to give him the word."

Julia couldn't see for the congealed dirt and tears that cascaded down her face. She didn't know where Carl was taking her.

"You need to come back to the paddock and see the doctor," he said. "You have a nasty lump on your head and you were unconscious for a while."

Julia felt terrible. Miranda's horse was going to die, and she was partly to blame. She couldn't stop crying. It had been such a bad day. For a moment she wondered how Carl had found out about what had happened. That was a silly thought. Word of tragedy had a way of spreading through the backstretch at lightning speed. Julia had stopped walking.

"I'm not going to see any doctor. I have to go back to the horse."

Carl held her. "You need a doctor, Julia. They put the horse down." Julia looked up at Carl. His eyes were moist. The words he spoke next were choked, and Julia had to strain to understand.

"What a fucking business," Carl said.

Chapter Thirty

The day that Miranda's filly died remained etched in Julia's mind for the rest of her life. The ambulance had taken her to the hospital following the tenth race. After a number of tests, Julia discovered Carl in the waiting room. He didn't say anything, but took her back to the racetrack. Julia felt Carl grasp her hand. It seemed like when she needed comfort the most, Carl was there.

Julia fed her horse, and then met up with Vern. Her friend sighed with relief. For Julia, the cruel reality of racing had reared its ugly head. She remembered when Vern had laughed at her last summer.

"You idiot!" Vern had said. "Those horses don't run because they love to. They run because someone is beating the shit out of them."

Julia and Vern walked down to the Pit Stop for supper. Julia dug into the Julienne salad and they drank beer, the cool air conditioning of the bar finally erasing the stifling heat of the day. The desire to get totally wasted coursed through Julia's veins. She needed to forget about what had happened. Sandra, Kyle, John, and Kristina joined Vern and Julia. Sandra and Kyle had just done a line of cocaine before entering the bar, and they flopped beside the others, immune to Julia's distress. Old Ned Nickelson, the backstretch drunk, sat down beside Vern, his speech already slurred.

"It must have been bad," Ned mused to the others. "I remember…,"

Julia tuned him out. She didn't want to hear the never-ending reminiscent stories tonight. The beer was making her angry at the unfeeling people who worked on the backstretch, at the cruelty of racing on the horses, and at the unrelenting weather.

Kyle's words worked their way into her fogged mind.

"It's so bitching hot. We need to go for a swim."

Julia came alive for the first time that evening.

"Let's do it. The old pier by the Walton."

"I don't have a suit," moaned Vern.

"You got your birthday suit," laughed Julia. "Sandra, drive us down there, will you? Let's go swimming."

With the exception of Ned Nickelson, the others thought it was a great idea. Julia was on her feet, the blood coursing through her veins as she reflected on the adventure ahead. Sandra, still high from the coke, opened a bottle of beer and picked up her keys.

It was funny trying to fit into Sandra's Volvo. Crazy Bill made an appearance at the last second, and Julia found herself squashed between Kyle and John. Sandra gunned the motor, and they set out down Thomson Road towards the old pier. Turning into the deserted beach parking lot, the group noisily disembarked.

Julia ran ahead across the vast beach. She quickly scrambled onto the cement blocks broken at the base of the pier. The summer evening breeze blowing off the lake rumpled her hair, and it cascaded around her shoulders. She held her beer in the air and howled at the moon. It was great just to let loose and be crazy. To forget the horrible things she'd just experienced a few short hours ago.

Running for the far end of the pier, Julia could feel Kristina close behind. As Julia made it to the pinnacle, she quickly tore her T-shirt and shorts away and jumped naked into the water six feet below, having no idea of the depth. As she hit the sand, Julia could her Kristina on the pier.

"You crazy woman!" Kristina said. "How big a drop is it? How deep is it? I can't even see you."

Julia laughed. "Nine foot drop with three feet of water. I don't suggest you dive."

She took a long gulp of her beer that she still clutched in her hand. She could see the outline of the others as they walked carefully along the old pier. Vern was calling for her.

"Julia, where are you?"

"Get your black ass in here," Julia said to her friend. "The water is beautiful."

She was serious. The water caressed her and carried her in its warmth. Julia threw her hair back and sighed. This was what she needed to end a bad day.

She watched the others tentatively get undressed, their bodies silhouetted against the moonlight. Julia stifled the urge to laugh. Too many scruples. They shied away from their own nakedness worse than a horse spooked by a blanket fluttering in the breeze.

"What the hell are you doing in the water?" asked Kyle. "I was hoping to see you naked."

"Loser," yelled Julia. "Next time don't do the coke before you come. You'll never catch me now." It was a challenge, and she laughed.

Crazy Bill was standing on the pier staring right at Julia.

"There's a hell of an undertow off this old pier, Julia. Don't swim too far out."

"Aw, Bill," Julia said. "You're going to have to get closer to me if you want to see some skin. That line won't work."

Julia could hear the splashes as the others jumped into the water. Crazy Bill didn't jump but remained fully dressed and standing on the pier. Kyle swam past Julia and into the current. He was a strong swimmer and seemed unaffected by the alcohol or drugs. Vern swam to Julia and splashed at her friend.

"You're crazy, you know." Vern grinned at Julia. "But so much fun to hang with. I'm beginning to think that you'd try anything."

Julia didn't get hangovers, thank goodness. The group didn't return to the racetrack until nearly midnight. Julia and Kyle had argued about humans running races all the way home, and finished with a challenge. Tomorrow night they would climb the fence and race from the quarter pole to the finish line. Vern had scoffed.

"What are you going to tell security when they catch you two?" she asked.

Julia had laughed. She was caring less and less about the consequences. She just wanted to have fun.

Cranky Dickson was munching on his hay when Julia lovingly stroked the horse on his nose. It was 4:30 in the morning, and the sheds were deserted. She dreaded going to work for Taylor and Miranda. The alcohol had done little to erase the guilt that she felt. She knew the signs of heat stroke, yet in her hurry to get back to the barn, she had written off the filly's behaviour as normal. Julia could still see Miranda sitting on the hard tarmac of the road, heat and dust drifting around her as she watched her horse die. Julia shook her head, trying to rid herself of the poignant images. She picked up the feed tin and dropped oats into Cranky's bucket. The horse eagerly lost his snout in the food.

The backstretch kitchen was quiet as Julia entered when it opened at 5 a.m. There were a couple of other early risers. She bought her morning coffee and headed back to her barn to clean the stall. The bump on the back of her head was considerably reduced, and she didn't seem to be feeling any ill effects from the incident.

Julia cleaned the stall around the horse, and then took him out to graze for the 10 minutes remaining before she headed to work. The walk to Barn 8 passed quickly, and Julia entered the shedrow to see Taylor scrubbing feed buckets. Miranda was sitting on a chair outside the couple's tack room. Julia walked towards the woman, not quite sure what to say.

"I'm sorry." Her words were quiet, and she knew that it wasn't good enough.

Miranda looked up at Julia.

"She was the last horse that we bred. I had such high hopes for her, but she was so crazy."

Julia didn't know what to say. She knew that Taylor was listening. Miranda rose and looked directly at Julia.

"It wasn't your fault. Both Taylor and I saw the horse go backwards when the tack came off. Eight horses went down from heat yesterday. We should have treated her, but you know what they say about hindsight."

Taylor had moved down the shed towards the women.

"If you're ready, we need to get going," he said, not unkindly. "There is a barn full of horses that need our attention."

By 9:30, Julia was back with her own horse. She stood watching Cranky, debating whether to find a rider to track the horse or simply walk him for his first day in his new home. The horse was acting like he wanted to train.

"*Bonjour, mademoiselle*," said a voice behind her in a lilting French accent.

Julia turned to see the tall man who helped with Miranda's filly yesterday afternoon. Despite his age and greying hair, he had the rugged good looks and fitness of backstretch workers.

"*Je m'appelle Maurice*," the man continued in French.

"I don't speak French. Your words are wasted on these ears." Julia laughed for the first time that morning. The man had a kind smile that was infectious.

"So sorry. My name is Maurice," he said softly.

"You helped with the filly yesterday," said Julia. "I want to thank you for taking her when I couldn't."

"Ah, a sad case. Horsemen should help each other. How are you feeling this morning?"

Maurice had penetrating steel blue eyes that belied his quiet voice and kind smile. Julia felt a strong presence emanating from this man and found him strangely attractive. She avoided his gaze.

"I've recovered."

"We will talk no more about yesterday's sadness. I came because I understand that you own a horse."

"What would you like?" Julia wasn't sure about Maurice's intentions.

"I am partly representing a new rider. I think that you know him—John Lawson. He still has the 10-pound allowance and would be glad to gallop your horse."

"So you're a jock's agent?" asked Julia.

"No, just a personal interest," Maurice said. "He is a friend of mine."

Julia contemplated what Maurice was suggesting. As a general rule, she didn't like green riders, but trying to get a horse out every day could sometimes be a problem. A young rider was more likely to show up at a specific time to gallop the horse.

"I'll consider your offer," Julia said. "Is he available to come by today?"

Maurice reached forward to shake her hand. Startled, Julia extended her right arm. The man grasped it firmly and looked directly into her eyes. The penetrating gaze locked into Julia's very being. Disturbed, she pulled her hand away. There was something about Maurice that was powerful, and she felt totally inadequate in facing the man.

"I'll be back with the boy within the hour," Maurice said.

Maurice sat down on his bed in his tack room and lit a cigarette. Inhaling deeply, he felt his body shudder from the excitement of approaching the woman he had been watching for nearly a year. She was magnetic, and he was deeply attracted. However, the attraction wasn't just sexual. Maurice had the feeling that Julia would blend well with his own ambitions and expectations.

It had been a week since he had mentioned John riding the horse, and John, true to form, had made it to the barn each morning by 10 o'clock. Julia seemed to accept the boy galloping the horse, and if the bow held, the horse might be worthy of a mount.

Maurice thought briefly of his own colt and then discarded the thought as he contemplated his next move. Julia obviously craved the excitement of racing and working with the high-strung thoroughbreds. He just needed an idea to attract her attention.

There was a knock on his tack room door which stood slightly ajar. John stuck his head into the tack room.

"Hey, boss."

"What's up?" asked Maurice.

"Just thought you'd want to know the latest. There's a group of them out there on the track right now: Julia, Vern, Crazy Bill, Kyle, and Kristina."

Maurice looked at him questioningly. It was an odd time of day to be on the track. He took a long drag from his cigarette and stood up. Maybe he should see what the group had in mind.

"Julia and Vern were causing shit down at the Pit. Ned Nickelson was telling his usual stories and those two pulled on his shorts.

There's the poor man, no underwear, standing in the Pit Stop with all those people. I think the girls were as surprised as Ned. Vern just about fell off her chair howling with laughter."

Maurice chuckled. Sounded like an interesting evening.

"What are they up to now?"

"Apparently some sort of deal Julia made with Kyle nearly a week ago. A race down the stretch in the dark."

"On horses?"

"No. They're planning to climb the fence. I'm not sure why exactly they are doing this."

Maurice had moved past John out into the dark shedrow. It was nearly 10 at night. It would be interesting to see what the group was doing. The cool air of the evening caressed his skin as he walked towards the gap only 50 feet from his barn. A group of people stood just within the gates. Maurice stopped as their voices became audible.

"Jeez, Julia, there's a lot of light on the stretch," Kyle said. "If security walks by, we'll be caught."

Julia scoffed at the man.

"You wimp. Don't you have any balls? Security won't give a shit about what we're doing."

"Could get ruled off," said Kristina.

"What for?" asked Julia. "We're not hurting anyone or anything. They're just security guards, not cops, and not the stewards."

"She's got a point," said Vern.

Julia walked out onto the stretch. She waved a hand at the quarter pole, the white stripes glowing against the black in the darkness.

"Weren't you guys sent for the key to the quarter pole when you were greenhorns?" asked Vern.

Crazy Bill was laughing. "I got her on that one."

Vern aimed a punch at her lover, which he expertly ducked.

Julia glanced back at the group. "Come on, you guys. I'm ready for some action."

Kyle finally moved out towards the centre of the track.

"Vern, can you be the starter?" Julia yelled to her friend.

Julia only made it halfway up the stretch. Her lungs were screaming within an eighth of a mile. Kyle was fast, and he easily ran 20 feet in front of Julia.

"Next time I get a head start!" Julia said as she flung herself onto the dirt. She looked up at the stars and thought about the last time that she lay in this dirt, under the hot midday sun, fighting for her life. Racing was a relentless business.

Maurice had been quietly watching the action on the stretch for a cool July evening. One of the security guards stood beside him, also silently watching the group on the racetrack. Finally the sergeant spoke.

"I got radioed from the officer in the grandstand that something was up on the stretch. If they are friends of yours, I suggest you tell them to vacate as soon as possible. I'll make sure the authorities are unaware that this happened."

Maurice quietly handed a bill to the officer. "Much obliged."

The group was heading back to the gate that surrounded the gap. Maurice moved towards them. Crazy Bill saw the man first. He squeezed through the gap in the gate and greeted Maurice.

"Was that security?"

The others were through the gate and stopped as Maurice nodded.

"It's all right. They have a guard in the grandstand that saw what you were up to and reported back to the office at the west gate. I talked to the officer in charge. We should probably move away from this area."

Maurice didn't wait for an answer but headed back towards Barn 9 and his tack room. John fell into step behind the tall man and Julia, curious, glanced at Vern and Bill.

"Let's check it out, guys. It's only 10."

"Some of us get up early," said Vern but she followed Bill and the others to Maurice's room.

The group piled into the little room. It was sparsely furnished, only the bunk bed and a TV set in the corner. There was a trunk and some buckets along with the usual horse tack. Maurice moved to one of the buckets under the sparse incandescent light. He held a hand out to his bunk.

"*Mademoiselles,*" he suggested to Vern, Kristina, and Julia.

Vern and Kristina sat on the bed but Julia preferred to stand in the doorway. Despite the beer, she felt the same uneasy magnetism from this strange, quiet man. John sat beside Kristina, obviously quite at home in the room.

"Got any beer?" asked Bill.

Maurice shook his head.

"I have some homemade wine if you would like to try," he said. The man looked at Julia who shrugged.

"Sure, I'm game."

Maurice found three plastic cups and poured the wine.

"I'm afraid that we'll have to share." He handed a cup to each of the women.

Julia took a sip of the heavy red wine. It was very strong but sweet like a sherry. She leaned against the doorframe and studied the inside of the tack room. Bill, John, and Maurice were talking about a poker game, apparently one recently played in this very room. Bill did most of the talking with John adding his own thoughts. Maurice was mostly quiet, and Julia had the feeling that he was watching her as she drank the wine. His brilliant blue eyes were intense, and she was unnerved when he turned them in her direction.

Naturally, the conversation turned to racing. John was inquiring about a colt that Maurice owned and he had apparently already ridden.

"I have to go to Finger Lakes in a couple of days," said Maurice. "There is another horse there that I want. I may need someone to come with me." The room was quiet for a moment.

"Not me," said Vern. "The authorities won't want to see me around that racetrack again."

"I'll go," said Julia softly from her spot in the door frame.

Vern raised her eyebrows and stared at her friend. Maurice smiled. He locked into Julia's gaze, and she stared back.

"I plan on leaving Thursday after morning training and don't intend on heading back here until early the next morning."

"I'll go," repeated Julia. She refused to be the first to break their gaze. It was as if no one else was in the room.

Kristina giggled, and Vern let the air out with a whoosh that she'd been holding.

"Julia, what about your job, your horse?" asked Vern with a sigh. "I haven't seen such crazy behaviour in you since Tony."

Julia glared at her friend for a moment. Vern was the only one who dared to bring up Antonio's name these days.

Maurice glanced at Vern. "She'll be back by six. Nice of you to be concerned."

"Jesus, Julia." Vern got off the cot and moved towards her friend in the door and hissed to her. "Don't you know this is a proposition?"

Kyle stood up from the bucket where he had been seated.

"I'm out of here," he said.

John and Kristina beat a hasty retreat after him. Julia moved out of the doorway into the room and Maurice closed it, looking around at Crazy Bill and Vern. The group stood quietly for a moment and then Julia spoke again, more confident now.

"Stop worrying about me, Vern. I know how to handle myself."

"It's nearly 11," said Bill. "I think I'll turn in." Vern looked at Julia as Crazy Bill opened the door.

"I'll be there in a moment." Julia tossed back another mouthful of wine and leaned against the wall, smiling.

Vern shook her head and followed Bill into the dark shedrow.

Julia was alone in the room with Maurice. She had been with a couple of men during the last year, and except for Carl, she liked to play games and leave them hanging. Maurice gave her a different feeling. Knowing that she was treading a line of excitement and danger, she couldn't escape the attraction she felt towards the man. It was almost like the first time a horse gets put in the starter's gate—unnerving, but an exciting unknown when the gates spring open to the new world of the race.

Maurice hadn't moved from the overturned bucket.

"What's in this trip for me?" she asked him. She noticed that he pulled a cigarette from his pocket. He held the cigarette out to her, and she shook her head, watching as he lit it. The door still stood open, and Julia could hear Vern and Crazy Bill arguing in the distance.

"Will you close the door?" asked Maurice.

Julia pushed the door shut and leaned against the wood, sipping the last of her wine. Maurice held the bottle out to the woman.

"You put on a brave front, young woman."

Julia let him pour more wine into her cup. The strong alcohol was helping to quell her fears. For a moment, she felt Maurice watching her as he contemplated her question.

"What do you want?" He was direct and to the point.

"I'm not sure what I want. I might disappoint you."

She wanted to be completely up front with this man. Finger Lakes was a long way from Fort Erie and in a different country. For a brief moment, she wondered about the wisdom of her decision. However, it wasn't the first time that she'd made an unwise decision. Taking a deep breath, Julia stared right at Maurice. He smiled.

"You won't disappoint me, Julia. I'm not expecting anything except someone to keep me company on a long journey. Hopefully you'll be willing to give your opinion on the horse that I'm observing."

"Just have me back for work by 6 a.m."

Julia wasn't convinced that he only had good intentions. She was certainly not the naive fool she had once been two years ago at Woodbine. She opened the door. Suddenly, she desperately wanted to escape.

"I'll talk to you tomorrow," she said.

Julia stepped into the shed with her cup of wine and walked away. Maurice didn't have the chance to say anything as the woman hurried away into the night.

Chapter Thirty-one

Julia dashed through the morning rain for the racing office. She passed by the red brick kitchen next door and then took the front entrance into the main foyer, a large room with two walk-in booths used by owners and trainers to enter horses into races. Pushing a conditions book into her back pocket, Julia moved through the office to the back corridor that housed offices for the racing secretary, bookkeeper and racing stewards. Julia entered the bookkeeper's room. The bookkeeper, a good friend of Vern's, greeted Julia enthusiastically.

"Vern tells me that you bought a horse," she said.

"Yes," replied Julia. "I want to put some money into an account to cover the jockey's mount."

The woman nodded and moved to her computer to enter Julia's name and start an account.

"How much do you want to put in?" she asked.

"Just 40 to cover the mount."

Julia knew that money sitting in a racing account didn't earn any interest. There was a race that suited the horse's conditions coming up on the weekend, and she was excited to at last enter her own horse in a race.

"You tell that Vern to come by and see me. She gets hanging around Bill, and it's nothing but trouble."

Julia laughed. Vern only got into trouble with Bill when they were drinking. Then Bill would call her names or say something to provoke her and she would retaliate. Julia had seen it happen often enough. One of these days, she suspected their play fighting might go too far. It was an odd relationship, but she was quickly discovering that most backstretch relationships weren't ordinary.

Julia stepped out of the office by the back door and ran through the rain towards the nearest shed. Friday morning she would enter her horse, and then go to the draw to make sure she got the rider that she wanted on the gelding.

Making her way through the barns, Julia came out at Barn 8 and quickly took the filly that Miranda was walking.

"Dreary day," said Miranda.

"I rather like the rain. It takes away the humidity."

"With this downpour, you're likely to be running horses in the slop on Saturday."

Miranda turned into the filly's stall and picked up her pitchfork. She had a point, Julia mused. Running horses in the slop was no fun. They came back filthy and leaned their hot muddy bodies all over the grooms so that she was covered in mud by the time she got back to the barn.

"Hot one coming in, Julia." Taylor interrupted her thoughts.

Julia put the filly into her stall and moved over to the rider who was pulling the saddle from the hot horse.

"We're done for today," Taylor said to the jockey. "Not worth sending them out in this crap when they're already racing fit."

The rider pulled his goggles from his eyes, leaving rings of white while the rest of his face was completely covered in mud. He grinned at Julia.

"Maybe I'll run under your hose before I go."

Julia laughed again. She was feeling on top of the world this morning.

"You entering that horse of yours?" he asked.

"Yeah. There's a race coming up on Sunday. He hasn't run in a couple of weeks, so I hope he gets in."

Julia held the horse in the downpour as Taylor lathered the sides and legs with shampoo. She was thinking about her trip to Finger Lakes with Maurice later that day. It still wasn't too late to back out of the proposition, but she was curious about both the racetrack and the man.

The morning finished, and Julia picked up an overnight bag at her room before wandering down to Barn 9 to meet Maurice. The rain had stopped but it was still overcast. Maurice was emptying feed from the back of his truck.

"I took the time to run up to the mill in Stevenson," he said as he lifted a bag of sweet feed onto his shoulder. His shirt was unbuttoned at the top, and Julia could see the curls of chest hair. She quickly averted her gaze.

"Like what you see?" he asked, laughing.

He took the bag to the feed room and dropped it into a bin. Julia opened the passenger door to the truck and tossed in her bag. She walked towards the track and waved to the ambulance attendant. The track closed for training at 11 a.m. The main gap was already shut and the outrider was waiting for the last horses to exit. Julia watched a gelding gallop by the quarter pole, the oozing slop splashing several feet into the air only to congeal back onto the track as though nothing had passed. The ambulance attendant had wandered over to where Julia stood.

"Easy day?" Julia asked pleasantly. The little man sipped on his coffee.

"Hasn't been any action for a week. Not that I mind. Don't like to see people hurt."

Julia nodded and watched as the gelding was pulled up past the wire. The rider turned the horse and began to jog towards where they stood.

"Be a muddy track this weekend," said Julia, "Hard on the ligaments."

"That's usually when riders go down," said the attendant.

Julia could hear Maurice calling her name. She was in no hurry and lingered a moment longer beside the ambulance before turning back to the barn.

Maurice leaned against the box of his truck as Julia came towards him.

"You ready?" he asked.

His voice still had the same soothing softness. Julia suspected his personality was far different from the quiet voice that he liked to use.

"Ready when you are."

Julia opened the passenger door and jumped onto the seat. Maurice watched her for a moment and then climbed behind the wheel and started the engine. The diesel motor came to life, and he put the truck into gear and drove out of the barn area.

Not a word was spoken between the two of them as they crossed the Peace Bridge and went through customs. Maurice pulled up to the booths for the New York State turnpike and grasped the ticket that the attendant handed him. Finally he glanced at Julia, who gazed out the window at the fields outside the Buffalo city limits.

"You need to know something about me," Maurice began quietly. Julia didn't answer. She was ready to play his game but had her own rules.

"I've done time. Six years in a federal penitentiary for armed robbery."

Startled, Julia turned abruptly to the man. Maurice continued to drive along the turnpike. This was the last thing that Julia had expected to hear, and she wasn't quite sure how to respond.

"How the hell did you get a racing licence?" she asked brusquely. If it was his desire to put her on edge, he'd succeeded.

"Full pardon. After so many years, they erase your record," Maurice said. "I'm trying to be up front with you, Julia. I hope you're not afraid of me now." He was looking towards her, his eyes momentarily distracted from the highway.

"What did you rob?"

"Banks."

Julia didn't say anything for a moment but studied the man as he drove. He still had that confidence, that magnetism that was attracting her. Maybe she was beginning to understand the source.

"Do I need to be afraid?" she asked quietly.

Maurice glanced at her again. "No. You have nothing to fear from me. However, I'm not entirely a nice person and sometimes other people need to be afraid. Do you understand what I'm saying?"

That comment didn't make her feel any better. Julia knew that she had chosen to go with someone whom she scarcely understood, and it was oddly exhilarating.

"What do you want from me?" she asked.

"Aside from the obvious," remarked the man drily, "I want a cohort, a partner of sorts. I think that you and I are very much alike."

Julia scoffed. "No way. You're sadly mistaken about me if you think I'm anything like you. Besides, I resent partnerships. I don't need them." She was irritated by the man's assumptions.

The flat land outside Buffalo had become rolling hills. Julia appreciated the beauty of their surroundings even under the cloudy skies. Part of her was wishing that she'd remained in Fort Erie, but it was only a small part. This was certainly an intriguing turn of events, a more formidable challenge than she'd previously considered. She reached to make sure that her knife was safely tucked in her pocket. Maurice glanced over at her and seemed to understand how she was feeling.

"I know you've been hurt," said Maurice softly. "I'm talking about a money-making partnership. You don't need to put any of your money into it."

Julia stared at him defiantly, not dropping her gaze. "What if I don't sleep with you?" She glared at him.

He glanced at her again and shrugged. "My loss. I won't force you. I'm not that sort of person."

Finally, Julia felt a little better. She felt that they'd reached somewhat of an understanding. The man appeared to be honest and was letting her know where she stood.

"Why do you need a partner like me?" she asked.

"You're street smart and a quick learner. I like to take the back seat, and I need someone to be the front runner."

Julia found his language confusing. What he was saying didn't make much sense. Again, Maurice sensed how she was feeling.

"You'll see. You've everything to gain and very little to lose in a partnership with me."

Julia reached across and touched his hand where it lay on his thigh. Maurice smiled at her and took her hand.

"You won't be disappointed. I promise."

To Julia, Finger Lakes appeared to be a barren backstretch when compared to Fort Erie. However, the surrounding landscape and town were very beautiful. She had seen pictures of upstate New York, but this was her first experience of the real environment.

Maurice pulled into the backstretch and had a trainer paged. It took about five minutes for a woman to drive up and call a greeting to Maurice. Julia stayed in the truck and watched as Maurice went to talk to the woman. He came back a moment later and leaned in the window.

"They claimed the horse three days ago. I hope my trip isn't wasted. There's another horse at a local farm I may go and see. So much for Finger Lakes."

Julia felt disappointed. She had wanted to explore the backstretch. She squelched the feeling and watched Maurice as he said good-bye to the trainer and climbed back into the truck. It was nearly 4 o'clock in the afternoon.

"Hungry?" asked Maurice. Julia had only grabbed a quick breakfast from the track kitchen prior to leaving, and was feeling famished. She nodded.

"I know a great little spot not far from here. It's attached to the motel where we'll stay. Might as well check in and eat and then we'll head up to the farm."

"Why did you come all the way down here just to see a couple of horses?" asked Julia.

"For a few reasons," explained Maurice. "They are friends of my wife and…." He stopped and glanced at Julia. Her mouth had fallen open and she stared at him.

"Did you say your wife?"

"Yes. Does that bother you?"

"Of course it bothers me. I didn't realize you were married."

Maurice reached for her hand again. "In name only. I haven't been with my wife for years. She was married previously when I met her and needed someone to raise her children. I needed respectability. It was a good agreement, however sexually inadequate."

Julia felt terrible.

"I'm beginning to feel really used."

Maurice pulled the truck over to the side of the road and looked directly at her.

"I won't lie to you, Julia. Anything that you want to know, just ask. I haven't been home for nearly two years. It's like we're separated. Does that help?"

Julia looked out of the window. "Just drive, please."

Maurice pulled her towards him and put an arm around her shoulder. For someone who appeared tough and strong, it was a tender sentiment. Julia leaned into the man, feeling him pull her towards his lean body. Despite the complications, part of her was still interested. Maurice used his left hand to shift the truck back into gear and turned onto the road, keeping his arm around her shoulder. She had a keen sense of safety, as though she would be completely protected with this man looking out for her, something that she never truly felt with Tony or even Carl.

A couple of miles down the road, Maurice turned into an old motel and restaurant.

"*Voila, mon amie,*" he whispered in her ear. He let go of Julia and stepped out of the vehicle. "Some dinner?" he asked cordially.

Julia took a deep breath and tried to pull together her taut nerves. Things were not going quite the way that she'd planned. This man was completely different from the wimps she had dated recently. It might prove a long night. She wondered how he'd respond if she turned him down, or even demanded to be taken back to Fort Erie.

Maurice proved to be more of a gentleman than she'd originally thought. Oddly, he handed her the menu, and asked her questions regarding the selections. When she looked to him inquisitively, he was perfectly frank.

"Some would call me illiterate. I don't like to read, and can't read English very well," he explained.

Toward the end of the meal, Maurice left to secure a room, and Julia toyed with the last of her potatoes. When Maurice returned, he briefly moved a strand of hair that was hanging in her eyes.

"Don't be unhappy, my friend. You are safe with me."

Julia looked at him, feeling desperately unhappy in many ways. "But am I safe from you?"

"*Oui*. You have nothing to fear."

Maurice stood and stretched. It had been a long aggravating drive. This woman had pulled more information from him than he was normally willing to give, and he could sense her backing away. He had to convince her that his intentions were real, and he did not want to simply use her body. It was so easy to get sex on the backstretch. He wanted so much more from Julia. His ideas were long term. He had spent more than a year finding the right partner for his plans. It would be fruitless if he scared her away this early.

Maurice was a man used to getting what he wanted. If people were not willing to give him something, he simply took what he desired. Julia was presenting a challenge to him that he had not enjoyed for many years. He needed to be careful never to let her see the side of him that was distinctly evil.

"If you're ready, we can head out to the farm. I need to pick something up there, and we can look at this other horse."

Julia followed him back to his truck. She climbed in, noticing that he taken her bag out. Maurice started the engine and extended his arm out towards Julia again. Knowing his intentions, Julia rather enjoyed the closeness of sitting against this confident man as he held her protectively.

It had been a long day and Julia was tired when they finally returned to the motel at 8 o'clock. Yet her nerves were locked with tension. It was the moment that she anticipated but dreaded. Maurice moved easily into the room and motioned to her bag.

"Make yourself comfortable," he said as he moved to the dresser and removed his belt.

Julia stood locked in place, unsure of how to proceed without losing her dignity. The man scarcely looked at her, sensing the uneasiness that prevailed in the room.

"You may want to remove your knife. You won't be needing it." Maurice locked eyes with Julia again, the vivid, forceful gaze understanding what she was hiding from him.

Startled, Julia stared at the man. She didn't want to admit that she carried anything to defend herself.

"I'll make you a deal," said Maurice. "Unload your knife and I'll unload what I'm packing."

He reached behind his back and drew out a gun. Showing it to Julia, he reached past her and placed the weapon on the dresser. Julia stood transfixed in place, afraid to move or say anything. Maurice moved away from her and stood by the bed unbuttoning his shirt. His back was towards Julia, as if he had simply dropped a few dimes on the bureau instead of a gun.

"It's a 38 special, police issue snub-nose revolver. The serial number has been removed. Six shots in the cylinder." The man's voice was directed at the wall as he still didn't face Julia.

She didn't respond but turned, wary of the gun on the dresser, almost afraid that it might come to life, have an intent of its own. She reached forward tentatively and picked up the heavy revolver, letting the weight land firmly in her right hand. She stared at the weapon as she rotated the gun, finally aiming it towards Maurice's stolid back. Suddenly, before she had the chance to realize that he was watching, Maurice spun around, his penetrating blue eyes locking onto her own nervousness. His expression was cold.

"It's loaded," he said quietly.

Julia had scarcely blinked, and the man was at her side. In a calm yet authoritative gesture, he placed a palm on her hand.

"You shouldn't point a gun at someone unless you intend to use it."

Julia was somewhat shocked at the force and swiftness of this man's movement. Maurice, until this point, had appeared a slow, lazy, laid-back type of individual. For the first time, she felt a true uneasiness.

"Have you ever shot someone?" Julia asked, her voice scarcely a whisper.

Maurice smiled, a trace of warmth coming back into his eyes, and took the weapon out of her hand. He laid it back on the dresser.

"The safety is on. You need to take it off if you intend to shoot." His hand had come back to rest on her right arm, preventing her from reaching for the gun again.

Julia looked up at Maurice, waiting, wondering what else he might release on her scattered emotions.

"Don't ask me something that you don't want to know, Julia. I won't lie to you, and you may not like the answer."

Abruptly, he let her go and returned to the bed, throwing back the sheets and sitting against the pillows. Julia pulled her knife from her pocket and laid it by the gun. It seemed insignificant next to so lethal a weapon. She wondered at her own futility in thinking that she could defend herself against an ominous force such as Maurice now appeared.

"Are you afraid of me?" asked Maurice, as if reading her thoughts.

"You'll not force me to sleep with you." She raised her voice.

Maurice chuckled. "I told you before; that's not my game. I only like the willing."

"Then what the hell is your game?"

Julia found solace in anger, and it was helping to calm her fraught nerves. The feeling of being alone with a potentially dangerous man was overwhelming. She was three hours from Fort Erie in a strange country. Maurice was turning out to be very different from what she'd originally thought.

"Sit down, and I'll tell you." There was an edge to his voice that wasn't there previously although Maurice still spoke in a hushed tone. His voice had almost become a command.

Julia refused to move. "Did you bring that across the border?"

Maurice took a moment to answer, and when he did respond, the answer was rhetorical.

"Does that bother you?" he asked.

It was a stand-off, and Julia wanted answers. She had learned to be bold in stressful situations, and was capable of reason despite the upsetting circumstances.

Julia moved towards Maurice so swiftly that he pulled back. Julia kissed him with a passion meant to absorb Maurice completely. Her technique worked as he responded with an equal force.

"Unless you're serious, you'd better stop," he whispered.

His words spurred Julia onward. The magnetism of the man was overpowering, and she had decided that it was better to control than to be controlled. It had been a hard lesson she had learned from life on the backstretch.

Just as suddenly as she had started, Julia stopped. Maurice was left breathless.

"You cunning cat," he whispered. "You know how to drive a man crazy, using the same manipulative manner that I use to control other people. My first impression of you was correct. We are similar in ways that would make a great team."

Julia ignored his words and ran her hands expertly down his chest, toying with the tiny hairs. She quickly curled a few strands and yanked them painfully. Maurice didn't say a word, but his blue eyes were laughing. Julia knew that she was playing with fire, but refused to be manipulated by this man. She refused to let her fears make her vulnerable.

"I want answers, Maurice. You told me that if I wanted to know anything, just to ask. Well, I'm asking. If you want an agreement, I need to know more about you." Julia moved to the opposite bed and waited. She hoped that he would come to her on her terms. Unless he'd been lying to her from the start, she didn't think that she was in any real danger.

Maurice was laughing again. "You're great. The more I see, the more I like. You're trying to con a con." He looked toward the TV stand and the sparsely decorated motel room. "Answers. Well, I didn't bring the gun across the border but I fully intend on returning with it to Fort Erie. I don't plan on keeping it for very long. I'm simply making a delivery."

Although he was no longer looking at her, Julia didn't dare take her eyes from this man. What little trust she had felt was quickly evaporating. She was wishing that she had listened to Vern. Julia was aware that she was hearing information that would make Maurice vulnerable. This trust would serve to pull their relationship firmly together. Julia suspected that this man would possess her in a way that made Antonio look like the warm-up before the real race.

"I want to know the rest," Julia said. "Have you shot someone? Have you killed someone?"

Maurice looked at her with something approaching sadness. "Come here and let me hold you if you really want to know the answer."

Fighting the urge to argue, Julia moved across and let him take her tenderly in his arms. The strength of his touch was different from the other men that she'd known. It was more than physical. The feeling of protection completely engulfed her body, despite her trepidations.

"If you really want to know the answer, I'll tell you." Maurice was speaking very softly again. "It was a long time ago in a different life. Yes, I shot someone. I had gotten out of a bank with the cash, and my partner wasn't waiting where I'd asked. I got on a bus, and one of the passengers decided to be a hero." He stopped momentarily, his eyes watching her closely.

Julia had closed her eyes, listening attentively. Her body was a rush of emotions. She willed him silently to continue.

Maurice bent his head and kissed her lightly on the forehead. "Don't ever be a hero. Bank robbers have very little to lose. They just want to get away. The movies don't show that side of the criminal mind. We will do anything to get away. We are not nice people."

Julia drew him down to her and kissed him again. Maurice responded, and his kiss seemed to be heightened by the memories.

"I don't think you're such a bad person," whispered Julia as she moved closer to him.

Maurice had pulled away, forcing her to open her eyes and look at him. The hard glint of blue was back. "I didn't kill him. I just shot him in the foot. It was enough to stop him."

"Did you get caught?"

"No, not that time. They charged me later for attempted murder. I didn't know that shooting someone in the foot was attempted murder."

Julia lay silently for a moment and studied this man who attracted her in some ways and terrified her in others.

"Maurice," she asked softly. He turned to look at her in his arms. "Can I change my mind?" She stopped, not sure that she should continue but wanting to find the right words. Maurice sat quietly waiting, just holding her as she struggled with conflicting thoughts.

"Will you make love to me?" Julia asked.

Maurice drew closer and tenderly held Julia.

"*Mais oui, mon amie. Je veux t'aime.*"

Chapter Thirty-two

When Julia returned from Finger Lakes, she walked with a lightness to her step. Vern asked her what had happened but Julia withheld the specifics, preferring to keep the intimacy to herself.

Julia spent most of her spare moments with Maurice La Chance. The couple often wandered down to the Pit Stop together later in the evening, picking up Vern on their way. Vern was great fun, spending less and less time with Crazy Bill. Bill and Vern had a bit of an on-again, off-again relationship. When they quarrelled, they avoided each other, choosing to sit at different tables in the Pit Stop. Julia suspected that they met up later at night in Vern's tack room but never mentioned it to her friend.

Julia ran her horse the Sunday after she'd returned from Finger Lakes. She took Cranky over to the paddock and watched Crazy Bill saddle the horse. Throwing John onto her horse, feeling in charge for the first time, she told him to just do the best that he could. The horse finished towards the back of the pack. Julia watched in disappointment, knowing that with a green rider, the horse was doing only what was necessary.

During the race, Maurice stood beside her at the rail. There was a fulfillment in their intimacy that had been lacking in most of her previous relationships on the backstretch. Maurice was someone that Julia felt she could trust completely. Even with Carl, there had been many things left unsaid. Against her better judgment, Julia knew that she was falling for Maurice, and the consequences of loving him were frightening. He was a married man with a sordid history.

Spending dark days watching the poker games in the smoke-filled tack room, Julia began to appreciate that Maurice, despite his quiet manner, manipulated and controlled others. She noticed that the game participants had little idea that they were being coerced. They would first lose the money in their pockets and then their next paycheque, and still begged to remain in the game. There was always the chance that their luck would turn. Yet Maurice did not play by luck, but rather, with a well-rehearsed skill, slowly milking the others of their assets, and then demanding loyalties that reached far beyond the dark tack room table. There was never a problem getting his horse out, or fed, or cared for if Maurice had the need. There were many people anxious to help.

It was a particularly hot race day one August evening when Julia finally made it down to Maurice at 7 o'clock. He was waiting in his room as she walked into his arms. She explained that she had run two tough horses for Taylor and Miranda, and had stopped by to graze Cranky for a few minutes before supper. Maurice listened respectfully. He was always gentle with her, but once Julia had seen a hint of underlying evil. She had been horrified to see the transformation in this quiet, kind man that she was growing to love.

Maurice kissed her and attempted to close the door. Instead, she grabbed his keys and ran from the room, taunting him.

"Come on. You know that Vern is waiting. You'll have me all night after we eat. I'm starving. I worked hard today." Maurice shook his head and sighed.

Julia was in his truck, the keys in the ignition. She had the radio turned to her favourite Buffalo station and curled against Maurice when he got behind the wheel. He started the engine and headed to Vern's barn.

Vern met them at the end of the shedrow. She opened the passenger door and Maurice pleaded with the black woman.

"Get her away from me, Vern. She's a tease and using me."

Vern chuckled. "You can handle yourself, you dirty old man."

Julia laughed and laid her hand on the inside of his thigh. "I'll leave you high and dry if you don't start driving."

"Kyle and Sandra are supposed to meet up with us at eight," explained Vern. "There was a horse with colic in Kyle's outfit today, and they had to take turns walking the colt."

"That's unusual," said Julia. "Track horses don't get colic because they are so closely watched by the trainers and grooms. It's a nasty stomach ache essentially, correct?"

Vern nodded. "Yeah, a horse can't regurgitate anything that it's eaten, so the indigestion can get really bad, causing a blockage in the intestines. They called the vet, and the horse was given muscle relaxants and oil was pumped into its stomach. Now they have to walk it continuously to try to prevent the bowel from twisting."

Maurice pulled into the tiny parking lot behind the Pit Stop, and the girls scrambled out of the truck and in through the back door of the establishment. They were seated at their favourite table in the corner by the time Maurice finally made an appearance in the dimly lit bar.

By the end of supper, Kyle, Sandra, John, and Kristina had joined the group at their table. Julia had fed some coins into the juke box. Sounds of Dire Straits filled the bar as they watched simulcast racing from the Ohio's Thistledown racetrack in Cleveland. Vern began to call out for Slammers. The owner brought the mixing bottle to the table and gestured for Vern to put her head back and open her mouth. Julia laughed as Vern let the liquid pour down the back of her throat. Within moments she was signalling for the man to stop.

"Enough." Vern coughed. "Julia's turn."

Julia had already had several beers.

"I don't think so, but a shot or two might help this heat," she said.

The owner moved to the bar and picked up some glasses to fill with the pink liquid.

Kyle seemed eager to move into the night.

"Hey, Julia, how 'bout taking that gorgeous body of yours for another swim off the old pier by the Walton?" he asked.

"You just missed it last time, and want a second chance, right?" laughed Julia. She knew that Maurice was studying Kyle carefully, and had an uneasy feeling that maybe she should make light of the incident. Kyle had done a line of coke and had no such misgivings.

"Sandra, you game?" he asked.

"Skinny dipping with you in the moonlight would be great right now. I've got a case of beer in my car. Who else is on?"

"I think that we're all going," said Julia. "Let's go party at the beach, Maurice. Time to see if you can swim." She knew the alcohol was talking but didn't care. She wanted Maurice to be there with her. She didn't trust Kyle, especially when he was high as well as drunk.

Maurice was silent. He seemed to be contemplating the invitation as he studied the group around the table.

"When did you do your last line, Sandra?" he asked quietly.

Startled, the woman glanced nervously around the bar but no one was paying any attention to the group.

"'Bout a half hour ago out back," she whispered. "Not very good shit. I think they cut it too much."

Maurice stood up. "I'll drive. I've only had a couple of beers and the rest of you are well on your way. You can all pile in the back of my pickup."

"Make sure you grab your beer," Kyle said to Sandra as the group made their way out behind the building.

Maurice held Julia protectively as they drove to the deserted beach behind the Walton. It was nearly midnight, and although tired, Maurice kept his arm around Julia and whispered to her as he drove.

"I haven't seen you this far gone before, Julia. You are definitely drunk. Remember, I will make sure that nothing happens to my newfound friend."

Maurice had scarcely pulled into the parking area when John, Kristina, Sandra, and Kyle were out of the box and racing for the water. Vern opened her door and Maurice grabbed Julia's arm before she had a chance to follow her friend.

She glanced at him, a little annoyed.

He kissed her. "I'll be watching your back," he said.

By the time Julia made the far end of the pier, the group had gathered to watch the waves, small whitecaps on top, glittering under the moonlight. There were a few scattered clouds in the sky, and the heat of the day had evaporated into a wonderful summer evening.

"What the hell are you waiting for?" shouted Julia as she began to take her clothes off.

The wind and spray caressed her skin, causing goose-bumps to spring up on her exposed breasts. Kyle was all eyes, devouring her body. Julia glared at him as Maurice walked up from behind.

"Take your clothes off, you invalid. If you hadn't done a line, you might not have that drooling problem." She touched the blade of her knife as she pointed it towards Kyle. "You touch me and I'll geld you." The alcohol was making her tougher than she really felt.

Maurice had reached around Julia and deftly removed the knife from her hand. "Don't be a fool," he whispered in her ear. "No one will touch you." He stared at Kyle, his eyes hard with a warning. "I promise."

Julia jumped from the edge of the pier. When her feet hit the sand and her body sank into the silky warm water, she knew something was different tonight. The waves had a mind of their own, and it felt as though something was tugging at her feet. She lay back in the waves letting them float her into deeper water, away from the pier. She could hear the splashes as the others jumped. Glancing back at the pier silhouetted in the moonlight, she could see no one remaining on the cement. Everyone was in the water.

Vern was swimming alongside Julia.

"Can you feel that undertow tonight?" she asked. "We'd better stay in close."

"I like it," replied Julia. "I like the feeling of the power of the waves. It's better than riding a racehorse. It's almost better than sex with Maurice."

Vern laughed and splashed her friend. "You're drunk, girl. And it's not just alcohol. He's got you."

Vern swam away towards the beach. Julia sensed someone else close by. Before she knew what was happening, she felt Kyle behind her, grabbing at her breasts. Julia struggled and pulled away.

"Fuck off, asshole. If Maurice catches you, you're a dead man."

"Your friend ishn't here to help you," said Kyle. "You're an open invitation, shwimming naked wish all these men. I think that's why you do it."

Julia swam as fast as she could away from Kyle towards where she could see Maurice.

"Why don't you go out there by the rocks," she yelled over her shoulder at Kyle. "You need to cool off, and the water out there is colder. Just stay away from me." She was panting for air and fear when Maurice caught her in his arms.

"It's all right, Julia. I saw what happened. He's swimming out for the rocks. You're safe." Maurice pulled Julia towards the shallower beach half carrying her in his arms.

Finally reaching the shallows, Maurice gently laid her in the sand and then turned to watch where the others were swimming. Julia, sensing that he was deeply angry at Kyle for approaching her despite the warning, became fearful for an entirely different reason.

"Maurice, you don't need to hurt him," she said.

The tall man beside her glanced down and smiled, but there was no kindness in his expression.

"He didn't heed my warning," he stated. His voice sounded cold.

"Maurice, he's drunk and he's stoned."

"He was sober enough to frighten you."

Julia struggled to get to her feet. "For God's sake, Maurice. Don't get yourself sent back to prison. I love you. Please, just let it go." She felt shaky, not sure that her legs would support her weight. The declaration had escaped from her before she'd had a chance to curb the words. They sounded hollow now. Did she really know what love was?

"If you love me, then you know in your heart that I can't let that man get away with this. I have no intention of going back to prison. But Kyle will know that he has crossed the line. You need to trust me, Julia. For us." Maurice reached and tenderly touched her cheek with the back of his hand. He kissed her and walked back out into the water.

Julia returned to the water and began floating on her back. Nearly 10 minutes later Vern joined her.

"Julia, I'm a little worried," Vern said. "Everyone else is around, but I haven't seen Kyle for some time."

Julia stared at her friend. She wasn't sure what to say. Had Maurice approached Kyle or was he still out by the rocks? Vern continued without waiting for an answer.

"Sandra said he was swimming way out in the deep water by those rocks." She pointed in the direction that Julia had recently indicated to Kyle.

Maurice was back, and Julia was dimly aware of the others close behind. They all seemed to know there was a problem. Maurice had taken charge, and the others were willing to listen to the authority of his calm voice.

"You people need to move up onto the beach," Maurice said. "I'm going to see if I can find him."

"No! No, you can't go out there!" Julia was unaware that she was screaming. She felt Maurice's arms around her. His grip tightened, and he whispered into her ear. Julia had to stop to hear what he said.

"No, Julia, you need to trust me. You aren't going to lose me. Only the good die young." The cliché seemed hollow. He pulled her head onto his shoulder as she cried and signalled to Vern.

Maurice was speaking over Julia's shoulder to her friend.

"Get her to the beach, Vern. You need to make sure that she has clothes on. Send John up to the Walton tavern to call the police. I'm going out there to see if I can find Kyle."

There was no sound except the waves crashing around Maurice as he stood chest deep next to the rocks. He held grimly onto a slippery rock, feeling the sand grasp his ankles and the water tug at his knees, oblivious of where he wanted to stand. Clouds filtered through the moonlight, causing shadows to be cast from the waves. Twice he thought that he detected someone swimming in the distance, but the moonlight was playing games with his eyes. The waves and undertow were powerful, and it was not a place for the meek. Finally, Maurice turned his back to the lake, satisfaction lurking in his grim smile. There was no doubt left in his mind. Kyle was gone.

It was 5.30 a.m. and Julia was walking a horse. She moved through the centre of the shed, not bothering to call out. It had been five days since Kyle had disappeared, and the body had finally washed ashore last evening. She held the horse loosely by the lead shank in her right hand. Her left hand gripped a beer, only half empty. As she reached the opposite side of the shed, she was startled by the presence of someone standing in the way. She pulled the horse up with a jolt and took a swig of her beer. It was Carl.

He reached out and took the beer from her hand, placing it on the rail behind them. He then took the shank away, leading the horse beyond where Julia collapsed into the dirt. He put the horse into its stall and quickly removed the shank. Julia sat in the shed. She had been drunk for five days, refusing to face the ugly reality that had become her life.

Carl took her hand and led her onto the grass beyond the shedrow in the early dawn sunlight. He handed her a coffee.

"It's time to sober up," he said and took a sip of his own coffee.

"I can't, Carl. I don't want to." Julia's voice had lost its lilt. She talked like a beaten woman.

"It was me, Carl. I told him to go out there. I killed him."

Carl stayed quiet for a moment.

"The police say that it was the undertow, Julia."

Julia didn't bother to reply.

"Drinking doesn't solve your problems, Julia," said Carl. "Eventually you have to face them. You can't spend your life running away."

Julia still didn't answer. She didn't want to hear what he was saying.

"You sold your horse." It was a statement more than a question.

"Gregory was looking for some horses, and the gelding wasn't running worth a damn. He didn't even want the papers." Her voice was bitter. It had been a move so against her love for horses.

"Where do you want to be in 20 years, Julia? In 40 years? On the racetrack backstretch? A Ned Nickelson? Living in a tack room? You're young. Don't you want marriage, or a family?"

For the first time, Julia looked at Carl, his words working their way into her muddled mind.

"You're digging a hole, Julia. It happens. It's called racing. It's a fucking depressing business unless you're hitting it big. So few of us hit it big. You can dig down Julia and bury yourself here, or you can build. The girl I knew that worked for the Weasel was a builder. She had hopes. She had dreams." Carl stopped and touched Julia under her chin. "The girl that I made love to last year had dreams. She was a wonderful woman. Don't let this cursed place change you, Julia."

For the second and last time in her life, Julia sensed that Carl was crying. She took a sip of the black coffee, the caffeine burning her throat.

"You're running with Maurice La Chance now. I'm not trying to tell you what to do, but I know that he was at Blue Bonnets when they closed the track. I think he knew what was going down. You need to be careful."

Julia answered him so softly, that Carl had to lean towards her. "He loves me, Carl." Carl looked at her for a moment as if trying to comprehend the change in her.

"It's time to turn your life around, Julia. Build up, not down. And for Christ sake, don't lose yourself in alcohol. Remember, there are more people than Maurice that love you and care about you on this backstretch. If you ever need anything, I'll be there."

Wearily, Carl stood and walked away into the gathering light.

Fort Erie Racetrack

May 1987

Chapter Thirty-three

Ricky VanNes was interested in only one thing: money. He had 24 horses in his barn to train and had built the pool across the road for swimming injured horses. The stewards had banned horses from being walked to his pool so he spent most of his afternoons shipping horses back and forth from the track to the building on the north side of Thomson Road. He was a man busy making money, and had a hard time keeping his own outfit in line, particularly when horses were entered at Woodbine. Then he would be gone for the day, hoping that the horses at home were at least fed and watered at feed time.

When Julia Reinhardt approached Ricky with her proposal, he had at first scoffed. It wasn't that Ricky didn't want to hire the woman. She was known to be reliable and dependable help on the backstretch. She also worked long, hard hours and could handle the most difficult horses.

"What the hell do I need an assistant trainer for?" Ricky had laughed when Julia had made her proposal. "It's a pain in the butt signing for someone to go for a licence. What if you fail the test? The racing stewards don't take kindly to women on the backstretch, especially women trainers."

"I won't fail the test," said Julia. "Besides, meanwhile you have me working for you all this summer. I'll turn this outfit into a well-run establishment, and you won't have to worry when you enter horses at Woodbine or when you're busy swimming horses across the road. The horses will be tracked and fed."

Ricky had looked at this strong, independent woman sceptically. "How much money do you want?" he asked in a gruff voice.

Julia stared the man in the eye. "Three hundred a week until I have my licence. Then it's under negotiation."

"Three hundred a week!" Ricky was aghast. "That's highway robbery woman! Even the best grooms only get $250."

Julia had stood her ground. "Let me clarify that. Three hundred a week clear. I'm better than a groom."

Ricky had studied Julia for a moment, debating her proposal.

"I have a lover, Ricky. No, I'll not go to bed with you."

Ricky glared at Julia. "Jesus woman, what gave you that idea? I never said a word about sex."

Julia laughed at the man. "Now you won't have to."

"All right." Ricky finally succumbed to the inevitable. The woman did have a point, regardless of how irritatingly manipulative she was being. He stuck his hand out to cement the contract. Julia ignored him.

"Let's go to the racing office," she said.

"Why?" he asked.

"You're going to talk to the stewards," Julia stated in a matter-of-fact tone. She laughed at the man again. "Besides, I don't fucking trust you."

Julia didn't start working for VanNes until the end of the week. It was a bittersweet good-bye to Taylor and Miranda who had held her position each spring. Taylor offered his congratulations.

"You come and see me as you get closer to the test. I'll ask you questions that the stewards might ask."

"Thanks, Taylor. I'll still run your horses when I can."

"Ricky VanNes wins a lot of races. He's got that good grey filly that runs for $16,000 at Woodbine. I think you'll be pretty busy," said Miranda.

When Julia finally walked down the shedrow of Barn 10 to view her new outfit, she was appalled by the carelessness of the workers. The grooms did as little as possible so that they could hurry to place bets through the windows in the grandstand. Some days the horses' feet weren't even picked. Saddle cloths were left dirty, rarely washed, and feed tubs had obviously not been pulled from their stalls in weeks.

Julia immediately fired two grooms and a hot-walker. Ricky was livid.

"What the hell are you doing? It's hard to get good help on the backstretch!"

"That's not my idea of good help," said Julia. "If you paid a decent wage, the help would find you. Stop being such a cheap bastard. You're winning races. I'll make sure that with some decent care, these horses will win a lot more."

Julia began making changes to the way the outfit was being run. She set afternoon feed at the end of morning training, and then rotated the duties of the grooms so that only one had to return to feed with her at 4 o'clock. The help quickly learned that if they got their work done, Julia treated them fairly. She made sure that they received what they wanted from the kitchen at break each day, and pressured Ricky into taking them out for lunch once every couple of weeks.

The horses were not fed an early morning feed, and Julia began to rise at 4 a.m. to slip some oats into the stalls before returning to Maurice who had his usual tack room in the next barn. It was a convenient arrangement living with Maurice who still treated her kindly. He didn't always feel the need to go out with Vern and Julia at the end of the day. However, Julia still frequented the Pit Stop after hours but drank less than last summer. One day Maurice handed her the keys to his truck.

Startled, Julia shook her head. "I don't drive."

"It's high time you learned. Take Vern with you. She drives. Try it out in the parking lot where there's lots of room."

"You trust me with your truck?"

"I've trusted you a long time, Julia. You know things about me that I've never told anyone. Of course, I trust you with my truck." Maurice dropped the keys into her hand.

Julia was reading and memorizing a book on veterinary care in anticipation of the first of the three tests she would undergo for her assistant trainer's licence. When the commission vets came by the barn just after break on race days, Julia would jog the horses entered for that day, harassing the vets with questions. They would laugh in a good-natured manner and point out where the stifle ligament was located, or explain that a bowed tendon was actually inflammation of the greater flexor tendon on the back of the legs.

Julia spent a lot of time sitting in the stalls of the VanNes outfit observing the horses as she studied for her trainer's test. Maurice would find this dynamic woman feeling along the shins of a filly's legs, counting bones or trying to determine the different ligaments in the leg. Even Gus seemed bothered by her questions. She would stand holding a horse for him to shoe, asking him questions about navicular disease and the use of bar shoes, or why did a horse founder?

Gus straightened his aching back and wiped the sweat out of his eyes. "Do you know what founder is?"

"Yes," Julia said. "It's also known as laminitis. That's when the inner laminae becomes inflamed and creates pressure on the outer laminae of the foot. The pressure can become so great that the coffin bone may turn, and if not corrected, can drill down through the bottom of the foot."

"I'm impressed. So answer your own question. Why does a horse founder?"

"Well, I know that they can founder if they are fed too much grain for the training they are receiving, or too hot a grain, such as corn or barley. They've also foundered from drinking too much cold water at once when they're hot. But Gus, what does drinking cold water have to do with the foot?"

"If you can answer that, woman, you won't need to work on the backstretch. You'd be a millionaire. I don't know the answer." Gus picked up the foot he'd dropped and continued to hammer nails into the racing plate.

Julia had an interesting conversation with Taylor about two-year-old racehorses and bucked shins. She'd just had a heated argument with Ricky about the hazards of bucking a horse right out.

"You need to break the youngsters out of the gate so they buck right out," Ricky had told Julia. "Otherwise, they'll buck as a three-year-old, and then you've lost the primary racing year."

Upset, Julia had asked Taylor his opinion regarding bucked shins. "Bucked shins are inflammation of the cannon bone and the books say that if you buck them out, it may result in hairline fractures in the cannon bone. Isn't that far worse than simply laying a two-year-old up for the year and hoping the bones are healed by the three-year-old year?"

Taylor had agreed with Julia's reasoning.

"That's the correct answer for the test. A two-year-old's shins are still undeveloped. The horse is really a baby. It's like sending a four-year-old human out to run a race. If you lay up a horse and wait a year, they are that much older and the bones are more developed. The cruel pounding of the track as they break out of the gate is less likely to cause fractures. Very few three-year-olds even buck their shins."

Taylor also took the time to show Julia the racing equipment that she had to understand how and when to use but had never seen before. She hefted the heavy lug-out bit, used when a horse lugged in or out badly in a race, running the risk of a foul. She knew that lugging out was usually the result of an injury on the opposite leg, or possibly faulty shoeing. Most of the time it was correctable through a variety of treatments, but occasionally a lug-out bit had to be used when the problem was so severe that the horse still pulled into the path of other horses during the race.

As May turned to June, Julia became more and more confident in her knowledge of horses and their problems associated with thoroughbred racing. She began to debate when to set the date for attempting her test. The first part of the three-part test was oral and tape-recorded; it ran for over an hour. She could be asked anything about anatomy and horse care, racing injuries and treatments, feeding, tack and equipment, or countless other topics in relation to horses. Ricky grilled her regularly. He had told her that she'd better pass since he was backing her.

"It's my reputation as well," he'd said.

Ricky found that he was relying more and more on Julia. On Fridays he handed her the paycheques so that he could go to the draw. He had to admit that the outfit looked cleaner, and the equipment was packed away properly at the end of each day. His owners had also noticed the difference. The horses were relaxed and well fed, and results were showing as he made the leading trainers list and his horses rarely missed the board.

One day when he was over at the pool, he didn't hear the morning run-down that announced how full the races were for the draw that day. Julia knew that he'd entered several horses and quickly copied down the numbers. When Ricky finally made it back to the barn, Julia asked for his conditions book.

"Why?" he asked suspiciously.

"To see where you entered horses, Ricky," she said. "I don't think the ninth in the book is going to go. There's only three horses entered. You said there was another race for Starlight Dancer. You may want to head up to the office to make the change. She's pretty high today. She needs to run this weekend."

Reluctantly, Ricky handed over his conditions book. Julia quickly turned to the page and noticed that he had scrawled the name of the filly across race nine. He also had a question mark above another possible race for Starlight.

"Entries close in 10 minutes. I don't think there'll be another run-down. Why don't you leave me your book in the future, and I can make whatever changes you want."

Ricky grabbed the book back and glared at Julia.

"I think I can handle the entries. Besides, you can't do it until you get that licence."

Nevertheless, Ricky VanNes moved quickly along the shed towards the racing office.

Julia knew the time had come. She headed to the office herself to book her trainer's test with the representative of the HBPA at Fort Erie, a woman who actually gave the first two parts of the test. As she passed through Barn 9, she stopped in front of the colt that Maurice owned. Sure enough, Maurice was busy with the rag rubbing down the horse's legs.

"Hey, Julia," he said. "You ready for lunch so soon?"

"In a little while. I have to book a time for my test."

Maurice leaned on the crossbar, his greying hair falling into his blue eyes. He smiled at Julia.

"You won't have any problem, girl. You know the horses well." Julia moved over to the man and let him hold her for a moment. His colt kicked the boards in the back of the stall.

"You need to have a talk with that youngster. He's jealous. Maybe he needs to break his maiden." She was laughing. She meant that the horse needed to win his first race, but she saw the humour in the double meaning of the words.

Maurice had pulled her closer to the crossbar. "You better get a move on to that office or you won't get there," he whispered in her ear. Julia laughed and pulled away.

"I'll see you in an hour, Maurice. I have to feed lunch when I get back to the barn."

"Do me a favour and check the number of horses in the seventh. I entered this scallywag," Maurice called after Julia's retreating back.

The day of Julia's test was set for the first dark day following the weekend's racing. That meant Wednesday. She was to appear at the HBPA office at 11 that morning. She helped Maurice with his gelding on Monday, and the two of them watched the horse finish dead last yet again. Maurice shook his head as Julia gathered the horse at the paddock.

"If that horse ever breaks its maiden, he will lose his best friend," he mumbled.

"Personally Maurice, I didn't think John was trying very hard," said Julia.

Maurice glanced at her hard for a moment.

"John did what he was told," he said.

Julia seemed startled at the fierceness of the remark, so unlike the way Maurice normally talked. Without another word, she headed back to the barn with the hot horse.

Chapter Thirty-four

Julia was a nervous wreck the morning of her trainer's test. She recalled vividly a time not so long ago when Tony had gone for the same test while she waited anxiously at the barn. She went through the motions of saddling horses and sending them to the track, bathing horses, and setting the lunch feed. Then she hurried to the showers and changed into a fresh blouse before she walked to the racing office. Ricky VanNes was inside talking to the racing secretary. He walked over to where Julia stood waiting to be called, and shook her hand.

"Good luck," he said gruffly. Despite her nervousness, Julia looked at him with determination.

"I won't let you down, Ricky," she answered.

The woman who gave the tests finally called Julia's name and led her down the back hallway of the building to a small room opposite that of the racing stewards. The bookkeeper leaned a head out of her office and called a friendly "hello" as Julia passed her door.

The door shut behind Julia, and she took a seat at a tiny table opposite the woman. A tape recorder lay between them, and as the woman gathered some papers together, Julia thought of the room as an interrogation room. She briefly wondered how Maurice would feel in this situation.

The woman pressed the record button.

"Today is Wednesday, June the fifth and the candidate is Julia Reinhardt for the licence of assistant trainer, Ontario Racing Commission. Are you ready, Julia?" The woman looked up at her and smiled as Julia nodded.

"Let's begin. Starting at the knee, name all the bones and ligaments found in a horse's front leg."

The test droned on, a long gruelling hour. As Julia answered questions, she gained confidence. She was asked about diseases, injuries, even the colour of the various poles around the track. The hour drew to a close, and the woman finally hit the stop button on the tape recorder and leaned back in her chair.

"I suggest we do the barn test after lunch," she said.

Julia stood up. She felt exhausted. She nodded.

"What time?" she asked.

"I'll be there at two." The woman also stood up and gathered her papers. She ejected the tape from the recorder.

"I'll drop this off to the stewards." The woman glanced at Julia. "By the way, congratulations. You've passed the first test."

The sunshine felt warm on Julia's face as she exited the racing office. She felt on top of the world. She had passed the toughest part of the whole exam. She knew that she'd be okay with the barn test, and, hopefully, the stewards would ask her decent questions. That meant by this time next week, she would have her trainer's licence. It was unbelievable. She wished she could flaunt it in the face of Jimmy Henderson. The creep never thought that she would amount to anything. Maurice and Vern were waiting outside the racing office.

"Well?" asked Vern.

"I passed. I bloody passed!" said Julia, not caring who heard. "Would you believe it?"

Maurice gave her a hug. "I never doubted you would."

Julia was walking and speaking so fast that her friends had to struggle to keep up.

"I have to be at the barn for two. It's the practical. Then the stewards tomorrow. Oh God, Maurice, what if they don't like me? What if they don't want me training?"

"You'll be fine. Ricky's backing you. You'll get your licence." Maurice's voice was smooth and caring, but Julia wasn't really listening.

Julia gathered equipment and bandages together for the barn test. She paced up and down the shed waiting for the woman to appear as the horses in their stalls munched on their hay, eyes following her movements.

The barn test went smoothly. Julia was first asked to put a bridle with a figure-eight noseband on a horse. Then she had to bandage a back leg with a polo bandage in a method similar to run-downs. The horse she chose stood quietly, and Julia easily passed the second stage of the test. The woman shook her hand before departing from the barn.

"The stewards want to see you at 10 tomorrow morning. Don't be late."

Sometimes trainers suggest that following the first two stages of the training test, the final session of questioning by the racing stewards is relatively easy. Yet for Julia, this part was perhaps the most intimidating. Other than signing her licences, Julia had avoided contact with the racing stewards as a truant student might avoid the watchful eye of the principal. She knew that these three men held the ultimate authority both on the backstretch and during the races.

Thursday morning the stewards kept Julia waiting for nearly half an hour. Entries were being made for Saturday's card and the racing secretary had outranked Julia's test with an issue for their attention. Finally, the stewards called her into their expansive office. Each steward sat behind his own desk set haphazardly against various walls in the room. One of the men asked Julia to close the door, and then she remained standing in the centre of the room as they began to question her regarding the rules of racing.

There seemed to be no semblance of order to their questions as each steward simply fired out another question while she was scarcely recovering from the last answer.

"What is a walkover?"

"Give me the time limit for the drug Acepromazine."

"How do you claim a horse?"

"What would you have to do if your horse gets put on the starter's list?"

"Why do you want your trainer's licence, young lady?"

The final question took Julia by surprise. She stopped, flustered. Why did she want her trainer's licence? Was it because just three years previously, she had walked onto the Woodbine backstretch terrified of horses? Was it to prove to Antonio Descartes that she was just as good as he was? Was it to prove to her friends and family that she could make it to the top of the racing world? Or was it because Carl had told her that she needed to turn her life around?

"Because I want to win races," she answered firmly.

The steward who had asked the question laughed. He smiled at Julia. "You'll get your chance to prove that. By the authority of the Ontario Jockey Club and the Ontario Racing Commission, we grant the licence of assistant trainer. After a period of one year, you may reapply, without testing, for the licence of public stable trainer. Congratulations."

Julia's heart was beating so wildly that she could scarcely hear the men talking. She vaguely remembered thanking each of them before she stumbled from the room. It was like a dream come true. She couldn't be threatened or pushed around anymore. She now held the power and the authority of a top position on the backstretch.

Chapter Thirty-five

Maurice quickly closed the door to his tack room. Julia wasn't due to stop by for at least an hour, and he didn't want to be disturbed. Lighting a cigarette, he reached behind the television set to a spot that only he knew existed. He carefully removed a revolver wrapped in an oil cloth. He pushed away the cloth and checked the gun. The cylinder was loaded and, like the other weapons, the serial number had been carefully erased with a file. He wrapped the gun in its cloth and placed it in a plastic grocery bag. He had already hidden a sawed-off shotgun behind the front seat of his truck late the previous evening. He was anxious to dispose of the weapons before Julia caught wind of his dealings. She was smart and observant, sometimes making it difficult for him to hide that side of his life.

Maurice inhaled deeply on the cigarette, tapping the ashes before he picked up the grocery bag and opened his door. He glanced into the shed. The morning work would soon be finished. He moved into the shed and slid the lock on his door. The motor of his truck turned over once and then started as he laid the bag on the seat beside him. He tossed the cigarette out of the window and shifted into gear, taking the back road towards the west gate. It would be less likely that Julia would see him on this route.

"*Tôt ou tard*," he thought aloud as he drove out of the gate and onto the highway. "Sooner or later, Julia will know."

Lighting another smoke, Maurice drove in silence towards Niagara Falls. Twenty minutes later, he turned off of the highway onto MacLead Road, making his way towards the motel where he was to make the exchange.

Maurice pulled into the parking lot of the motel and stepped out of his truck. He glanced at the numbers on the room doors, the memorized number firmly in his head. Moving to a particular room, he tapped lightly on the door.

The door opened to reveal an older, blonde woman. Maurice moved into the room, glancing around to make sure that no one else was present. The woman nodded at the empty room. Maurice pushed the door shut.

"*Tu l'as dit à ton père?*" asked Maurice, his blue eyes penetrating into the woman's face. ("Did you tell your father?")

She quickly dropped her eyes.

"*Oui,*" she answered quickly. "*Il viendra quand il pourra.*" ("He'll come when he can.")

Maurice looked at her fear thoughtfully. "*Très intéressant.*" ("Very interesting.") She cringed as he reached a hand towards her.

"Why are you so afraid?" he asked quietly in English, but he knew the answer. Her father kept her informed. His link with Maurice was long-standing, and she knew just how cruelly Maurice could treat those who crossed him.

The woman didn't answer. Lines of worry and age creased her forehead.

Maurice's voice was quiet. "*Il est peu probable qu'il viendra.*" ("It's unlikely that he'll come.")

"*Il m'a parlé de toi,*" the woman whispered. ("He told me about you.")

Maurice smiled. *Quel dommage! Elle avait beaucoup souffert.* (What a pity! She had suffered a lot.) He leaned forward and drew her to him. "*Souvenez-vous de ceci?*" he whispered in her ear. ("Remember this?")

Maurice kissed her, drawing the woman away from her fear, reminding her of the type of man he had once been to her. He glanced briefly at the bed, and then discarded the thought. He was here on business, and the woman had aged. She was not as beautiful as she had once been. *Principalement en raison de ses actions.* (Mostly because of his actions.)

"Do you have the money?" asked Maurice, his question this time in English. He released her and lit a cigarette. Her fear was probably a good thing considering the circumstances. He handed her the cigarette and she took it, inhaling in quick puffs and finally looking directly at him. The woman nodded briefly and moved towards the dresser to retrieve an envelope. Maurice took the envelope and quickly counted the bills.

"*N'aie par peur*," he told her. ("Don't be afraid.") He opened the door. He had left the weapons in his truck.

"*Tu viens?*" he asked. ("Are you coming?")

She nodded again and followed him out of the room. Maurice retrieved the items from the truck and handed her the bags. She glanced nervously into the grocery bags. Maurice sat behind the wheel and placed his key in the ignition. He had not said hello to her, and he didn't say good-bye. He started the engine and shut the door as she backed away with the bags. Her eyes dropped to the ground and Maurice drove out of the parking area.

Chapter Thirty-six

Julia made several new demands from Ricky VanNes once she safely had her assistant trainer's licence. Ricky grumbled but raised her pay to $400 a week and $50 a win. Julia knew that with the two or three races the outfit was winning each week, it would prove a lucrative addition to her pay.

"Just think of it this way, Ricky," Julia had said. "If you come up with a positive, I lose my licence as well. I'll be watching this outfit that much closer."

Vern had teased her friend about the increased demands. "You should have asked for $50 across the board," she said. "You know damn well that man's making 10 per cent for win, place, or show."

As Julia continued to work for the outfit, she found that she often disagreed with the training choices that Ricky was making. She tried not to argue with her boss, but as she had a primary interest in winning races, she often added her opinion. Ricky had entered a colt by the name of Local Connection into a race that ran 6 ½ furlongs. Julia knew they had previously discussed that this particular horse seemed to want to go farther than 6 furlongs. When Julia discovered the horse in the shorter race on the overnight sheet, she was irritated.

"Why the hell didn't you enter him for the mile and a sixteenth?" Julia asked that evening.

"They didn't write a race for him." Ricky scowled. "That was the only place that I could enter him."

"They did write a race with his conditions on the very same day and look at this..." Julia pointed to the overnight. "It went as the 10th."

"He's running farther than last time, Julia."

"Yeah right, by half a furlong."

"Can you get off my case?" Ricky looked annoyed and grabbed the overnight. "I'm the trainer here, and you work for me."

Julia gave up. The next morning she went into the stall to pull the bridle off the colt after he tracked, and asked the exercise rider how he'd trained.

"Like he's sitting on a win." The man grinned. "I hear he's entered tomorrow."

"For 6 ½ furlongs. We both know that he wants to go farther." Julia shrugged.

The rider gave her a quizzical look as he pulled the saddle from the horse and took the bridle.

"What do you want to do, Julia?" he asked.

She stopped putting the shank on the horse and glanced at the man, a plan beginning to form. She stepped to the door of the stall and looked up and down the shed. Ricky was nowhere in sight.

"How about we warm him up?" she asked the rider quietly. "I'll make sure there's 10 to win on him for you."

The rider nodded. "Ricky'll have your head if he finds out. Better keep it quiet. If the horse doesn't run well, you can blame it on the distance, but if he wins…"

"We both go to the bank," said Julia, smiling.

The rider smiled back. "I'm going to like working with you. What time do you want me here?"

"Come by at two. The horse is entered in the sixth race. I'll post one of the grooms at the end of the shed to watch for Ricky, but I doubt he'll show. He likes to watch the races from a comfortable chair in the clubhouse."

Julia was nervous the next afternoon. VanNes was in an exuberant mood, and Julia thought that he would never leave the barn for the grandstand. Julia knew better than to act any differently from normal race-day procedures. She made it a point never to run any of the horses, but stayed at the barn and listened for results from the loudspeakers. The groom running the horse knew what was going on, and Julia knew that he was struggling to keep from blurting a hint to the boss.

"If you want to cash a bet, keep your mouth shut," Julia had said to the man.

True to his word, the rider appeared at two, and Julia tacked the horse. The unusual pre-race treatment excited the colt. Julia gave the rider a leg up onto the dancing colt. She took him a turn while he tightened the girth.

"Just jog him lightly around the shed for 20 minutes," she said. "I hope that's enough." The rider grinned down at her as he took a racing hold on the horse. "Whatever you say, boss."

Julia had the uneasy feeling that people were watching. She cleaned the stall and set out bath water. She knew it would only be a matter of time before Ricky got wind of what they were doing. She'd have to tell the man herself before someone else had the chance.

Coming out of the freshly disinfected stall, Julia just about jumped at the sound of a voice from behind. Maurice was leaning on the outside rail as the horse jogged between them.

"Do you want me to make a bet?" he asked quietly. Julia quickly glanced around. "It's all right. The sheds already know what you're doing." Maurice chuckled.

"Can you put 10 to win on for the exercise rider?" asked Julia. She dug into her jeans pocket. "And 50 to win for me?"

Maurice smiled. He took the money from her outstretched hand.

"I'll make the bet late so the crowd doesn't realize there's something going down," he said. "It'll keep the odds high."

When the tack came off the horse, Julia could scarcely hold the animal on the ground. The rider dropped the saddle across the shed.

"I gotta run, Julia," the rider said. "I want to make the windows."

The groom grabbed the shank.

"We'd better bathe him," said Julia. "I can see the sweat mark from the saddle. It's a warm day. He'll be dry by the paddock."

The colt was bucking and lunging. Julia hoped that she hadn't made a mistake.

"Try not to lose him," she said nervously to the groom.

"Don't worry, Julia. I've got him. I'll see you in the test barn." He waved to her and moved down the road toward the gap.

The colt went off at 40 to one odds and won the race by nearly 10 lengths. Julia didn't know whether to laugh or to cry. Part of her wished that she'd boxed the exacter with the rest of the field. Regardless, she had made a pile of money. Maurice handed her the mutual's ticket after the race, and she shoved it in her pocket. She'd cash it tomorrow before the races, early when no one was watching.

Maurice held and kissed her tenderly, igniting the passion of shared conspiracy. Racing was a terribly exciting business. The stakes were high, but when you came out on top, the feeling of euphoria had no comparison. The only people who truly understood the overwhelming thrill were those who worked in the business.

Vern and Crazy Bill met up with Julia and Maurice at the end of the day. Bill ribbed Julia about the win.

"You could have given me some idea that you were going to win that race," he said. "I would have loved to have even $2 on him. It paid over $80 for the win."

Both Julia and Maurice remained silent.

Maurice drove them to the Pit Stop, holding Julia possessively against his body.

Ricky VanNes made an unusual appearance at the bar. He walked over to the table where the four friends were eating.

"Don't be cheap, Ricky. Why don't you buy your assistant trainer a beer?" asked Vern. "We all know that you had money on that horse."

Ricky had obviously been drinking. He held his beer loosely and grinned at the four people seated at the table. Julia's back was turned to her boss. She didn't have the desire to speak to him about the horse or the race at that time. Maurice was leaning against the wall, quietly studying them in his usual manner.

"She hashn't had her inishiashon yet." VanNes swayed. "Kinda like the key to the quarter pole. A blow job for the trainer."

Julia froze. Vern stared at the hard glint in her eyes.

"Oh, shit," Vern mumbled.

"Yeah," Ricky said. He didn't seem to realize that he'd crossed any type of line. "I had a long talk last year with your old buddy Tony Descartes, and I think…"

Julia was on her feet, holding her beer in her right hand. She glared at the man who was her boss. He grinned back and adjusted his tie. He was still wearing the suit that he proudly wore each race day to saddle horses. Julia could feel Maurice stirring beside her.

"Let me handle this asshole," she said quietly to her lover. Maurice stayed put.

"Oh, shit," said Vern. "There's going to be a fight. Nobody ever mentions Descartes around Julia."

VanNes was laughing at his own humour and the reaction that he'd obviously gained from Julia. There was a hush in the immediate area of the bar, as the patrons realized that something was about to happen.

Julia glared into the laughing eyes of her boss and then lifting her beer above his hair, calmly poured the remains of the bottle over his head. His laughing expression turned to disbelief.

"Sorry, Ricky. Seeing as how you're such a dick and want a blow job, I thought you needed cooling off." She smirked at him. "Now who's laughing?"

The beer ran down his hair and onto his suit, drenching the tie and neatly pressed shirt. Ricky's hands were clenched into fists.

"You bitch!" he yelled at Julia.

The owner of the bar had moved from behind the counter. Maurice stood up. Julia braced herself. She knew that Ricky would probably strike out. He brought his fists up in an angry gesture.

There was a sudden crash. Startled, Julia glanced over her shoulder. The back window of the establishment disintegrated as Sandra's heavy Volvo crashed through the wall. Patrons ran to get out of the way. Maurice grabbed Julia and pulled her back, towards the counter. Behind the wheel was Ned Nickelson, his eyes glazed over in a drunken stupor. Ricky's anger was lost in the chaos of the moment.

Chapter Thirty-seven

There was a sick filly in the barn. Julia was very concerned, checking the temperature of the two-year-old every two hours. She finally called Dr. Nichols just before feed time.

"Doc, I'm worried. The temperature of this filly has risen steadily for the last four hours."

Now in the stall, the veterinarian used his stethoscope to listen to the horse's lungs and heart. "Did she eat her lunch?" he asked.

Julia shook her head.

"Hasn't touched any hay or water either. She just hangs her head."

"Use the oral syringe to try to get her some water. I'll give her some Banamine to bring down the fever."

The vet went to get the needle, and Julia put a shank on the filly, leading the reluctant horse out of its stall.

The Banamine didn't work. The filly's temperature continued to rise, and Julia called the vet back at 7 a.m.

"A hundred and five," said the vet. "This horse should be dead. I'll give her a vitamin jug and some more Banamine. It's a virus, Julia. There's not much more I can do."

The legs of the filly were swelling. Instead of the smooth curves of a thoroughbred racehorse, the legs were stumpy pegs, nearly three times their regular size. The vet said it was unusual for the fever to move into the extremities.

"You better get a cold water hose on her legs," he said. "The fever could crack the feet. At best, she'll founder. Her racing career may be over."

Julia pulled the horse onto the grass, hoping that it would show some interest in grazing. Turning on the hose, she began pouring water onto the filly's legs from the knees and the hocks down. The frigid water made her hands ache. It was going to be a long night, but she knew that she had to bring the fever down.

It was nearly one in the morning when Maurice took the hose from Julia. "I'll keep it going 'til morning. You go get some sleep."

Wearily, Julia rose from the overturned bucket where she'd been seated and stretched her aching body. Her hands were numb with cold. The young filly remained fixed in the same spot, its dark bay head resting within inches of where Julia had sat hunched on the bucket. Julia looked sympathetically at the horse.

"The fever has stopped rising, but it's not going down yet," she said softly to Maurice. She handed him the thermometer. Maurice kissed her gently.

"I won't let her die. Go and get some sleep. I'll see you at morning feed."

Julia fed the outfit at 4:30 a.m. As she walked over to where Maurice held the hose on the filly's front legs, she ran a hand down the enlarged limbs. Despite the cold water, Julia could feel the heat radiating from the legs. She knew that unless they could get the heat out of the legs, the horse was sure to founder. Taking the hose, she relieved Maurice of his night-time post.

The vet returned at 5.30. Ricky VanNes came to the back side of the shed. Julia had not bothered to tell him about the horse last night. He scowled at Julia.

"We have horses to track."

"When the grooms arrive, I'll get them to spell me off on the hose," she answered wearily.

VanNes studied the sick horse. Its head hung listlessly on Julia's left shoulder, the eyes partially closed. The vet had an IV line in the neck and was administering another jug. He had started the filly on massive doses of antibiotics.

"Maybe we should just let the thing die," said Ricky gruffly. "She's insured for $60,000."

Julia was too tired and shocked to respond. Doctor Nichols was leaning on the filly's neck holding the jug. He glared across at VanNes.

"I'm going to pretend that I didn't hear you say that. No insurance company will pay if they think that the horse could have been saved."

The vet pulled the IV line from the filly's neck and pressed a thumb onto the site to stop any further bleeding. He completely ignored Ricky and turned his instructions to Julia.

"I'm going to draw some blood samples and send them to the lab to see if we can identify this virus. Get one of your grooms to go through the stall and try to recover a stool sample." The vet looked at Julia kindly. "You're doing a good job. It's because of your care that this horse is still alive. I wish there were more trainers with that type of heart on the backstretch."

For three more days and nights, Julia and Maurice kept the cold water constantly on the filly's legs. The swelling reduced in the back limbs but the front legs weren't responding to the cold. The skin on the legs split, and large gaping wounds of pink and white flesh appeared. Flies buzzed around the open sores as Julia continued to pour cold water onto the legs.

The fever finally responded to the vet's ministrations. Slowly, the front legs reduced in size, and the filly took her first handful of hay, eating directly from Julia's hand as she stroked the sick horse between the ears. Gus came by and pulled the shoes, studying the bottoms of the feet for signs of laminitis. The blacksmith showed Julia a pink line just inside the wall of the hoof.

"That's founder," he said, "but it's not bad. Your cold water treatment stopped the inflammation from becoming too severe."

Doctor Nichols still appeared every few hours to see how the filly was doing, and VanNes, mercifully, stayed away. The flies around the open wound were troublesome, and within a week, the flesh on the filly's front legs was crawling with fat, white maggots. Julia spent every spare hour with the filly, letting her graze on tender shoots of grass. She sat on a bucket and pulled the hundreds of maggots from the filly's legs.

One dark afternoon, as Julia was pulling maggots from the open wounds, she looked up to see Carl standing in the shed.

"I'm glad to see you," he said. "I heard about your sick horse. You are the talk of the backstretch."

"I couldn't just let her die," answered Julia wearily.

"No," replied Carl softly. "You wouldn't let a horse die if you could save it. I hear that you not only saved its life, but Gus says that you stopped her from foundering."

Julia stroked the filly on her neck. The horse followed her everywhere without a lead shank attached. There was a connection that had appeared with the constant care.

"I have a horse for sale" said Carl. "He has excellent conformation but doesn't want to be a racehorse. He's sound, not a scratch on his legs. You said once that you had friends in the hunter business. The owners want a thousand for the horse, but I'll tell your friends $1200 if you can get them here today. The other two hundred is yours."

Julia was a little startled at this offer. She hadn't even talked to her friends in over a year and wasn't sure if they'd be able to drop everything and make the three-hour trip to Fort Erie today. She wondered why Carl was making such a kind offer when there were many people on the track who would gladly purchase the horse for a thousand, knowing that it was easy to make money on so cheap a deal. It was as if Carl was reading her thoughts.

"Julia, you deserve to get some breaks. You've been handed the shitty end of the fork too often on this track. Make the call as soon as you can. I can only hold the horse for you for today. There have already been others inquiring."

Julia picked up the lead shank and led the filly back to her stall.

"I'll go make the call right now," she said.

She hooked up the webbing and crossbar, making sure the horse had lots of hay in the stall. She moved back to where Carl stood waiting in the sunshine.

"I don't know what to say, Carl." Julia's voice broke and she shook her head to clear it of the intense emotions. "Thanks for being my friend."

Carl sold his grey gelding to the hunter friends that Julia called. True to his word, after they'd loaded the horse onto the trailer and said good-bye to the new owners, Carl counted out $200 of the cash he'd been handed and gave it to Julia.

"Did you make any money on this sale?" asked Julia.

"No, I promised the owners a thousand. Your happiness is more important. I don't need much."

"Well, thank you," replied Julia. "I guess I owe you."

Carl studied her intently for a moment.

"You don't owe me anything, Julia. You don't owe anybody anything. Just do me a favour and look after yourself."

Julia smiled and stretched her hands into the warm summer air.

"Things are going pretty good right now, Carl. I have money, a job as assistant trainer, and a man who is pretty good to me. I also have a very good friend named Carl who seems to care."

It was nearly a month before the filly was well enough to be loaded onto a trailer and sent to the farm. At the peak of the illness, she had lost so much weight that Julia could count every rib. Her hips stuck out in sharp contrast to the considerable lack of flesh and muscle tone. Julia fed the filly hot mashes of barley and corn with molasses so that she could regain the nearly 200 pounds that she'd lost. Doctor Nichols gave her some zinc oxide ointment that was the eventual miracle that allowed the horrible leg wounds to heal with new baby skin.

Julia watched the trailer pull away with the filly, glad that the horse had survived. Ricky VanNes, standing just behind her, cleared his throat.

"Maybe you can pay more attention to the rest of the outfit now." He sounded annoyed, and Julia turned to look at her boss. "I want you to take some horses to Greenwood for the fall meet. You will train them so that I can stay here at the pool."

Julia was waiting to see if Maurice was going to Greenwood. One day when she'd finished afternoon feed, she found Maurice diligently studying the racing form in their room. When she sat down on the bed beside him, he put the form down.

"Well, my dear, I think that it's time we claimed ourselves a horse."

Maurice stared at Julia, his blue eyes reading right through her. It made her uncomfortable when he studied her in this way, but she was a little surprised at his announcement.

"It's just about the end of the season, Maurice. What exactly do you mean by 'we'?"

Maurice smiled.

"I've already put five grand in the office," he said. "I want you to make the claim. I don't like being the front runner. I'll put up the money. You officially own and train any horses that we acquire."

"You trust me not to run away with your money or horses?" Julia asked.

Maurice's eyes turned cold. The look he gave her was truly frightening. She knew in a flash that even if she wanted, she would never dare to double-cross this man. Sometimes Julia saw a level of evil in him that was terrifying. As quickly as she saw Maurice's answer, he smiled and the look was gone.

"Of course I trust you," he said. The answer had been clear.

Maurice picked up the racing form and pointed to a race for Saturday. "We need a horse such as this gelding. Hitting the board to make us look legitimate. My colt is set. I'm going to make the equipment change that you suggested and then plug him in. The odds will be high."

Julia shook her head at his confusing language. She couldn't believe what she was hearing, if she was reading through Maurice's words correctly. She was astounded.

"But Maurice," she said. "That's illegal! You're talking about fixing races!"

Maurice put the form down and walked over to shut the tack room door. He turned and smiled at Julia, the cold, hard look frightening her deeply.

"I always knew that you were a smart girl."

Chapter Thirty-eight

"I can't do it," said Julia. "That's extortion, fraud. If we're caught, we'll go to prison."

Maurice's silence was ominous. Julia couldn't believe that he'd try to push her into something like this when he claimed that he was in love. Maurice sat down close to Julia. She tried to back away from the man who was intimidating in a way that she'd never experienced.

Maurice was frightening Julia. She felt that he wasn't giving her a choice. He touched her hair and drew her towards him. Part of Julia was fighting him, but there was still a well-founded trust that wasn't easily removed with the present behaviour. She let him kiss her, astounded with the fierceness. It was as if he was a different man. She pushed against his chest, trying to draw away from the powerful embrace.

"Please Maurice, you're scaring me," she said in a soft voice.

Maurice obliged, releasing her from his grasp. He lit a cigarette, filling his lungs with the smoke and exhaling abruptly. His eyes had not lost the hard glint and Julia, for the first time in their relationship, wanted to avoid this man.

"I really don't want to be a part of this," Julia began quietly.

"You already are," Maurice said. "Don't think that half the backstretch doesn't know how you set that colt up, shedding him before the race so that he could run the distance that was necessary. Everyone that saw you ran for the windows. You made over two grand on that bet, Julia."

"That's not really the same thing as what you're suggesting," Julia replied.

"You are my partner, Julia," said Maurice quietly. "There's going to be some things that you don't like, but you're still my partner. Together we can make a lot of money."

Maurice pointed to a horse in the third race. "Look at the form on this one. Non-winners of three in a lifetime, non-winners of two this year. He still has conditions and has been picking up checks almost every start."

Reluctantly, Julia glanced at the form on the horse. He was right. The horse did appear to be a good claim, in for only 2500. Her interest in claiming a horse was there, Julia had to admit. She began to study some of the other horses in the race.

Maurice finally seemed to relax. This time he took her hand tenderly. The man that Julia knew and loved at last reappeared. She put down the form and glanced at him.

"Why are you doing this to me?" she asked. "I don't understand, Maurice."

"The rider has been bought. John will do whatever we tell him. He has too much to lose if he does otherwise. If you want, I'll keep the colt in my name, but I want you to sign on as trainer. Julia, you have nothing to lose from this partnership and everything to gain."

"But what if we get caught?" she asked.

"How are they going to prove anything?" Maurice put his arm around her shoulders. He was gentle, and she leaned against him.

"But you said that you were going to plug your colt in."

"I have the device. We'll give it to John tomorrow. The perfect race is this weekend. The one with the most to lose is John."

"But what if he says something?"

"You need to stop thinking about the 'buts' my dear girl. I've already got that covered. He won't turn us in."

Julia was quiet, sceptical. She knew that she either stuck with Maurice or she refused to be a part of his plan. Despite knowing him for more than a year, there were still parts of this man that she didn't trust. She had to ask one last question.

"Maurice, what if I turn you in?"

He looked at her.

"You're my partner. You won't turn me in." He took a long drag on his cigarette.

"What if things changed between us? What would you do?" Julia knew that she shouldn't keep persisting but she had to know the answer.

Maurice bent and kissed her on the cheek. "The same thing that I'd do to any two-timing partner." He drew on the cigarette again and stubbed it out in his ashtray before he grasped her chin and looked directly into her eyes.

"I'd kill you."

Julia needed some fresh air. She walked away from the room and into the late September evening. Her running shoes made little noise on the surface of the road. Part of her didn't want to believe that Maurice could possibly be serious, but part of her was afraid that he meant what he said. Until now, he had always been completely honest with her. Yet tonight he had been strangely different, detached, manipulating her in a way that she saw him use on other people. It bothered her that perhaps he had been using her from the start.

His threat did not really frighten her. She looked on it as a warning to tread carefully around the man. She would never turn him in, and she knew that she would join him in his plans. However, Julia also knew that she had to make sure that he could not control her and that she always had the upper hand. Her relationship with Antonio had taught her to always keep part of herself independent in a racetrack relationship. She still had her own tack room, her own private escape in a barn far from Barn 9.

Julia unlocked her tack room door and lay on the bunk, contemplating the proposal that Maurice had presented. She would accept his proposal on the condition that she had control over the training and entries of the horses. She would also tell him that she intended to go to the Greenwood meet to train Ricky's horses, and planned to gallop horses on a farm in Milton for the winter. Any serious claiming or entries would have to occur the following spring.

Julia knew that Maurice still desired her as a lover, and she would use that to bait the man. She fully intended to make this relationship a true partnership. Julia stood up and began to search for the right clothes. It was time to give Maurice a taste of the new Julia. He had to realize that she wouldn't be frightened by his threats, and wasn't going to let a man push her into a corner.

Julia and Maurice talked to John the next morning following training hours. Maurice dropped a small metal circular object into the jockey's hand. John appeared sceptical.

"They video-tape every inch of a race from a lot of angles, boss," he said. "The tail moves in circles when you hit a horse with voltage. What if I get caught?"

Julia moved up to the rider. "I suggest that you don't get caught. Light him up just before the quarter pole. I've been up the stretch tower. The angle is bad there and they won't be able to see what you've done."

Maurice handed John the racing form, pointing to the horse they were interested in claiming. "Know anything about that horse?"

John shook his head. "I don't gallop for that trainer, but one of the guys who works on the gate walks hots for the outfit. I'll ask him for you."

Julia left the men talking. She had to make the draw. They had entered the colt for Saturday. When Julia entered the racing office, the large front room was filled with trainers and jockeys' agents. The racing secretary sat behind the glass, organizing the entries.

"The sixth in the book will go as the first race," he announced as the room grew quiet. "Three and four-year-old maiden fillies. Claiming set at 4000. Exacter betting; first half of the early double." He paused as he loaded the numbered disks. He drew a number and turned over the first entry. "Logan's Secret, four; Sunshine On My Shoulder, two; Buster's Landing, five."

The voice droned on and Julia watched the other trainers. After drawing post positions for the first race, the racing secretary called out the rider's names for each mount.

"I've got Daryl on two different horses. Who do you want to ride?" He glanced up at the jockey's agent who represented the rider.

The agent checked his notes and gave the name of one of the horses.

"Is Tyler here?" asked the secretary. "He needs a rider."

The woman taking down notes and organizing the entries went to page the trainer. Julia knew that it was important to be at the draw. Sometimes jockeys' agents would tell the racing secretary to put a rider on a horse without consulting the trainer. It was extremely difficult to change a rider once the overnights came out at 2 o'clock in the afternoon.

The colt's race went as the seventh. Julia had been hoping for a triactor race, but it was at least a full field. The colt drew the fourth post position, an excellent post for the six-furlong race. John was riding, of course, with the five-pound weight allowance given an apprentice jockey. Julia left the draw to tell Maurice the news. He'd want to see the overnight so that they could study the competition. Even with the horse being set up, sometimes a trainer entered a superior horse that was being dropped from a higher claiming price to steal the win and be eligible for the starter allowance races. They would have to study the form before making their final decision. Julia knew that with the addition of a tongue tie, an equipment change that didn't have to be announced at the time of entry, the horse was likely to win regardless of any device that John might use. She had suspected a couple of starts ago that the horse was swallowing his tongue at the top of the stretch.

Vern and Julia arrived back from the Pit Stop by 9 o'clock to find Maurice playing cards with John and Crazy Bill. There were a couple of new faces at the table, rough-looking individuals even by racetrack standards. Maurice ended the game shortly after the girls arrived. The men left, grumbling about lost money. Crazy Bill gestured to Vern but she shook her head. They were in the middle of one of their numerous lovers' spats and Julia chuckled as Maurice chased him out of the room.

"I'll run your colt on Saturday," said Vern. "You don't have to pay me. One of these days he's going to win."

"I hope so," said Maurice, lighting a cigarette. He glanced at Julia, his eyes asking if she'd said anything to her friend.

She ignored him. Julia had made it a point not to let him near her since he had made his threat clear. She flirted with him and teased him, but when he tried to hold her, she turned him down. She was sleeping elsewhere, but knew that it didn't stop him from wanting her. She was playing a game, and for a change, he was the victim. In some ways she found the situation amusing.

There was a tap on the door and Crazy Bill stuck his head into the room. "Maurice, we need you. There's a fight, and John just got hit."

It still astonished Julia that Maurice could move so quickly when necessary. He stubbed out his smoke and was out the door before Vern or Julia had a chance to comprehend what Crazy Bill had announced. The women followed them out into the shed, Julia watching as Maurice sprinted for the far end where the commotion had occurred. One of the men from the gambling game was holding John while the other was about to hit their rider.

Maurice didn't stop. His fist smashed into the face of the man holding John and with his elbow he viciously jabbed the other man in the side of the head. Both of the strangers fell. The one man was holding his nose.

"Son of a bitch, I think you broke it!" he said.

The other stranger jumped back onto his feet. Maurice hit him twice more before he had a chance to strike.

"Stay down." He scowled at the man.

Julia and Vern had moved down the shed towards the fight. Maurice turned to the girls. His hands were covered with blood and his eyes flashed. Vern had never seen this type of behaviour from the man, and took an involuntary step away from Maurice.

"Julia, you need to leave," said Maurice quietly. "I don't want you to see this." Julia stood where she was until Vern pulled at her arm.

"He's right, Julia," she said. "Let's get out of here."

She tugged at Julia's arm again and reluctantly, Julia followed her down the shed. Crazy Bill also had the good sense to disappear, taking

John. The black woman kept glancing at her friend as they moved in silence away from Barn 9. Finally, Vern had to say something.

"Jesus, Julia, that man is scary." Her friend's voice was hushed. "He acted like he was going to kill those two. I sure hope that he never loses it around you."

Julia was quiet. Maurice had scared her with the intensity of his sudden violence. She was terrified that he might.

Chapter Thirty-nine

Julia grasped the tongue of the gelding and pulled it out the side of the mouth. The horse tried to draw back its head in protest but Maurice had a firm hold on the opposite rein of the bridle. Julia dipped the canvas strap into the water pail and then wrapped the moistened tie around the gelding's tongue. She released the tongue but kept a firm hold on the ends of the strap and tied it in a knot under the gelding's chin.

Vern doubled the shank back on the D-bit and led the horse out into the cool October day. It was overcast, and the heat of the summer was a distant memory. Julia and Maurice followed Vern to the gap. There was no need to stop for the number as Maurice had already acquired the clip from the gap attendant and hooked it onto the bridle. Julia threw the gelding's halter on the ground beside the gap. It would be there when they returned from the race. Never again would she loop a halter around her neck.

The walk to the paddock was uneventful. The gelding played with the tongue tie, trying desperately to unknot the irritating piece of cord. Julia moved to the paddock stall that indicated the fourth post position and nervously waited for the paddock judge to tell the grooms to "put them in."

At the call, Vern entered the stall with the gelding, and John's valet placed the numbered saddle cloth on the horse's back. Julia reached up and straightened her side of the cloth. The saddle was put next on the back and the colt stood calmly, though twitching with excitement. Julia reached below the horse's belly and took the elastic girth that the valet held. She pulled down and then up to avoid catching the skin of the animal. She drew the single saddle leather into the buckle and pulled the girth all the way to the top and hooked it into the last hole.

"I'm right up," she told the valet. Julia felt the valet tighten the girth on the opposite side of the saddle.

"Right up on this side as well," he announced in return.

He placed the overgirth on the saddle. Taking the strap end in her hand, Julia pulled the elastic away from the horse and then brought the leather down and under the belly of the animal into the waiting valet's hand. He put the leather strap through the buckle and Julia then pulled with all her strength on the strap, finally looping it into a hole when she thought it was tight. The valet secured the end of the strap so that it wouldn't flap against the horse as he ran.

"Take him a turn please, Vern," Julia told her friend.

John had come out of the jockeys' room and stood beside Julia and Maurice. He was smiling, and flexed his whip in his hand.

"Any last minute instructions?" he asked.

"Just win the race," said Julia.

John laughed as he glanced at Maurice. "I intend to do just that," he replied.

Vern had stopped the horse in front of the group.

"Riders up!" yelled the paddock judge.

Julia gave John a leg up onto the gelding and Vern led them away. Maurice touched Julia's arm briefly.

"I have a bet to make. I'll see you at the rail."

Julia moved through the crowd of horsemen to the track. The post parade had just finished and she watched closely as John warmed up the horse. Vern was standing at the rail chatting with the ambulance driver. The paddock security guard pulled back the rail to let the ambulance onto the track, effectively ending the conversation.

Julia checked the mutual board. The horse was at 99 to one, the longest odds that could be displayed on the board. Vern had moved over to her friend.

"Think he has a chance today?" she asked.

"You never know in a horse race," replied Julia, a standard backstretch reply.

"Has he ever worn a tongue tie before?"

"No."

"Might make a difference."

Julia glanced at her friend. "I hope so."

Maurice wandered out to meet them as the race caller announced that they were at the post.

"And they're off!"

The gelding broke cleanly and was sitting around fifth, three lengths off the lead. He was in a good spot if they didn't get boxed in by other horses. By the far turn of the backstretch, the gelding had moved into third and was only a length off the lead. Julia felt excited. It was beginning to look good. As they rounded the turn at the quarter pole, John was crouched over the gelding's neck, hitting the animal every stride.

The crowd roared as the horses raced up the stretch, the gelding now in the lead by more than a length. Julia began to shout.

"Come on! You can do it!"

She was dimly aware of the others around her yelling. As the horses flew under the wire, the gelding was in front by half a length. Julia was jumping in the air, tears of joy and disbelief falling from her eyes. She looked at Maurice, standing at the rail and smiling.

"We won, Maurice! We won!" Julia yelled over the thunder of the crowd and galloping hooves. Maurice put his arm around her and pulled her close.

"You bet we did," he told her happily. He leaned towards her and whispered in her ear. "And we made thousands."

Winning a race with a horse that you have worked on for countless hours, and had hoped and dreamed would make it to the winner's circle filled Julia with a euphoria that she had never experienced. She had scarcely heard Maurice's words as she gazed in wonder at the gelding still running down the backstretch. Finally, she turned and smiled at Maurice.

"Would you see that?" muttered Vern. "John got run off with after the race. The outrider has to pull them up."

Julia laughed as she again looked at the backstretch of the track and saw the outrider with the gelding. She was aware of Maurice pressing a ticket into her hand. Julia glanced down at the mutual ticket, her hand beginning to shake as she comprehended what she held in her palm. She looked at Maurice, who kissed her tenderly and then turned to watch the gelding pulling up in front of the group. He had bet $100 across the board on the horse.

Vern glanced at the ticket that Julia held.

"Holy shit!" she said. "That horse went off at 80 to one. You guys are wealthy!"

"Easy money, easy game," said Maurice quietly.

John's valet had taken his whip and Maurice grabbed the rein of the horse. He smiled at Julia again.

"Don't lose it," he said and led the gelding into the winner's circle.

FORT ERIE RACETRACK

June 1990

Chapter Forty

The winning mutual ticket that year built Julia and Maurice an outfit. They claimed four more horses the following spring and managed to be in the money most of that summer. Julia loved training. It presented problems that challenged her mind, and gave satisfaction with the correct solutions. Although they never cashed a bet as substantial as that first winning ticket, there were other opportunities to fix races, and John was always a willing accomplice. For the most part, Julia forced Maurice to play the game legitimately, the horses themselves pulling in thousands of dollars in purse money each racing season.

Life on the backstretch never lost its exciting edge. There was always a loose horse, or a crazy horse, or a horse that simply needed that extra attention and love. Julia never sold another horse to Gregory. Although she had forgiven herself for selling Cranky Dickson to the man, she didn't forget. Horses that were finished with racing she sold privately to her friends in the hunter business.

Julia had left Ricky VanNes after the Greenwood meet the year that Maurice's gelding finally broke its maiden. She'd had enough of the man and his uncaring ways. She went back to walking hots for Taylor and Miranda, and running horses on race days. This left her time to train her own horses in the latter part of the morning. Maurice usually had the stalls cleaned and the cold ones walked by the time that Julia reached their barn. John would arrive to track the horses each day immediately following break and Julia would walk down to the gap with the horses, leaning on the rail and chatting with the other trainers as they watched the late morning workouts.

Julia had made a particularly good claim late the previous summer. Vern complained about the gelding Stand Proudly that dragged her back from the paddock, but Julia was surprised they'd gotten the horse for only $2500. They ran the gelding back for $3200 and he ran second. Julia entered him again for $3200 and he ran another second. He ran second for $4000 the following weekend. Julia began to tease the horse, suggesting that he had "seconditis."

"Nothing wrong with seconds," Taylor had said to her. "That's $1000 a week in purse money, and he keeps his conditions."

However, the horse finally won and then won twice more before the end of the meet. He quickly became a barn favourite. He was sound and easy to handle. Julia loved to pull Stanley from his stall on dark day afternoons, and scratch him behind his ears as he grazed.

The spring had begun with Vern and Crazy Bill in another heated argument. Vern had lost her temper and slugged Bill, who responded by reporting his girlfriend to the stewards. The stewards were not impressed with the female black American, and put Vern on a probationary licence.

"You better watch your moves," said Julia to her friend. "It sounds like they have it in for you."

Ironically, it was Julia who would partly cause the trouble that got Vern ruled off.

The two friends had gone for dinner at the Pit Stop. Crazy Bill had walked into the bar, and seeing Vern, had approached her, ready to continue their current argument. Vern had complained as the two women walked back to the racetrack.

"That old pain in the ass. I've a right mind to go to his tack room and steal his beer. Nothing like taking an alcoholic's beer. That'd really piss him off."

"Why don't you?" asked Julia. "You know that he's still down at the Pit. We've got lots of time to slip by his room."

Vern looked at her friend. "You instigator. I think that I just might do that. I still have his combination."

Entering the backstretch by the east gate, the two friends headed towards Barn 2 where Crazy Bill had his tack room. The room was located on the wing of the barn. Vern stopped in front of the door and twirled the combination in the barn lights. After a moment of trying to unlock the door, she dropped the lock and turned to Julia, upset.

"That son of a bitch changed his lock. Some of my stuff is in that room, and I can't get in. I wish I had something to break the lock, that no-good bastard."

Julia, always ready to help, leaned against the door frame of the tack room.

"I got a chisel in my room," she said. "How 'bout we go get that?"

"You're crazy, girl," said Vern. "Don't tempt me. I'd love to break in."

Julia thought of the beer in the room. Far from drunk, it might be fun to obtain another cold one in a clandestine manner. Furthermore, Bill seemed to be getting the upper hand in her friend's relationship recently, and that fact irritated Julia. She wanted to see her friend even the score.

"Come on, Vern. I've got beer in my room and even if you change your mind, at least we can drink to the asshole."

Julia led the way up to Barn 8 where her tack room was located. When they entered Julia's room, she found the heavy chisel and handed it to Vern.

"Well, what do you want to do?" she asked.

Vern turned the tool over in her hand. She grinned at Julia.

"Let's do it."

Julia grabbed two beers out of her fridge, handed one to Vern, and locked the tack room door as they left. It would make for an interesting night in an otherwise dull week.

It didn't take long for the girls to pry the lock from the door frame. Vern entered Crazy Bill's sparse tack room and found the clothes that she had left there. Julia couldn't stop laughing. The whole situation struck her as enormously funny.

"You gonna take his beer?" she asked.

"Shh...," Vern hissed. "I heard something. I bet he's back. He's probably watching."

"You didn't hear anything, Vern. It's just the wind."

"I know I heard something. We're gonna have to get out of here. That bastard wants to get me and this is just the excuse that he needs."

"You gonna take his beer?" Julia asked again.

She couldn't help laughing at Vern's fears. Vern and Crazy Bill were lovers. It was unlikely that he'd turn her in. Little did she realize how thin the line of love could be between two people. It was a lesson that she had yet to learn.

Vern grabbed the beer. "I'm taking the whole damn case. Now let's get out of here."

She followed Julia to the door. Before Julia stepped into the shed, she stopped and listened.

"Vern," she whispered back to her friend. "I think I hear the security van. We're going to have to be quick."

Sure enough, as Julia glanced around the cement block wall of the tack room, she could see the van stopped on the road at the end of the barn. It was unusual for this time of night. Julia could scarcely suppress a giggle. This was turning out to be loads more fun than she'd first imagined. She was getting into this cloak-and-dagger game. She thought briefly of Maurice.

"Head through the washroom when I say 'run.' We'll make for Barn 9. Maurice will help us. He has security paid off."

The girls slipped out of the room. Vern pulled the door closed. The escape went well. They moved through the barns until they were outside Maurice's room, breathless with laughter and the excitement of the chase. Pounding on the door, Julia and Vern tumbled into the tack room to tell Maurice about their adventures.

He quietly listened to their tale. "I was wondering where you'd got to," he said to Julia.

Julia's hand came up to her mouth. "Oh, Vern, the chisel! I left the chisel outside Crazy Bill's room. We have to go back. I want my chisel back!"

"We can't go back," said Vern. "By now Crazy Bill is there for sure, and knows that we've taken his beer. Besides, I think that security is on to us."

"I want my chisel back," said Julia.

"You should never go back to the scene of the crime," Maurice said.

"Come on, Vern, where's your backbone?" asked Julia. "We escaped security once tonight already. They aren't the brightest ones on this backstretch. We can slip by them again."

"I'm on a probationary licence, Julia. I can't afford to get caught running through the barns at 1 a.m." said Vern. She looked at Julia's expectant face and gave in to her friend's whim. "Oh, what the hell! Let's go!"

Maurice shook his head at the two girls as they ran back into the shed. He said that the mission was doomed, but Julia wasn't about to listen to reason.

"I'll be waiting for you girls when you decide to come back and keep me awake half the night," he called to their retreating backs.

It didn't take long for Julia and Vern to reach Crazy Bill's room. Julia opened the door and walked into the room, searching for her chisel in the dark.

"He's been here," said Vern quietly.

"How the hell do you know that?"

"I know. I didn't leave this pile of clothes here." Vern pointed to some of Bill's clothes on the bed.

"They were there before," said Julia.

"No, they weren't. I was sitting there searching for my own stuff."

The sound of an engine stopped both girls from talking. The security van was moving quickly up the main road. Julia stuck her head out the door at just the wrong moment. The driver slammed on the brakes, and the van skidded on the gravel. They heard a door slam and footsteps.

"Oh shit," whispered Vern.

"Run!" yelled Julia and the two friends leaped out the door of the tack room and raced down the shed. The bobbing flashlight of the security guard pursued them from close behind.

"Stop!" shouted the guard. "Security!"

Julia was laughing. This was just too much fun. Fit from walking and running horses, it was easy to keep ahead of the guard.

"That's the damn sergeant," said Vern. "There's no way I'm stopping."

"I know that's you, Veronica," shouted the guard. "You need to stop right now."

The girls cut through the washroom and doubled back around the far wing of the tack room block, temporarily fooling the sergeant. Vern was winded.

"I'm not sure how much longer I can run, Julia," she whispered. "I'm carrying too much weight. I'm not as thin as you."

"Can you make Barn 9?" asked Julia.

"No. Let's hide in the can while I catch my breath."

The girls could hear the guard searching on the other side of the shed. It would have been too easy to slip out of the barn without being caught, but Julia had spent the whole evening making unwise decisions.

"Okay," she said and led the way back into the washroom.

The girls went into the stalls and stood on the seats. The sergeant eventually made his way back into the washroom, his flashlight shining around what appeared to be a deserted area. He was about to leave when Vern began to whistle. Julia was astonished as her friend flushed the toilet and walked out of the stall to wash her hands.

The sergeant smiled and shone the light on Vern's face. "I've caught you," he said.

"Do you mind?" Vern glared at him. "I'm trying to wash my hands."

"This is a man's washroom," said the guard, pointing at the urinals.

"That's all there are on this backstretch. I'm not walking all the way to the kitchen just to have a pee."

Julia heard the water running at the sink. She took the opportunity to jump off the toilet seat and walk out of her own stall.

"Ah, there's the other one. I'm surprised at you Julia, running with this one."

Julia didn't bother to answer the man. The security sergeant looked as if he'd been dragged out of bed. His hair was a dishevelled heap instead of its usual neatly combed coiffure. He was still panting, obviously winded from the chase.

"You need to get fit," said Julia. "Can't run a race when you're blowing after the first furlong."

The man scowled at her remark. Vern turned off the tap and calmly dried her hands on a paper towel, taking her time. She turned to leave.

"Where do you think you're going?" asked the guard.

"Back to my room," replied Vern, holding her hands out. "I start work early in the morning."

Julia grinned, enjoying the showdown.

"No, you're not," said the guard. "You girls are coming with me."

Vern rolled her eyes at Julia who couldn't take it anymore and began to laugh.

"He thinks he's a cop," Vern said. "Been watching too much TV."

However, the friends followed the sergeant out of the washroom and piled into the back of the van.

"You can ride up front with me," said the guard to Julia.

Julia was disgusted with the insinuation.

"Fuck you," she said and climbed in beside Vern.

The guard drove back to the security room at the west gate.

"Wait here," he said as he left them to enter the brightly-lit building.

"Oh shit, Julia," said Vern. "I'm screwed. I'm going to be ruled off for this shit."

"Would you shut up," said Julia. "I can't believe that idiot left us alone. We have a moment to get our story straight. Quick. This is what I'm going to say to that bastard when he starts questioning me. Make sure that your story matches."

Vern stopped whining and listened to her friend. By the time the guard returned, the girls were waiting in silence.

"You first, Reinhardt," said the sergeant.

Julia grinned at her friend and gave her the thumbs up salute. She followed the guard into the security office. He led her into the back room and closed the door. Julia didn't like the situation as the man looked her over.

"Nice pad," she said, looking around the room.

"Where's your licence?" asked the guard.

"In my tack room. I don't usually need it to take a pee."

"I've a mind to search you."

Julia glanced at the clock. It was 2 a.m.

"If you lay one finger on me, you asshole, Maurice will cut your balls off and serve for breakfast." Her voice was quiet but the threat was clear.

The guard walked over to his desk and sat on his chair, leaving Julia standing in the middle of the room.

"What were you doing outside of Bill's tack room?" His voice was angry.

"Walking to the washroom," replied Julia.

The guard glanced at this defiant woman.

"Have you been drinking?" he asked suspiciously.

Julia laughed. This was the backstretch. What the hell did he think?

"I'm fucking wasted," she said, although she was far from drunk. The man stood up, obviously disgusted. He opened the door to the front office.

"Wait there," he said. "I'm going to talk to your friend."

The next morning Julia saw Vern going into the stewards' office, followed shortly by the trainer she worked for. Later, Vern told her that her boss had pleaded her case, and the stewards relented, stating that as long as she was off the backstretch by nine each night, she could still work the morning training hours and afternoon races. Then something happened that Julia found unbelievable. Crazy Bill moved in with Vern in the cabin that she rented off the backstretch, and the two lovers got along fabulously for the rest of the season.

The racing stewards never questioned Julia. Vern had been their scapegoat. She was the wrong colour, citizenship, and status. Julia knew that because she was a trainer with horses running consistently, the stewards were willing to overlook a single night's craziness.

Despite the consequences, it had been an enormously amusing experience. It had shown Julia that she could handle herself with any man. They couldn't force her, hurt her, or push her into a corner. That is, with the exception of Maurice. It was scarcely a month later when she unwittingly turned loose the evil that her lover struggled to keep in check. This time she was the victim.

Chapter Forty-one

One of the fillies that Julia had recently claimed was proving to be a handful to keep sound. During a race, the splint bone on one side of her leg shattered and pieces of the bone became embedded in the suspensory ligament and ankle. As a consequence, her ankles were proving a constant source of trouble, and Julia found that she had to alternate between mud and sweat treatments to keep the ankles tight. The feet on the horse also seemed tender, and Julia suspected that she might have navicular disease, but without x-rays, didn't know for certain. The horse was a good runner and had made them more than $1200 since they'd claimed her nearly six weeks ago. However, it was always hit and miss whether she would pass the commission vets on race day.

Julia wanted to drop the filly back in for 2500 in hopes of stealing a win and losing the horse. She leaned against the shed rail and watched as her vet ran a practiced hand down the filly's front legs. Maurice held the shank and listened to the discussion.

"I'd like to tap the ankles and block the feet," said Julia to the vet. "Do you think there's anything left in the ankles, doc?"

The vet put pressure on the ankles with his fingertips. "We could try, but they've been tapped a lot, Julia. Might only get blood."

Maurice spoke up. "Why don't you cut the nerve? We're hoping she gets claimed anyway."

The vet nodded. It was a possible treatment.

"No," said Julia. "I will not nick a horse. It's cruel and inhumane. You know that this filly has so much heart she'd run down the stretch with a broken leg."

"It's a legal procedure," said Maurice.

"That I will never do," said Julia. She looked at the vet. "Tap and cortisone the ankles and block the feet."

The vet nodded again and went to prepare the needles.

"Sometimes I think that you are too soft for this business," said Maurice.

His eyes had that hard glint in them, and Julia knew that he wanted to argue with her decisions. She refused to let him back her into a corner with his intimidating tactics.

"Sometimes someone has to give a shit about the horses," said Julia. "They're the ones doing all the work."

The next week they ran Stand Proudly in an allowance race. A claim had been in for the horse when they had entered him for 4000, and Julia, catching wind of the claim, had forced John to gate scratch the horse. The suspensory ligament had been a little spongy that morning and the commission vet, though unwilling, had obliged. However, the stewards were not impressed. The horse had been the two to five favourite and the mutuals had to return thousands of dollars in refunds.

The allowance race produced a tough field and Stanley was no speedball. Studying the form, Julia realized that without a muddy track, the horse would never run a quarter in 21 seconds, like some of the competition. A muddy track would be a mixed blessing. She was still concerned about the suspensory ligament on the horse. A muddy track could result in blown suspensories and the end of Stanley's racing career. She debated scratching the horse but knew that was nearly impossible with a six-horse field.

Race day was an anxious time for Julia as she prepared the gelding. She knew that the horse was probably in over his head. Vern came by to run Stanley. The big horse was difficult to paddock because he was so strong. He literally dragged her over, bucking and squealing, and then dragged her home again after the race.

The day was hot, and John only jogged the horse for a warm-up, not wanting to over-exert the animal before the tough race. Stand Proudly broke cleanly and held his own toward the back of the pack. Julia watched as the horses rounded the quarter pole, Stanley in his favourite spot on the outside as John moved him into position. Julia couldn't help feeling the excitement of the race as the horses galloped down the stretch. Her gelding was running third.

It happened so fast that Julia wasn't sure initially what had caused the horse to suddenly slow. It was like he'd hit a brick wall. A half furlong from the wire, Stanley stopped galloping and it didn't matter what John did, the horse was going slower and slower. He crossed the wire dead last. When John pulled up in front of them, Julia looked at him expectantly.

"I don't know what happened, Julia," the rider said, jumping off the horse. "He just stopped. He's never done that before."

Julia was suspicious. "Let me take him back, Vern," she said grabbing the shank from her friend.

The horse didn't appear to be acting much different from normal. He began his tiring trek along the stretch towards the gap, pulling Julia along. She glanced at the horse's front legs, cautiously studying the suspensory ligaments. He appeared to be sound. As they moved off the track through the gap, the horse coughed.

Julia looked quickly at the animal, hoping that the cough was only dirt in his nose. In her heart she knew otherwise. By the time they reached the barn, the horse had coughed three more times. She felt tears stinging her eyes. It wasn't fair. The horse was her favourite. She shouldn't have run him over his head in that allowance race.

Maurice was waiting at the barn with the bath water. Julia entered the shed and threw the dirty blinkers under the rail.

"Page the vet, Maurice," she said as she took the animal into his stall and pulled off the bridle. The horse coughed again.

Maurice stood in the doorway of the stall and watched her put the halter on the hot horse. "What's the matter?" he asked quietly.

The horse coughed as she put the shank through the halter. Julia glanced anxiously at the gelding.

"You hear that? He's bleeding."

"Oh shit," said Maurice and left for the racing office to page the vet.

The vet didn't even need to get the endoscope down to the lungs. Halfway down the windpipe, there was so much blood that he quickly withdrew the instrument. He looked sadly at Julia and Maurice.

"Did the commission vet have any indication?" he asked.

"No, he didn't start to cough until we were nearly at the gap," replied Julia. "At least he won't be on the bleeders list."

"He's bleeding bad," said the vet. "I'll treat him. He needs a break for a couple of weeks so that his lungs will heal. Just light training. He may have lost his heart."

Julia adjusted the cooler and looked sadly at the horse. It was her worst fear. Sometimes when a horse bled, they refused to run again. Stanley was such a good racehorse. She didn't think that she'd ever see that happen to this particular horse.

"We'd better drop him in and hope that someone takes him," said Maurice.

"He can run on Lasix," said Julia positively. Maurice looked at her sceptically.

"That's an illegal medication, Julia."

"Only for twenty-four hours," replied Julia.

"You'd have to pull the water and all feed," said the vet. "Otherwise the medication doesn't work."

"You can't pull the water for 24 hours before a race," Maurice said. "Especially in 30-degree weather, Julia."

"Yes, we can," she said. "I'll bed him on peat moss and put him on the bleeder feed, Respond, for training. We can treat him with Lasix and I'll make sure to pre-race him for heat."

Maurice shook his head.

"I hope you don't come up with a positive test," he said. He looked at the horse. "And I hope that he hasn't lost his heart."

Stand Proudly lost his heart. Julia put him on steroids, turning her quiet horse into a grunting stallion. She ran him twice more and then laid him up. Maybe the winter on the farm would help the gelding to forget. Maurice wasn't impressed. It was true that the gelding had earned them nearly $40,000 in the last year and a half but he told Julia he didn't see the financial point of keeping a bleeder.

It had not been that good a summer for Maurice and Julia. They'd made a couple of bad claims, and the outfit was showing the strain. Maurice managed to cash a couple of bets, setting up John to hold horses before they were dropped in for the win. Julia knew that some of the things Maurice was involved with were not strictly legal, but had long since stopped asking the man questions. As long as he continued to treat her well, she didn't want to know the answers. Periodically, rumours filtered back to her about fights and late night poker games.

One night when Julia walked into their tack room, she happened to glance at the top of the fridge and was astounded to see a gun partially hidden by the conditions book. She picked the weapon up and turned it over in her hand. She was acutely aware that Maurice was watching her movements. She had not seen him with a gun since their trip to Finger Lakes many years ago. Part of her had hoped that he had left that type of life behind, and she felt sadly betrayed to find a weapon here at Fort Erie.

Julia felt Maurice pull the gun from her hand.

"Julia, you know that it's loaded," he said softly.

It was a 22-calibre weapon, and he pulled the clip out to show her the bullets. Julia shook her head and sat on the bed as Maurice replaced the gun on top of the bar fridge.

"Why Maurice?" she asked. "I thought that our life here was good enough. Why do you have to be involved with that?"

"I have other interests, Julia. You know that."

Julia fumed. "What about me? What about us? Don't you care if you go back to prison? I sometimes wonder if you lie to me."

It was very hard to read through Maurice's look. He stayed quiet while she said her piece and then a moment later he answered.

"You know that I won't lie to you, Julia. I'm not going back to prison. I've learned how to play the game. If you want to know something, just ask."

"I don't want to know, Maurice. I don't want to know what you're doing with the gun. I don't want to know how you've influenced people to be so loyal to you. I don't want to know what happened to Kyle." Julia put a hand over her mouth. She hadn't meant to say that. She could almost feel the tension in the air.

Maurice remained very still.

"Sometimes you scare me," she said. "I wish I could leave you."

That's when she saw the drugs. Maurice had carefully hidden them behind the fridge but as she realized what she looked at, she gasped and stared. It was all there: the needles, the syringes, acepromazine, clenbuterol, flunixin, furosemide, and even phenylbutazone. As she recognized the name of every illegal medication, she knew that Maurice had set her up. She was the one named as trainer. He didn't care if they came up with a positive so long as he could cash the bet. It would be her that would take the fall, her that would lose her licence, be fined, and ruled off. He didn't really care about the horses. He just cared about winning races.

Maurice was so fast that Julia didn't even see it coming. She felt him on top of her, his thumbs closing over her windpipe. She stared up at him in horror. She couldn't breathe! He was choking her! His blue eyes bored into her mind. They were so cold.

Julia tried to grab at the man's hands, but he was strong and she was weak from lack of oxygen. The hands gripped her throat, bruising the skin and she tried to speak but couldn't. She couldn't cry. She couldn't scream. She was completely helpless in his grasp. Just as suddenly as he'd started, Maurice released his hold on Julia.

"*Qu'est-ce que je fais?*" ("What am I doing?") He was shouting, swearing at her in French.

Julia put her hand on her throat, terrified of this man, the evil that she had inadvertently released. Maurice picked up the gun and his keys and stormed out of the tack room. She heard the sound of his truck starting and the gravel spitting out from beneath the tires as he left. Only then, in the utter silence that followed, did she finally turn on her side, sobbing from the physical and emotional pain that tore at her heart.

Chapter Forty-two

Maurice didn't return to the track for three days. Julia moved back to her own room. She trained the horses each morning and grazed them under the hot afternoon sunshine. The second day, Carl came down the shed to visit. She put a hand up to her throat in an attempt to cover the bruises but knew it was useless. Carl was well aware that they were there.

"Are you going to Greenwood?" he asked, avoiding looking at the dark bands on her neck.

"Yes, but only with two horses. The rest I'm shipping to the farm next month."

Carl was quiet for a moment. Then he looked directly at Julia. She sat on a bale of hay, trying to avoid what she knew was coming. Carl always made her face what she was doing, how she was living.

"You don't have to take this. You could press charges."

"Please, Carl," she answered him wearily. "It's my bed. I have to lie in it. I knew the type of person that he was the day I met him. He never lied to me. I just crossed the line that he warned me about."

"God, Julia, you don't have to do this." Carl was clearly upset. "You could leave him. He is married to someone else."

"You're wrong, Carl," Julia said, staring at him. "I can't leave him. He won't let me."

Julia came out of Stanley's stall early the next afternoon to discover Maurice standing outside the shed. She put down her brushes, not sure what to say to the man. Her hands were shaking, partly from fear, and partly from knowing that she'd been used. His blue eyes were soft, having lost the cold, calculating look she'd last seen in them. She walked outside the shed and stood in front of the man. She hit him as hard as she could.

"You bastard."

Maurice didn't flinch. He didn't try to stop her.

"I trusted you," she said. Julia tried to hit him again. She was so angry. Maurice grabbed her wrists and pinned them to her sides. He pulled her towards him.

"I know," he said quietly, "and I let you down."

She didn't want Maurice to touch her, but he was holding her the way he had so many times in the past. The familiarity of the gesture was somehow comforting.

"You used me." Julia's voice cracked as she said what was closest to her heart. "You set me up from the start. I was just a pawn to you. A toy. A game. You bastard." She had stopped shouting, grateful that the sheds were still empty. She was so hurt.

"I won't deny anything, Julia."

"And now you won't let me leave."

Maurice was quiet for a moment as he grasped her hands.

"You are right, Julia. I have always been a cruel, possessive bastard. I knew that it was only a matter of time before you saw the real Maurice, the one people run from in fear." He led her over to the straw bales by the shed and sat down. "What do you want to know? I'll tell you and I won't get angry at your questions. I promise."

Julia didn't know whether or not she could trust him. She felt that there were some questions about his past that needed answering.

"Blue Bonnets," she began. "Tell me about Blue Bonnets. Were you there?"

Maurice let go of her and lit a cigarette. He was quiet again, obviously contemplating her question about what had happened in his distant past.

"It was a long time ago. That track has been closed for years."

He glanced at the woman beside him. Julia waited, not sure that she wanted to hear about the details, but she had asked anyway.

"Yes, I was there. I knew what was happening. I was a part of what was happening, a big part. You probably already know that, Julia. I left the day before they set the grandstand on fire. Someone told me what was going to happen and I got out so that they wouldn't look to me."

He was quiet again, and Julia had a chance to absorb the information. She didn't ask him about Kyle. It was better not knowing some things.

Maurice pulled back and looked at her, studying her in a way that Julia hadn't felt for some time. She froze as he touched the bruising on her throat.

"Loving you is dangerous," she said quietly. "You're very demanding and possessive."

"I know," he replied. "You need to have some fear, Julia. You have become a part of my life, and I don't part easily with those people."

Chapter Forty-three

It was the last race of the day and the sun cast long shadows across the dirt of the stretch as Julia paused at the gap to get the race number for the filly. The filly pranced, excited by the prospect of the race, and Maurice cast an anxious look at Julia. Must have money on the horse, Julia mused. Her mind wandered over their last argument, her harsh words not even cracking the ice of his anger. Their relationship had changed, obviously. The trust that Julia had once warmly felt had been replaced by misgivings, and a sense of unease. Perhaps even more important was that Julia knew that Maurice was very aware of her feelings. The latest argument had ended similarly to the others. They would do things as planned; Maurice had been forceful, and Julia had backed down.

Leading the filly onto the racetrack, Julia started the arduous journey towards the paddock, letting her stride carry her confidently forward along the dirt. She was aware of Maurice walking several paces behind, his eyes always on the filly, noting her excitement or anxiety about the race.

Julia approached the fence that surrounded the grandstand. It was a mediocre fence, only four feet high and made of simple page-wire. This end of the grandstand was normally deserted, as most patrons wanted to be close to the wire. Today, however, there was a young boy playing with pop cans, crushed and clamped to his shoes as he strutted about the grandstand cement. He was laughing at his game, slamming his noisy shoes against the asphalt in delight. The filly at Julia's side cast a look at the lad. The boy stomped towards the fence, as Julia watched the filly carefully. The lad grasped the loose metal fence and shook it, laughing again as he stomped his feet. Julia could feel her body tense.

Leaping backward, the filly caught both Julia and Maurice off-guard. Julia, jerked by the lead, stumbled and fell onto the thick dirt of the track. The filly spooked—turned and bolted for the gap. The shank slid through Julia's hand, and her mind took a moment to comprehend the situation. Yet in that moment a plan formed. She could feel the knot at the end of the shank, and the filly hesitated.

Julia felt the shank slacken, but she let go. Only a brief instant prior to the filly's release, Julia heard her own voice in the distance calling, "loose horse!"

Maurice was breathing down her neck.

"What the hell?" he yelled. "I was right behind you! Couldn't you hang on for another instant?"

The dust from the filly spilled into the air as she raced for the gap and the barns in the distance.

Julia's mind numbed with the repercussions of what she had just done. Maurice was no fool. As if emphasizing that fact, he stood for an instant with a look of anger and disgust on his face. Julia could feel his hands on her throat in her mind, and she shuddered just before she chuckled.

"Jeez Maurice, hope you didn't have too much money riding on her today."

What the hell was wrong with her? Had she completely lost her mind? Why was she provoking Maurice in this way? Julia could see the outrider galloping down the stretch towards her as Maurice turned and stomped towards the gap.

It was late after the last race and Julia has managed to cool out and bandage the filly. The horse had run third, but Maurice had not said a word to her in the paddock as she saddled the filly before the race or at the wire as the horses rushed by. Third was not so bad considering that the horse had run loose back to the barns prior to post. The barns had emptied quickly and she waited alone in the gathering darkness of the October evening.

Julia was nervous that Maurice would still hold her accountable for losing the race. There was a very real reason for her fear. Maurice appeared suddenly in the shed as she stood against the cement block foundation of the barns. He didn't even hesitate as his hand rose and struck her across the face.

"Don't you ever cross me like that again!" His voice thundered.

The blow was hard, and Julia could scarcely keep her balance. Although a dreadful fear rushed through her, her first reaction was anger. She was unaware that her hand rose in retaliation until she felt Maurice's powerful grip on her wrist. Julia could hear her own voice as though it was in the distance.

"Are you threatening me?" Julia's cheeks burned from shame and anger. It was hard to avoid the cold, calculating fury in her lover's eyes. Of course it was a threat.

Maurice pushed her backwards as he released her. Glaring at Julia, he stopped to light a cigarette; the sudden flare of the lighter illuminating the cold blue of his eyes. Julia could tell that he was barely containing his anger.

"I still can't believe that you let go of that horse. You try my patience with your defiance, Julia. You are lucky that I am so fond of you." Maurice glanced at her, a slow smile spreading across his face. "You are also lucky that I hadn't yet made my bet."

Julia stood her ground, unwilling to back down. The implication of his words was not lost on her. Maurice would not hesitate to punish anyone who stood between himself and his ultimate goals. God knew that Julia had seen the level of his violence more than once. Yet somewhere deep inside, Julia was finding a new strength and felt the wall of the shed behind her as Maurice strode across the dirt to the filly's stall.

It was nearly two minutes before Maurice glanced back at Julia. She could see that the smoke had helped to calm his anger, but for the first time in their relationship, Julia was willing to stand up to this man. Although she had taken the lead in training the horses, she had always been aware that he held the ultimate power.

Maurice tossed the butt of his cigarette into the gutter.

"I thought we had an understanding, Julia," he said quietly as he walked back towards her. He reached up and carefully traced a line across her cheek to her lips. Julia didn't move, but there was a flicker of fear in her eyes. "Good. You need to be afraid of me, Julia. I've told you before: don't ever try to con a con.

"You are a smart woman, Julia. I do have a soft spot for you. You have willingly joined forces with me, and given me considerable pleasure as a lover. It is regretful that our relationship has come to this. I am partly to blame because you should not have seen the medications. I should also have held my temper that night. However, it's done, and ultimately you will have to know that I must have control, Julia. Even if it hurts you."

Julia scarcely heard what he said. She had worked so hard for them, for their horses. She was angry that Maurice thought that he could control her like he controlled others. Yet her heart was pounding at the soft violence of his words. And, yes, she was very afraid. She knew without a doubt that Maurice would hurt her if she ever crossed him again.

"Are you threatening me?" she asked for a second time.

Maurice leaned over and kissed her, his lips brushing against her resistance. "No threat, *mon amie,* but a promise."

Julia sensed Vern lurking in the gathering darkness. Her friend was once again pushing the time limit imposed by the stewards. Maurice must have also known that Vern was close.

"We will continue this conversation later," Maurice said.

It was somewhat of a dismissal, but Julia did not move away. Brushing her braided hair lightly with her right hand, her left arm moved swiftly, striking Maurice across the face with all her strength.

Maurice, caught off guard, stumbled backward, surprise and anger in his eyes.

"Don't you ever hit me again!" Julia said, amazed at her own power. Julia braced herself for Maurice's retaliation, but it didn't happen. Instead the man chuckled.

"I love your spirit; it makes the challenge even more interesting."

Vern materialized from around the corner. She glanced with concern at Julia.

"Let's get out of here," said Julia. "The conversation is over."

Aware that Maurice was watching, she strode defiantly down the shed.

The tension between Maurice and Julia did not diminish. Julia found it difficult to work with the man each morning, and few words passed between them. There were not many races left in the conditions book so Julia took most of the horses out of training. October was nearing an end, and Maurice would ship most of the horses to the farm for the winter.

Julia sat down on a bale following afternoon feed one of the final dark days of the racing season. It had been a beautiful day, and she relaxed, watching as Maurice locked the feed room door. He came over to where she rested and sat beside her.

"My brother is sick, Julia. I need to go home earlier than usual this year." Maurice turned to look at her sitting in the autumn sunshine.

"You go home every year anyway". Julia replied. "This year, that may be a good thing."

Maurice placed a hand on top of Julia's fingers, and she didn't pull away. She was sorry that their relationship had come to this. Perhaps the distance of winter would help to mend their issues.

"Can you handle the horses at Greenwood without me?"

Julia breathed a sigh of relief. "Of course."

"John will be there if you need anything," said Maurice.

"I won't need much. I'll ship the last two to the farm at the end of the meet."

"Julia." Maurice wrapped an arm around her shoulder and drew her towards him.

Julia closed her eyes, remembering the old Maurice, the man who had held her tenderly and could make love to her so passionately. The man who didn't hit her or try to kill her, force her under his control. She wondered if she could ever trust him again.

"December at Greenwood," Maurice said. He looked at Julia. "I won't see you until the spring. Please come to me tonight, Julia."

Julia turned away. Despite what he'd done to her, there was still a part of her that loved him. He had always been a kind, thoughtful lover.

"When are you leaving?" she asked.

"Next week."

"I'll come tonight," Julia said.

Maurice smiled.

Maybe things would be all right after all, she thought.

Chapter Forty-four

Greenwood in the spring is a land full of promise. There are new horses, new faces, and a new season of racing. Greenwood in the fall is the last stop of a long year. It is lonely, dark, and cold. Julia settled easily into the routine of training the two fillies that she had brought from Fort Erie. They were already racing fit and didn't need much attention. She entered them into races and was glad when Carl appeared to give her a hand running them. It was nice to have a friendly face close by in the big city.

The races were tough, and neither filly hit the board. As December approached, Julia decided to take them out of training and wait for the van to ship them out the following week. She spent her days in the backstretch kitchen or over at the grandstand watching the races. It was a miserable fall, and blizzards seemed to rage off the lake nearly every night. Late one particularly nasty evening, she found herself wandering through the old rambling barns. Her mind was years back in the same spot when she'd felt so overwhelmed by Antonio Descartes.

Julia paused outside a tack room door and then reached up to knock on the wood. The door opened and Carl was standing inside the dimly lit room. He held the door open and she entered. Neither of them said a word as Julia reached for him and Carl took her into his arms. It was a passion built from friendship and mutual respect. Neither of them mentioned Maurice.

Afterward, Julia lay against Carl's chest listening to his heart beat while the blizzard raged around the barn, rattling the windows.

"I love you, Julia." It was the first words that had been spoken. Julia reached up and placed a finger on the man's lips.

"Please don't," she whispered. "There's too much tied up in those words. Just be my friend, Carl."

Carl reached down and kissed her on the forehead. "I will always be your friend," he promised.

They were quiet again for a few moments, listening to the wind. Julia felt comfortable and safe. She didn't regret for an instant being with Carl. Maurice was at home with his wife.

"Where are you wintering?" asked Carl.

That was a good question. Julia remembered other off seasons, winters breaking babies on the farm or training at racetracks in the States: Cleveland, Ohio or Birmingham, Alabama. Julia especially remembered the winters at Woodbine, by herself in the big dormitory, walking through deserted barns in the blistering cold. She remembered galloping yearlings on the training track when her hands could barely feel the reins or walking horses on Christmas morning. It had been a lonely existence.

"I think I might go home, Carl. Back to see my parents. Maybe take a trip somewhere warm with my mother." The idea sounded good. She wondered if it really was time to go back.

"What do you want to do with your life, Julia?"

"Train racehorses." Julia was surprised. It was such an easy question and there was no doubt in her mind about what she wanted.

Carl had pulled her closer. "No other desires?" he persisted.

"Well, at one time I wanted to go to university. But that was a long time ago. Before the racetrack."

"You're young still," said Carl. "There is life beyond racing. The track will always be here, as long as people want to bet on horses."

"I don't want another life, Carl. I love racing."

"You can love racing and still be something else. You don't want to be 50 years old and still living in a tack room. You should think about it, Julia. You've overcome impossible odds on the backstretch and succeeded. On the outside, you'd be invincible. I would feel sorry for the person who stood in the way of what you really wanted."

Julia fell asleep in his arms, and when she woke up the next morning, Carl was still there, and he was still her friend.

Chapter Forty-five

Julia knew that she had no choice as the summer season started in Fort Erie. Maurice arrived at the track with the horses at the beginning of April, and there was no avoiding him. Although they were still occasionally lovers, Julia was wary of their relationship. She chose to stay primarily in her own room, yet she knew full well Maurice, through his network of spies, was aware of everything that she did. Not that she wanted to try to cross him again. She knew better than to push Maurice too hard.

Julia brought back Stanley on the bleeder medication and he appeared to be running, but certainly not true to his old form. They claimed a couple of horses and won some races. By July, Julia was running more horses for Taylor and Miranda each week than training herself. An onslaught of problems had forced her to lay up three of the five horses she and Maurice owned.

Towards the end of July, Carl came by the shedrow as Julia was hanging up the freshly cleaned saddle cloths from the morning training.

"I've been looking for you, Julia," said Carl. "I was up at the racing office and noticed that the HBPA is giving grants for horsemen that want to pursue their education: $1000 for university or college. I thought that you might be interested."

Julia wasn't really interested. The horses and the backstretch were her life. Yet she found herself considering the idea, wondering if she might be able to get a grant. Going to school was an easy way to spend the winters, and she could still train horses during the summer racing season. Rumours had recently surfaced about the

Jockey Club closing Greenwood and tearing down the barns, which would effectively shorten the racing season.

A couple of days after Carl told her about the form, she found herself in the racing office filling out the document. She handed the form to the HBPA representative, and didn't consider the grant again as August racing started.

Julia suspected that Maurice was still medicating the horses behind her back. She had seen him with considerable cash—probably from bets—but she had no desire to ask him what he was doing until she saw him walking out of Stanley's stall late one afternoon. Julia had entered Stanley into a race on the weekend, reluctantly dropping the horse to a claiming price of only 2500. Already upset about the gelding, she immediately confronted Maurice.

"What the hell are you doing?" she asked.

Maurice ignored Julia as he walked past her to their tack room where the equipment was stored. He made no attempt to hide the needle and syringe in his hand. Julia followed him into the tack room, her anger mounting.

"This is enough, Maurice. I want you to stop!"

Placing the used needle into a bucket in the corner, Maurice finally turned to face Julia. "No," he said.

"I thought that you understood how I felt last fall, Maurice. Why are you still doing this? Why are you using me like this?"

It was more of a plea. The year had run quite smoothly with no major confrontations and Julia had temporarily forgotten the feelings of frustration from last October. She had forgotten the false impression Maurice gave that he cared about the horses, the false impression that he loved her.

"You know that I have ultimate control of this outfit, Julia. That was decided last fall. If I choose to use a medication, then you need to deal with the consequences. I regret that you saw me."

"You are a bastard, Maurice La Chance."

Julia was furious as she whispered the words. Was there no way out of this nightmare? Her friends were sympathetic, but had no clue as to the level of violence in this man. Carl had simply told her to walk away. That was impossible. Vern knew more, but chose not to interfere. She was leery of Maurice, and had too much to lose on a probationary licence.

"You knew that the day you met me, Julia."

Why was she so attracted to these men? Initially, she had found Maurice romantic and exciting, but she had never dreamed that he would twist their relationship into such madness. She had never dreamed that she would have to fear for her career, or her life. Julia knew that she needed to find a way to be rid of Maurice, before it all came crashing down around her. She didn't know that the thought was too late.

It was a dark day, around 3 o'clock in the afternoon, and Julia was lying on her cot just two days after her confrontation with Maurice. However, the bitterness and feelings of helplessness still remained very real. A soft knock sounded on the door.

"Come in," she said, not bothering to move.

She knew everyone on the backstretch, and didn't ever worry about complete strangers. Maurice made sure that she would be protected. It was one of the few benefits to their partnership. The door opened; the afternoon sun pouring in across the tack room floor. One of the new workers from Barn 2 stood in the light. Julia sat up quickly, unsure why this stranger was bothering her. He was thin and wiry, his dark eyes staring into the dim light of the tack room.

"Julia, ma'am," the man began politely. He reached into his back pocket and pulled out a thin wallet. He flipped it open to reveal a badge. Julia's eyes widened in dismay. "I'm an undercover detective, ma'am. Been working on the backstretch for the last couple of weeks. I have some questions regarding Maurice La Chance, a friend of yours."

Julia's heart pounded in dismay. She quickly stood, but was unsure that her legs would hold, she was shaking so badly. Her nightmare scenario had always involved the stewards and being ruled off. This was far worse than anything she could have dreamed. The detective held his spot, obviously watching her reaction. Her recent anger with Maurice dissolved as she realized the power she now held. Did she have the nerve, the strength for a final act of defiance?

"What do you want to know?"

Chapter Forty-six

Julia knew that he would come for her. She had hoped to God that the police would pick him up first, but knew in her heart that Maurice would not let that happen. She lay in her room, dreading the moment of confrontation. She had been home for only half an hour when she heard his truck, and then his footsteps across the cement. There was no doubt in her mind that he was angry but how angry remained to be seen.

The door slammed back against the wall as Maurice stormed into the room. Julia cringed from fear as the sound vibrated down the shed. She couldn't see his face; the sun was low in the sky, casting an extensive shadow across the floor. It was probably just as well. She jumped up to meet him, but she was shaking worse than when the detective had entered only three hours previously.

"Where the hell have you been?" asked Maurice.

"None of your business," Julia said. Her bravado was false, and she was aware that Maurice knew it.

"What did you tell them?"

"Nothing." Too late, Julia realized her mistake. "I don't know what you're talking about." Of course Maurice knew. His boys would have reported everything.

Maurice had always been lightning-quick, but Julia did not see him move as he grasped her wrist, yanking her towards him.

"That was a very foolish thing to do, Julia." His voice was barely above a whisper. "You and I are going for a little drive. Move out the door in front of me. No wrong moves or I will kill you. I promise."

Julia's heart pounded. She was absolutely terrified of this man that she thought she'd known so well. She had dared to cross Maurice again, and this time it could very well mean his return to prison. He would stop at nothing to prevent that from happening. Julia didn't know his intentions, but she knew her prospects of returning to the backstretch unscathed were low. She was desperately afraid of his anger.

Maurice pushed Julia out the door. Julia stumbled, feeling his hand hard against her back. There was nothing gentle about his touch, and the anger reverberated through his fingers. It took only a moment to reach the truck. Maurice forced her into the passenger seat before he slipped behind the wheel, the engine roaring to life in the silence of a sleepy backstretch afternoon. Julia fought back tears, unwilling to let Maurice know the intensity of her terror. She was rigid in her spot, not daring even to put on her seatbelt as he drove towards the west gate of the backstretch. Security was oblivious of her plight and the uniformed man raised the bar with a friendly wave to Maurice.

Maurice turned onto Thomson Road and headed for the highway. He drove silently, as Julia contemplated her fate. She knew he had never dreamed that she would go to the police. They had been partners, and he had always thought that Julia would be true to their partnership. His anger was real, and she was deeply afraid that he might be ready to kill her.

Taking the first exit, Maurice followed the road partway to Stevenson, finally pulling over onto the gravel shoulder by a deserted laneway into the brush. There were no farm houses in this area, and Julia glanced out the window at the bleak landscape.

"Get out," Maurice said.

Julia didn't move. This had turned into a surreal reality. She couldn't have moved if he'd pushed her. Her terror left her that helpless.

"You're going to kill me," she said hoarsely, afraid to even glance at the man who had once been her lover.

Maurice had switched off the engine.

"No, Julia," he replied. "Other people do that for me. Maim, rape, kill. I'd rather not get my hands dirty. You know that's the way

I work." His voice was calm and collected, much more frightening than the anger had been. He pushed in the lighter on the dash, pulling a cigarette from his pocket.

"I can make arrangements. Acid in the face is my preference, but rape works equally as well. You do know what it is like to be raped, don't you Julia?" Maurice lit the smoke and sat back in the seat, watching her carefully as he'd done so often in the past.

Julia felt the unbidden tears welling in her eyes. How could he possibly know? She had never told anyone. How could he possibly know?

The cruelty of his threats bothered Julia. Maurice had never lied to her. Julia knew that he would use every method at his disposal for her submission. The comment galvanized Julia into action. Reaching across, she grasped his arm.

"Please, Maurice." She was pleading. "Please don't do this."

"Don't beg, Julia. You are far too strong for that."

Maurice carefully pried her fingers from his arm, and then reached across to the glove compartment. Snapping it open, he grasped the pistol that lay on the top of vehicle paperwork. Julia's eyes widened in horror. Sensing her new-found fear, Maurice paused and glanced at her face.

"I want to make sure that you don't run," he said. He slipped off the safety, making sure that she saw the movement.

Maurice opened his door and glanced down the road.

"Out," he said, waving the gun.

Julia edged across the seat and, a moment later, stood beside him in the sunshine. She was acutely aware of the gun in his hand as Maurice pointed to the laneway across the road.

"Start walking, *mon amie.*"

Time stood still. Each step sent a pounding into Julia's ears as she moved slowly across the road and down the trail. She was unaware of Maurice following. Instead, she wondered how it had come to this. She was smart. She had planned worst-case scenarios. Yet it had still happened. Maurice still held the upper hand. The unevenness of the farm laneway skidded beneath her feet, and Julia was reminded of the first time she had walked a horse along the shed. How she longed to be back even in Jimmy Henderson's barn. Anywhere but here and now with Maurice.

Julia became aware of her own heartbeat, the feel of the late afternoon sun on her back, the light sweat on her palms, her jeans tight with every stride, and her hidden knife safely tucked into her pocket. Her knife! In the fear of the moment she had forgotten that she always carried the knife, partly because it was handy to open bales in the shed, but also for protection. Maurice sharpened the blade regularly. Julia knew that she had to think quickly, but her mind was fuzzy. Fighting for clarity, she straightened her shoulders and shifted her left hand up towards the pocket. She had to move so slowly, so slowly.

Maurice fired the gun past her and Julia froze. She had never known terror so full, so all-encompassing. Had he been aiming for her? Was this the end?

"Don't bother, Julia," said Maurice, his voice still very calm. "Turn around. Leave the knife alone."

Julia turned to face her lover. He seemed relaxed, the gun held loosely in his hand. Yet there was no end to the coldness of his blue eyes. She had seen him like this before. There were no good intentions in his mannerism. Julia fought for clear thinking. It was the only thing that could save her now.

"You need to reach an understanding, and I don't have much time." Maurice continued, "Your friend Carl saw us leave the track, and it will not take the police long to find my truck."

"Why are you doing this, Maurice? I thought you loved me."

He studied her for a brief moment. His answer was soft, a look of disappointment and regret in his eyes.

"I thought you loved me, Julia, but you still turned me in."

It was true. Julia glanced away, her emotions in turmoil.

"They will arrest me, Julia, but unless you testify, they have no case. You will not testify against me. Do you understand?" His words were forceful.

For a brief moment, Julia saw an opportunity to escape the nightmare that was engulfing her.

"Answer me!" Maurice yelled.

Julia stared at him. So this was his demand?

"I will not shoot to kill, Julia, but I will shoot you. A shot in the kneecap will cause considerable pain, and you will be a cripple for a long time."

Maurice still surprised her with his willingness to hurt, his level of cruelty. He had once warned her never to be a hero with a desperate man. She had thought that she understood those words then, but the true meaning was much more apparent now. He raised the gun, taking aim at her leg.

"Maurice, please." Julia's voice was hoarse, pleading. For a brief second she saw a softness in his eyes, but just as quickly, it was gone.

They could hear the sirens in the distance. A new-found hope welled in her heart as she faced this madman who had once been her partner and lover. It seemed simple. She would give him the answer that he sought.

"I will not testify against you, Maurice." Julia's voice was calm and controlled.

Maurice smiled and primed the weapon. "That was too easy, Julia. You are far too calm. I don't believe you."

"Drop the gun!" yelled a police officer.

Maurice continued, his eyes meeting Julia in a deadlock. She could smell her own fear once more.

"Have I lied to you, Maurice?" asked Julia. "Haven't we always been completely honest with each other? I said that I will not testify against you." Julia kept her voice calm as she reiterated the statement.

Behind, the police were still yelling. Some of them rushed forward, taking cover in the bushes. Julia could sense their fear. Fear for themselves and fear for her safety. Yet for the first time in the last five hours, she felt somewhat in control.

"I had every intention of punishing you, Julia. But for what we had, I will trust your words, and leave you alive." Maurice kept the gun aimed on her leg, his hand steady. He stared directly at her, locking into her gaze. "However, should you choose to go back on those words, I will find you. *Au revoir, mon amie.*" His last words were a whisper.

Smiling, Maurice laid the gun on the ground and put his hands in the air. The police rushed forward, tackling him to the ground in their frenzy. Julia looked away, not willing to see this happen to the man that she had loved so deeply. Her emotions were torn and frazzled. Yes, she had once loved him, but Maurice was the man who had also caused her such anger, and ultimately, such fear. She couldn't believe that she had persuaded him to let her live.

The detective who had questioned her earlier moved to her side. Julia's face was a ghostly white. The man grasped her arm in reassurance.

"I'll help you, ma'am." His voice was polite as always.

He guided her past Maurice as they pushed him into the patrol car, his hands firmly behind his back. Julia stopped and glanced at the man inside. He met her gaze and smiled. An insane anger rushed through Julia. Never again would she allow this man to use her, to control her.

"Fuck you, Maurice!" she yelled. "I will testify. I'm going to see you rot in hell!"

Julia turned quickly away, but not before she saw the look of murder in his eyes.

Chapter Forty-seven

Julia pulled Stanley from his stall and unwrapped the overnight bandages from his legs. Carl was holding the horse in the morning sunshine. He had held Julia all night. She had relived the horror of that day's events over and over in her dreams, and it had never ended well. Carl hadn't asked each time that she awoke, the unspoken terror in her eyes. He had simply pulled her closer.

"I need your help, Carl," Julia said. She had never asked him for anything, but desperation was driving her to new heights. She thought briefly of the conversation that had ensued with the police officer following Maurice's arrest. They couldn't hold him for long. There would be a restraining order, but on the backstretch…,

It was strongly suggested that she leave and live elsewhere for a while.

"I have to sell the horses. Quickly."

Carl didn't ask her for details. "I will help, Julia. I think we can get a good price for them."

"Thanks, Carl," she replied gratefully. "Except one. Don't sell Stanley. The gelding—I'm taking him with me." She stroked the animal gently on his muzzle. If she had to leave the track, at least she would have Stanley as her memory.

She glanced at her favourite horse, and fought the tears that were forcing their way to the surface. Memories of a kind-hearted Maurice, their partnership, the horses, racing. It tore her apart.

Vern found Julia a week later to tell her that the office was looking for her. "Something about the HBPA," said her friend.

Julia was mystified. What would the HBPA want? Maybe there was an issue associated with her dealings with Maurice. Julia sprinted for the office. Sure enough, there was a message.

"Roger Dongals will be down from Woodbine with your cheque next week," said the racing secretary. "Looks like you've been chosen to receive the thousand dollar scholarship. Congratulations."

It took Julia a moment to remember filling out the forms a few weeks ago. She had never expected to receive any type of scholarship. She hadn't even applied to the university. As Julia realized that she had been given money to go back to school, she began to see the implications. Suddenly there was a new direction to her life. She now had somewhere to go, a reason to look forward to a new future, however different and perhaps intimidating. There was a lightness to her walk as Julia stepped out of the racing office.

Vern was waiting outside.

"What's up?" she asked. "You're grinning like you just breezed a quarter in 21."

Julia smiled. "I think I'm going back to school, Vern."

Vern just stared. "Did the stewards rule you off?"

Julia laughed. "No. The HBPA has given me some money to take a university or college course this winter."

Vern continued to stare. "You gonna quit racing?" Her voice was scarcely a whisper.

Julia took a moment to answer as she contemplated the question. She didn't want to quit racing, but the backstretch would be the first place that Maurice would look.

"I don't know, Vern."

Vern ran a hand through her black curls, the warm afternoon sun making the sweat glisten on her face and neck. Racetrackers had long ago nick-named the friends salt and pepper.

"Are you ever afraid, Julia?" Vern asked quietly. "Are you ever afraid that he'll come back for you?"

Julia stared off into the distance, studying the barns and the blue sky beyond. She turned back to her friend, sorrow etched in her eyes.

"Yes."

Julia sat in her tack room taking the braids out of her hair. It seemed like such an odd thing to be doing in the middle of the day. Roger Dongals was due at the racing office at 1 p.m. and wanted to personally present her with the cheque. She changed her blouse, threw her horsemen's cap onto the bed and walked out into the sunshine. She locked the door.

The shedrows were deserted as she wandered down the road towards the office. Julia walked slowly, her eyes wanting to take in everything. She looked down every shed, studying the horses, the barns, willing herself to remember. She knew that she was never coming back.

The August sun was warm on her back, and she could hear the sounds of horses moving in their stalls and birds singing in the trees. The backstretch at Fort Erie was one of the most beautiful places on Earth. Taking a breath of fresh air into her lungs, Julia opened the door to the racing office and walked in to meet Roger Dongals.

Glossary

Glossary terms are based on the Daily Racing Form Glossary of Horse Racing Terms online at www.drf.com/help/help_glossary.html

Across the board: betting a horse win, place, and show.

Allowance race: a non-claiming race in which the racing secretary allots weights based on a horse's conditions.

Also eligible/A.E.: a horse entered in a race, but not allowed to start unless the field is reduced by a specified number of scratches.

Apprentice rider/Apprentice jockey: a rider who has not ridden a specified number of wins, or for a specified length of time; allowed a 10-pound weight allowance for the first five wins, and then five pounds for one year following the first five wins.

Backing up a horse: taking a horse clockwise around the track on the outside rail; only permitted during morning training.

Backstretch: the far side of the racetrack between turns; also used to mean stable area.

Bandages: strips of cloth wrapped around a horse's legs for support or protection against injury.

Bleeder: during a race or workout, a horse that bleeds from the lungs due to ruptured blood vessels.

Blinkers: devise placed on a horse's head to restrict vision.

Blocking: a procedure in which medication is injected at a point on the horse's legs to reduce pain.

Blown suspensories: inflammation of the suspensory ligament.

Bookkeeper: racetrack official who oversees horsemen's accounts.

Bow/Bowed tendon: inflammation of the greater flexor tendon.

Breezing: working a horse at a moderate speed; usually slower than an official timed workout.

Bucked shins: inflammation of the canon bone often seen in young horses; may result in hair-line fractures.

Bullring/Bullring racetrack: a track shorter than a mile; usually has tight turns and long stretch and backstretch runs.

Cast: a horse lying down too close to a wall so that the horse cannot get up without help because of risk of injury.

Claiming race: a race in which horses may be bought for a specified price prior to post; transfer of ownership occurs immediately following the race.

Cold horse: a horse not sent out to train but walked around the shedrow.

Commission vet: hired by the racing commission to ensure that only sound horses are running in the race; horses are checked on the morning of the race day, in the paddock, and prior to loading into the starting gate.

Conditions book: book issued by the racing secretary specifying the conditions of races to be run.

Daily double/Early double/Late double: type of wager in which the winners of two consecutive races must be chosen; usually the first and second races, or the last two races of the card.

Exactor/Exactor box: a type of wager in which the first two finishers must be picked in the exact order; an exactor box allows the picked horses to finish in any order.

Fast track: track condition describing footing at its best; dry and even allowing for fastest race times.

Furlong: an eighth of a mile; 200 metres.

Furlong poles: poles placed around the racetrack which are colour-coded to indicate the distance to the wire; sixteenth poles are red and white, eighth poles are green and white; quarter poles are black and white.

Gate/Starting gate: mechanical device having partitions (stalls) where horses are confined until the starter releases the doors at the beginning of the race.

Heat/Heat exhaustion/Heat stroke: when a horse over-exerts itself in hot humid weather and collapses; life threatening condition.

Homebred: a horse bred and raised by its owner.

Hot horse: a horse that has trained or run a race and requires walking to cool out.

Iron halter: a metal device used to restrain a particularly fractious horse.

Irons: stirrups.

Jockey's agent: a person who represents a jockey and organizes which trainers/horses a particular jockey will ride; agents may represent up to three jockeys.

Lasix: bleeder medication.

Lugging in/Lugging out: bearing in or out during a race; may result in an inquiry against the offending horse.

Maiden: a horse who has not won a race

Muddy track: deep condition of racetrack after heavy rain.

Nerve line: a piece of twine or wire placed over a horse's gum and poll to restrain a particularly fractious horse.

Nerving/Nicking a horse: an operation that severs a vital nerve, allowing horses to run without pain; illegal procedure in most jurisdictions.

Off track: a wet racing surface.

On the bit/Taking hold of the bit: when a horse is eager to run.

Outrider: racing official who oversees morning training; responsible for safe practices of riders and horses, catching loose horses, and leading post parade in the afternoon.

Overnight: a list of post positions and riders for the upcoming racing card in two days

Paddock: place where horses are saddled and kept prior to post time.

Photo/Photo finish: a result so close that a finish-line camera must be used to determine the order of finish.

Place: ran second in a race.

Pony/Pony person: a horse and rider used to help control horses during warm-up prior to post; also often used in the morning training hours.

Post/Post position: starting point or position in starting gate.

Post time: designated time for race to start.

Racetracker: a person who works on the backstretch.

Racing card/Card: races/race conditions set for a particular day.

Racing form/Form: a newspaper published prior to each racing day listing horses starting in races, their racing history, and the betting odds of performance in the race.

Racing plates: an aluminum shoe used on racehorses; has ridge at the front (toe grab) to help slipping in off-track conditions.

Racing secretary: racing official who designs races and assigns handicaps/weights; also responsible for entries and the draw.

Rubbing horses: a person who grooms horses; also responsible for general care like bandaging and feeding.

Run-downs: bandages, normally on the hind legs with pads, to prevent a horse from "burning" or scraping his heels while he is racing.

Scratched: a horse taken out of a race.

Shed/shedrow: a row of stalls in the stable area.

Show: ran third in a race.

Sloppy track: track condition following heavy rain; wet on the top with a firm bottom allowing for firm footing; generally considered a fast track.

Stallman: person who allocates which horses/trainers get stalls on the backstretch; also allocates tack rooms to trainers.

Stall walker: a horse that walks in its stall, fretting rather than resting.

Starter: starts the race by cutting the power to the starting gate and allowing the doors to open.

Starter allowance race: an allowance race restricted to horses that have started for a particular claiming price or less.

Stewards: top officials at the racetrack responsible for enforcing the rules.

Tack room: a room assigned to trainers on the backstretch to store tack and supplies; often used as sleeping accommodations for backstretch workers.

Tapping: a procedure in which fluid is extracted from swollen joints such as knees and ankles. and replaced with a medication, usually cortisone.

Tattoo: a letter and group of numbers applied to the underside of the upper lip of all registered thoroughbreds.

Test barn: a barn where the winner and another horse from each race is sent to cool out following a race, and a urine sample is taken by racing officials to test for illegal drugs.

Toe grabs: the ridge at the front of a racing plate to help slipping in off-track conditions.

Tongue tie: a strap cloth used to tie down a horse's tongue to prevent it from choking during a race.

Tracker: a horse sent out to train in the morning.

Triactor/Triactor box: a type of wager in which the first three finishers must be picked in that exact order; the triactor box allows the picked horses to run in any order.

Valet/Jockey's valet: a person who tends to jockeys, and keeps their racing clothes and equipment in order.

Walking hots: a person who walks horses.

Walkover: a one-horse race in which the horse simply has to gallop the length of the race.

Windows: betting mutuals; where patrons can place a bet.

Wire: a wire stretching across the finish line (usually 20 feet in the air) to indicate the end of the race.

Working/Timed workout: to gallop a horse at a specified time so that it is eligible to start in a race.

.